AF552398

ArcheBooks Publishing

IMMORTAL BONDS

A Novel
by

DAWN SCOVILL

To Cathy —

Thank you so much for the support. Enjoy!

P.S. Rochester Rules!

IMMORTAL BONDS

By

DAWN SCOVILL

Copyright © 2007 by Dawn Scovill

ISBN-10: 1-59507-161-X
ISBN-13: 978-159507-161-3

ArcheBooks Publishing Incorporated

www.archebooks.com

9101 W. Sahara Ave.

Suite 105-112

Las Vegas, NV 89117

All rights reserved, including the right to reproduce this book or portions thereof in any form whatsoever. For information about this book, please contact ArcheBooks at publisher@ArcheBooks.com.

This book is entirely a work of fiction. The names, characters, places, and incidents depicted herein are either products of the author's imagination or are used fictitiously. Any resemblance to actual events or locales or persons, living or dead, is entirely coincidental.

First Edition: 2007

DEDICATION

To Mom and Dad
for not only giving me life,
but for passing on the tools with which to live it.

ACKNOWLEDGMENTS

Without guidance, support, and encouragement, this book would only be a file on my computer.

First and foremost, I have to thank my husband Scott, for his blind faith, justifiable impatience, and indestructible love—the foundation upon which everything in my world is built; my son Chris and daughter Casey, who remind me every day that someone is watching; my parents—and biggest fans—Judy and Orville, who went against their better judgment and let me live to experience adulthood; my brothers Jack and Jamie and sister "George" (a.k.a. Jill), for constantly reminding me that the "big sister" thing is nothing to take for granted; my grandparents Vera and Leroy, who believed in me when they shouldn't have and who continue to do so despite the barriers of geography and time (*I miss you, Grandpa*); *The Bloody Pens* (Graeme, Joe, Joel, Tina, Peter, Randy, Joan, Maria, Jay and Prudy), who consistently—sometimes painfully—forced me to write better than I ever thought I could; my dear friend Robin, for the countless hours of brainstorming that, among other things, flushed out the vampires; Officer Mick Keehan and the rest of the Palm Beach Police Dept., for being so hospitable in showing me around the place; and everyone who types, scans, downloads, uploads, and in some way, shape, or form contributes to the glorious information highway that is the Internet, who by taking it beyond the realm of porn, have truly raised the bar for those of us who crave knowledge, and if *you* can't end the world's suffering, God help us all.

IMMORTAL BONDS

PROLOGUE

With equal parts hope and terror, Jane fumbled the pay phone's receiver from the hook and jabbed at the digits. First the phone card number. Then the password. Then the New Orleans number she'd known since 1971.

"Thank you for choosing us," the recorded voice said.

"You're welcome," Jane mocked as the phone started to ring. She'd driven ten miles from her Palm Beach home to stand in a phone booth along Congress Avenue. *This better be good*, she thought. Thankfully, he was quick to answer.

"Janie?" Oliver's voice betrayed his own anxiety.

"Tell me something profound, Oliver, or it'll be another fifteen years before..."

"I found him." The connection was awful, but she heard every word clearly. "You need to run."

Run? she thought. *Now?* No. No one was nearby, but Jane closed the door anyway. "What are you talking about? Who did you find? Why do I have to run?"

"You know how we've always thought it was a disease, a virus, that did this to us?"

"Yes."

"It wasn't something we touched or ate at all, Janie. It was a man."

A man?

"Not an ordinary one," he added, "but a man, nonetheless."

"How could a man have caused this? Who is he?" She thought of Rand, the husband who'd shared her bed for twenty years. "And why do I need to run now?"

"There's too much to explain. Get to New Orleans as soon as you can. We're meeting him in Malta on Friday."

"Friday? But that's..."

"I know, short notice."

What an understatement. The ninety-degree Florida heat and high humidity suddenly made the glass box feel like a sauna. "I can't just forget everything and leave. What do I tell Rand?"

"You act like this is your first time. Tell him you're visiting a friend or something. What does it matter?"

"It's not that simple." She wanted to tell Oliver she'd found love this time, but the news would have fallen on deaf ears.

"You and I have prayed for this moment for a hundred and fifty years, Jane. This trip isn't negotiable."

He was right, but she didn't want to admit it. "You've really found the one responsible?"

"Yes."

She sighed. "Give me 'til Wednesday."

"To decide whether or not to go?"

"No. That decision was made long before today." Jane pushed the door open, but no amount of fresh air would lighten her heart. "You've just told me that life as we know it could end in five days. All I'm asking for is time to tie up loose ends."

"Fair enough."

She didn't wait for "goodbye" to hang up.

Jane slumped to the concrete floor of the phone booth, overcome with self-hatred. Rand didn't deserve the pain she was about to put him through. She wished there was another way. But even in her sadness she knew there wasn't time for self-pity.

She rose slowly to her feet, wiping at her eyes and brushing the sand from her shorts. Whether it hurt or not, tomorrow she would say her last goodbye to Rand and reenter a world she had deliberately forgotten. It was ironic, she thought as she exited the phone booth, that she would have to die to get there.

DAY 1

CHAPTER 1

Anxious for the break from work, Rand set the cordless phone on its base and shouted up the stairs. "Hey, babe! They'll have the *Sweet Mystery* ready in half an hour. Still wanna go?"

"Absolutely," Jane said, gliding down the staircase, "unless you'd rather be alone on your therapeutic deep-sea voyage."

"We've discussed this before," he said, pulling her close and plunging his fingers into her dark, satiny hair. "You're welcome aboard every time the boat leaves the marina."

"*Every* time?" she asked, batting her deep green eyes at him.

"Yes, *every* time. In fact, I like it better when you're with me. Especially when your bikini-clad body graces the bow."

"You're a devil."

He kissed her hard, and the woman who inspired him to name his boat the *Sweet Mystery* kissed him back. What had he ever done to deserve her? "Like to go upstairs for a quickie?" he whispered. "The kids are out of the house."

"We don't have kids," she giggled as he kissed her ear.

"All the more reason," he said, taking her hand and beginning his ascent up the staircase.

She stopped him, smiling mischievously. "Why go upstairs when we have a perfectly suitable kitchen counter?"

"And you call *me* a devil." He didn't protest as she pulled him into the kitchen.

•

"You sure we should go out today?" she asked when they'd come up for air. "What about your photos for *Details*? Aren't they due this week?"

Rand shrugged, slipping his shorts on. "Three days from now. I'll develop them in the morning, make my picks in the afternoon, and have them ready for the 'Pony Express' no later than Wednesday."

"If you're sure."

"I am." After years of similar conversations, he knew her persistence was rooted in concern for his well-being, not to mention his tendency to put things off until the last minute. "The shoot in Nassau was crazy. I need to get out and clear my head. And it might do you some good, too. You seem preoccupied."

"Me? What could possibly preoccupy me?"

"Don't know, my dear, but something's on your mind."

Gathering her clothes, she seemed to be thinking of something clever to say. It was so her, so *Jane*, to gloss over her problems with wit or sarcasm.

"I'll give it some thought while I'm changing," she said, as she started up the stairs.

Here it comes, he thought, as he watched her turn her head toward him and smirk.

"But if I can't figure out what's bothering me," she said, "maybe you can shag...I mean, drag it out of me later."

He smiled. "I'm sure something can be arranged."

Rand crossed the Mexican tile floor of the kitchen and gathered crackers, cheese, grapes, water, and iced tea from the refrigerator and pantry—and a bottle of red wine for the sunset. Janie loved sunsets. From a lower cabinet, he pulled out a tote bag and placed the items inside. Later, after the sun went down, they could dock for dinner at the Waterway Café or, if they were too tired, somewhere on Singer Island.

Rand already wore boat shorts and a long-sleeved pullover. The only difference between his summer and winter wardrobes, his friends would say, was the length of his sleeves. All that was left was to wait for Janie. He'd suggested the boat ride earlier that day for selfish reasons. He'd felt overwhelmed with the mountains of requests from fashion and travel mags. He'd been swamped for months, and he and the *Sweet Mystery* hadn't been out for a run since early November. He also hoped the ride would pull Janie out of the blue mood she'd pretended not to be in. Something was obviously troubling her, and maybe time away in the sea air could pull it out.

"You ready?" Jane called from the stairwell.

"Yup." He looked up at her. She'd put on a white top and Navy blue shorts. He loved her ass in Navy blue.

"Then why are you just standing there?" She grinned and pecked him on the lips.

•

On the drive to the marina, Janie was quiet, almost melancholy. She'd suggested earlier that they take the Chevelle instead of Rand's BMW, which wasn't unusual—she loved her car—but the way she seemed to pet it and sort of take it all in while Rand drove the short jaunt to the docks was unsettling. But he didn't want to talk yet. Not until they were away from the rest of the world.

The *Sweet Mystery*, a thirty-six-foot white fiberglass Century with dual outboards, was cleaned, gassed, and ready to roll when they arrived. The spring air off the intracoastal felt cool, but not cold, and the sound of the salt water splashing against the dock posts relaxed Rand almost instantly.

"Thanks, man," he said to the young attendant as he passed him a ten dollar bill, "she looks great."

"She missed you," the kid answered.

"Feeling's mutual. We'll bring her in sometime after nightfall."

"The old man'll be here. Just honk."

They climbed aboard and Janie crept down into the small cabin to stow their tote bag. Rand took his post under the center console's T-top and turned the key, bringing the twin two-fifties to life. "And she still runs," he called out to the attendant who scrambled dockside to release the lines. Rand shifted the throttles and pulled away from the dock.

He idled through the channel's no-wake zone, heading north toward the Palm Beach Inlet. Tall buildings of the West Palm skyline gave way to smaller, private residences as they neared the Port of Palm Beach. Along the opposite, or starboard, side of the waterway, and farther away, Palm Beach's estate homes—theirs included—graced the shoreline. White clouds dotted the blue sky, and sunlight shimmered on the water.

Janie emerged from the cabin and took her seat next to Rand at the console. "It's so beautiful out here, isn't it?"

"Yes."

"Are you going to fish?"

"Not today."

"But it's the best time for dolphin, isn't it."

"Yeah, but I think we'll stick to reconnaissance and just cruise around." He looked at her sitting next to him. She'd put her dark glasses on. Her hair flowed freely around her face and neck, and her tanned shoulders contrasted her white sleeveless shirt. God, she was beautiful. Like a movie star.

"It's okay by me. I'm content just being here with you."

"Well, that's a good thing."

"I've always thought so."

He put his arm around her and steered past Peanut Island to the now visible inlet. "Ocean looks good. Not too rough." With favorable currents and few boaters, Rand easily guided the vessel one-handed through the inlet and out into the deep blue of the Atlantic.

Rand stayed a mile or two off shore, cruising north toward Jupiter, beyond the condos, to admire the unspoiled coastline of John D. MacArthur State Park. They spoke little during the first hour, breaking the silence only to point out large, lumbering turtles paddling through the surf or schools of flying fish that erupted from beneath the skimming hull.

"Look," Janie said excitedly, pointing northeast and just off the bow, "it's Flipper!"

"Wonder if he wants to race." Rand throttled up from their cruising speed. "Wanna race, Flipper?" The bottlenose kept up, gliding easily and playfully in and out of the water alongside the boat. The dolphin was almost immediately joined by two pals and, for a few minutes, the three porpoises raced the motored craft. Janie giggled, and Rand smiled. But, as quickly as they had appeared, they dove beneath the surface and turned toward the deeper ocean, racing only each other toward the horizon.

"That was fun," Janie commented when the dolphins were out of sight.

"Yeah." Rand slowed down and steered the boat into a turn. "Wanna cruise back south?"

"Sure."

"It's about four-ish, so we'll stop and drift near Lake Worth for a snack."

"Sounds good."

Small whitecaps made the ride south bumpier than traveling north, but the *Sweet Mystery* sliced through easily enough. Rand eased into the backrest of the two-person seat and turned to Jane. "How're you feelin'? You hungry?"

"No. I'm good."

But she wasn't. Not really. He could tell.

"How are *you* feeling?" she asked. "You're the one who suggested this trip. You over your photographer stresses?"

He chuckled. "That shit's easy to turn off out here."

"You're a different person on the water."

"I think there's an...*energy*, a different kind of energy. It makes you feel as if nothing on land is that important."

She paused and looked thoughtful. She'd told him early in their relationship that she had tried being a writer once, "in another lifetime," as she'd put it. He often wondered if, behind her thoughtful looks, there were words battling for the chance to be spoken.

"I know exactly what you mean," she said.

He had to ask. "Is there something bothering you, Janie?"

"No," she answered too quickly.

"Are you sure? I think you're not telling me something."

"No, really, I'm fine. I…I came across something the other day that made me think of my family, that's all. Sometimes I just miss them. It'll pass."

"And that's all?"

"Yes," she wrapped her arms around him and squeezed, "that's all."

He doubted that was the end of it, but she'd talk in her own time. He'd known her to fall into slumps before over memories of her parents. She didn't talk about them much, but he knew she thought of them. His parents were alive and well in Cleveland, and likely plotting their next attempt at driving him nuts. He couldn't imagine what it must be like going through most of life without a mother and father who tormented, nagged, and endlessly loved. Kicking up the throttles toward forty miles-per-hour, he guided the pleasure craft through the chop.

•

Rand cut the motor forty minutes later, drifting in two-hundred-feet of water off the Lake Worth coast. Sunset was still more than an hour away, which gave them a chance to snack and possibly adjourn to the cabin for a late afternoon rockin' on the waves. Sex on the boat was fantastic. Almost weightless. And free. Especially on the bow, as opposed to in the cabin. But they were too close to shore to get it on above deck, so below deck would have to do. He felt a stir in his shorts just thinking about it.

"Ready to eat?" Jane asked.

"Oh, uh, yeah."

From the cabin, Jane appeared with a plate displaying the crackers, cheese, and grapes he'd packed earlier. Two cans of iced tea were clenched beneath one arm. They made their way to the cushioned rear seat that spanned the length of the stern, and Jane plopped the food in the center between them.

"This is perfect," she said.

"It is nice."

"I wish it could always be like this."

"It wouldn't take much to get out more often. We used to be here three or four days a week."

"And it's always been good for us."

"Yeah."

She'd stopped eating and was looking at him…no, *studying* him. He could see her eyes behind the dark glass. "I love you, Rand. Do you know how much I love you?"

He stopped eating, too. "If you feel half as much for me as I do for you, then, yeah, I have some idea."

She reached up and caressed his face. She'd done it many times before, but he never tired of her touch. When she spoke, her words traveled only as far as his ears, their echoes deafened by the salted breeze and swallowed by the rolling waves. "You've been so good to me. And *for* me."

"That goes in reverse, as well."

She leaned over the tray of food and kissed him. And just as she had responded to him earlier, he kissed back. The stirring he'd felt only moments before returned with a vengeance.

Jane spoke first. "I think we *should* come here more often. Get away from the snowbirds and the town meetings and the photo shoots. Even in the house the phone rings constantly, and a thousand little things steal our attention."

"You have my full attention now." He raised his hand and cupped her breast. Her body always felt so good, so right, beneath his fingertips.

"Do I?" She had a playful smirk.

"Completely."

"Shall we go below deck?"

"I thought you'd never ask." He stood up and held his hand out for her.

"I'll follow," she said, gathering the plate and partially-consumed cans of tea.

"I'll be ready."

Rand moved forward toward the bow, steadying himself on the T-top frame and gunwale as he advanced to the cabin door. He bent down and descended the single step below deck, and crawled onto the mattress. He kicked off his deck shoes and pulled his shorts and underwear down his legs, chuckling to himself at the recollection of how a friend of theirs once described their on-board bed as being big enough to "sleep two or fuck four." God, that was funny.

That's when he heard the splash.

"Janie?"

No answer.

Nude, he bolted through the cabin door, clipping his right knee on the frame, and stood to check the scene on the deck.

"Janie, you okay?" Then more urgently, *"Jane?"*

Where the hell could she go? He scanned the water near and around the boat, but saw nothing. Their snack plate was upside-down on the rear seat cushion, half-covering the scattered cheese slices, crackers, and grapes. Rand started when one of the tea cans rolled off the seat and hit the fiberglass deck with a crack.

"Jesus, *Janie!* Where the fuck *are* you?"

This couldn't be happening.

He dove into the water and swam around the underside of the hull. He looked down at the ocean bottom, but without a mask he saw only shadows. None of them looked like his wife. He came up for air twice, swimming 'round and 'round the *Sweet Mystery* until the first urgent thoughts of a worst-case begged him to stop. He climbed aboard using the prop and engine as a ladder, and rushed to the overhead compartment of the operator's console.

Opening the door, he reached in, removed the VHF radio mike, and depressed the talk button. "Mayday, Mayday, Mayday. This is the *Sweet Mystery* drifting in...approximately one-hundred-fifty-feet of water, south of the Lake Worth Pier. There's been an accident." *Oh God there's been an awful accident and hurry please hurry.* "I repeat, there's been an accident. Mayday, Mayday, Mayday."

He scanned the water surrounding the boat. He looked into the cabin, as if she'd somehow crept around behind him and snuck in.

"*Sweet Mystery*, this is the Coast Guard at Boynton Beach. Please confirm your distress and location."

Confirm my distress? My wife—whom I was just about to *bone*—has disappeared into *thin* fucking *air*. *That's* my distress. How do you transmit *that* over the radio?

"*Sweet Mystery*, I repeat, this is the Coast Guard at Boynton Beach. Do you read me?"

He thought about diving in again and checking under the hull one last time. But he knew he'd find nothing. Drifting silently along the slow-moving ocean current, Rand had no other place to look.

"Yeah, I read you, Coast Guard," he choked into the mike. "My wife has just fallen overboard."

And there's not a fucking thing I can do about it.

CHAPTER 2

On a wrought iron bench in New Orleans' Jackson Square, Coop sat with his companion and gnawed on his fingernails. Normally, he and Ozzy would be at Oliver's, working on the website and laughing at nothing. But Oliver had told them to stay away today. Tomorrow, too. With nowhere to go and half as much to do, Coop was out of his mind with boredom.

"You shouldn't do that." Ozzy's short, stout frame was perched on the back of the bench. His feet, clad in scuffed, red Converse high-tops, were planted on the seat to Coop's right.

"Do what?"

"Bite your nails. You'll dull your teeth."

Coop leaned his head backward and squinted in the late afternoon sun as it hovered above the city's former town hall and Spanish colonial gem, the Cabildo. *Like I'd listen to a guy with a missing tooth,* he thought. "Thanks for the advice, Fang de Uno, but I'll take my chances."

Ozzy slapped him hard on the shoulder. "How many times do I have to tell you? I'm self-conscious enough without your cracks."

Coop straightened in his seat. "The woman had a collar on, dumbass. How could you bite a silver chain collar?"

"It was dark."

"We can see in the dark." Coop looked down at his fingernails. Not much left. He brought a finger up to his mouth and started nibbling again.

"I'm not discussin' this anymore. When we get some money, I'll have it fixed. Until then, just shut up about it."

"Whatever." God he was bored.

The day had been typical for May. Sunny and seventy-eight degrees. Prime conditions for noisy-ass kids and their Yankee tourist parents. He thought for sure that last year's hurricane and flood would keep the tourists away for a while, but here they were back again. There'd been a time when proceedings in the Plaza d'Armas were more interesting than watching ice cream drip from the chins of whining children. When Coop and Ozzy had first arrived in New Orleans, public torture and executions entertained hundreds in the square by the river. And then there were the slave auctions. The place was always crowded, but early arrival guaranteed a good spot. Coop gazed up at the statue of General Jackson and wished things could be more like they used to be.

"Hey, Coop." Ozzy shook him from his thoughts.

"Yeah."

"I've been thinkin'."

"Shit. That's the first sign of Armageddon."

"Shut up, asswipe."

"Just fuckin' with ya', man. What's on your mind?"

"I was sittin' here thinkin' about how long it's been since we started over. It's time we came up with new names again."

"Didn't we just change 'em? God, this gets old."

"We're supposed to start over every ten years or so, right? Pontchartrain Beach closed in 1983. That's like twenty years already. Remember the big celebration and the rocker bitches we nailed under the Zephyr?"

"Yeah. They talked rough, but when it came time to dance they screamed like babies."

"They all scream like babies, but that's not the point. We need to pick new names."

"Twenty years, huh? Guess we should." Coop stopped nibbling his nails and moved to the end of the bench to sit facing Ozzy. "Have you thought of any?"

"Well," Ozzy hopped off the back and sat opposite Coop, "I thought maybe we could do it like last time. Get names off the girls' shirts next time we feed."

Not a bad idea, Coop thought, but even good ideas had a down side. "What if they're wearing the same shirts as the last girls?"

"Coop, nobody knows Ozzy Osbourne and Alice Cooper anymore. They're dead."

"Are they? I thought I just saw one of 'em on the tube at the Rose."

"Probably a rerun."

"I think it was live."

"It doesn't matter. If by some astronomical coincidence we find women with the same shirts, we'll move on to different women, okay?"

"Okay. Hey, but what if their shirts don't have anything on them? What if they're blank?"

"Don't make this difficult."

"I'm just sayin'..."

Ozzy's cell phone rang and Coop stopped talking. He watched Ozzy reach quickly into the pocket of his denim jacket to answer.

"Here," Ozzy answered.

Coop tried to read his friend's expression, but the face beneath the scraggly brown hair was stoic.

"We're gone." He hung up the phone and returned it to his pocket as he stood up. "We gotta go to Oliver's." Hitching up his jeans, Ozzy strode down the circular sidewalk toward the gate.

Coop rushed to catch up. "But Oliver said..."

"Plans change." Ozzy's pace quickened as they drew closer to the park gate and St. Louis Cathedral. Coop followed him past the street painters and tarot card readers dotting the streets along the fence. They rounded the Cabildo's architectural sibling, the Presbytére, and marched into the growing shadows of Saint Ann Street.

"So why are we going?"

Ozzy kept walking as he yelled back. "This is exactly the reason why I have the cell phone and you don't. You ask too many fuckin' questions."

"I'm just wonderin' why we're interrupting Oliver when he told us not to."

"Because we are."

Crossing Saint Ann, they neared Royal, narrowly avoiding a collision with a dark green sedan. The driver honked. Coop gave him the finger and hollered, "Welcome to the Crescent City, Yankee bastard."

"Don't attract attention," Ozzy called out over his shoulder. "We need to keep moving."

"Yeah, well, just let that sonofabitch turn 'round and get a piece of me." Coop turned his head to see if the Yankee bastard was following. "I'll kick his..." Coop's head and chest collided with an iron balcony pole. He lifted his hand to his forehead. "Hey, look. Blood!"

"For Christ's sake, Coop, hurry the fuck up."

A horse-drawn carriage was making its way up Royal toward Coop. As he moved along the sidewalk, still hurrying to catch up to Ozzy, he listened as the driver prattled to his passengers about the old house across the street.

"Commissioned one hundred sixty-five years ago by an early owner for his new bride, the fence is made of cast-iron and incorporates the signs of harvest." The guy sounded like such a douche. "The cornstalks were of particular interest to the bride, as her native home was Iowa."

"What a bunch of crap," Coop mumbled to himself. "Who gives a flyin' fuck?" *Fuckin' tourists.*

Ahead on the left, Oliver's house stood at the corner of Royal and Prince Avenues. It was a two-story, French-style structure common in the Vieux Carré, with a balcony that wrapped around the entire façade. Coop knew it well since he and Ozzy had been taking care of the paint and small repairs for most of the previous century. Not that Oliver cared about the house. It could crumble around him and he wouldn't notice. Every five years or so, the city sent threatening letters about the home's disrepair and neglect. Like it was any of their business. To shut them up, and to avoid the hassle of relocating operations for the website, Coop and Ozzy pounded in a couple of nails and slapped a coat of burnt orange paint on the bricks and dark green on the shutters. Oliver would slip them some pocket money and the city would leave them alone. 'Til the next time.

Up ahead, Ozzy turned and disappeared up Prince Avenue. Coop dodged a taxi crossing Royal and rounded the corner in time to see his friend slip through the wooden gate to the alley.

"*Compadre*," Coop called out, "*mira esto.*" He dashed through the gate behind Ozzy and secured the latch. "*Espera*, fat ass. Hold up." Coop grabbed Ozzy's shoulder and spun him around. "Check it out." He pointed to the spot where the iron pole collided with his forehead. "I knocked it so hard it drew blood. See?"

"All I see is an idiot who can't keep up. Let's get inside."

"You mean it's gone already? Shit. I haven't had a gash like that in a while."

Ozzy pulled a key from his pocket and unlocked the courtyard door. "If you're that disappointed, I could rap you in the head with a brick and make a new one."

"Nah. That defeats the spontaneousness."

"It's *spontaneity*, dumbass. Leave the big words to those of us who don't have shit for brains."

"Fuck you."

"That's more like it."

They entered the courtyard and followed a well-worn path over the cobblestones to the back stairs. The overgrowth of plants and vines made it impossible to venture through any other way without a machete. Making no attempt to conceal their arrival, the two tromped up the creaky stairs and into the second floor hallway. A left turn, followed by a right, brought them to the doorway of the music room.

Coop slid past Ozzy and barged into the room. "Hey, O-Man, we came to..." He stopped. All that lit the room were a few slivers of sunshine that penetrated the closed, time-worn shutters. But that was all he needed. Oliver wasn't there.

"What's the matter?" Ozzy asked, stepping into the room. "Where's Oliver?"

"Right here." Oliver appeared behind them, having entered the hall from the opposite direction. "I told you both, the house was off limits today."

"That's what I said, but..." Coop was silenced by a hard blow to the back of the head. "Aah. Why'd you do that?"

Oliver squeezed past the two companions.

"Sorry, O." Ozzy followed Oliver as he navigated through the dusty, abandoned instruments and music stands. "I realized this morning I skipped a critical step uploading the message board last night."

"It can wait." Oliver was showing an uncharacteristic amount of impatience.

Coop followed Ozzy through the room and wondered why his companion hadn't mentioned the upload problem this morning. "Oz, we ran through the checklist twice last night before...OW!" Ozzy had backhanded him. "Jesus. That was right where the post hit."

Ozzy ignored him. "The board's not live unless we fix it, O. It'll only take me a minute, man, I promise."

For the second time that morning, Coop felt for the wound on his forehead and discovered blood. He needed a mirror. Casting his gaze to the far wall on the left, he spotted one. But, in order to reach it, he'd need to carefully maneuver around delicate instruments and wooden chairs and music stands discarded and silent for decades.

Piece o' cake.

The only portions of Oliver's estate Coop had seen since the three partnered up were the courtyard, the back stairs, the hallway, and the music room. He'd heard there was more—a library even—but he was most familiar with the room in which he now stood.

Oliver had told them of the recitals and rehearsals conducted here, in what was intended for a grand ballroom. Lit by a hundred candles, musicians played to crowds that sometimes spilled downstairs and into the streets. Peering up, Coop couldn't imagine the dark chandeliers casting a glow on anyone.

He advanced toward the mirror and listened as Oliver continued his conversation with Ozzy. "I'd really prefer to be left alone, gentlemen. The board can wait."

"You're the boss, O. Your call. I just thought it was important."

"Under normal circumstances, it would be."

Ozzy kept talking, but Coop stopped listening as he skirted the vacant orchestra rows, anxiously progressing toward the mammoth, gold-trimmed mirror for a good ogling at his wound. He wasn't close enough to see himself, yet, but the reflection did offer a perspective Coop had never seen. It was as if he were hovering above the room. The abandoned violins. The flutes. The dust-covered chairs. The silent sheets of music. Reminders of what had been. But, he reminded himself, nostalgia wasn't why he'd shuffled over here.

Lunging forward on his final step, Coop's hand brushed against a saxophone strap. The instrument crashed to the floor. Coop recoiled and backed into a flimsy wooden stand laden with sheet music, toppling it into the row of chairs behind. The stand split in half when it struck the floor. Dust billowed in every direction.

"What the hell are you doing over there?" Oliver snapped. His words echoed off the walls in the expansive room.

Coop felt like he'd stepped out of the john with his pants around his ankles. He looked apologetically to his companions. "I was tryin' to get to the mirror."

Oliver responded, "You obviously fell short of the task."

Coop brought a hand to his forehead. "There's a nasty bump on my head I wanna look at."

Ozzy yelled from across the room. "Can you be careful about it? You're actin' like a fuckin' moron." Since he was sitting behind a computer, Coop assumed Oliver had relented to Ozzy's request sometime before the crash.

"You don't need your best behavior here, gentlemen," Oliver said from a Louis XVI chair in the far corner, "but I do expect a certain reverence."

"Reverence?" Ozzy said. "You'd never get that dumbass into a church."

"Yeah," Coop retorted, "well at least I didn't break my tooth on a fuckin' collar."

"Would you shut up about that!"

"Gentlemen," Oliver interjected. He sounded annoyed. "Make a note to look into the definition of 'reverence' before embarrassing yourselves any further."

"What's that supposed to mean?" Ozzy sounded confused. Coop was right there with him.

"Nothing," Oliver said. "It's not important." He stood up from the upholstered chair and approached Ozzy at the computer. "What *is* important is that you leave. Are you finished?"

Oz looked up from the screen. "Why? You expecting company or something?"

Coop thought it a strange question, considering Oliver never had guests. Except for Coop and Ozzy, of course, but they hadn't been considered *guests* since 1932.

"Not that it's any of your business," Oliver said, "but yes, I am expecting someone."

Coop felt his jaw drop. Ozzy, on the other hand, continued to look at the screen in front of him and exhibited no surprise at all.

"That's big news, O," Ozzy commented. "Were you ever going to tell us?"

"I hadn't planned to."

Ozzy stopped typing and stood up to face Oliver. "Well, I guess we should let you be, then."

We're leaving? Coop wondered. "But, Oz..."

Ozzy interrupted. "Can't you see the man wants to be alone?"

Bringing his fingers to his forehead, Coop felt for the gash he'd traveled to the mirror to see. Finding nothing, he scratched his head, bewildered his companion had switched gears so quickly.

"I think the bulletin board's okay, now, O." Ozzy skirted around Oliver and ambled toward Coop and the exit. "Sorry for the interruption."

"Shouldn't I clean some of this up?" Coop asked, surveying the damage that surrounded him.

"Leave it," Oliver instructed, following Ozzy.

"It'll take just a few minutes." Coop squatted and began gathering sheets of music. A violent tug at the back of his neck sent them fluttering again to the floor. "Hey!" Coop stumbled, but stayed on his feet.

"O wants us out, dumbass, didn't you hear?" Ozzy's grip held firm as he pulled Coop toward the door.

"But coming here was your..."

Ozzy pulled harder, shutting off his air supply. "Shut up and keep moving."

Shuffling backward, Coop watched Oliver trail them into the hallway and shut the music room door. He tried to say goodbye, but all he could manage was a faint gurgle as Ozzy dragged him by the collar through the hallway and down the stairs.

CHAPTER 3

The South Florida sun had set by the time Jane pulled herself from the water near the pier, but enough light remained for her to tell she'd not been noticed emerging from the surf. A few diehards—or maybe just lovers or tourists—remained scattered along the Lake Worth beach, which was good because it kept her from appearing suspicious.

She'd held her breath, of course. It was a trick she'd learned decades earlier after a boating accident. *How ironic*, she thought. What made it difficult on this occasion had been the constant urge to cry. Had she relented, her lungs would have filled with water and she would have erupted in a coughing fit that would have drawn attention to her arrival on the beach.

But she could breathe now, and she spit out the water that *had* rushed in during the moments when she couldn't hold back the sobs. Like now. The can of iced tea that helped her sink to the bottom, the one she'd filled with rocks when Rand wasn't paying attention, was still in her hand. She threw it into the ocean as far as her strength would allow. She tossed the goggles aside, too. The ones she'd slipped into her pocket before they'd left for the marina. He loved her so much. What hell must he be going through right now, while she shivered and cried only a few short miles away? Was his pain worth it? Was hers?

"There was no other way," she whispered through clenched teeth. Their years together had brought more happiness than she'd ever imagined possible. She was still crying when the security officer approached her and asked, "Are you okay, ma'am?"

She instinctively tensed. "You startled me."

"Sorry, just checking to make sure you're all right."

She looked around and saw that the beach was empty. The sun had disappeared. "Yes, I'm fine. I had a…a bad break-up today." True enough. She stood up and wiped at her eyes, then brushed the sand from her shorts and shirt. She was dry. How long had she been there? "I'll get myself home."

"No rush. Take your time. I just worried that you might be hurt or something. Can I walk you to your car?"

"No. Really. But, thanks."

"I'll be around, down that way," he pointed. "Be careful."

"I will." She waited until the man was far away, then trudged through the sand in the opposite direction. Jane hoped the kid who found the goggles in the morning would enjoy them more than she had.

Tonight, she would go to one of those efficiency-type motels, the kind that say they're within walking distance of the ocean, but aren't close enough to have a view. She'd pay cash for the single night, check out early in the morning, take a cab to the bank Rand never knew about, then board a train for New Orleans. It had been sixty years since she'd ridden a train, but the connection she'd developed as a little girl had not left her. And, for this task at this time, what mode of transport could be more appropriate? Trains were anonymous. Not sleek or high-profile like airplanes, and they didn't have the reputation buses couldn't shake. They were neither blue collar, nor white. Trains just *were*. Like part of the landscape. Like Jane had become.

The one she loved was behind her. *Like a broken record*, she thought, her life—her *lives*—kept repeating. But Oliver had come through. Obviously, he'd picked up where she left off all those years ago. Maybe there could finally be an end to the running. She was afraid to hope. Then again, when had Oliver ever been wrong?

She made her way on foot under the streetlamps, across the bridge, and along closed storefronts to Federal Highway. Ahead, the sign on a fifties-style motel advertised vacancy. Jane rang the bell when she reached the office door. With so many heavy thoughts, she would have preferred walking the lamp-lit streets, but she had more crying to do.

And she couldn't be seen.

Through the office window, Jane watched a tall figure cross the lobby toward the door. She fished in her back pocket for cash. In less than forty-eight hours, she'd be with Oliver and the truth about who she was and who she'd become would swallow her whole. But hadn't Rand been worth pretending it away for a while?

The man opened the door and invited her in. Jane stepped inside and followed him to a recently re-surfaced and painted counter. *It's not the Ritz, but it's fitting*, she thought, and she prepared for her journey back in time.

Chapter 4

Northern Texas – June 1861

E. Clifton Dougharty snapped to consciousness and sat upright in his seat. Shaking off a brief but wonderful dream—his wife Catherine had been gone six years, but her memory was never far—he took a quick inventory of the rocking, dimly lit coach to remind himself of where he was.

The children, seated across from him, were stirring, but thankfully still asleep. Eddie, only ten, had sprawled across the length of the padded bench, his head resting comfortably in his older sister's lap. And Janie—his beautiful Janie—sat directly in front of her father, with her head leaning against the side of the coach and her hand placed lovingly on her brother's shoulder. Seated there, with her dark locks hanging down, her pale skin reflecting the filtered afternoon sun, it was evident, even at age twelve, she would one day be as striking as her mother.

The heat was unbearable, and the dusty terrain of the middle states had coated everything with a thin layer of what looked like gray soot. It was due to pure exhaustion that they were able to sleep at all. For two months they'd endured extreme discomfort, and, if all went along as scheduled, three more months lay ahead. But so far the overland journey had been uneventful. Thanks, in part, he supposed, to the man with the gun seated up top next to the driver. Dougharty had voiced his concerns about the weapon in the beginning, but the two men in charge said they'd all "die fools" attempting the trip without it. He wondered how many of the stories he'd heard along the way were to be believed.

The vision of a transcontinental railroad may have originated with his superiors, but the realization—the strategies of actual construction—had been placed in his hands. Mr. Charles Crocker, one of the project's key financiers, had written Dougharty personally, requesting he join the managers "post haste" in California. Crocker strongly recommended in his letter that he not make the journey by sea as it was perilous, disease being cited as the most frequent affliction. So Dougharty and the children had traveled first by train from Philadelphia to St. Louis, as far west as the railroad could go. From there, they'd endured various coaches, seldom gaining more than eight or ten miles each day. If the trip had done nothing else, it had shown Dougharty the tremendous need for safe and timely transport from east to west. In essence, and considering the mounting unrest in the southern territories, the modernization and union of this great country depended on him. He was determined to do everything in his power to see it happen. But first, he reminded himself, they must safely reach Sacramento.

A rap on the side of the coach jerked him quickly from his thoughts, and, as the children wrestled awake, he lifted the window shade. Broad, empty plains surrounded them, but, up ahead, the outline of a vast mountain range was not far distant. The change in landscape would be a welcome one.

"Mr. Dougharty," the driver called from his seat above and behind Janie.

"Yes," he answered, peering out and craning his neck to see.

"How you folks fairin'?"

"We're fine, thank you. A bit warm, but fine."

"Yup, it's a nasty heat in summer, but the night'll cool you down. We'll be stoppin' soon. Small camp ahead. Last settlement before El Paso. Just wanted to tell ya'."

"I'll see that we're ready. And thank you again." He started to return the shade over the window, but Janie protested.

"No, Papa, leave the window open. It's awfully hot in here." Eddie had removed himself from her lap, and Janie was fanning her face and neck with her thin, robin's egg blue hat as she pulled up the shade on her own window. She looked at her father's face and giggled, "Papa, your hair and mustache nearly match your suit."

Dougharty wiped at his head and face, sending dust in every direction. "Better?"

"At best an improvement."

"We'll all get cleaned up soon."

Eddie scrambled around the coach, pulling up the two shades opposite his father and sister. "Wow," he shouted, hanging his torso too far outside, "Janie, look! You gotta see this."

Dougharty watched his children, Eddie on the left and Janie on the right, as they leaned out the coach's windows to get a glimpse of the approaching terrain. "Be careful, now, both of you. We didn't come this far to have you fall and break your necks."

"Oh, Papa," Janie said without turning around, "you worry too much."

"Come look, Pa," Eddie turned and motioned to his father, "the mountains are closer. I swear they are. Will we be going through them soon?"

"Yes, I believe we will," Dougharty replied, looking out the window next to Eddie. *One way or another*, he thought.

"Those are the Rockies, boy," the driver called out. "You folks'll have to get by 'em to make your way to California. Used to be treacherous, but it ain't so no more. Oxbow route runs through the passes. You'll likely be ridin' with Doc Fenton. One of the best. Used to drive Denver to Salt Lake."

"There's a town ahead, Papa," Janie said, barely concealing her excitement. "Not another one of those relay stops."

She had good reason to be anxious. They all did. They hadn't seen much that passed for civilization in weeks. There'd been scattered forts and settlements, but nothing like St. Louis. Or home in Philadelphia.

All the more reason, Dougharty thought, to push proceedings in Sacramento.

"Children, gather your coats and hats."

"Ah, do we have to, Pa?" Eddie sighed, climbing back into his seat.

"I'll have none of that, Edward," Dougharty chided. "We proudly represent the state of Pennsylvania and the founding colonies of this great nation, as well as the interests of the Central Pacific Railroad. You will portray yourself to the people of this settlement accordingly."

"Yes, sir." Eddie reached for his hat and wool coat, brushed away some of the dust, and grudgingly put them on.

"And be careful not to fall into manure getting off the stage," Janie added, after placing her own hat atop her head and reaching for her small, waist-length coat.

"Hey, that was an accident," Eddie whined, obviously irritated by the reminder of his *trip* in Sioux Falls. Janie aggravated his embarrassment by sticking her tongue out at him.

"That's enough, Jane Marie," her father advised.

"Yes, sir," she said, flashing a smile and fastening her coat.

•

A quick glance at his pocket watch told Dougharty it was just past four when the coach rolled to a stop in front of what was likely the only hotel. And that was fine. The prospect of sleeping in a proper room, as opposed to the inadequate bunks at most stops along the trail, did boost his spirits. The door of the coach opened, and he stepped gladly down onto the hard-packed street. "Ah, firm ground," he said to no one in particular as the driver assisted his children down the step.

"Welcome to the gate of the west, Mr. Dougharty," bellowed a voice behind him. He turned to find a long-haired, bearded man, dressed head-to-toe in black. His left hand clenched a black wide-rimmed hat close to his chest, and his right hand was extended. "I'm Rudolph Porter, the soul who passes for Sheriff in this camp, and the gentlemen behind me," he gestured to two similarly-clad deputies after shaking Dougharty's hand, "are Matt and Ray Stone." Porter's men tipped their hats first to Dougharty, then to the children. "It's an honor to meet you, sir, and to welcome you and your family to Devil's Eye."

"Thank you, Sheriff, this is, uh, a pleasant surprise. I hadn't expected a reception. You say this is Devil's Eye?"

"Indian name. To be honest, we're considering a change when the town incorporates."

"Of course." Dougharty wondered if he should be concerned. "But, where are my manners? Children? Step here, please, and meet Sheriff Porter." The children moved obediently forward. "This is my son, Edward."

"Good to meet you, Sheriff," Eddie said proudly, offering his hand. Sheriff Porter had placed his hat on his head, revealing the badge on his lapel. Dougharty immediately noticed the sparkle in his son's eyes as they were drawn to the shiny insignia.

"And this is my daughter, Jane Marie."

"Pleased to meet you, sir," Janie said equally as proud as she dipped into a short curtsy.

"Fine children, Dougharty," remarked Porter. "And your wife? Has she come along as well?"

"I'm afraid my wife passed some years ago."

"Oh, I'm sorry."

"So are we all."

The awkward silence was broken when the stagecoach driver asked, "Mr. Dougharty, where shall we deliver your bags?"

"Here," the Sheriff instructed, "we'll take care of those for you. I've taken the liberty of reserving the finest room we have...that is, if you don't mind."

"Oh, no. Not at all. I'm sure whatever's been arranged will be fine."

"And, Mr. Parker," the Sheriff called out to the driver, "many thanks to you and Hayworth for seeing to it that these folks arrived safely."

"Yes," Dougharty added, "that goes for myself and the children as well, sir. We thank you kindly for the service." Ordinarily, coaches carried six passengers. Parker had been the only driver who'd not required a bribe—along with the additional fares, of course—to transport only the family of three. Dougharty tipped his hat to underscore his gratitude.

"You take care, Mr. Dougharty," Parker replied as he strode forward to lead the horses away, "and keep an eye on the young 'uns."

"You know I will."

"Goodbye, Mr. Parker," Eddie called out, "and thanks."

"Me, too, Mr. Parker," Janie chimed in. "Goodbye."

"Now," said the Sheriff, "let's get you settled in. The boys will see to your things."

Porter led the family across the boarded walk and toward the hotel door. Dougharty thought the Sheriff's reception strange, considering they'd met with no similar welcome anywhere else. But offering to carry the bags? And lodging secured prior to their arrival? He wondered if other motives lurked beneath the hospitality.

The hotel lobby was small, but elaborately appointed with elegant, wide-striped wallpaper and a large chandelier. To their left was a staircase, and directly in front of them stood the hotel desk.

Sheriff Porter stopped to greet the clerk. "Jacob, this is the gentleman from Pennsylvania we've been expecting. Please see to it that he and his family are shown your utmost hospitality."

"Without question, Sheriff. Jacob Winslow at your service, Mr. Dougharty. Welcome to the Winslow Arms."

"Thank you. All this…fuss has been somewhat overwhelming, but my children and I certainly look forward to our stay." He nodded to Winslow and the Sheriff and to the deputies who'd stepped through the door carrying the luggage.

"I'll take them up, Winslow." The Sheriff took a key from the desk. "Your room is this way," he instructed, and he led them up the stairs.

At the end of the hall on the right-hand side, Sheriff Porter reached out and opened the door marked with a wood-carved number seven. He then stepped aside, allowing the family entry. The simple, yet suitable quarters, furnished with two beds, a sitting area, and a washbasin atop a chest of drawers, was a welcome sight. Two broad windows, facing north, overlooked the street below, and one additional, smaller window looked to the west. All were open, presumably, to allow for better air circulation.

"This will do very well, Sheriff," Dougharty said.

"It's our pleasure, sir. Oh, and here's your key."

"I thank you again."

"Come look, Pa," cried Eddie, his feet nearly off the floor as he hung over the windowsill. "There's a gallows going up in the square."

"Where, Eddie?" Janie asked, pursuing her brother.

"It's better from over here," Eddie instructed, and he motioned for his sister to follow him to the smaller window in the corner. He looked away from the spectacle below to turn and ask, "Are you gonna hang somebody, Sheriff?" But he didn't look away long.

"Sheriff, is this true?" Dougharty hoped his mild distress wouldn't be noticed. "Will there be a hanging here today?"

"As a matter of fact, there is. History in the making. We were hoping you would join us later, Mr. Dougharty, on this special occasion. We'd be honored to have a man such as you participatin' in the festivities."

"Festivities? You refer to public execution as if it were a carnival."

"Oh, Pa, can we go? Please?" Eddie was beside himself with enthusiasm.

"Son, I don't believe a hanging is an appro..."

"If you'll pardon the interruption, Mr. Dougharty," Porter interjected, "the children are most certainly welcome to come along. Might do them some good to witness the wheels of justice. Why, I expect most of the townspeople will bring their children."

Before Dougharty could answer, Porter's deputies appeared through the doorway carrying the luggage. "Shall we drop these over here, sir?" one of the brothers asked.

"Yes, that'll do fine," Dougharty answered, "and the rest can go there as well." He offered the gentlemen the most sincere smile he could muster, but his unease was difficult to mask. How many more surprises would there be in Devil's Eye?

"Sheriff Porter," he said, returning his attention to the man with the badge, "perhaps we should continue our conversation downstairs. I'd prefer to discuss this matter away from the children."

"Whatever you wish."

"Janie, Edward, I'm going downstairs for a bit with the Sheriff. Please remain here until my return."

"Yes, sir," Janie answered first, sneaking a glance in her brother's direction.

"Yes, sir," Eddie mimicked, his enthusiasm visibly deflated.

"That's good, then. Now, there appears to be fresh water in the basin, so wash up and change. We'll be having dinner soon. I won't be long." Dougharty started to follow Sheriff Porter through the doorway, then turned to his children and added, "And stay away from the windows."

If they protested, they did it quietly and behind the closed door where Dougharty couldn't hear them.

•

Once downstairs, the men stepped outside onto the boarded walkway. Dougharty looked west to the mountains, guessing the sunset to be at least three hours away. He removed his hat briefly, both to examine it for wear and to brush away the dust, then patted at his coat and vest.

"Can I interest you in a drink, Mr. Dougharty? We have a fine saloon in town, and it's just across the street there."

"I'm really quite tired. It's been a long journey, and there's still many days ahead."

"Well, let's not waste another minute, then." The Sheriff stepped down from the boardwalk and Dougharty reluctantly followed.

"Is there always this much activity here?" Dougharty asked, dodging a horse-drawn cart. There wasn't much to the small settlement—the main "street" was comprised of six two-story wooden buildings, three on each side—but what there was buzzed with activity. People crowded the boardwalks on his left, heading toward the west end of town, and a half dozen horses or more were tied to hitching posts outside the saloon and the adjacent mercantile.

"Preparations for this evening are keeping a good deal of the locals occupied. They've come from miles around. We get a lot of trade, mostly supplies headed west. Devil's Eye's the last civilized camp this side of the Rockies, and the only place to properly whet your whistle within a hundred miles."

"Where does everyone stay?"

"Oh, right around back there, behind the mercantile, there's a hundred tents or more. Most folks are only here for the night, and there weren't enough rooms at the hotel to accommodate them." The Sheriff stepped up onto the boarded walkway leading to the saloon and added, "Not that they could afford the rent anyway."

Dougharty followed as Porter pushed open the swinging double doors to the saloon and greeted the man behind the bar.

"Aye, Sheriff," welcomed the man wiping the counter with a dirtied towel, "and who might yer friend be?"

The Sheriff puffed out his chest. "Martin O'Donnell, Broken Wheel owner and barkeep extraordinaire, I'd like you to meet Mr. E. Clifton Dougharty of the Central Pacific Railroad."

O'Donnell slung the towel over his shoulder and offered his hand. Dougharty marveled at the man's fire-red handlebar mustache and at the strength of his handshake. By the looks of the men crowding the tables throughout the room, he guessed O'Donnell likely had as much opportunity to act as peacekeeper as he did barkeep.

"Good to make yer acquaintance, Mr. Dougharty. I take it yer a fellow Irishman?"

"Indeed, second generation born in Philadelphia. Pleased to meet you."

"Marty came to us straight from the motherland near five years ago," Sheriff Porter said as he pulled a stool up to the bar. "What was it, '55, '56? Ah, hell, not that it matters. He's the best thing ever to happen to folks in the Eye."

"He only says that 'cuz his drinks're on the house." O'Donnell produced three large shot glasses from underneath the bar and filled them with a bottle he took from a locked cabinet.

"To the railroad," Sheriff Porter announced, holding his glass in the air, "may she come 'round swift and sure..."

"...and may her payload always stop at the Broken Wheel," O'Donnell added with a wide grin.

"To the railroad," Dougharty finished. The three men downed their glasses in unison.

"Ye'll surely join us for the hangin' later, won't ye, Dougharty?" O'Donnell asked, refilling two of the three empty glasses and wiping the third with the towel from his shoulder.

"The Sheriff and I were just discussing that, and I'm afraid, on account of my young children, I may have to decline the invitation."

"But ye have to be there," O'Donnell protested, "the Sheriff was tellin' me only this mornin' that yer attendance makes things look more official. Ain't that right?"

"Official?" Dougharty asked. "I'm afraid I don't understand."

"Let me explain," Sheriff Porter replied. "The Eye's not recognized by the state of Texas as a town. Not yet, anyway. We got laws, but no recognized way to enforce them. We're unprotected. Most camps out west are still that way."

"And we should be, too," a man from a table near the bar called out.

"Yeah, let us at Dickens," shouted another man from the next table. "We'll see that he gets justice." Several men in the crowded saloon cried out and laughed in agreement, but the Sheriff cut them off.

"That's enough boys, you know the way it is now. We've heard your arguments and the matter's been settled. Keep quiet or I'll see to it that you're not even allowed to watch."

Dougharty mused that if towns *with* laws in the west treated public hangings like harvest festivals, what was to be expected from towns *without* law enforcement?

"Henry Joe Dickens' execution represents the Eye's first act of real, official justice," the Sheriff continued, "and, aside from these few idiots within earshot, it means a lot to the locals who depend on the mercantile and the kitchen. Havin' you here as a witness, and what with it goin' down on the record books as havin' a kind of government representative in attendance, the whole business just comes across as...well, more official."

"I see your point," was all Dougharty could bring himself to say.

O'Donnell filled their two glasses again, and tended to the other patrons around the room. Dougharty took a sip. After a brief pause, he finally asked, "How is it that you consider me a representative of the government, Sheriff?"

"You're the closest thing we got, and that's the truth. We expected a Marshall near a week ago, but he got...well, let's just say he was *detained* in Omaha. Day or two later, we heard you was comin', so we held off the execution a few more days."

"If I were to attend," he said quietly to the Sheriff, "and it would have to be only myself, you understand. I can't allow my children to witness such a...severe act."

"Of course not," coddled the Sheriff. "Why, I was just thinkin' earlier to myself that I might not bring my own young 'uns."

Dougharty hesitated, looking for the right words. "In what capacity, or rather, at what level would I be expected to participate?"

Sheriff Porter's quizzical look was brief. "Oh, you don't think...why, Mr. Dougharty, I'd certainly not expect you to pull the lever. Just stand in the crowd and give a wave to the folks. Let 'em know you're here."

"Hmm. Then, I suppose I shall agree to...attend your...act of justice. But I must insist I return to my children directly after."

"Certainly."

"Well, that's settled, then. At what time should I arrive, and in the town square, I presume?"

"Yes, sir. You'll find me near the gallows, right about six o'clock."

"Of course. Near the gallows."

•

It looked to Dougharty as though every settler within a hundred miles had come to witness the execution. Throughout the town square, men were engaged in boisterous conversation about the accused. Women corralled children. All were aflutter with anticipation, pushing their way to the gallows for a better view. Dougharty identified Sheriff Porter in the crowd without much difficulty, as he maneuvered toward the lawman as quickly as possible. After greeting the Sheriff and his deputies (in addition to the Stone brothers, Dougharty noted, four other deputies were joyfully in attendance), Dougharty stole a glance toward the hotel's second-floor corner windows. Eddie had been especially argumentative earlier at dinner when his father informed him of the evening's plans, but Dougharty had remained firm in his instructions. The children were to close the windows, close the shades, and sit on the beds until their father's return. As far as he could tell from where he stood, they'd remained obedient.

The Sheriff, followed by two of the deputies Dougharty had met only moments before, ascended the steps built into the side of the gallows, and called out for the crowd's attention. "I believe we're ready to start, folks, if you'll all turn yourselves this way."

The people gathered closer to the main event, and the murmurs bounding through the crowd dulled. Sheriff Porter stepped to the edge of the platform and called down to the deputy standing closest to Dougharty.

"Sanford, it's time," he said.

"Gotcha, Sheriff," the young man replied, looking up. He strained his eyes against the sun as it perched atop the mountains. Dougharty watched the boy exit the crowd and run down the street and into the jail.

"Welcome, esteemed citizens of Devil's Eye," Sheriff Porter began his oration, now reading from a slip of paper he'd produced from his breast pocket.

The crowd cheered in response to the greeting.

"We have come to this spot today to witness the execution of Mr. Henry Joe Dickens..." Despite Dougharty's close proximity to the gallows, shouts and boos from the crowd made it difficult for him to hear. "Mr. Dickens was found guilty...ad-hoc court of law...Thursday, the fourteenth...May, in...eighteen hundred and sixty-one...sentenced to death by public hanging."

The noise subsided, replaced by a ripple of whispers as Sanford and yet another deputy led the prisoner, hands tied behind him, through the door of the jail and down the street toward the gallows. Dickens was assisted up the wooden stairs and brought to the center of the platform, next to the Sheriff, and near the trap door. The crowd silently waited for Sheriff Porter to continue.

"Henry Joe Dickens, you have been advised of your crime and its punishment under the laws of Devil's Eye. Have you anything to say for yourself before the sentence is carried out?"

Dougharty, wishing he'd been able to hear what the man's crime had been, watched as the condemned man's expression turned from sorrowful into a crazed and angry sneer.

"All I have to say is that you can *suck* my *nuts* you fuckin' phoney lawman. You ain't *never* done *nothin'* in this *shithole* and you… nnnt… nnrr… nnrrnnt…" A quick-thinking deputy stuffed a handkerchief in Dickens' mouth before more obscenity spewed over the crowd.

Sheriff Porter tried desperately to regain the attention of his audience. "Please calm down, ladies and gentlemen. Calm down, please. We'll cut through the prayer and formalities, given the, uh… extenuating circumstances, and get right to it." Aggravated, he waved his arm at the presiding deputies, one of whom had placed a black hood over the prisoner's head, and positioned himself at the furthest corner from their activity.

The two lawmen placed Dickens atop the trap door, and the hangman's noose was fitted tightly around his neck.

"Ready?" asked the Sheriff. The man grasping the lever nodded. "Then take 'im down."

The air had noticeably cooled as the bright ball of the sun vanished behind the ridges of the Rocky Mountains. When the trap door clicked open, Henry Joe Dickens' body hit the ground with a thud. At first, no one realized anything had gone wrong. As the first screams shot out, echoing along the wooden façades of the main street, Dougharty glimpsed the ground below the gallows as the retreating crowd disbursed. In the dirt, directly underneath the platform and the gently swinging noose, was Dickens' body, blood spilling rapidly from his neck. Approximately eight feet away, and resting against the support post of the gallows, was Dickens' hooded, severed head.

Dougharty brought his fist to his mouth and quickly turned away. He'd heard of this happening before. It was rare, but possible. If the knot wasn't placed correctly, if the rope were too long and the body too heavy… He ran toward the hotel, dodging men, women, and children as they scurried frantically from the scene. Arriving safely on the boardwalk near the hotel door, he turned to watch the mayhem. He didn't have a clear view of the gallows themselves, but he could make out the Sheriff and his deputies as they huddled together near the steps to the platform. They seemed to be the only spectators remaining in the town square.

"Why don't you step inside, Mr. Dougharty," came a voice through the opening hotel door.

"Ah, Mr. Winslow, you...surprised me."

"Come in. A terrible mess, that, isn't it?" Winslow gestured toward the end of the street as he shut the door behind them.

"Yes, it certainly is." Dougharty again remembered reading that accidental beheadings were rare, but not unheard of. Still, seeing it firsthand sickened him. He considered flying straight upstairs to check on the children, but his curiosity begged him to ask one last question. "Mr. Winslow?"

"Yes, sir."

"What was it that Henry Dickens did, exactly, to warrant such a spectacle?"

"Oh, he shot a horse."

"A horse?" Dougharty repeated, afraid he hadn't heard the proprietor correctly.

"Mighty fine horse. Belonged to the Sheriff. Outright act of defiance was what he done. That man was a menace."

A horse. "Thank you, Winslow," Dougharty said as he slowly made his way to the staircase, "I appreciate the information."

"My pleasure, sir."

Speechless, Dougharty ascended the stairs and moved down the hall, musing over Sheriff Porter's words earlier that evening. *Devil's Eye's the last civilized town this side of the Rockies*.

"God help me," he whispered under his breath as he turned the knob on door number seven. *What kind of world have I brought my children to?*

Chapter 5

"I want to leave." Rand's body ached. The last moments of the cruise played over and over in his mind. If only he hadn't gone below deck. If only he'd jumped into the water sooner. Or looked deeper. "You have no reason to keep me."

He'd followed a marine officer to the Palm Beach police station for a few questions after the Coast Guard had cleared him. They said it would be brief. Rand's stomach was telling him it had been longer. Hours longer.

"We're simply trying to confirm the events surrounding your wife's disappearance." Sitting in an upholstered armchair in what looked like a petite version of a living room, Detective Janson had been cordial, but his inquisition had worn away the little patience Rand had left.

Rand shifted his weight on the beige couch. "But I've already told you," he looked at the two detectives in the small room and at the conspicuous mirror built into the wall, "that I don't know anything. One minute she was there. The next she was gone." He wanted to cooperate, but *Jesus*.

The female officer, Griffiths, spoke from her position next to him. "Mr. Ackerton, we're sure you want to get back to your home and your work..."

"I have no one to go home to, Detective, and I'm not exactly in the mood to work. I'm hungry, I'm exhausted, and I'm tired of answering the same questions. What I *want* is to get out of here, call my lawyer, and get something to eat."

"That attitude won't help us, Mr. Ackerton," Detective Janson chided, "and we've told you there's no need for a lawyer. You're not under suspicion at this time."

"I wasn't threatening you. My lawyer also happens to be my best friend. I've had a tough day, Detective." Rand reached for the white Styrofoam cup on the coffee table in front of him. The coffee was awful. He took a sip. It hadn't improved since it cooled. "I'm sorry. I'm just... What else can I possibly help you with?"

Detective Griffiths answered. "Tell us one last time exactly what happened. You say you anchored offshore at Lake Worth around four-thirty?"

"It was around four or four-thirty that we stopped, yes, but we drifted. We didn't anchor."

"And your wife was with you when you stopped the boat?"

"Yes."

"You're sure?"

"It's a small fishing boat, Detective, not a damn cruise ship." Rand stood up and stepped around the table to the mirror. The muscles in his ass were on fire, his knee throbbed, and he needed a smoke.

"Mr. Ackerton." Janson played the referee role well.

Leaning his head against the one-way glass, Rand continued. "Yes, I'm sure. Janie was with me in the boat when we stopped. She went into the cabin and grabbed a snack. We ate on the stern."

"For clarification," Detective Griffiths interjected, "the stern is the back?"

"Yes. It's the back." What good were all the notes these people were taking if they didn't read them?

"You said your wife brought two cans of...iced tea with her." Griffiths had an open file in front of her.

Rand watched her reflection in the mirror as she scanned the contents of the first sheet. *At least someone referred to notes.*

"The Coast Guard reported," she continued, "that only one can was found on the deck."

Rand turned his back to the mirror and faced the mauve wallpaper. "What difference would it make if we'd had one or two or seventeen cans of iced tea? We each had a can, I remember that. She brought two out of the cabin, not one."

Detective Griffiths maintained her tone. "So you sat down and ate for...fifteen, twenty minutes. Did you talk?"

"Yes."

"What did you talk about?"

"I don't know. Stuff. The shit married people talk about when they're floating on the ocean eating grapes."

"You said the mood of the afternoon turned romantic."

That wasn't exactly what he'd said, but it meant the same thing. "Janie suggested we go below deck."

"Meaning she wanted to have sex."

"We're married."

"And you're sure it wasn't you who suggested it?"

"I remember my wife wanted to have sex with me on the boat. A man approaching fifty doesn't forget something like that."

"And that's why the Coast Guard found you naked."

Why did they have to bring that up again? "I'd gone into the cabin first. I thought she was right behind me."

"But approximately twenty-five minutes passed between the time you alerted the Coast Guard and the time they arrived alongside your vessel."

"I wouldn't know. I'd kinda lost it at that point."

"Mr. Ackerton," Detective Janson interrupted his thoughts, "you said your wife seemed 'preoccupied' that day. Do you think she might have been depressed?"

"You mean like suicidal?" Rand couldn't imagine it. "Janie got blue now and then, but she wasn't nuts. She was happy. Happy people don't throw themselves overboard."

"Were you getting along? Would she have any reason to run or hide from you?"

"Shit. You've already asked me these questions. Yes, we were getting along fine, and no, she didn't have any reason to run."

"Just one more, Mr. Ackerton. Do you have any enemies? Anyone that might want to harm or kidnap Mrs. Ackerton?"

"No. Everybody loved Janie, and I...I'm just a guy with a camera." What the hell was happening to him?

"Well," Janson stood up, "if there are no more questions." He looked at his colleague.

"I'm satisfied." Griffiths closed her file and stood.

"Thank you, Mr. Ackerton, for your patience." Janson picked up his pen and notebook. "Oh, and thank you for the photograph."

"Of course." Rand remembered the tinge of guilt he'd felt taking it from his wallet and turning it over to the police earlier. But, he reminded himself, when he'd promised Jane he'd never share her photographs, they hadn't foreseen this shit.

Janson retrieved his coffee cup from the table, then gathered his clipboard. He looked like an honest guy. White shirt and tie type just doing his job. Rand wondered if every day were like this for him. Sitting in an interrogation room, drinking bad coffee, and asking questions of people who didn't want to talk.

"Thank you, Mr. Ackerton." Detective Griffiths extended her hand.

"Sure." Rand spoke politely, shaking the detective's hand. If not for the discreet holster on her hip, Griffiths looked like she could have been a retail clerk. Or an insurance salesman.

Janson motioned for Rand to follow him to the door. "I'll escort you out."

"Then we're done? I can go?" He moved toward the door, leaving the Styrofoam cup.

"Yes." Janson opened the door. "After you."

Rand stepped out of the dimly-lit, mauve interrogation room and into the bright second floor corridor. He trailed the detective beyond a row of cubicles and around a corner to an electronically secured door.

"We may need to speak with you again, Mr. Ackerton, so I have to ask you to stay in Palm Beach." Janson pressed a button on the wall. A buzzer sounded. The detective pushed the door open and held it with his foot.

"My wife disappeared today, Detective. I'm not going anywhere until I find out what happened."

Janson offered his hand. "Just take the elevator to the first floor." The men shook. "Thanks for your time, Mr. Ackerton. We'll be in touch."

The men parted and Rand entered the landscaped mezzanine lobby overlooking the polished tile floor of the station's main entrance. The door behind him closed. Rand looked up and noticed only darkness pouring through the circular skylight. What time was it? He approached the elevator doors and pressed the call button.

Once outside, he reached into his jean pockets and pulled out his keys, cigarettes, and lighter. His BMW was parked in front of the station. He lit a cigarette, descended the steps to the sidewalk, and wondered what he should do next. Janie was gone. His boat was "in custody." And the police, instead of looking for *clues*, had spent an entire evening asking the same questions the Coast Guard and marine officers had asked at the scene. Should he appreciate their efforts to be thorough? Or be offended by their misuse of his time?

Or, Rand thought as he pressed the unlock button on his key chain, did their barrage of questions mean the police thought he had something to do with Janie's fall?

He climbed in behind the wheel and slid the key into the ignition. Not so long ago, Rand remembered following the news of a man in California accused of killing his wife and unborn child. He'd believed then that the man was guilty. "Guilty as shit," he'd said to Jane. The evidence pointed right at him. Under Rand's current circumstances, feeling the pressure of police and the confusion over how things had gone so wrong so quickly, he could sympathize. Maybe the guy had been telling the truth all along and no one believed him.

Maybe he hadn't been guilty as shit after all.

•

Inside the station, Detective Patrick Janson had retreated down the corridor to the group of cubicles outside the interrogation room. Randolph Ackerton didn't seem the type to run, so he felt comfortable letting the guy go home. But then, Janson had been surprised before. Like he was with that Kennedy thing. And the guy a couple years back who'd stuffed his wife in a refrigerator. These Palm Beach people had a way of thinking themselves above the law.

Detective Adriane Griffiths was seated at her desk with the phone to her ear. Janson pulled a chair out from under the desk behind her and sat, tapping his notebook with his pen, pondering Ackerton's interview, and wondering how Griffiths managed to keep her space so neat. Two chairs down, Janson's desk looked like a family room on Christmas morning after three kids had pillaged their gifts. It was amazing Janson knew where everything was.

Griffiths hung up the phone and spun around in her chair. "Just checking voice mail. Did you notice it's almost midnight?"

Janson stopped tapping his notebook. "I know we should have left an hour ago, but what do you think about the Ackertons? Think the husband's telling the truth?" It was late and Janson was tired, but he wanted to be sure they were on the same page before their meeting with the Sergeant in the morning.

"I expected as much when I agreed to work with you on this case, Janson." Griffiths grinned, then swiveled in her chair to rifle through the few sheets of paper in the file on her desk. "But sleep's overrated, isn't it?"

"Here you two are." Detective J. B. Davis appeared from the corridor. As always, his shirt and slacks were perfectly pressed. His aqua tie likely purchased on Worth Avenue. Despite being his polar opposite, Janson liked the guy. Davis shot a grimace toward Janson's desk. "I've been meaning to tell you, Janson," Davis looked at the seated detective, "if a hurricane dropped a Buick on this desk of yours, it would be an improvement."

"Thanks, man." Janson stood up and mock-saluted the young, black detective who followed them on the night shift. "I'll take that under advisement."

Griffiths chuckled.

"On a more professional note," Davis continued, "Sergeant Benson asked me to help you with the Ackerton case. I saw a bit of the interview. The guy seemed agitated."

Griffiths spun her chair again. "We were just doing a recap when you showed up, Davis. We're looking at either drowning, abduction, foul play, or a simple missing persons. The guy says his wife fell over while he was below deck. Nothing aboard the vessel indicated foul play. Divers found nothing. They'll resume in the morning, but currents have been strong and they don't expect to find anything. Without a body, it's hard to tell which way to take this case. But for what it's worth," she craned her neck to look Janson in the eye, "I don't think the husband was lying."

Davis unfolded his arms and leaned against the side of the cubicle. "But how do you lose someone on a clear day in calm seas? Unless she was weighted down, it's hard to believe the guy's story."

"Yeah, but it happens," Janson argued, returning to the chair. "How long you been in paradise now, Davis? A couple of months? We see three or four of these every year."

"But don't forget," Griffiths added, "in most cases the boat is moving when the fall occurs."

"True," Janson replied. "So for the sake of argument, let's say the guy's lying, and the boat was moving at the time."

"Or," Griffiths said, "let's say he had something to do with it."

"You think he pushed her overboard?" Davis asked.

"Not necessarily, but we should consider every possibility. Maybe something went wrong, and to save himself the embarrassment he's covering it up. Maybe they were drinking and she fell and he couldn't save her in time. Or maybe they were moving when she toppled out and he didn't notice until he was too far away. Ackerton's a fashion photographer with friends in high places. It wouldn't exactly help his career to look like an idiot. Wine *was* found on board, so we know they're drinkers."

"But it was unopened," Janson added.

"Who's to say there hadn't been another bottle?" Davis asked. "Maybe it got tossed. The glasses, too. Maybe something else happened on that boat and, like Griffiths says, Ackerton's just too scared to say."

Until they were able to rule something out, Janson knew every scenario was theoretically possible. He also knew, given Ackerton's near celebrity status, the media would want to get involved. Janson absentmindedly started tapping his pen on his notebook again. He wanted to believe the guy. Ackerton had broken down several times during their interview. Not that Janson always fell for tears. But he had good intuition, and the man's grief seemed sincere. The guy had grown irritable as the night wore on, but who wouldn't have?

"So how're we gonna play this?" Griffiths asked, looking at Janson.

"Well," Janson shook off his thoughts and stood up again, "it's still a drowning unless we discover otherwise. Davis, scan the tape of the interview and make sure it's consistent with the marine officer's report. Maybe Ackerton's story has a hole."

"I can do that." Davis retrieved a small leather-bound notebook and pen from his shirt pocket and started scribbling. "Anything else?"

"A background check wouldn't hurt."

"On the husband?"

"Actually," Janson replied, "run both of them. Maybe there's a motive somewhere."

"Gotcha." Davis stuffed the notebook back into his pocket and tucked the pen behind his ear.

"Griffiths?"

"Yep."

"Get some sleep and meet me here tomorrow morning at six."

"Six? Roll call and briefing's not 'til seven."

"Right, and our meeting with the Sarge is immediately after. I want to hear what Davis has come up with before we see him."

Griffiths shrugged. "Fine. Your call. You getting some shut-eye, too, Janson?"

"Eventually." *But first*, he thought, *I want to get a closer look at that boat.*

"Suit yourself." Griffiths reached in a desk drawer to retrieve her purse. "I'm outta here."

"Thanks for your help," Janson said as she brushed by.

Griffiths waved without looking back. "See you at O'dark-thirty."

"Girl likes her sleep," Davis said once the exit door had closed.

"She's a good detective." Janson meant it.

"That's what I hear. I'm looking forward to working with both of you."

"Back at ya'." Janson stood. "See what you can find tonight and we'll talk in the morning."

"Will do. Goodnight, then."

"Goodnight." Janson stepped around the young detective and exited down the back stairs, anxious to uncover any secrets the Ackertons might be hiding.

DAY 2

CHAPTER 6

Rand woke on the couch, accompanied by a pounding headache and a throbbing right knee that instantly reminded him of the accident on the boat the previous day. He pulled himself up and rubbed the sleep from his eyes. He was still dressed in the shorts and pullover he'd worn to the police station. On the coffee table in front of him, the house phone, Jane's cell, and his palm pilot sat silent. He'd spent half the night talking with family and friends. The conversations drained him. He wanted to believe his wife was still alive. She was a strong swimmer. If she hadn't been hurt in the fall from the boat, she could have made it to shore and…

And what?

She hadn't called home. Hadn't contacted anyone. The fact that she might really be gone was sinking in, and the pain was excruciating.

With her near, their Key West-style estate felt warm. Comfortable. Without her, the house was cold and cavernous. So last night, Rand had fallen asleep with the large plasma television tuned to HBO. The volume was set low, but Ian McShane was still audible. The *Deadwood* star was screaming something about loyalty and how he wanted everything the way it was. Rand could relate. On a table to the left of the screen, the cable box's digital display read 6:22 AM. Would there be answers today? Or simply another parade of questions? Rand buried his head in his hands and thought how quickly his happiness had turned to hell.

A loud ring shook him from his thoughts. He reached for the home phone and pressed a button. "Yeah."

"Detective Janson, Mr. Ackerton. Please excuse the early call. I wanted to catch you before the reporters did."

Reporters? Was it standard procedure to bring in the press? "Have you found something? Have you found Janie?"

"Unfortunately no, but it seems the marina and the Coast Guard have spoken to the media. The story's in the Post this morning and..."

Rand didn't wait to hear the rest. He dropped the phone, bolted to the front door, and flung it open. In his bare feet, he darted across the small stones of the circular driveway and stopped at the mailbox. The morning paper was in the bin below it. As he reached in, two men jumped out of unmarked cars parked along the roadside. "Mr. Ackerton? Rand Ackerton?" They had notepads. And cameras. "A moment of your time, sir?"

"Fuck off." Rand seized the newspaper and hurried back to the house.

"Please." They were following.

"Get off my property." He shut the door in their faces. This wasn't the kind of press he needed right now.

He returned to the couch and opened the newspaper on top of the items on the coffee table. His picture was printed next to the headline:

WIFE OF FAMED PHOTOGRAPHER RAND ACKERTON MISSING

Was Foul Play Involved?

Palm Beach, Fla.—Police are investigating the mysterious disappearance of Jane Ackerton, young wife of celebrity and fashion photographer Rand Ackerton, a long-time resident of Palm Beach. According to

> sources at the West Palm Beach Marina, the couple set off on a pleasure cruise aboard their power boat, *Sweet Mystery*, shortly after one o'clock on Monday afternoon. A distress call three hours later, overheard by fishermen monitoring their radio's emergency channel, sent the Coast Guard to the scene near Lake Worth.
>
> "The guy was hollering that his wife fell overboard," stated a Boynton Beach fisherman, who requested his name not be used...

Rand couldn't read anymore. His private hell was about to become public.

"Ackerton." Rand thought he heard a voice. "You there?" The phone was lying on the floor next to his feet.

Rand recovered the receiver. "Yeah, I'm here. I grabbed the paper. What's up with the 'foul play' headline?"

"They're guessing."

"Doesn't really matter, does it? It's in print, people believe it's true. I didn't do anything to my wife, Detective. You're supposed to be finding out what happened, not coming after me."

"We're holding a press conference this afternoon. Three o'clock. You should be there. Show them you're not in custody."

Rand wondered if this wasn't some kind of trick the police used to get someone *into* custody. "Am I a suspect?"

Janson's pause was brief, but his words offered little encouragement. "Mr. Ackerton, we have no immediate plans to arrest you."

Was that true? Could he believe Janson? After all, he was the police, and the police were there to "protect and serve." Right? Besides, there couldn't possibly be evidence of guilt. Rand had done nothing wrong.

"If I can get out of my driveway," Rand conceded, "I'll be there."

"There's one more thing I should tell you."

"This gets better?"

"A body...well, a substantial part of one, washed up on Juno Beach about an hour ago. No I.D. yet."

"Juno? That's miles north of Lake Worth. You don't think..."

"We don't think anything right now, but once the media learns of the discovery, they might try to connect the dots."

"What am I supposed to do?"

"For now, stay home and stay calm. The press conference should put everybody on the same page. This'll blow over in a few days."

Blow over? His wife of twenty years was missing, presumed dead, and the newspaper made it look like Rand had something to do with it.

"I'm praying you're right," he said as he scanned the article and picture again, this time noticing an obvious omission. "Hey, Janson?"

"Yeah."

"Why would the paper print *my* picture instead of Janie's? Shouldn't there be…"

"You know," he interrupted, "I asked 'em that myself this morning. It seems the local press has no file photos of your wife. They were planning to run the next edition using her DMV photo until we passed along the picture you gave us."

That was odd, Rand thought. The press didn't hang on to pictures of average citizens, but Jane was an active member of the community. "Don't they keep charity and society photos on file?"

"They do and they've looked."

"Strange." Surely they'd misplaced them. "I'll scan some images and put them on a disk for you. Even if they print bullshit, at least Janie's picture will be out there."

"I'll call if I learn more."

"Thanks." Rand jabbed the OFF button and tossed the phone onto the couch. On the television screen, Kevin Costner was building a baseball diamond in a cornfield. Rand lifted the newspaper, found the remote, and changed the channel to a local news station. There it was. He turned up the volume.

"…fallen overboard during an ocean cruise." A picture of the *Sweet Mystery*, on blocks at the marina, was displayed to the left of the newswoman's head. "When Coast Guard officers responded to the Mayday call around five o'clock Monday evening, her husband, famous photographer Rand Ackerton, was reportedly found aboard the vessel speaking incoherently." One of Rand's PR shots replaced the picture of the boat.

"Rescue divers have been unable to locate any trace of the missing woman, and it's expected that search efforts will not resume this morning, due to the outgoing tide." Her expression of sympathy looked forced. "Mr. Ackerton's work has graced the covers of such magazines as *LIFE* and *People*. More details on this story are expected at..."

Rand turned off the television and stared at the darkened screen. *Why run a picture of me? Janie's the one that's missing*. Janson said the media could access Janie's DMV photo, so why wasn't it out there? Had he missed it? If they showed her picture, maybe someone would see it. Maybe someone would call.

But that call wasn't coming, was it? It had been fourteen hours and Jane was still gone. Sooner or later, he would have to face the inevitable.

•

Detective Janson hung up the phone and looked down the cubicle row at Detective Griffiths, who'd just arrived. "He's seen the paper. You think of anything new last night?"

"Maybe, but it's a stretch."

"I spent three hours on that goddamn boat and found zilch. I'll take a 'stretch' to nothin' any day." Janson leaned back in his chair and brought his hands behind his head.

"I was thinking about what Davis said last night, and it's just speculation."

"I'm listening."

"Let's say Ackerton's lying and he's responsible for what happened. Had things really gone down the way he said, the divers would have found something, or the wife would have washed up by now."

Janson wondered if Griffiths had heard about the body in Juno. He decided to ask after he heard her theory.

"What if he knocked his wife unconscious, weighted her down somehow, and tossed her overboard. The current in the Gulf Stream is pretty swift and she could have been dragged farther north."

Janson scratched his head. "That would mean the position of the body today would depend on where it was initially dumped. If Ackerton's lying, how do we know where the boat was?"

"There's a GPS on board, isn't there?"

Janson was a devout land-lubber and handled few boat-related cases, but he had made a list of the equipment on the vessel's console. "Yeah, there was. You think there's some kind of memory on it?"

"Not *some* kind of memory, an *exact* memory. A GPS unit remembers where you've been so you can trace your path exactly."

"I never knew you were so boat-savvy."

Griffiths smiled as color rushed to her cheeks. "I'm not. I made a call last night to one of the officers who responded to the Mayday."

"Keehan?"

"No, the Fish and Wildlife guy."

"Ripley? Why'd you..." but he stopped, realizing why the mention of a late night phone call would make a woman blush. Janson was many things, but naïve was not one of them. "Never mind. So can you follow-up on this theory?"

"Already started. Keehan's checking the GPS right now and I'm speaking with a tides specialist this morning. His answering service said he'd be in at seven-thirty."

Janson looked at his watch. "It's almost seven now. Let me know what you find."

"I will. But that's not the only scenario I've considered."

"What's the other..."

"You two have a minute?" Detective J. B. Davis appeared.

"That's why we're here," Janson answered. "What ya' got?"

"The husband's story seems consistent, and I've been digging into the Ackertons, looking for anything they might have done to piss somebody off. For a high-profile couple, they're pretty low key, and painfully average."

"So if they pissed anyone off—including each other—they kept it under the radar."

"Right. But I found a couple of things that don't make sense. Like the newspaper article this morning. Did either of you notice the story didn't include a picture of the missing woman?"

"I spoke to the husband about it a few minutes ago," Janson said.

"The paper said they didn't have any."

"Did they tell you what they *do* have?" Davis asked.

Janson shook his head.

"The Ackertons have been mentioned in the archives dozens of times. The husband's mug showed up in dozens of the media shots, but his wife, despite being on the guest lists, was nowhere to be seen."

"Maybe she's camera shy," Griffiths offered, "it's not like *no* photos exist, because the husband gave us one yesterday. It's right here." She dug through the file on her desk and removed a color snapshot.

Janson looked briefly at the picture his partner held up. Ackerton had caught himself a real looker. With a face like that, why would she be nervous in front of a camera? "It might be a good idea to make copies of that for the press conference. Ackerton's bringing more, but it won't hurt to be prepared. We'll pass them around. If it turns out she did somehow get back to shore, maybe someone spotted her." Then to Davis he added, "What else you got?"

"Jane Ackerton, maiden name Williams, wasn't who she said she was."

Janson shot a brief glance at Griffiths before turning back to Davis. "Then who was she?"

"Well, that's the problem. There's no record of a Jane Williams born in Westchester County, New York, in 1952. I checked '45 through '62, just in case Ackerton didn't have the year right. You know how women can be about their age."

"I still can't believe," Griffiths broke in, still holding the snapshot, "that this woman was in her fifties. Ackerton said this was a recent picture."

"There's something to be said for good genes," Janson responded.

Davis continued. "She *did* start teaching at Flagler in '78, but her original application no longer exists and none of her former co-workers remembered her mentioning any previous employers. They also remembered her saying she'd gone to school at Yale, but the records office there didn't show her on the alum list."

Detective Griffiths broke in. "So we don't know who she was prior to 1978?"

"No." Davis leaned on the cubicle frame. "Never worked. Never banked. Never voted. Ackerton said yesterday her parents died when she was young and she doesn't talk much about her childhood. I get the impression she'd been hiding something."

Maybe that's it, Janson thought. "Maybe she had a past her husband didn't know about. If it was bad, something that would hurt his career or his family's reputation, he might not like it if he found out."

"If we knew what that past was," Griffiths said, "we might have a motive."

"Or maybe," Davis leaned in, "Mrs. Ackerton bailed on purpose."

"That's something we'd considered yesterday," Janson remembered.

Griffiths added, "Which ties to the other theory I was going to tell you about, Pat. Suppose Ackerton is telling the truth. If his wife held a weight while she swam from the boat, it would have kept her below the surface and virtually invisible from her husband's perspective. By the time the Coast Guard arrived, she could have easily covered half the distance to shore. It would explain why we don't have a body."

Davis argued. "But after Janson's comment last night, I checked our archives. We don't always find a body in these overboard cases. It's rare, but it happens. Besides, they were at least a mile out, according to Ackerton, and their dive equipment was accounted for."

"Not necessarily, Ackerton admitted he wasn't sure how many pairs of swim fins were kept on board. With fins and a breath of air every couple of minutes, she could have done it."

Janson felt more confused than enlightened. Were they dealing with a drowning, a missing persons case, or a homicide? Had Ackerton tossed his wife into the water, or had she jumped in herself? "Why would a woman like Jane Ackerton go to such lengths to disappear?"

"Why do men with beautiful wives cheat?" Adriane Griffiths commented. "Some questions have no reasonable answer."

Maybe not, Janson thought, but the reporters—and the Sarge and ultimately the Chief—were going to want something. "Adriane, follow-up with this specialist on your first theory, and call the friends and family. Maybe the Ackertons weren't as perfect a couple as the husband says."

"You got it."

"Davis, see what else you can dig up on the wife and look for anything that resembles a motive."

"No problem," Davis said.

"You guys head downstairs for roll call. I'll meet you in a minute. I'm going to check with the M.E. about a body that washed up in Juno this morning. If it's our lady, maybe we'll get a break. Unless we uncover something extraordinary, I'll push the missing-presumed-drowned scenario at the press conference this afternoon and hope our friendly neighborhood reporters haven't heard about the Juno find."

"What are the odds of that?" Griffiths asked with thick sarcasm.

Janson didn't answer.

Davis and Griffiths left the second floor, and Janson dug through papers for the phone number to the Medical Examiner's office. Someday he'd get around to cleaning his desk, but it wasn't going to be today.

CHAPTER 7

Scheduled departure had been 7:45 that morning, but it was closer to eight when the train finally pulled away from the platform in West Palm Beach. Jane's cabin was disappointing, despite the achievements of the twenty-first century. It had all the comforts promised—armchair, fold-out bed, private facilities—but it lacked the charm she remembered from childhood travels with her father. He'd been so proud of the railroad. His heart would break to see how much neglect the past century had brought.

She was certain that behind her Rand mourned. As the miles grew between them, she ached for the ability to reverse time, erasing his sorrow and allowing her a little more of him. More of his touch. His embrace. More of his scent and his humor and the reassurance of his presence.

But what was the point? She had cried all night in the small motel and still her options hadn't changed. True, there was hope, but in the end—and as always—Rand would merely be another love lost in an unending stream. She'd been so naïve to have wasted decades searching for something that, once found, she couldn't keep. How long would it take to forget him?

How long did she have?

As the train rocked along the rails, Jane closed her eyes and thought of Michael in St. Louis. Summer of 1917. He'd been forward, approaching her in a café as if they'd known each other.

"Excuse me," he'd said, "but I wonder if I might join you this morning?" His uniform was new. Crisp and creased. He was clean-shaven, with a sincere face, and she guessed he'd recently finished high school. A boy trying desperately to be a man.

"I ship out in three days." He'd gone right to the point after she'd let him sit down. "I don't have a girl to spend my last few hours with, and I..." The young soldier struggled for the right words.

No matter his rationale, she allowed him to love her for three days. Their intimacy was honest. Their passion was free. He left for France having filled his need for the attentions of a woman. The knowledge that she'd helped calm his fears was gratifying. But the war took him anyway. When news of his death came, Jane was struck with the painful truth: as long as her mysterious condition continued, every relationship she fostered would be temporary. Every love she found would be lost.

Please, Oliver, she wished, *be right.*

But after all this time, it was hard to believe.

•

The Silver Star—or was it Meteor? Jane couldn't recall—slowed then lurched to a stop. Out the window, South Florida was awash in the morning sun. Several yards away, a man who looked in his sixties walked along the roadside and stopped at a parked car. Jane watched as he opened the door. Paused. Looked to the train. Waved. Wiped at his face with his sleeve.

His granddaughter is on board, Jane thought. She had an uncanny way of knowing things that went beyond women's intuition. *Her name is... Laura...yes, and she's going home to a husband who beats her*. Jane watched the man climb into the car and drive away, afraid he might never see his granddaughter again. From her armchair onboard the train, Jane envied them both for being able to say goodbye. In every case that mattered—her mother and father, Eddie, Rand—she'd not had the luxury.

Still, after a century and a half of moving from one place to the next, she'd had her share of sorrowful partings. Lou in Seattle had been difficult. And sending soldiers off to fight a world war wasn't any easier the second time around.

The train pulled away from the station. Paved roads and sidewalks gave way to open fields. In seventeen hours, she'd be in New Orleans. With Oliver. Jane thought of the news he'd relayed on the phone the day before. Could he really have found the one responsible for their condition? Was it some type of spell that could be reversed? And should she risk disappointment in hoping so?

It's best not to yearn for the impossible, she thought. But was it really impossible?

Jane reached above her head and pulled the shade down over the window. In the now dim cabin, she leaned into the chair, laid her head against the backrest, and wondered for the millionth time what she had done to deserve the curse of immortality. Had she been targeted since childhood? Or was her fate changed as a result of some cosmic accident?

Across from her, sitting indiscreetly on the floor against the wall, was a tattered red shopping bag. Inside were the only reminders of her past she'd dared hang on to. All but one, she thought. She'd left her suitcase behind, knowing Rand would notice its absence. It was enough risk bringing what she did, but some mementos were simply too difficult to part with. Like her father's railroad certificate. Her mother's jade necklace. The handkerchief she'd used to wipe Eddie's tears in the hospital. These were things that proved Jane hadn't imagined it all—that she really *had* lived a century and a half. And that as long as she remembered where she came from, she could overcome even the most difficult of situations. Even this one. After all, she remembered, her education had started early.

Jane's first experience with the supernatural—for lack of a better explanation—happened the day her mother died. She was six. Their family lived in the Belmont neighborhood of Philadelphia in a large Victorian overlooking Fairmount Park. In the large backyard, her father had built a shed in the far right corner to shelter wood for the winter. A cabinet held his tools and her mother's gardening supplies. A tall maple tree stood sentinel in the opposite corner. It served as an end for the clothesline that ran the length of the fence. The tree's single low-hanging branch supplied perfect support for a rope swing.

Jane remembered the inside of the house perfectly because her father later brought the blueprints to Sacramento and built an exact replica to help his children with the transition of moving across the country. Edward Clifton Dougharty had been a caring and hard-working man who provided well for his family.

Catherine Jane Dougharty, Jane's mother, was an active member in the Ladies' Guild of St. Joseph's. Jane suspected her mother missed the home and family she'd left behind in Ireland, but she never let on. Her hobbies—or "diversions" as she called them—kept her busy.

On one particular summer morning in 1856, Jane and four-year-old Eddie were chasing one another around the back yard. Their father was away at work. Mary Beth, their nanny, sat under the towering maple with a book, not paying the least attention. It was Tuesday, her mother's quilting day, and Jane had been expecting her to call them any moment to leave.

A child's sense of time cannot be trusted, so Jane couldn't be sure how long they waited. Maybe thirty minutes. Maybe more. Regardless, she grew curious and wondered why her mother had taken so long to get ready. She excused herself from Eddie and told Mary Beth she'd return directly.

With practiced skill, she caught the door behind her before it banged shut and eased it gently into the latch. She'd been scolded enough for slamming the kitchen door. Her raven pigtails bounced atop her shoulders as she stopped short in the center of the room, aware that the house was too still. Where was her mother? Her ears strained to detect any noise. She heard only the sound of her breath.

Before her was a long hallway to the front door and the base of the stairs. She wanted to call out, but she didn't like the way her voice bounced off the walls and ceiling in an empty house. It made her feel alone. At such a tender age, the prospect sent a shiver up her back.

She crept ahead slowly, careful not to make a noise on the hardwood floor. On her left was a closet. On her right their father's study. Both doors were closed. No sound came from behind them. But someone was in the house. She was sure of it. And her mother was...in distress.

At the left end of the hallway, next to the staircase, a set of doors opened onto the parlor. Unless the family had guests, the doors were closed. As she approached the foot of the stairs, Jane could see the double doors were ajar. She glanced to her right, through the archway into the dining room. Nothing looked amiss. Ahead of her, the front door was shut but not bolted. Whoever was in the house was confined to the parlor. Young Jane quietly drew a deep breath and inched forward around the banister.

And froze.

Like a chilling wind, the presence of malice wafted from the parlor. Jane felt it to her toes. There was movement behind the doors. The hair on the back of her neck prickled. If she'd been able to ignore the sense that her mother was in peril, she would not have gone farther. She would have run back to the yard to Mary Beth and Eddie and the safety of daylight. But something was wrong.

She buried her fear and tiptoed to the narrow opening between the parlor doors. Placing her forehead against the painted wood surface, she peered in. Her heart pounded. Nothing was out of place near the windows. The table and fireplace mantel seemed untouched. She strained to see further to the left, into the rear of the room, but a high-backed chair blocked her view. If she wanted to see more, she would have to open the doors and go inside.

A muffled cry convinced her she'd wasted enough time. She threw the doors open and rushed into the room. "Mama! Mama!"

Evil permeated the air. Jane would swear she could taste it. The scene near the sofa stopped her cries. She stood still. Fits of rage gathered at the pit of her stomach.

A dark figure leaned over her mother on the sofa. Large, muscular hands pulled slowly away from her mother's neck. With the mannerisms of someone rudely interrupted, the figure stood and turned to face the intruder. But Jane was looking beyond him. Catherine Dougharty's arm had fallen limp to the floor. Her new blue dress cascaded over the edge of the sofa. Her eyes were wide and lifeless.

"No!" Jane wanted to beat the man who'd hurt her mother. Pound on him with her fists. Kick him as hard as she could. But her feet seemed anchored to the floor.

He said nothing. Without looking back at the damage he'd done, he strode past Jane, towering over her, through the parlor doorway and out the front door into the afternoon sunshine.

Jane bolted to her mother and fell to her side. Her body was warm, but Jane knew she was already dead. Mary Beth and Eddie barged through the back door, letting the door bang hard behind them. When they reached the parlor, Mary Beth screamed and rushed to hold Eddie back from the scene.

Young Jane had been anxious to describe her mother's killer to the authorities. They could catch him. Punish him. He should pay for his crime. But, despite having been in the same room, she couldn't remember. No matter how hard she tried.

Jane shuddered against the memory as she sat upright in the cabin's uncomfortable vinyl seat. She opened the window shade and looked out, wondering how close she was to Orlando. There, she would change trains and ride the Sunset Limited to New Orleans.

The "Sunset Limited." *Papa would have liked that.*

Closing her eyes again, she blocked out the sorrows that trailed behind her, along with the uncertain fate ahead, and remembered a time when none of it mattered: a life forged in the American frontier, where her father was her beloved enemy and her brother her involuntary best friend.

CHAPTER 8

SACRAMENTO, CALIFORNIA – OCTOBER 4, 1867

Sixteen-year-old Eddie walked alongside his older sister, relieved the days of wearing a coat in mid-summer heat were gone. They turned right off P Street onto Front, where stately Victorian homes gave way to two- and three-story merchant buildings built of brick and granite. But the banks and stores and rooming houses here in Sacramento's west end were of little interest. It was the commotion along the swift-moving riverfront—the *embarcadero*, as his father called it—that Eddie loved.

It was harvest time, and Eddie could already see that the thoroughfare ahead was lined with horse-drawn carts. Tall, menacing ships sat tied along the riverfront, one behind another, waiting to be loaded or unloaded. Men who spoke in strange tongues and dripped sweat transferred cargo to and from the docks. Eddie would give anything to be one of those men, to travel the world in seek of adventure. They had such ambition. His father wouldn't allow it while he was in school, but he was sixteen now and that was behind him. As he and Jane progressed along the storefronts, he silently reaffirmed his intention to leave before the first signs of winter.

"I don't understand why you insist on traversing this insufferable route," Jane remarked, "it reeks of river sludge and rotting fish."

"Ah, but that's part of its charm, don't you think?" He switched a heavy basket of fruit and sandwiches from his right hand to his left.

"'Charm?' You're surely joking. How you manage to find charm amid the stench and vulgarity of this place is beyond comprehension."

"I suppose that's why you're walking so quickly?"

"You're lucky I agreed to accompany you in this direction at all. These people you idolize here are quite uncivilized and in dire need of attention. When I become a teacher, I believe I'll make the instruction of manners and etiquette my priority."

A familiar merchant came along, heading in the opposite direction. The siblings nodded in passing, offering him a cheery, "Good morning."

"So, I should thank you, then," Eddie continued, "for enduring the 'stench and vulgarity' for my sake?"

Jane stopped short and grabbed his right arm above the elbow. "You can be sure, dear brother, that when supper ends this afternoon and time rolls 'round for dishes to be cleared and scrubbed that your debt will be repaid."

"But that's woman's work," he said to her back as she continued on the boardwalk without him. "Margaret sees to the cleaning."

"I've decided to give Margaret some time off after she's finished cooking. With father gone, there's no need for..."

"I'm to repay you for walking with me to town? And in that fashion? The stroll itself has been punishment enough, I'll not lower myself to—"

"Oh, yes you will," she hollered back to him, "or I'll tell Papa of your secret hiding place."

"You wouldn't!" He rushed to catch up to her as she turned the corner to K Street.

"Wouldn't I?" She flashed a devious smile.

He would have challenged her further, but they were too near the hardware and general store where their father occupied offices. The boardwalk abounded in activity and familiar faces as men labored with wheelbarrows and carts, hurrying to stock grocers' shelves before the town's early crowds shuffled in. Brother and sister exchanged greetings with shop owners who stood by overseeing the chaos, until they eventually reached their destination.

Huntington, Hopkins & Co. was a grand structure, remodeled from what had originally been three separate buildings. Eddie had watched bits of the reconstruction himself, albeit as a young boy. The store was enclosed on only three sides, with the fourth opening out onto the boardwalk, adorned with a dozen elaborately carved wooden columns. Eddie bowed mockingly, gesturing that Jane should step in first. She did, relieving Eddie of the basket she'd made him carry from the house. *While walking in town, a gentleman should always carry a lady's packages*, she'd lectured. Did that still apply if the 'lady' was your sister?

"You're welcome," he said, sneering.

She flashed him a wry smile in response.

"Good morning, Mr. Johnson," Jane called to the man standing near the back wall, "is my father upstairs?"

"He is, indeed, Miss Dougharty, and a good morning to you." The man, a friendly Swede who'd managed the store for seventeen years, walked toward them down the aisle. "I see you've accompanied your brother today."

"I have. I've come to wish Papa a safe trip to the mountains, and to bring him this." She held up the basket.

To make Johnson think she'd carried it herself, Eddie thought.

"Ah, that's right. Your father leaves today. Young Edward, I'll need your help in gathering and loading supplies into wagons for the trip."

"And I will, sir, but, if you don't mind, I'd like a few moments with my father first."

He seemed to consider, then said, "Of course. The loadin' can wait another ten minutes."

"Thank you, Mr. Johnson." Eddie tipped his hat. "I'll gather my apron when I come back."

Eddie once again followed his sister, this time up the staircase near front and center of the store. He watched her ascend above him, bitter that she'd taken credit for their father's travel basket as if she'd lugged it herself. Sure, she'd prepared and placed the items inside, but he'd done his part, too. She was always making him out to be the *little brother*. The boy who tags along and does her bidding. He'd show her.

"Say, Janie," he said as she crested the top of the stairs and started down the hall to the left, "maybe Mr. Dinklesnort will be in the office this morning. Did you bring him a basket, too?"

She stopped and turned, her cheeks as red as her dress and matching hat. "Mr. *Dimmelthorpe's* whereabouts are no concern of mine, and I'll warn you not to speak that name again."

"Sorry," he lied. When she resumed her way toward the office door, she stomped more than walked, and Eddie grinned at his success.

They approached the last set of double doors on the left, upon which were inscribed the words:

CENTRAL PACIFIC RAILROAD
Construction Office #2

Jane knocked as she opened the door, but instantly halted. "Oh, excuse me, sirs. I didn't know you were busy."

"Nonsense," came a voice Eddie had heard few times before, "come in, Miss Jane. Your father and I were simply tying loose ends before his departure."

Eddie walked through the office doorway and found his father standing behind the room's large, oak desk alongside Mr. Charles Crocker, the man who'd summoned the Doughartys to Sacramento six years earlier. Eddie removed his hat and greeted the two men. "Good morning, sir. Father." He pivoted to the left and addressed his father's guest directly. "Mr. Crocker, sir, I trust your trip to San Francisco went well?"

"It did, my boy," he chuckled, "and thanks for your concern."

Mr. Crocker was a pleasant, middle-aged man, with a round face and graying beard. He stood framed by the window behind him, wearing a smart dark jacket and vest. According to Eddie's father, he'd originally traveled to California—like thousands of others—to hunt for gold. An adventurer. When he didn't find it, he turned his attention to business, and had amassed a considerable fortune supplying hopeful miners still in the hunt. He'd been a model citizen and member of California's state government before joining the cause of the western railroad.

"You're here to see your father off, too, young Edward?"

"Yes, sir, but I'll not linger. I'm needed downstairs to help load the wagons."

"Of course, then I'll not keep you from your goodbyes." He shook hands with Eddie's father. "Oh, one last thing, Dougharty. You'll be taking the chemist along with you?"

"Yes, sir. He's meeting me downstairs within the hour."

"Good." Crocker crossed the room, and removed his top hat from the post near the door. "I'll expect a full report of the new techniques on your return."

"Without question, sir. I'll call on you as soon as I'm back in town."

"Miss Jane, it is a pleasure seeing you again." He held his hat to his chest and nodded.

"Thank you, sir, it's nice seeing you as well."

"And, Master Edward," Crocker held out his hand for Eddie to shake, "I presume we'll meet again on the morrow?"

"It's likely, sir." Eddie proudly shook his hand.

Mr. Crocker closed the door behind him, leaving the Dougharty family alone in the room.

"Papa, we brought you a package for your trip." Jane wasted no time, but at least she used *we* instead of over-glorifying herself. "It might not last long, but you'll not need to suffer camp food for a day or two."

He walked around the desk and took the basket, kissing his daughter on the forehead. "Thank you, my dear. It's very thoughtful. You, too, Eddie."

"You're welcome." *Just don't expect to kiss* me *on the forehead, or anywhere else, for that matter.*

The elder Dougharty peeked into the basket, then placed it on the desk. "Before I go, Janie, have you given any more thought to what we discussed last night? I'll be seeing Mr. Dimmelthorpe along the construction line, and I wonder if you have a message I might pass on to him?"

"My *message* is as it was last night, Papa, and I don't intend to discuss it any further this morning," she turned to sneer at Eddie, adding, "in mixed company."

"But, Janie, I wish you'd reconsider. He's a fine man." Eddie felt awkward, if not invisible, as he watched his father and sister argue. But their bickering was not a display to which he was unaccustomed.

"I don't care about pedigrees or bank holdings or...political aspirations. I will not marry Melvin Dimmelthorpe because I don't love him. I will marry only for love, and only after I've completed my education."

"But you should marry, raise a family, settle down..."

"...or I could learn to teach. I'm eighteen, Father. Old enough to decide things for myself."

The two stood, eyes locked and postures firm. "I hate to interrupt this...parlance," Eddie broke in, "but I'm needed downstairs. Father, enjoy a safe and successful trip."

"Yes, thank you, son." His father broke free of Jane's hold and stepped close. "I'll see you in three days. Five at most." Eddie gripped his father's hand tight. "Take care of your sister."

"Yes, sir." He let go, tipped his hat, nodded to his sister, and left the room. Eddie didn't want to hear the rest, because he'd heard it all the night before. Through the keyholes and beneath the doors of their two-story home. He didn't have an opinion either way, as long as it ended the bickering.

Eddie heard them mutter on as he descended the steep stairs and returned to the ground floor. He strode along the storefront to the register counter, and stepped in behind to hang his hat and coat atop a hook on the wall. He retrieved an apron, hung on an adjacent hook, and slipped it over his neck as he made his way to Mr. Johnson.

For four years, Eddie's free time had been divided between working at the store for Mr. Johnson and running errands for his father. He was aware of his father's hopes that Eddie would study structural engineering and assume the career the elder Dougharty had so successfully pursued. But sitting at a desk day after day, pouring over plans and reconciling budgets, had no appeal for him—with or without men like Charles Crocker. Instead, he planned to use the money he'd saved to travel. He'd seen how easily men secured jobs aboard ships, their Captains eager to replace crew members who'd chosen to look for gold rather than return to the sea. As soon as his father returned, Eddie would inform him of his intentions.

"Edward," Mr. Johnson's voice came from outside the front of the store. Eddie hurried out to the boardwalk and found his boss offering directions to a cart driver. Satisfied with whatever the old Swede had told him, the driver shook the reins and pulled away. Mr. Johnson waved, then turned to Eddie. "I need you to gather the items on this list and arrange them at the back. The carts are bein' brung 'round."

Eddie took the handwritten list. "Yes, sir." He turned on his heel and strode back into the store with Mr. Johnson behind him.

Footsteps on the stairs, paired with the high-pitched sounds of grumbling, alerted him to his sister's descent from the second floor. Eddie knew she'd won the argument with their father. If she'd lost, she would have been wailing—not because she'd been hurt but to heighten the drama. She appeared at the foot, her feathers visibly ruffled.

"Father is being completely unreasonable," she shouted at Eddie, who stood in an aisle at the center of the store.

"You going home, then?" he asked her.

"I've one stop at the dressmaker's. Shall I tell Margaret to have supper ready at four?"

"Has there ever been a day I've told you different?"

"Oh, you are as insufferable as Papa." She stomped out of the store, nose held high, and disappeared down the boarded walk. Miss Know-It-All off to buy a dress.

"That's a feisty one, your sister," Mr. Johnson commented.

"Yes," Eddie agreed. He'd had to tolerate her high and mighty behavior his entire life. As he moved about the store, collecting the items from Johnson's list, he imagined what kind of suffering she would doubtless inflict on *Dinklesnort*, or whomever the unlucky bastard was who came to marry her. As a wife, she'd have her husband running circles. Unless, of course, a man were to deal with her firmly.

Yes, Eddie decided, as he went about collecting supplies, his sister was going to need a considerable amount of discomfort to knock her from her self-made pedestal.

CHAPTER 9

In the wake of recent events, Rand knew one thing for sure: he was going to need a lawyer. The newspaper had come dangerously close to accusing him of murder. The police had found a body. Reporters were camped outside his home. He'd hung up the phone three hours earlier after speaking with Detective Janson, and done little more than stare blankly at the empty television screen listening to his breath. How had things gone so terribly wrong so quickly?

He reached for the phone on the couch and dialed David Fristoe's home number. As a lawyer, Dave had handled Rand's legal affairs for fifteen years. As Rand's college roommate and best man, Dave's friendship went back even farther. They'd spent hours on the phone the night before.

Dave answered quickly. "Were your ears ringin', man? I was about to call you. How are you doing?"

"If my ears had been ringing, the banging in my head would have smothered the sound. I talked to the police this morning. Have you seen today's *Post*?"

"Not yet. We're running late in the Fristoe household this morning. Coffee's still brewin'. Why?"

"It's on the front page, and they're not painting a nice picture."

"No shit? You said last night they were keeping this low-key."

"Yeah, well, that didn't happen." Rand lay back onto the couch and crossed his bare feet on the coffee table. "And it gets worse."

"Worse than the story leaking to the press?"

"The police found a body in Juno. It washed up onto the beach early this morning."

"Jesus. Do they think it's Jane?"

"They don't know yet, and I…I really don't want to think about it. I'm supposed to go to a press conference at the station at three. I assume they'll know more then." Rand leaned forward and retrieved his cigarettes, lighter, and an overflowing ashtray from the table.

"You're not under suspicion, are you? I mean, they don't think you had anything to do with this?"

"I think they might." He sat the ashtray on the couch and lit a cigarette. "Detective Janson said the press is guessing, but I'm not convinced."

There was a long pause. Rand thought he heard clanking on the other end of the line. Dave was pouring himself some coffee. "Well," Dave said finally, "number one, you and I need face time before this press conference. I've got a meeting at ten in Vero Beach, but I'll reschedule and head south instead. I was coming down anyway. I can be at your place before noon."

"Sounds good. I could use some company."

"And, number two, don't talk to anybody about the accident—not the press, not the police, not even your mother—until we've had a chance to chat."

"Okay. Hey, wait. You said you were about to call me. Was it anything important?"

"Huh? Oh, I wanted to tell you I called *Details* for you and left a message. I knew you were due to send photos this week."

"Thanks. Shit. I completely forgot."

"No problem. And I also had a few questions about Jane's medical history and birth records. Lawyer stuff. But we can talk about it later. Current events are a bit more important."

"Is there something wrong?"

"No, well, I don't think so." Dave sounded unsure. "I guess we might as well do all this at once, though. Do you keep your birth certificates and things there at the house or in a safe deposit box?"

"At the house, I think. Why?"

"Good." Rand heard Dave sip his coffee. "This shit is hard enough on you without having to deal with this routine stuff, too. I've tried to handle it for you, but I ran into a snag. All I need is her birth certificate, I.D., Social Security card, and any medical and dental paperwork you might have."

"I think I know where to find all that, but I thought you had copies in your office. And what do you mean by 'a snag?'"

"I do have copies, except for the medical records, but they're old, and some of the numbers have faded. It's nothing, Rand, and if you'd rather wait 'til I get there to go through Jane's things, that'll be fine."

"No, I'm all right. I'll have it ready when you get here." Rand tamped out his cigarette.

"Hang in there, man. This can't be easy for you, but we'll get through it. I'll see you before lunch."

"Thanks." Rand pulled the phone away from his ear, shut it off, and dropped it onto the couch. Again, the silence of the house consumed him.

He rose and stumbled into the kitchen. Coffee sounded good. The patter from his bare feet on the cold tile bounced off the walls. Maybe he should turn the TV back on so the place didn't seem so empty.

Grounds were still in the coffee maker from the last pot brewed, so Rand removed the basket and opened the cabinet below the sink to dump the old filter into the trash. He hadn't made coffee the previous day, so the grounds must have been a couple days old. His hand stopped over the plastic garbage can as the damp filter and its contents fell. Jane had made the last pot. Yesterday morning. The *Today Show* was playing in the background. She had her blue satin robe on and her favorite "puffy slippers," as she called them. She'd worn nothing underneath.

Was this what he should expect for the rest of his life? Remembering moments with her? Not even being able to make a simple pot of coffee without seeing her face? He fumbled with the rest of the process, fighting tears and strong mental images. Finally, dark brown liquid dripped successfully into the carafe.

He took a quick shower upstairs and changed into an old pair of khakis and a faded red Flagler College sweatshirt. Back downstairs, he filled a large cup with black coffee and retrieved his cigarettes from the living room. Jane had been the manager of the household ever since they'd exchanged vows, so Rand wasn't exactly sure where he'd find the items Dave asked for, but he guessed the most obvious place to start looking was the den.

Before walking past the front door, Rand stopped to peek through the slim pane of beveled glass and saw the two reporters outside had been joined by three more.

"Vultures," he said aloud. "How do they sleep at night?"

He sipped from his cup and trudged beyond the foyer and down a short hallway. The door at the end on the left was ajar. He pushed it open with his foot.

The den was modestly appointed but well lit by two large windows. Sheer curtains kept the reporters outside from seeing in, and Rand was grateful for that. He set his coffee and cigarettes on the small maple desk situated in the center of the room. From the bottom drawer, he retrieved an ashtray. Jane always kept one there for the few occasions she felt like having a smoke. He'd always envied her ability to pick up a cigarette only when the mood struck her. Rand didn't have it so easy. He'd been hooked since his first puff at seventeen.

The room was barely used, and only by Jane when she had "business to attend to," which meant she either planned to write a letter or had let the filing pile up. They had an accountant who handled their financial matters, but Jane insisted on keeping track of a few things personally, like the department store and credit card accounts. The accounting firm sent copies every month. She didn't feel right about spending money without knowing where it went. She'd quit teaching when they got married and hadn't worked a "real" job since, so he supposed it was her way of feeling like she contributed to the relationship. He'd never been able to convince her that she contributed plenty. And in more ways than he'd ever been able to explain.

Aside from the desk and file cabinet, the only other objects in the small room were a trash can and a silk palm tree, and two prints of Rand's early work that were framed and hung on the wall. Jane hadn't even wanted a computer in here, which was another thing he couldn't convince her of.

He lit another cigarette and moved the ashtray to the top of the filing cabinet, then opened the top drawer. *American Express. Bank of America. Burdines. Certificates and Licenses.*

"Hmm."

He slid the ashtray back and opened the file on top of the cabinet. Inside, Rand found the original, as well as a copy, of their marriage certificate. He couldn't remember seeing it since the day it was signed. Dave hadn't asked for it, but he removed the sheet from the file and set it on the desk, anyway. Also in the manila folder was a copy of Rand's business license and the originals of both his and Jane's birth certificates.

"That was easy." He turned and placed Jane's certificate on top of the other paper on the desk. "Now, the medical stuff would be..."

He looked under "D" for doctor or dentist. Nothing. He opened the next drawer, checking "M" for medical, then "P" for physician. What was her doctor's name? Rand had seen Jay Bishop for years, but there'd been nothing in the top drawer. He hadn't been Jane's doctor, anyway. Still, she must have had a gynecologist, if nothing else, but Rand couldn't remember if she'd ever mentioned a name. He rifled through the remaining files in the second and then the third drawer, but found nothing that hinted at medical or dental files.

The bottom drawer contained only office supplies, including a box of envelopes, several pens, and a bag of paper clips. Since they'd both been healthy, he thought, having visited doctors only for routine appointments, maybe she hadn't kept anything. Later, he'd try to remember to ask Karen, Dave's wife and Jane's closest friend, if Jane ever brought up the name of her doctor.

For her I.D. and Social Security card, Rand would have to retrieve Jane's wallet from the Chevelle. Thankfully, it was parked in the closed garage and also away from the prying eyes of the media. He took a drag from his cigarette, then put it out and retrieved the two certificates off the desk. Slipping his Marlboros into the front pocket of his khakis, he grabbed his coffee cup and exited the den.

As he moved through the kitchen toward the garage door, he tossed the papers on the island countertop and, after taking a long sip of coffee, set his cup next to them. He opened the garage door, flicked on the light, and stepped down onto the concrete floor.

The blue Chevelle sat silent, seemingly waiting for Jane to hop in and take it for a spin.

"We're both at a loss, there, old pal."

Rand's tears surfaced again. The car's convertible top had been left down, and Rand slipped easily behind the wheel. Jane loved this car. He remembered how she'd stroked the dash on their way to the marina two days ago. Had she somehow known she wouldn't see it again? Was that possible? He doubted it. How could she?

Rand had argued with his wife on several occasions concerning her tendency to leave her wallet in the car as opposed to keeping it in a handbag. Her excuse was that she switched handbags frequently and she was afraid she'd forget her money and license one day. Rand knew better. Jane carried a purse only when she had to, and the rest of the time she was in too much of a hurry to run upstairs and get one. Having her wallet in the car meant she could jump in and go. He thought she was asking for trouble, that she put too much faith in her fellow man, but it fit her personality. He wiped at his eyes and plodded on.

Leaning over the passenger seat, Rand opened the glove box and rummaged for Jane's wallet. When he pulled it out, several napkins fell onto the floorboard.

"Burger King, huh? Oh, and Wendy's." Health food had never been up Jane's alley. She would have chosen Burger King to Café' L'Europe any day. Among the scattered napkins was a business card. *Jonathan L. Singer. Klassik Kars.*

Where—and *when*—had Janie picked this up?

Rand returned the napkins to the glove box and climbed out of the car, but his curiosity was killing him. Back in the kitchen, he sat Jane's wallet on top of the certificates he'd found in the den, lit another cigarette, then walked to the living room with the business card in his hand. He reached over the couch, picked up the phone, and dialed the printed cell number, hoping the guy would answer. He did.

"John here."

"Hi, uh, Mr. Singer?"

"You got him."

"Yes, I'm...uh..." He cleared his throat. "I'm calling on behalf of my wife. Well, sort of. I found your business card in the glove box of her car just now and..."

"Hey, man, if you're calling about the other night, I didn't know that chick was married."

"Oh, no," he hadn't expected that response. "I'm sure my call has nothing to do with whatever happened the other night. You see, my wife has a classic Chevelle, and I think..."

"You mean the blue '68 convertible? That car is a beauty. Did she change her mind about selling it?"

"Well, no. I mean yes, I mean..." Rand took a deep breath. "Sorry. Yes, that's the car, but no, I don't think we'll sell it anytime soon. That's sort of why I'm calling." Had Janie been thinking of selling the car? Why would she save the guy's card? "I was just wondering how long she'd had your business card. Did you speak to her recently?"

"Sure did. Couple days ago, I think. She stopped in at one of the stores I own. Congress Avenue in Lake Worth. I was filling in for the limp dick manager who didn't show half the time. I fired the asshole. You know how hard it is to find people in this town who actually want to work?"

"I can imagine." Rand was wondering if the call had been a waste of time. "Do you happen to remember why she stopped in?"

"Yeah, she was looking for a pay phone. I remember 'cuz I offered her the phone behind the counter, but she wouldn't use it. She bought a phone card, and I gave her directions for the booth down the street. Nice ride, that Chevelle. Good condition, too."

"Yes, it is." A phone card and pay phone? Why would Jane go to such trouble to make a call when she always carried her cell with her? "Um, Mr. Singer, do you mind my asking what kind of store it is that you own?"

"Not at all. I've got six 7-Elevens from Riviera to Pompano. Helps fund my real obsession, you know? Sure you don't want to sell?"

"No, I mean, yes. Yes, I'm sure we don't want to sell. Not now, anyway. Thanks for your time."

"No problem, man."

Rand disconnected the call. Why would Janie need a pay phone and a calling card? She hadn't mentioned it, but then they didn't talk about every detail of every day. Who did? She *had* been preoccupied, though. Hadn't that been one of the reasons for the boat ride?

Phone still in his hand, Rand stood behind the couch and wondered what Jane had been up to prior to the accident. It was possible she'd been planning some type of surprise for him. His birthday was in a month, and their anniversary wasn't far off. If the scheme was grand enough… But that couldn't be right. She would have behaved differently. Sneaky and playful, maybe, but not solemn or melancholy. No. Whatever it was hadn't made her happy. Could she have had an affair? No. He couldn't believe that. He would have noticed something different about her. Wouldn't he? Could she have been sick? Maybe seriously? That might explain why there were no medical files in the cabinet. But wouldn't she have told him? Or maybe she planned to, but never got the chance.

He couldn't believe she'd meant any harm in her actions, whatever they had been. Still, he was sure the not knowing would haunt him. What bothered Janie before her disappearance—her *death*—would now bother him, instead. Unless…

Rand dropped the phone on the back of the couch and hurried to the stairs. There had to be something she'd left behind. Something that explained her mood and behavior. A scribbled note. A hidden letter. Something. He'd look in her handbags, her drawers, her closet, until he found it. He wouldn't stop looking until he knew the secret that had weighed so heavily on Janie's mind.

CHAPTER 10

The train was slowing. Another stop must be ahead. How many more would there be now? Five? Seven? More? After changing trains in Orlando, Jane had settled into her private cabin on the Sunset Limited and fell against the window, lost in thought. She wondered how much time had passed. Had they reached the Florida panhandle yet? Outside, forest had given way to houses. Would it be Jacksonville ahead? Or Tallahassee? Probably neither. The houses were spaced too far apart. Maybe a suburb. Not that it mattered.

Her cabin was a more recently constructed copy of her previous accommodations. Only the commercial color scheme had changed. She'd gone immediately to the chair near the window and immersed herself in the memory of where her troubles began. The first time she'd been alone, after her father and Eddie had gone.

In the beginning, she and Oliver believed the root of their condition was some type of communicable sickness or disease, like the smallpox epidemic that had taken Eddie. Like food poisoning people caught from eating bad meat. Oliver's recent theory that their immortality was instead caused by a man didn't change their current situation, but it did compel Jane to rethink the origins of the dream she associated with the condition's onset. Over the years, she'd become certain that the two were connected. But what had triggered them? What power was behind them?

It had started in November of 1870. She'd just turned twenty-one. She'd awakened intensely ill and with the vague recollection of a terrifying dream. By that time, she had lived alone in her family's Sacramento home for more than a year, but she couldn't shake the feeling that someone else—someone who meant harm—was in the room that morning.

She'd tossed the bedding aside and reached for the chamber pot, taking care to heave away from the bed. Her first thought that something odd had happened came when she noticed she was stripped bare. At no time would she have slept that way. Especially not in winter. When the worst of the vomiting subsided, she laid back and found her rumpled nightclothes beneath the blankets.

Physically unable to do anything else, and fearing the nausea would return if she moved, she slept most of the morning. No figures appeared before her and no demons haunted her sleep, but a feeling—a presence—she'd associated with the death of her mother hung in the room like a blanket of smoke.

Intense pain in her groin area came next. There'd been discomfort earlier, but the soreness from retching had preoccupied her. She hadn't urinated, so she assumed the dull throb in her belly was the result of not making water, or possibly some female dysfunction. When she stood up, still unclothed, burning tendrils shot through her legs and torso. Her bladder emptied. Urine pooled around her feet. She stared at the floor and chamber pot and cried, knowing no one would be coming to help.

Foregoing her corset, ruffled petticoat, and slip, Jane chose the simplest dress with the fewest buttons and dropped it over her head. She wiped her legs and feet with the bedding, and clenched her teeth against the pain of putting on her stockings and lacing her shoes. The journey into town wouldn't be easy, but it was one she'd have to make if she was to see a doctor.

Progress on the stairs was slow. She clung to the railing and took each step carefully, placing her feet side-by-side before descending to the next level. Retrieving a coat and hat from beside the front door, she stepped outside into the chill of winter.

Her legs cramped, unaccustomed to exposure, but the cold brought a welcome numbness to her stomach and pelvic region. She stopped twice along 2nd Street, relying on the young oaks to keep her from swooning. Had her hat blown off, Jane decided, she'd not attempt to bend and retrieve it. Etiquette be damned! She plodded on, determined to find answers to her sickness and an end to the discomfort. What could possibly have happened to her in the night? Could the dream have been real enough to convince her subconscious to act out? What other explanation could there be?

As she turned into the alley behind Front Street, Jane paused, stricken with an overwhelming sense of relief. Whether preoccupied by the powerful dream and its haunting effects, or simply riddled with shock, she had traveled the full six blocks to town without realizing it. She was standing comfortably upright. Her hand no longer clenched against her belly. How long had she been lost in thought? Fifteen minutes? Twenty? Could her body have righted itself in such a short time?

She wasn't imagining it. Her soreness lessened. Her legs no longer felt chilled. The remaining stroll was astonishingly painless. Jane hiked the collar around her neck and stepped onto the boardwalk in front of the doctor's office.

Dr. Iverson saw her quickly. He asked personal questions and performed an examination that left Jane feeling violated. Then he announced everything appeared "perfectly normal." No cuts or tears. No rash or other abnormality that would explain the burning. He suggested Jane might have been temporarily disturbed by the nightmare. Jane got the feeling the doctor believed she'd made it up. If the problem persisted, he'd instructed, she was to call on him immediately.

Three months later, she saw him to report her menstrual cycle had stopped. There were blood tests and another uncomfortable examination. He said it was unusual for someone to enter menopause at only twenty-one, but not unheard of. Then he told her without her cycles she couldn't have children. There was pity in his voice.

The horn on the Sunset Limited shocked Jane to the present. The car rocked from side to side. Again, the train was slowing. She opened the window blind and saw only a sliver of daylight remained in the east. Passengers on the train's west side were likely being graced with a majestic Florida panorama as the sun bid its last farewell. Jane wished she could see it. From the rooftop balcony of their home overlooking the intracoastal. With Rand. She closed the shade against the pending night and switched on the overhead lamp. She had to think of something else. Something happy. There were places she could imagine, but every landscape recalled a face. And every face inevitably met with death.

Glancing across the cabin at the shopping bag propped in the corner, Jane was reminded of how few things she'd held onto through the years. *Things* didn't matter like they did when she was young. People mattered. Love mattered.

The only constant had been Oliver. A man who had entered her life as the result of an unimaginable event and proceeded to remain for the same reason. With the exception of his having abandoned her and broken her heart, Jane's memories of him were among her most treasured. Particularly their introduction.

As the train squealed and rolled from the station, Jane let herself remember the first moment she and Oliver had come face to face.

•

Thousands of miles away, Sir Moncado LaCassiere DeSain stood alone in the dark, thinking about the very same thing.

CHAPTER 11

SACRAMENTO, CALIFORNIA – OCTOBER 7, 1867

From the railing of the paddleboat's upper deck, DeSain watched the crew lower the gangway to the dock. Passengers crowded the exit, anxious to put their twelve-hour voyage from San Francisco behind them. DeSain had reason to be impatient, as well, but he elected to wait for the frenzy to subside. *After all*, he thought, *I'm not a spoiled, eager child*. He'd waited this long. Another minute wouldn't matter. *Right?* He detoured his gaze to the land beyond the river's edge, gathering an impression of the town.

With the Sierra Nevada mountain range as its backdrop, the young city appeared raw and rugged. The packed-dirt thoroughfare of the wharf was a swarm of activity. Carts and wagons lined two-story warehouses for several blocks. Dust swirled about the boots of the workers as they transferred barrels and wheat sacks to buckboards. Along the river, a dozen ships awaited cargo. *She's here*, he thought. His sentinels had done well. Having seen enough, DeSain abandoned the railing and descended the steep stairs to the main deck.

He followed the last passengers across the wooden gangway and dock and stepped up to the hard-packed earth of the busy thoroughfare. From somewhere on his left, melodic strains of a piano playing something unfamiliar but cheerful wafted by in the calm, cool air. A recital? No. Not at this end of town. He strained to hear more clearly. Only a barrelhouse, or *saloon*. But behind the sound, there was something else. Panic? Yes. And horror. His interest diverted, DeSain hurried across the dirt street, climbed onto the boardwalk, and turned north as the sun began its twilight journey into the rolling hills behind the Sacramento River.

The immortal had long ago acquired the ability to hear and manipulate minds. After five-hundred years it had become second nature. But he was especially keen to powerful emotion, and somewhere ahead—coming ever closer—a man was carrying heavy news. A lone rider from the Sierras. An explosion triggered a landslide. Hundreds of railroad workers were dead. Ordinarily, DeSain would have no interest in such matters. This was not his home. These were not his people. However, a familiar name was prominent in the rider's thoughts.

A name he associated with betrayal.

And anticipation.

DeSain pivoted right, following the boardwalk around a corner, and peered forward. Moving swiftly up the center of the dirt street was a man on horseback. Riding as if it pained him to do so. DeSain halted his advance and watched the man bring his horse to a sudden stop. The rider dismounted, relying on gravity more than strength, and stumbled onto the boardwalk directly ahead.

To gain a better view, DeSain relocated to the thoroughfare. He watched the man disappear through the wide entryway of a long, two-story structure. Painted in block letters above the first floor awning was "Huntington, Hopkins & Co." A hardware store. DeSain crossed the remainder of the street and leaned against one of two granite pillars flanking the entrance of a bank. With his mind, he pursued the man upstairs and into the office of the Central Pacific Railroad.

He tugged his dark hat over his right brow to reduce the glare of the sunset and listened intently to the conversation across the street.

"Mr. Crocker?"

"Yes."

"I've come from the tunnels. Somethin' awful's happened."

Speak the name, DeSain suggested, wanting to hear it aloud.

Winded, the rider continued. "Mr. Dougharty, sir, and the chemist...they were tryin' something new, but...they didn't make it...so much of the mountain...they was too close."

DeSain loosed his concentration. *Mr. Dougharty*. His interpretation of the rider's pained mind had been correct. The girl's father—the witch's husband—was dead. *What splendid timing.* The girl would be grief-stricken.

Oh, how he ached for her pain—her vulnerability.

The immortal had traveled these fourteen months to the New World to see the girl—the *woman*—with his own eyes. Not for the first time, but back then... He paused his thoughts, reminding himself of her face as it was twelve years ago. She'd only been a child. Her features foretold exquisite beauty, but that hadn't intrigued him most. She had discovered him in the throes of a most unsettling business, but she'd not been afraid. Instead, she looked at him with rage, her eyes illustrating a strength of spirit DeSain had not encountered before. Few mortals were capable of repelling his powers of the mind. He suspected immediately she was the one the ancient oracle had seen.

The conversation across the street had concluded. Presently, two men emerged from the shadows of the general store. The rider, in his rumpled, sweat-stained shirt and suspenders, and an older man wearing a dark three-piece suit. The contrast, DeSain thought, was amusing. He watched as the men crossed the street and approached the boardwalk, but he didn't bother turning to see them enter the bank behind him.

They reappeared five minutes later, joined by another dark suit and top hat and a young gentleman in a light suit and brown bowler. The four men descended the boardwalk onto the street and trudged east, away from the river. None of them spoke, but DeSain knew their purpose. To deliver word of Dougharty's death to his children. *A lucky coincidence*, he thought, and followed them.

The immortal knew how to be unseen when it suited him, but he felt no reason to expend the effort this evening. This burgeoning river town was accustomed to strangers, and few people remained on the streets and boardwalks since the sun had set. Instead, he concentrated on masking his presence from the men directly in front of him as he followed them around a corner store to the right.

The two men in black were high-level representatives of the railroad; although, DeSain noted, one was of higher rank. Both had held respect for Dougharty. Neither reveled in the task of conveying unpleasant news. The youngest man in the group was an accountant. He felt uncomfortable, but not having known the deceased, his chief preoccupation was mustering the confidence to perform without embarrassing himself. And then, there was the rider. Exhausted but determined.

The men crossed a service road that ran along the shops' back entrances, and emerged from the shadows of the town's center of commerce. In single file, they strode silently down a footpath beneath transplanted oaks lining the residential street. Ten houses down, the men stopped in front of a large two-story Victorian, painted white with green shutters and trim.

While DeSain lingered on the footpath, the men climbed the steps to the covered porch. A man in black rapped on the doorframe. Within seconds, the door swung open and an elderly woman appeared. The men removed their hats. The spokesman addressed her. She stepped to one side, gesturing for the men to enter.

For a split second, DeSain considered following them in, but his instincts froze him. The woman was inside. How much had she learned since her childhood? Thinking it best to fall back, DeSain crossed the narrow dirt street and propped himself against the base of a young oak tree. He felt comfortable with the distance. The men and the housekeeper had disappeared inside the house. DeSain shut his eyes, following the scene inside as the reluctant officials awkwardly relayed the news of Dougharty's death to his children. Their cries of pain flooded DeSain's soul.

•

Dougharty's death hadn't been entirely lucky for DeSain. True, he had been escorted almost immediately to the home of the woman he'd come for, but grief had not made her vulnerable, as he'd anticipated. It had, instead, hidden her away. The windows of the home were veiled within hours after the family received the news. For weeks he'd tried to gain a clear look at her, standing tirelessly in the rain and the cold. But she didn't come out, not even for the funeral, and her mind wouldn't bend to his. He tried entering the house once as she slept, but he felt her defenses before he approached the stairs. Since then, he'd contented himself to observe from a distance and wait for her sorrow to fade.

After hours of standing on his feet, DeSain removed his overcoat and tossed it to the ground beside the young oak. He sat down with his back against the bark and his legs extended into the edge of the street. His boot heels imprinted half moons in the dirt. The afternoon sun shone bright overhead.

Yes, he thought, she'd been stronger than he expected, but he refused to believe too quickly that an untrained mortal—albeit a gifted one—could so easily ward him off. He'd traveled a great distance to see her face and to what end? To stand in the mud and gawk at endless parades of mourners? Before his arrival in Sacramento, he'd thought it would be enough to simply know that the time of the prophecy was upon him. But he'd already confirmed that, and still, after coming this close, being on her doorstep wasn't enough. He wanted to see her. He wanted to smell her.

But, of course, he reminded himself, he had competition now.

Since Dougharty's death, a curious development had unfolded. The young accountant who'd helped deliver the news had established a friendly rapport with his new customer. A *very* friendly rapport.

The young man visited the Dougharty home twice each week. DeSain watched his approach from beneath the shade tree near the house across the street. Although the young woman's thoughts were guarded, the young man's were not, and DeSain had gathered quite a comprehensive description of the maiden from the boy's mind.

On cue, the young accountant appeared rounding the corner of the distant main street. He walked with a confident but mindful gait.

Without paying heed to the spying stranger, he strode to the front of the neatly-kept Victorian, ascended to the porch, and knocked on the door.

Expecting the servant woman to greet him, DeSain observed the activities across the street with mild interest. But the old woman wasn't coming. The young Dougharty woman was approaching the door. DeSain leapt to his feet, not caring that he ripped his coat in the process.

The door opened and a figure emerged from the unlit recesses of the foyer. Her ebony hair was gathered neatly behind her head, and DeSain traced the outline of her face as she stood in the doorway. She'd grown more beautiful than he'd anticipated. A rare prize.

She has to be the one, he thought.

The young accountant stepped into the house, blocking DeSain's view of her, and the door was shut behind them. It would be an hour or more before the door opened again.

DeSain stayed on his feet.

Their meetings routinely began with trivial reports of bank account activities and generally ended with invitations to call on the bank if any needs arose. Dougharty's son, Edward, stopped attending the meetings after the second week. He'd returned to duties at the general store, his thoughts on other matters. That left only the lady of the house and the accountant to carry on the conversations. And, of course, the servant woman who occasionally made appearances in the room.

The couple's conversation began as usual with Mr. Chatham, as she called him, delivering a sermon on the ease with which Miss Dougharty could access her funds. Taken at face value, Chatham's words might have led one to believe he was interested only in the young woman's money. It had its appeal. Taken in context with his emotions, however, it was obvious the nervous young man was taken with the beautiful young woman.

It made sense given her station and outward sensibilities that she was a virgin. Pure and uncharted. Through Chatham's mind, he'd searched the woman's mannerisms and speech for clues of her virtue, but it was impossible to detect. She would eventually belong to him, virginal or no, so it didn't impact the final result. But there was something else. She was the chosen one. And she was extraordinary. If her innocence was to be taken, to whom should the honor fall?

He focused again on the meeting across the street. Their words weren't clear—DeSain wished he could draw closer—but the meaning was easy enough. Chatham asked how she and her brother were getting along. She said they were fine. Small talk was unusual this soon, but DeSain had noticed its introduction occurring earlier and earlier with each of Chatham's visits. Then he noticed a peak in the young man's energy level. The woman had said something that made his body tense. The boy's brow beaded with perspiration. His heartbeat doubled. *What did she say to him?* DeSain reached deep into the accountant's thoughts.

She'd confessed her feelings for him. He was overcome with rapture. He would marry her. With her brother's approval, of course. How long was her period of mourning? His breathing halted when she answered. Months, maybe years. Customs were different in the east. *But*, he was begging, *they weren't in the east anymore*.

Being in the habit of making hasty decisions, DeSain decided he wouldn't let the courtship continue between Mr. Chatham and Miss Dougharty. There were benefits and losses to consider. Losses DeSain was unwilling to assume. He stood up and shot a brief glance at the Victorian, then, leaving his coat, struck a course for downtown. The thought of a mortal laying hands on what was rightfully his suddenly made him furious.

•

The room was smoky and a bit loud, and the piano needed tuning, but the young man was glad he'd chosen to stop for a drink this evening instead of rushing home. And the stranger who'd offered Oliver an empty seat three drinks ago had up to now been a pleasure to talk to. They'd discussed topics of wide range: business and economics, even philosophy. Their exchange had been so exhilarating that he hadn't thought of Miss Dougharty—*Jane*—all night. Oliver wondered, though, if the man seated across the small table hadn't suddenly crossed into some realm of madness—or maybe egotism—with his last assumption.

"Five dollars says you're wrong, sir," Oliver said.

The stranger smiled and shook his head. "It would be a foolish bet, my boy." His accent was exotic. Oliver could ask the man where he'd come from, but the not knowing made him more interesting. Come to think of it, he hadn't even asked his name.

Oliver leaned in over the table and lowered his voice. "I can't believe, sir, that any woman of my choosing would *at your command* fall to her knees before you and...um, place her mouth...well, I just don't believe it."

After what appeared to Oliver as a pause for second thoughts, the man spoke. "If you don't mind losing your money, I will prove it to you here and now."

Oliver was dumbstruck. At twenty-five, he wasn't embarrassed or offended by the language of the man's declaration. And he'd enjoyed the attentions of a whore at the age of twenty-two, so was familiar with the act to which the stranger was referring. What struck him as most unusual was that the man believed he could summon a crude sexual deed "on command." What choice did Oliver have but to show the man his folly?

"You're on, sir." He pulled out a modest money clip from his breast pocket and laid a bill on the table. "But the woman must be of my choosing, remember."

The man sat back, unfettered. "If that is what it takes."

All Oliver had to do was produce a woman who would decline the stranger's request. He scanned the crowded saloon, but quickly discovered the only women inside its confines were for hire. "Under the circumstances, sir, may I choose from outside the saloon?"

"Of course. It won't matter." Oliver couldn't tell if the man spoke with arrogance or insanity.

Oliver excused himself from the table and shuffled through the crowd to the door. Outside, the street was quiet and drenched in shadow. The sun had gone down. The air was crisp. A fire burned on his right near the railroad yards, and Oliver hastened his steps toward the glow.

"Excuse me," he said, arriving at the fire's edge. Several figures huddled in its warmth. "Are there any women here interested in an easy five dollars?"

"Maybe," a voice croaked from the shadows. "'pends on what ya' mean by 'easy.'"

Oliver pointed. "Step inside that saloon there with me, and let a gentleman ask you a question."

"That all?"

"That's all."

The figure rose and stepped through the fire's light, revealing a haggard and repulsive woman. "You sure there ain't nothin' else involved, boy? I 'spect more'n five dollars for particular favors, if you get my meanin.'"

"I do, ma'am, and I don't think it will come to that."

The woman followed Oliver back into the bar. Oliver approached the stranger who'd been his companion for the evening and introduced him to the woman he'd brought in from the yards.

"This is the one I've chosen." He smiled triumphantly. "Still up to the challenge?"

Without hesitation, the stranger stood up from the chair and faced the woman. He was taller than Oliver expected. His vest looked like armor, and his dark shirt and pants made his figure ominous. Oliver stepped aside and watched as the stranger's eyes locked on the hag.

"Woman, I'd like you to show this young gentleman how eager you are to please me."

The woman from the rail yards took a step forward and fell to her knees. Her hands reached for the buttons of the stranger's trousers. She hadn't protested, nor did her expression let on that she was anything but anxious to serve.

"This is a joke," Oliver said to the man. "You must have prearranged this."

The man's countenance didn't waver. "I assure you I did not."

"There must be a trick." Oliver watched the woman reach into the stranger's pants. "Tell her to stop. There's no need to continue."

"Would you like to stop?" The stranger asked her.

She looked away from her task and into his face. "No, sir."

Oliver could swear she was pleading. "This is crazy. You can't do this in the middle of a saloon. We'll both be tossed."

But no one appeared to notice. Men at nearby tables continued their drinking and card games as if nothing was out of the ordinary. Even the whores seemed unconcerned with the loss of a paying customer.

The kneeling woman bobbed her head as if her life depended on it. Oliver couldn't look away.

"Do you believe?" the stranger asked.

Oliver didn't know. "There must be some kind of deception."

"You chose the woman, as was your condition."

"Yes, but…" Oliver looked around the room again, bewildered. Wasn't anyone watching this? "You could have made prior arrangements. You must have."

"Then surely this could not happen again?"

"Are you suggesting I choose another woman? But there aren't any. Only whores."

The stranger tilted his head down. "That's enough, woman." The hag stopped her chore and stood. Without a word to Oliver about the money he'd promised, she turned and left the saloon. Leaving his pants unfastened, the stranger picked up his drink. "So choose a man, then."

Oliver shivered at the suggestion. "It's obscene enough that you stand there…exposed as you are." Oliver gestured, but didn't look. He wasn't about to lower his gaze and risk encouragement of the wrong assumptions. "I'll not choose a man."

"A whore, then."

"Why must we continue this at all?"

"This was *your* challenge, remember? You were the one who asked for proof. I demonstrated my ability, and yet you're unconvinced. Am I expected to leave this business unfinished?" He gestured with both hands toward his erection, which, through his peripheral vision, Oliver could see was more than average size.

"That could be easily remedied upstairs."

"But you would still not believe."

Oliver thought about the situation. It was possible that the man had a prior alliance with the hag from the rail yards. She was, after all, the only woman Oliver had come across outside the saloon. It was simply unbelievable to think that any man had such power of persuasion. But then, it was equally unbelievable to imagine a man could stand in the center of a crowded room with his manhood exposed and not be thrown out.

"Let's agree to this," he said finally, "I will choose a whore. *But*, before she's brought to you, I must be given the opportunity to discourage her from obeying your command. If she defies you, I get my five dollars back and we'll end square. If she surrenders to you as the old woman did, I'll be out ten dollars—double or nothin'—and you will have convinced me."

"Fair enough."

"Could I get you boys another round?" A blonde had appeared before the two men. She smiled politely, and made no mention of the stranger's exposure.

Are these people blind? Oliver thought. "Yes, ma'am, thank you. I believe we'll be having one more." He reached over the table for his unfinished drink and poured it quickly down his throat.

"She seemed pleasant." The stranger should have been growing impatient, but he seemed as relaxed as he had all evening.

"That was too easy. Too coincidental." Oliver looked around the room. "How about that one there? The redhead?"

He didn't look. "Whomever you like."

"Or maybe her," he pointed, "in the corner with her breast exposed."

"It won't matter."

Was he laughing?

Oliver retrieved money from his coat pocket again and laid it on the table. "That's five for the bet and a dollar for the round. I'll not be long."

He stepped away from the table and approached three prostitutes standing at the foot of the stairs. This charade would end here and now. "I'll pay one of you ladies fifteen dollars if you'll tell that man over there to go fuck himself."

"I'm up for it."

"Me, too."

"Which one is he?"

Oliver pointed. "But, I need only one of you. You choose however you like."

A fair-haired woman stepped forward. "I'll go. There's nothin' I can think of that would be more satisfyin'." The women giggled.

"All right, then. It'll be you. Now, this man and I have a bet, and I need you to understand the terms. He's going to tell you to do something. If you refuse, you'll get the money. Plain and simple. But if you do what he says, the deal's off."

"I get it, okay? Let's go."

Oliver led her to the table where the stranger stood, his manhood still at attention. "No way this one'll fall for your parlor tricks." He turned to the whore. "You remember the deal?"

"I ain't no dumbshit, mister. I know the deal."

Oliver picked up his fresh drink from the table and held it up triumphantly at the stranger. "Give it your best shot."

Just as before, Oliver watched as the man locked eyes with the woman. "My dear, do you see the predicament I'm in?"

"Yes."

"And you know what to do?"

"Yes."

"Then waste no time."

She dropped down as the hag had done. No objections. No hesitation. No "Go fuck yourself."

Oliver slumped into the chair, clinging to his glass, as the whore finished the job and returned to the foot of the stairs without uttering a word. He was no longer surprised that no one protested the act.

The stranger straightened his clothing and resumed his seat across the table. "You believe now?"

"I believe I'm out ten dollars."

"I was never interested in your money. You can keep it."

"No. You earned it square, and I'll not decline payment on a bet."

"Suit yourself." The stranger tipped his glass and drank, but he didn't move to gather Oliver's money from the table. "What would you say if I told you I could give you that same power to persuade?"

"Teach me the art of getting a woman to suck my prick? Ha! I can understand the need, sir, in the most desperate of situations, but I can't see it as a useful talent."

"*Persuasion* is so much more than what you may think you just witnessed tonight. Did you not find it a wee bit strange that our public display wasn't halted?"

"I did, but we're surrounded by drunks and prostitutes."

"Indeed. Still, there is a code of conduct to be followed, even in a place such as this. Not even the proprietor—I believe that's him there by the bar—stopped to warn us of our infraction."

He had a point. "So you're saying you 'persuaded' every individual in this room to permit you to carry on without interference? That's ridiculous."

"Is it? Imagine what you could accomplish, not just as a financier as you aspire to be, but as anything. Or anyone. Take your Miss Dougharty, for example. Would it not be worthwhile to convince her to wed immediately?"

Oliver's neck grew warm. "What do you know of Miss Dougharty? And how dare you speak her name in this place and after what's transpired."

"I only use her as an example. Her mourning must certainly be a hindrance to you."

Oliver raised his voice. "I ask again, sir, what do you know of my affiliation with Miss Dougharty?"

"I know she is the woman of your heart."

"How do you know? I've not spoken of her, and you and I met only tonight."

"It's of no concern precisely how I know these things, only that I speak the truth. She is but one woman in a world of many. I can offer you them all."

"What kind of man are you?" Oliver wasn't sure if he should be offended or intrigued.

The stranger's dark eyes seemed to twinkle in the bright candlelight. "The kind that can make your most fantastic dreams come true."

That was all he could take. He finished his drink quickly and stood.

"I have enjoyed our conversations tonight, sir, but I will not stay longer."

"Oh, but you will."

Oliver sat back down. Images of Miss Dougharty passed through his mind. How beautiful she was on their first meeting, dressed in yellow with dark curls falling against her neck. Her green eyes danced with youthful vibrancy. How even in black her cheeks looked blushed and not ashen, and how envious he was of her tears each time he saw them falling softly over the curves of her face.

"Come closer, boy."

Oliver leaned in.

"You'll forget this Miss Dougharty in time as I have a special purpose for you."

Forget Miss Dougharty? Never. But the words refused to be spoken.

"You will leave here tonight and travel east until no memory of her remains."

That would be impossible. He would never agree to that.

"And to be sure these instructions are followed, allow me one simple act of insurance."

The stranger reached across the table and placed a single fingertip against Oliver's right temple. His touch was cool at first, but then it erupted into an intense burning that spread quickly through his head. Oliver fell back into the chair and brought his hands to his ears. He pressed hard, as if the force could somehow alleviate the pain.

His eyes were shut tight, and he felt the burn travel like hot, thick liquid through his body, passing behind his face, down his neck, and into his shoulders and chest. Within seconds, he felt as if he were engulfed in flames.

But then a cooling started in the pit of his stomach. Icy tentacles wove their way through his extremities until the fires burning inside were vanquished and replaced with the lifeless cool of snow. He opened his eyes, then, and suddenly felt violently ill. The stranger was gone, but Oliver's concern over his disappearance was secondary to the more immediate need to vomit.

He pushed through the saloon and rushed to the street outside. He fell to his hands and knees, coughing and choking, believing that surely his intestines and other inner workings would follow. He wondered if he'd been poisoned. He prayed the end would come soon.

His sickness hovered for several minutes, until he fell exhausted onto his side. He rolled onto his back and wiped at the corners of his mouth with his coat sleeve. The stench of regurgitation hung thick around him as he lay in the dirt street. What in the name of hell had come over him?

Then he remembered. He'd been in the company of a stranger whose name he hadn't ascertained. They'd made some kind of bet. Oliver had lost. At some point late in the evening, the man offended him, invoking the name of a woman. But what woman could it have been?

Oliver struggled to recall specific events of the night. The harder he thought, the less he remembered. He stared at the stars, wishing for answers, but none came. Obviously he'd fallen in a drunken stupor. And with a hard-on that would wait for no one.

He stood and brushed himself off, and realized he'd lost his hat. His temple was throbbing. He reached up to rub his head and felt a wound. He looked at his fingers. No blood. *Must've hit my head on something.* He staggered toward the swinging door or the saloon, intending to grab onto the first whore he saw. Then he made a mental note to look for his hat before continuing his journey east.

CHAPTER 12

Dave Fristoe's scarlet Jaguar purred into the Ackerton driveway and stopped. Rand unfastened his seat belt and reached for the handle on the door. "Thanks for bein' there today, man."

"Hey," his friend smiled, "it's my job as your lawyer. At least they didn't arrest you. Wasn't that your big worry?"

Rand had to admit he'd been relieved to walk away from the press conference a free man. "They make me feel guilty, Dave. How can they do that when I've told them the truth?"

Dave shifted the transmission to Park and dropped his hands in his lap. "Feeling guilty around the police is something that's ingrained, my friend. It comes from driving seventy-five in a thirty with a bag of weed trying to get back to the dorm before lights out."

If Dave was trying to lighten Rand's spirits, it was working. "I suppose you're right."

"This has got to be hard on you. It's too bad this town has such a shitty bedside manner."

"Yeah."

Rand noticed a car pull up alongside the road. What looked like a teenager climbed out of the driver's side door. Over the hedge, Rand caught the slogan on the back of the kid's green t-shirt: *Up Yours*. The media.

"I thought a press conference was supposed to satisfy the press."

Dave shifted the car into Drive. "I'd better run if I'm going to miss drive-time traffic. I hate leaving you here alone, though, buddy."

"I'll be okay. I've got plenty to do before bedtime."

"Don't talk to these guys."

"Promise. Thanks again, man."

"You're welcome. I'll call you when I get home."

Rand opened the door and stepped out of the car, wincing at the pain in his knee as he hurried to reach the front door.

•

It was after four o'clock and Rand had nothing but time. His search for Janie's secret had been put on hold when Dave arrived that morning, but with the day's activities behind him, Rand was anxious to recommence.

He stood before the walk-in closet, taking inventory of Jane's things and praying he would find a clue as to what had troubled her before the accident. For a moment, he only stared, trying to remember what his wife's closet was supposed to look like. He was surprised to realize he hadn't paid that much attention before.

A mirror of his side, Jane's half of the walk-in was separated into four sections, each with a large drawer on the bottom and a cabinet door at the top. As far as he could tell, nothing was disturbed. Her clothes hung neatly in the three cabinets to the right. On the left, her shoes were tucked in, two-by-two, into a dozen or more cubbies. One pair was missing.

And it wouldn't be back.

He bent forward and opened the first drawer. Winter clothing. Scarves. Gloves. He placed his hand on the soft wool of the sweater Janie had worn the previous year in Switzerland. She'd been so beautiful with the snow as her backdrop, her cheeks flushed from the cold. He pulled his hand away and closed the drawer, then opened the one to its right. Swimsuits. Tank tops. Beach shorts. Items, he recalled, she hadn't owned when they married twenty years ago. But then, neither of them had much at the time.

Rand could never say he'd been poor. Not while he had a mother who made up for her constant butting-in by shoving bundles of cash into his pocket. Rand was reminded of the day he'd discovered an envelope full of twenties in the freezer while preparing to move with his new wife from St. Augustine to Palm Beach. His mother later admitted to hiding the money there ten or eleven months earlier. With Rand's discovery came his mother's realization that Rand, their only child, didn't need her help anymore.

But the money hadn't been the only discovery Rand made on moving day. There had been something in Jane's Charlotte Street home. He had reached down to pick up a battered suitcase and an open carpetbag when Jane rushed over and uttered too quickly, "Let me get those." She explained the items had belonged to her family and were precious.

They must be here somewhere, he thought.

Rand shut the drawer and stood, rubbing his knee where he'd bumped it on the boat. He cursed his aching bones for reminding him that, although he wasn't *old* yet, he wasn't twenty-six anymore. He half-limped to a tall hutch on the far right, marking the end of the closet. Opening the cabinet door, he saw the old suitcase on the bottom shelf. The initials C.J.W. were etched in a tarnished metal plate near the handle. A relative? Wedged alongside the suitcase, and obviously empty, was the worn carpetbag.

The phone rang and Rand was swept from the memories of moving day. Although the ring's sharpness was muffled by the thick silence of the closet, a shiver tickled the back of Rand's neck. Maybe the police had something new. Maybe the body Janson mentioned earlier had been identified. He hurried through the awning into the master bedroom and grabbed at the phone atop the desk near the window.

"Hello?"

"Yes," a man with a deep voice and southern drawl replied, "is this

Missus Williams' residence?"

A wrong number. Rand's heart rate started its descent toward normal. "I'm sorry. There's no one here named Williams."

"Then I hope you'll excuse the inconvenience, sir, but are you sure no Missus Catherine Jane Williams can be reached at this number?"

"I'm sh..." *No. It couldn't be*, he thought. *Catherine Jane Williams. C.J.W. Williams had been Jane's maiden name.* "Wait," Rand said abruptly, "who is this?"

"Sampson Delano. I work as a conductor on the Silver Star."

"Silver Star? Is that some kind of tour company?"

"No, sir," the man chuckled, "the Star is a train. A passenger in one of my private cars this morning left something behind when she got off. This was the phone number recorded with her reservation."

Jane said she had no living relatives. Could there have been someone she never mentioned? The initials were too coincidental for the call to have been the result of a random, misdialed number.

"Sir?" the man spoke. "Are you familiar with Ms. Williams?"

"I'm not sure, I... I've just been through a rough few days." If that wasn't an understatement. Rand pulled the high-backed, leather chair out and away from the desk and sat down. "I suppose it's possible that one of my wife's relatives used our phone number as a contact."

"Those things happen. In my house, I'm always the last to know what's goin' on, you know? Wives are like that. They don't always tell you everything."

No wisdom could be more true. "Are you allowed, sir, to say what the woman left behind?"

"It's not anything perishable, and it's not a pocketbook or anything like that. Just a piece of paper, or a ticket, I should say. Something like what you get from a baggage claim or a locker box."

"Pardon my indifference, but a piece of paper doesn't sound like anything important. Not important enough to make a phone call."

"In my business, you learn not to make guesses on what's important and what's not. One man's trash is another man's treasure, so they say. I watch out for the passengers on my train. Some of 'em got no one else to depend on."

Rand took an open package of Marlboro Lights and a lighter from the drawer of the desk. "You're right." He lit the cigarette. "Who am I to say what's important to someone else?" Rand slid the ashtray closer and shot a cursory glance at the photographs spread out across the desk. Pictures that marked momentous occasions in his life with Janie. He thought he'd known all there was to know about her. "Just so I can figure out which one of my wife's relatives I should pass this message to, could you tell me where she got off the train?"

"Well, I'm not generally supposed to, but I don't see where it would hurt. She got off in Orlando so she could change trains on her way to New Orleans."

New Orleans. Rand took a drag from the cigarette. He'd tried several times to convince Jane to accompany him to New Orleans, but she'd always had some schedule conflict or other reason she couldn't go.

"So you'll tell her, then? Your wife's relative?"

"Yes, certainly. But, if you wouldn't mind one last thing. I think your passenger may have been my wife's mother," he lied, "to be sure, it would help if you would describe her to me."

"Well now, I don't know that she could have been your wife's mother. She couldn't have had no grown and married children. This was a young white woman, early thirties maybe. Friendly, but preoccupied. Black hair tied in a ponytail…and bright green eyes that could 'light up a room' as my mama would have said, God rest her."

Rand didn't respond immediately. He'd been gazing into the faces of the people in the pictures on the desk when he realized the train conductor at the other end of the line was describing Janie. Could that be possible? Could Janie be alive?

He tried to sound calm. "Thank you, um, Mister…"

"Delano."

"Right. Sampson Delano." Rand was trembling. "Thank you, Mr. Delano."

"Would you like me to put the ticket in the mail?"

Should he? If Janie really was alive, maybe it was a clue that would lead him to her. But if this was nothing more than a bizarre coincidence, and the stranger *did* need that piece of paper Delano had recovered…

"Thanks for offering, but no. Maybe the woman will call and retrieve it herself." *But*, his mind still argued, *what if you need it to find her?* "Should I hear from the careless relative, however, I'll be sure to contact you."

"I would appreciate that, and I thank you. Have a good day, sir."

"You, too." Rand hung up the phone.

What was going on? Jane's blue mood. The accident. The police. The body washed ashore in Juno. The old monogrammed suitcase. The phone call looking for a young woman with the initials C.J.W. Catherine Jane Williams. Jane Catherine Williams.

Jane Catherine Ackerton.

Rand dropped the lit cigarette into the ashtray and sprang from the chair toward the closet. *Where was the box?* The one he'd first seen in the carpetbag in St. Augustine. The same one he'd secretly opened years later when he came across it while looking for a pair of hiking boots. Inside he had found nothing more than what appeared to be cheap souvenirs—theater tickets, fading playbills, a lace handkerchief—and a handful of old jewelry and coins. Items Jane prized, he assumed, more for their sentimental value than anything else.

He approached the opened door of the first cabinet and pulled out the suitcase and bag. Both were empty. He reached up and pulled items off the remaining three shelves. Travel bags, toiletry kits, and hat boxes, among other things, cascaded to the floor. He opened the next cabinet above the hanging clothes, and then the next, until every item from every cabinet was cleared from the shelves and added to the pile. *It's not here.* He wished he'd asked the conductor if the woman had any baggage.

You should have asked him what the woman was wearing.

Where else would Jane have kept the antique box?

She took it with her.

No. Rand's mind was playing tricks. That couldn't be the answer. Janie was gone. He was there when it happened.

But you didn't see her go in the water.

I heard the splash. She never came up.

What about the pay phone call?

It was unrelated.

And her missing medical records?

Maybe she doesn't keep them at home.

Yours are here, why not hers? Maybe she doesn't have any or maybe she took them *with her, too.*

"Enough!" Rand brought his hands over his ears and yelled. "Janie's gone. She's dead. The police have recovered a body."

You know it's not hers.

I don't know that. Not for sure.

Yes. You do. She's gone, but not dead.

Gone to New Orleans.

Go to New Orleans.

Rand picked up the phone.

"Change in plans," he said to Dave when his friend answered. "Turn around and come get me."

"What the fuck, man? What's wrong?" Rand could hear Tim McGraw singing on the radio in the background.

"Just turn around, okay. I need to stay with you tonight. I'll explain when you get here."

"You know, if you're thinking of doing something stupid, this police shit's nothing to fool around with."

Among the photos before him was a snapshot of himself and Jane with Dave and his wife Karen. Their friendship had been priceless. "Dave, how well do you trust me?"

Dave hesitated. "Probably a damn lot more than I should."

"Then turn around."

"You'd better know what you're doing, Rand."

Rand clenched his teeth and took a deep breath. "I do." He hoped it wasn't a lie.

DAY 3

CHAPTER 13

PORTLAND, OREGON TERRITORY – APRIL 14, 1881

Jane paused on the last step before the station platform and, grasping the car's handrail, drew in her first breath of the crisp northwest air. Behind the smell of cooling iron was a thick and natural scent that reminded her of Philadelphia and the carefree days of her childhood. The tension in her shoulders and neck eased. Any doubts she'd harbored about her decision to leave California melted away. In less than a week, she would be in Alaska—"the furthest point north," she'd said when buying the ticket four days earlier—and there she would start a new life. With renewed purpose, Jane stepped down onto the wooden platform, joining the hundred or so other rail passengers as they disembarked to await ferry transport across the Willamette and Columbia Rivers.

Overcast skies betrayed the early hour of the day and cast a dim light on what passed for the train station. It wasn't much to look at, being nothing more than a square wooden building that could have easily been mistaken for public toilets; but the San Francisco station had been the same, and Jane reconfirmed to herself for the hundredth time that the west would forever be decades behind the east.

The planks beneath her feet were wet, so Jane chose her steps carefully, modestly hoisting her skirts as she made her way toward the baggage car near the end of the train. Ahead, just beyond the platform, a heavy man covered head to toe in mud backed a horse-drawn cart toward an opening railcar door. The heavy door squealed along its track as two workmen jumped down into the cart and immediately began barking orders to one another and catching bags thrown from the car. Jane stopped at the end of the platform and waited for her trunk to emerge.

"Beautiful, isn't it?" A male voice from behind startled her. Jane swung around, instinctively reaching for her hat in case it slid from her head, and recognized the train's young porter.

"Beg pardon?" she asked.

"The view. Just there," he pointed to the caboose, "beyond the river."

Jane raised her eyebrows and strained to see what the young man was pointing to. "I'm sorry, but I see nothing but warehouses, hills, and trees."

"Well, I guess you can't really see the river from here, but it's just there, behind that row of buildings."

"Oh."

"And the cloud cover's a bit thick, but if it wasn't, you could see the peaks of four mountains from this spot. Volcanoes, really. They're quite a spectacle when the weather is more accommodating."

Again, Jane looked into the distance, but saw only gray skies and approaching thunderclouds. If there was beauty out there, it was well hidden.

"It will be a few hours, Miss, before the ferry is ready to depart." He pointed this time to the sky. "With rain likely coming, you might want to seek cover in the station or have an early lunch in town."

"Thank you for your concern," Jane nodded, then returned her attention to the workers, "but I would like to ensure the safe transfer of my belongings onto the ferry."

"These men will see to your baggage, ma'am," the porter said, referring to the workmen on the cart. "I can attest to their trustworthiness."

"It is not necessarily *their* trustworthiness I hold in question." Jane turned her head to look the porter in the eye. "This territory does not have the most stellar of reputations, you know." In fact, rumors she'd heard on the train had let on that the bustling river port town was one of the world's most dangerous.

He winked. "All the more reason to stay with the crowds." His boyish face reminded Jane of her brother, Eddie, and she recalled confessing that fact to the porter the previous day on the train. During their brief conversation, the porter had offered his own confession, explaining how he'd come to be the youngest porter in the short history of the railways by "simple right of birth." His father was an engineer. His uncle a conductor. Jane found the young man cocky, but harmless.

She returned her gaze to the baggage car and considered abandoning her post to leave the fate of her trunk and its contents—everything she had in the world—to the small band of railroad workers who were currently tossing bags haphazardly onto the growing pile. She decided she couldn't do it.

"Again, I appreciate your concern, sir," she smiled sincerely at the porter, "but I prefer to attend to this first."

"As you wish." He nodded.

"Thank you." Jane expected him to turn and walk away, but when he remained, awkwardly shuffling his feet and fussing with his coat sleeves, she asked him, "Was there anything else?"

"Huh? Oh, no, ma'am. I only..." he stuttered, "well, uh, if you need someone to escort you into town for lunch or, uh, I..." He cleared his throat and grabbed at his collar. Blood rushed to his cheeks.

Jane suddenly felt as if she were reliving the first time someone tried to ask her to dinner. "I believe, sir, that an invitation such as the one you're attempting to propose is most inappropriate under the..."

"Oh, no," he interrupted as the color drained from his cheeks, "I didn't mean to offend... I only..." He brought his hands together as if preparing for prayer and cleared his throat again. "Please don't misunderstand, Miss. I mean no disrespect. On the contrary, in fact. It's just that a young woman shouldn't travel alone here."

A young woman, he'd said. At age thirty-two, Jane likely had five years or more on the railroad's youngest porter. The hairs on the back of her neck stood on end. Jane was growing sick and tired of men—and boys—treating her as if she were a helpless child. She gathered her five-foot-two frame and squared off firmly before the slightly taller young man.

"I have already traveled alone quite a distance, *sir*. You of all people should know that. I am perfectly capable of seeing myself across the street."

The porter lowered his head and said nothing.

"Good day," Jane huffed and, turning her back on the young man, renewed her supervisory position as gentle raindrops began to fall. *How old must a woman be*, she wondered, *before she's considered by the opposite sex as being capable of taking care of herself?*

•

An hour passed before Jane finally entered one of the downtown restaurants, drenched to her core in what had become a chilling downpour, but satisfied that her belongings were safely aboard the paddle ship. Attempting to rid some of her discomfort, she ruffled her skirts and swept at her sleeves, until a brief glance about the room told her she was succeeding only in drawing attention to herself. Mindful not to lower her head like an embarrassed puppy, as the porter had done earlier, she exited the growing puddle at her feet and sloshed across the floorboards to an empty table at the back of the restaurant. There, she sat down with a *squish* that she suspected was audible to everyone in the now hushed room. For a person supposedly desperate to be anonymous, Jane was failing miserably.

From over her right shoulder, a woman's voice confidently broke the silence. "You look like you could use a good wringin'." Pockets of muted laughter erupted about the room, softening the awkward moment. "But here's my napkin instead."

Jane watched as the thirty or so diners offered a final apologetic glance in her direction, then returned to their meals and conversations, likely relieved that someone other than themselves had offered a helping hand. *People*, Jane thought. *They're the same here as in California: quick to judge and too busy with their own pursuits to consider the needs of anyone else.* But that wasn't entirely true, was it? Jane turned in her seat toward the voice she'd heard seconds earlier and came face-to-face with a lightly-stained, white cloth napkin hanging beneath three long red fingernails.

"It's not pristine, mind you," the voice behind the napkin reported, "but it'll take care of the waterfalls on your face."

Jane reached out and plucked the napkin from the bright red talons, revealing the extended arm, striking face, and drawn-up blonde curls of a woman in her late thirties seated at the next table. With her disarming features and the confident way she carried herself, the woman seemed part of a theatrical troupe, like the ones that visited the San Francisco college Jane had attended.

"Thank you," Jane said. "You're very kind."

"Don't mention it." The woman waved her hand. "You obviously need it more than I do. I was finished eating anyway." The blonde woman stood, patted at her peach-colored dress, and, to Jane's astonishment, cupped her oversized breasts—one in each hand—and jostled them. When her eyes again met Jane's, the woman burst into laughter. "Oh," she chuckled, "the look on your face is priceless."

Jane quickly erased the expression she didn't know she'd made and brought the napkin to her forehead and started patting.

Momentarily, she felt the woman's hand on her shoulder. The woman leaned in close, bringing her bosom to Jane's eye level. Her low-cut bodice left little to the imagination. "You can't tell me," she whispered, "that with that rack of yours you've never felt the urge to settle 'em in a bit."

Jane unconsciously stiffened and brought her arms forward, as if protecting her breasts from watchful stares. The drowned fabric of her dress clung to her skin.

The blonde woman in peach silk straightened and removed her hand. "They're just tits, honey. Every woman's got 'em. They're nothing to be ashamed of."

A few feet away, Jane watched a couple scramble from their seats and quickly usher their young boy from the restaurant. The mother's hands were held tightly over the boy's ears.

"Careful, Lou," a passing busboy carrying a tray of dirty plates interjected. "You'll get my father all worked up again."

"Bollocks to your father, Ernest," the woman blurted with theatrical zeal, snatching her handbag and feathered hat from her table, "and bollocks to his attempts at ridding the world of sin."

"I'm serious, Lou," the busboy, a teenager, shouted as he disappeared behind a set of saloon-type doors.

"Serious, ha!" Lou replied toward the swinging doors. She tapped on Jane's shoulder, then pointed with her thumb. "The man finds God and suddenly he's a saint. A hundred bucks says he's back at the whorehouse beggin' for credit before summer." Lou laughed at her own joke as she positioned her hat on her head.

Never having met any woman like Lou, and consequently unsure as to how to respond, or if she should respond at all, Jane sat quietly in her chair, busily patting her face with the napkin and wondering what life experiences could prompt someone to speak and act with such abandon. Until now, Jane believed only men could be as outspoken. Even the woman's name suggested a more masculine persona. Was Lou her real name? she wondered. Or had she adopted it for the stage? But then, none of the speculation mattered, anyway, because soon Jane would be miles away from Portland and Oregon and Lou and Ernest *and* his God-fearing father.

"It's been nice chatting with you," Lou's voice tore Jane from her thoughts.

"Oh, of course." Jane rose from her chair. "Thank you again for the napkin."

"Least I could do," she replied. "By the way, what's your name, honey?"

Caught off guard, Jane opened her mouth to answer and actually let out a kind of chirp before catching herself. "Ch…uh, I'm sorry. Must be the cold," she lied. "My name is Williams. Catherine Jane Williams to be precise." In the commotion, Jane had temporarily forgotten she'd been traveling under her mother's name.

"Well, Catherine Jane Williams, it's been a pleasure." Lou's eyes shot briefly up and down Jane's body, as if she were sizing her up. "Look me up if you're ever in need of a job." Turning back, she called out, "Bye, Ernest. Give your pa my regards." With that, and a small wave of her hand, Lou was out the door, past the window, and gone.

Before Jane could sit down again, Ernest appeared at her side. "We got beef stew, beans and cornbread, or chicken pot pie. Which can I get ya'? And you want a blanket or something?"

"Thank you, but no," she turned to the proprietor's son who, despite the coolness in the spring air, was sweating like a mule. "And I regret I'm not as hungry as I thought." She pushed her chair in. "The ferry will be leaving soon, anyway."

"You got more'n an hour before that tin can pulls out. Say, you're not leavin' on account o' that whore, are ya'? No way she'll be let back here if she's runnin' off customers."

Jane was shocked by the teen's casual disregard. "Whore? The kind woman who gave me her napkin? Your father should count himself fortunate to have any patrons at all with his son referring to them in such a manner."

"Beggin' your pardon, Miss, I don't know 'bout any napkin, but a whore's just what Miss Lou is. Owns the Blue Goose at the end of town. Everybody 'round here knows her *and* her business."

"Still..." Jane started, but thought better of drawing out the conversation any farther. This part of the country, along with the queer, rude customs of its inhabitants, had turned out to be more foreign than she'd anticipated, but she hadn't come to correct or condemn them. Nor did she want any more attention. "Never mind," she told the sweating busboy. "Please give my apologies to your father for my not staying to eat." She fished into the damp handbag dangling from her wrist, pulled out two dollar bills, and dropped them onto the table. "Thank you for your trouble."

"But you didn't—"

Jane raised her hand to stop him. "Have a pleasant afternoon," she told him and strode to the door, her stocking feet still sloshing within her shoes from the torrential rains.

Once outside, Jane was relieved to see the rain had stopped, but surprisingly disappointed that Lou was nowhere to be seen. She had hoped to catch up with her and...and what? Jane wondered. Compare breast sizes? Discuss current events? What practical reason did she have for tracking down this stranger? Especially if what Ernest had said was true. But Jane couldn't believe it. Could she? Lou, that nice, stylish woman in the restaurant, a...*whore*? Her clothes and makeup had been admittedly more shocking than Jane's conservative preferences, but her taste was impeccable and nothing was noticeably *over*-done. Except maybe for her tone of voice.

And her colorful choice of words.

And the fact that she "settled-in her tits" in a public house.

An uncontrollable giggle took hold and Jane had to steady herself against a framing post to keep from stumbling. What a delightful and refreshing woman Lou had been. Had they met under different circumstances, Jane was convinced they would have become fast friends. She wondered if Lou, the boisterous woman in peach silk, would admit the same conviction. It was funny how strangers sometimes instantly, and for no inexplicable reason, just took to one another, as if they'd been friends for years. She'd felt that way about Oliver the year her father died and, until he disappeared, she thought he felt the same about her.

But she wasn't going to ruin this day like she'd done so many others, pining away at what could have been. Her father and Oliver had been gone for fourteen years. Eddie for twelve. Her mother for twenty-six. Jane had been alone long enough to come to terms with it. She even enjoyed it most days. And she had a university degree behind her and teaching career ahead of her that she refused to let melancholy steal away.

But, then, melancholy wasn't all she was running from, was it? Something else had happened to her in Sacramento. Something beyond the loss of family and kinship. Something that defied explanation. She could go weeks without food and water and never lose a pound or feel any adverse effects, and only after hours of vigorous activity did she feel the urge to nap or even lie down. One winter, two years after Eddie's death, she'd attempted suicide by trekking into the Sierra Nevadas on foot and covering herself in a snow bank. Death should have overtaken her within hours, but she stayed there, weeping and begging God to take her for three nights. After she returned home, neighbors and once-upon-a-time friends began acting differently toward her. Suspicious, but with a touch of fear. Life in Sacramento hadn't been the same after that.

"Which is why I'm here in Portland," she said aloud, shaking the images loose from her mind.

A woman leading a small boy by the hand—Jane recognized them from the restaurant—hurried past her on the sidewalk. Twice the woman looked back at Jane, as if she were making sure she wasn't followed, before she dragged the boy through the nearest open shop door. The sign above it read, "Gunsmith."

Not a typical destination for a mother and son, Jane thought, and suddenly the giggles returned. How odd she must look, laughing and talking to herself. And soaking wet, at that. Not wanting to further distress the mother and child, Jane burst down the boardwalk at a brisk walk toward the docks and the awaiting ferry. Once there, she'd bribe one of the deckhands to take her to her trunk so she could change into dry clothes before other passengers arrived.

"No need to scare them, too," she said, mocking herself, and her impulsive lack of decorum transformed her giggles into outright laughter as she sped along the Portland storefronts toward the southern shore of the Willamette River.

•

Jane traveled three or four short blocks along D Street before the laughter subsided. Her shoes and the hem of her dark blue dress were caked with mud from the wet thoroughfares, but Jane was oblivious. Until this morning, so many things had weighed heavily on her mind. Her brief stop in Portland had brought on an unexpected confidence in her future and a calm toward her past. She might never understand how it happened, but she was grateful. Within an hour she'd be continuing her journey north, over the Willamette and Columbia Rivers, through the Washington Territory and Canada, and finally into Alaska. Pressing on at her brisk pace, she suddenly couldn't wait to get started.

As she neared the riverfront, the pungent smells of timber mills grew stronger and the twangs of a banjo grew louder. She hadn't heard music earlier when she'd ridden to the docks with the railroad crew, but as she turned onto Third Street she knew she'd come the right way. The brick and mortar landmarks—the bank, the jeweler—were familiar. One more block and a left turn would bring her within sight of the ferry. *And*, she thought with a sigh and a smile, *a promising tomorrow.*

Ahead, smoking and tying a horse to the hitching post outside a quiet saloon, a tall, unshaven man looked up and tipped his wide-rimmed hat. "Mornin', ma'am," he said as she approached. Within the shadows of his face, his eyes scrolled quickly down then back up her frame.

Not slowing her gait, Jane responded with a shallow nod and a wide berth, sensing his lingering stare even as she passed. An uneasy chill coursed through her, as if she knew the malice that lurked behind what would normally have been a benign greeting. Then, seconds later, Jane's optimistic mood took a spiraling dive when she realized—by the sounds of boot heels and the trembling boards beneath her feet—that the man was following her.

Of course the idea of a stranger following her in broad daylight was ridiculous, so Jane struggled to calm her nerves and forget her paranoia as she stepped off the boarded walk and crossed to B Street. The ferry was in view now, so the last thing she wanted to do was break into a run and call attention—again. *Besides*, she thought, *it's only coincidence.* But when she left the muddy street and ascended the boardwalk on the other side, she knew his footsteps were growing closer. He was maybe three feet behind her.

Beyond caring what she ducked into, Jane briefly caught the words "Snug Harbor" on the hanging sign overhead as she departed the boardwalk and burst through the swinging doors. She hurried to the small counter, noting that only a bartender and two patrons occupied the simple wood-framed space. All three men watched her curiously as she scrambled alongside the barstools to the end of the counter and whispered to the bartender, "Could you help me, please?"

Before he could answer, the saloon doors opened again and four sets of eyes looked over to watch the bearded stranger enter the dimly-lit room. The swinging doors creaked to a stop. The stranger spat on the floor, then wiped at his nose with his shirtsleeve. The two men across the room temporarily suspended their card game.

"Hi ya' Piedmont," the bartender called out. Jane swung her attention from the stranger back to the bartender and wondered if the recognition was a good sign. "This young lady come runnin' in here all spooked. You wouldn't know anything about that, would you?"

Jane questioned his blatant approach, but assuming he knew what he was doing, she remained silent, waiting for the stranger's reply.

"I tell ya'," the stranger started, removing his hat and displaying a knotted, greasy head of hair, "I was out to the west end this morning and I spied this pretty little thing getting off the train." He brushed his hand through the matted mess atop his head a couple of times, firmly replaced his hat, and adjusted a gun belt that held a pistol on each hip. Jane's uneasiness returned. "Looked fresh outta the big city, she did, and it didn't look like nobody was with her."

The bartender spoke up, startling Jane. "That *would* be a shame. 'Specially 'round here."

Suddenly afraid and not wanting to listen to more of their small talk, Jane turned from the bar to leave, but an iron hand—the bartender's—clasped around her arm and held her fast.

"Let me go," she cried. "I'm expected on the ferry." She tried to pull away from him, but his grasp was firm. "This is absurd. What is it you want? Money? Unhand me and you can take all I have."

"It ain't your money I'm after," the stranger said, stepping close enough to Jane that she could smell the liquor and tooth decay on his breath, "but it's a good start."

The bartender let go and Jane bolted to the right, but the tall, bearded man swept her effortlessly into his arms and held both her hands tight against her chest. The strap of her handbag dug into the flesh of her wrist. She kicked back at his legs.

"Help me," she screamed to the other men in the room only to realize, with terror, that their card game had resumed as if nothing out of the ordinary was happening. *Oh my God*, Jane thought as the stranger tightened his hold with one hand and brought his other hand up to cover her mouth. *What's happening to me?* The stench of the man's palm as it pressed against her lips nauseated her. She recalled how he'd stroked his filthy hair with that same hand and struggled as he dragged her along the floor, but her efforts were futile.

"Pull it, Tom," she heard the stranger say, apparently to the bartender. Jane couldn't imagine what he meant.

But she didn't have to.

In an instant, and with a faint click, the floor beneath her gave way and she and her captor plummeted into the darkness below. They landed on their feet, but rolled to one side as gravity and the unevenness of the straw mattress beneath them stole their balance. The man rolled on top of her and straddled her at the waist, still intent on keeping her mouth shut and her hands still. Her muffled cries were lost in the dank, cold air around her, but Jane continued to scream, even as she watched the trap door above her slowly close, shutting out all traces of daylight and eliminating any hope she had of reaching the ferry on time.

"You scream again and I'll slit your throat faster'n you can blink," the man snarled.

Having watched her skin heal itself on at least a dozen occasions, Jane was optimistic she'd live through such a slashing, but decided she'd not press her luck just in case. And who would hear her anyway?

"You gonna stay quiet?"

In the pitch black, Jane nodded.

"You don't get no second chances, understand?"

She nodded again and was relieved when the man withdrew his palm from her lips. Without thinking, she turned her head and spat.

Apparently, the stranger didn't approve because a stinging blow from the man's open hand struck Jane's nose, left eye, and cheek. Shocked, she drew in a breath as her eye began to water and the first waves of pain pulsed in her head. Whatever ailment she had contracted in Sacramento that kept her from dying had most definitely not granted her immunity to pain.

"I said quiet, you little cunt."

He'd also said "no second chances," Jane remembered, and she braced herself for the imminent attack. Instead, the man climbed off her and shuffled onto his feet, then grasped her by the hair and pulled her upright.

"I'm gonna find us some light and you're not gonna move from this spot." To underscore his point, he shook her with the fistful of hair. "You can't find your way outta here on your own, anyhow," he let go of her hair, "so stay put."

For no more than a minute, her captor shuffled in the dark, knocking over objects with a thud as they struck the dirt floor, until finally she heard the unmistakable sound of a matchstick striking a hard surface. A soft glow poured into the room as the man lit an oil lantern and Jane found herself in a low-ceilinged, stone cellar, surrounded by wooden crates, casks, and bottles.

Holding the lantern at eye level, and looking eerily like the insane old miner that had plagued Sacramento when Jane was a teenager, the man stepped over to the mattress that had broken their fall, retrieved his hat, and slapped it against his leg before returning it to his head. Spying her own hat on the floor, Jane sidestepped toward it.

"Wait," the man commanded. To her surprise, he bent down and picked up her hat, then courteously brushed it off and held it out to her.

She snatched it quickly and without any show of appreciation.

"Come this way," he instructed, motioning her to follow him behind a column of boxes. She obeyed and found a brick-framed archway about three feet wide built into the wall. "You first," he said, grabbing her hand and shoving her into the passageway. "When you get to the end, turn left."

Jane inched forward several feet until she came to the end of the passage, but the darkness to the left and right made it difficult to see more than two or three feet in either direction.

"Keep going," the man barked.

"I can't see."

"Don't need to see. Just need to do what yer told."

He shoved her and she stumbled to the left, catching herself on the stone wall. The pounding in her head was nearly gone, but the corresponding beat in her chest was making it hard to breathe and her face still stung. Jane had never been so scared in her life.

She felt her way along the wall with her left hand, clutching her hat and skirt in her right, until the lantern light exposed the tunnel before her. It seemed to go on for hundreds of feet. *Where does this lead?* she wondered. *Where is he taking me?* Something scurried past her foot. Jane shrieked.

"Shut up!" He whacked her in the back of the head. "It's just a wharf rat. He ain't gonna bite ya' 'less you bite him first."

The man chuckled and Jane thought of the crazy old miner again. More than anything, she wished the wicked man behind her would get a bullet in the temple like the miner in Sacramento had.

They crept through the tunnel beneath what Jane guessed must have been four or more city blocks, passing countless archways that likely led to various other tunnels or basement cellars like the one Jane had fallen into. The air was cold and thick with the smells of earth, urine, decaying food, and spilled whiskey, and from time to time Jane could hear faint sounds of laughter or music. The dirt floor was littered with chips of something that clicked against her heels and sometimes stuck to her soles. She had no idea in which direction they traveled.

"Hold up," the man finally spoke. Jane stopped and the man shuffled by her and ducked into a shorter, narrower passage that spurred off to the right. She watched the lantern light flicker and fade as she was once again plunged into darkness. Something stirred in the tunnel ahead and Jane hoped the man would return with the light soon. As dangerous as he was, she didn't want to be left here—*alone*—to single-handedly battle the rats.

And only God knew what other creatures resided beneath the streets of Portland. Shivering and clinging to her handbag and hat, Jane stood in the blackness and waited for her captor to return.

CHAPTER 14

PORTLAND, OREGON TERRITORY – APRIL 14, 1881

Would the ferry leave without her? Jane wondered, her head slightly bent as she crept through the dark tunnel, straining to see the dim glow of the lantern ahead. The man who'd tracked her into the Snug Harbor Saloon and subsequently kidnapped her and left her in the darkness had returned before the wharf rats had a chance to descend upon her, but as she entered her second underground room of the day, she began to wish he'd left her behind to grope for an exit in the dark.

As in the first cellar she'd seen, there were crates and whiskey barrels stacked as high as the low ceiling would allow, but this room had a new feature: a roughly-built tin cage, measuring maybe five-foot square, with a hinged door that locked and no visible windows or ventilation ports. *What could this be used for?* she pondered.

As if in response to her query, her captor spoke. "Already had a tenant in the hold, but I chucked 'im to the corner there. Didn't think he was the type of company yer used to keeping." Behind his scruffy mustache and beard, Jane thought she saw him smile.

Since her line of vision was blocked by the man holding the lantern, she stepped to the side and craned her neck to see the corner. Sticking out from beneath a short stack of burlap bags was a man's bare foot. Jane gasped and brought her hand to her face. She suddenly knew what the small tin cage had been used for.

"Gods be damned, but yer a tender one," her captor said. "He ain't even gotten to smellin' yet, and yer all a fright."

"You're not putting me in there." She pointed to the cage and absent-mindedly took a step backward, away from the corner and the bearded man.

"Gimme one good reason not to."

Jane struggled for an answer and settled on the most obvious. "I'll give you fifty reasons if you let me go." It was all the cash she had on her. She wished she had more.

"If yer talkin' money, I'll be havin' that anyway. Yer gonna have to come up with somethin' better'n that to convince me to change yer accommodations. In the meantime, take off yer shoes."

"What?"

"You heard me. Take 'em off or there ain't gonna be no negotiating at all."

To this man, what could be better than money? she thought. But the answer chilled her. "You can't mean..." she started, but couldn't finish. The very idea repulsed her.

"I said take off yer shoes or I'll do it for ya'." The man, slightly bent at the shoulders to keep from bumping his head on the ceiling, sat the lantern down on a crate. "I got two cells, pretty lady. This one here and that other'n over there." He took off his hat and gestured with it, showing her a prison-type door with a small, barred window near the entrance they'd come through minutes earlier. "Ain't no way I'm lettin' you go, but I'll let you choose yer room." He moved closer than she would have liked and stood between Jane and the exit. "Which'll it be? The suite with the bed and the view or the cage our friend over there drew his last breaths in?"

Terrified, but willing to protect her virtue from the hands—and other unmentionable appendages—of the filthy madman before her,

Jane held her ground. "I'll not be a prisoner. What will you take to let me go?"

"Ha, ha, but you're a spunky one, aren't ya'?" He stepped closer, tossed his hat aside, and reached for her shoulders. "I just don't think you're getting' the big picture here."

"Get away from me," Jane screamed, backing up. She hoped she could summon the strength to fight this man off if it became necessary.

"You got nowhere to run, missy, and once I cut the tongue outta yer head, ain't nobody gonna hear you scream." From a sheath strapped to his thigh, the man produced a large hunting knife. "Now, I don't wanna hurt you, and I really don't wanna toss a pretty little thing like you into this box here, so why not make it easy on yerself? Take off yer shoes, gimme a little poke, and maybe I won't come back again tomorrow night."

The back of Jane's legs struck a solid object. She felt with her hand and discovered she'd backed into the tin cell. With all the conviction she could muster, she stared deep into the man's dark eyes. "I'm warning you. Don't touch me."

Slowly, the man snapped his gun belt off one-handed and dropped his weapons to the floor. Then, with a speed Jane wasn't expecting, he snatched her purse and hat from her grip and tossed them as well. He lunged at her, grabbed her throat, shoved her onto the cage, and touched the tip of the hunting knife to her cheek. "You gotta figure how much it's worth to you."

Jane struggled to breathe, temporarily forgetting that she didn't need her air supply.

"To me, you'll bring in three times what I get for the crews, whether I leave you pristine or not." Steadying the knife tip close to her skin, the man loosed his grip around her neck and moved his hand to her skirts. He grasped a handful of the material, jerked it upward, and began clawing his way underneath.

Her breathing now unrestricted, Jane tried to push against him, but the man's chest was pressed too heavily upon her. She tried to kick, but his legs held hers tight against the cold tin box. He tugged on the laces of her right shoe and pulled it from her foot, then, with a practiced skill, he shifted his weight and removed her other shoe. When his hand moved up her leg and his icy fingers started groping with the bow-knot of her undergarment, she screamed and spit in his face. The knife slid against her cheekbone and the warmth that followed, trickling slowly down her chin and neck, convinced Jane she'd been cut.

But she didn't dwell on it.

Instead, taking advantage of his having moved slightly to the side, Jane shoved against him again. The man staggered backward, holding the hem of Jane's skirt. She brought her foot up and into his groin. He let go of her clothing and dropped straight down to the dirt floor.

Jane gathered her dress and darted from the room, running in her stocking feet through the low passageway as fast as her hunched frame could manage. Rounding the corner into the main tunnel, she sped right, in the opposite direction from where she'd come, but sharp pains in her feet quickly halted her progress. She held herself steady against the wall with one hand and reached down to quickly brush her foot with the other. It took two pats to realize the debris scattered on the dirt floor of the tunnel—the scraps that stuck to her shoes earlier—were bits of broken glass.

Oh my God. How could she run farther? She glanced back, turning her shoulder and shifting her weight on the one foot that remained on the ground. Piercing jabs sent shivers through her toes and heels and up the back of her leg. She could go or she could stay. Charge ahead or go back for her shoes. Either way, it would be painful.

But only one way promised freedom.

Still holding one foot, she gritted her teeth and took a deep breath. Then another. She couldn't be certain her affliction would ward off the scars, but she was sure she'd survive a little glass. With one last breath, she released her foot and bolted down the tunnel, her arms outstretched, praying she'd find an exit very soon.

•

Jane connected with a glass shard every second or third step. Tears of pain streamed down her face and soaked into her dress. After ten minutes, her pace had slowed considerably, and she had begun to wish she'd taken the chance and run back for her shoes. *How bad could it have been?* she thought. Losing her virginity to a criminal and getting slapped around could never have been as painful as this. And would it have brought the end of the world?

But Jane stopped. She heard voices. And music. Chopin, she thought. Her mother had taught her several of his delicate and enchanting works. But how could strains of Chopin reach the depths of this underground prison? This hell? With her feet stinging and her teeth still clenched, she groped along the wall toward the sounds.

Only four or five feet ahead, a tiny ray of light stabbed through the darkness into the earth. She panicked at first, wondering if her angry captor had somehow come up on her from the front. Glancing over her shoulder and finding nothing but darkness behind her, she relaxed. She looked again to the beam of light before her and saw that it didn't move or shake. It couldn't be the lantern. She drew closer, trying not to step on more glass, but knowing it didn't matter anymore. The light, she could see now, was coming from an auxiliary passageway.

Could this be a way out?

Moving faster, and wincing at the pain in her feet as she swung left into the corridor, she ran to a door with a small decorative window. The silhouetted figures behind it were blurred, but the light coming through the small pane was warm and inviting. Jane felt for the door handle and turned. It didn't move.

She pounded on the door with both fists. "Help, please. Somebody open the door." She pounded harder. "Please. Somebody help."

The voices continued, louder now, but the door remained closed. Jane couldn't tell if anyone inside was moving closer. She brought her fist up to pound again when she heard a noise behind her.

The sound of shoes clicking on broken glass.

She turned and saw shadows dance in the tunnel behind her. Her kidnapper had found her!

Had the pounding on the door attracted the wrong attention? Should she risk doing it again, now that her pursuer was so close? But he would find her, anyway, wouldn't he? He had the advantage of light and, considering her torn feet, she was at an extreme disadvantage. Besides, where else could she go? There was nothing to lose.

She balled her fists again and smashed the window. "Help. Somebody. Help me." She kicked with the top of her foot and resumed banging with her fists. "Somebody! Please!"

"You ain't getting away, you little bitch." His voice echoed, but he wasn't far.

"Hurry, please! Somebody, please!" Jane didn't stop banging until she realized the door was swinging open.

The woman standing before her spoke with bewilderment. "Good God, child, what in the..."

But Jane wouldn't let her finish. Nearly blinded by the flood of daylight, she pushed through the doorway and grabbed the woman's hand. "Shut the door and lock it. There's a man chasing me. He'll kill us both."

"Now, hold on," the woman started again.

"Lock it now," Jane commanded, stepping forward and slamming the door.

With a shaky hand, the woman slid the key in the lock and turned. For peace of mind, Jane grasped the knob and rotated it back and forth. Satisfied her pursuer wouldn't gain entry, Jane slumped to the floor, short of breath and dizzy, and let her body collapse at the feet of the woman who had saved her.

•

Jane didn't know she'd lost consciousness until a man's voice, angry and desperate, woke her from her temporary slumber.

"Open the door or I'm gonna start shootin'."

The sudden recognition brought Jane to her feet. "No!" Still blurry-eyed from the fainting spell and the hour or more in the dark, Jane grappled for a hold on the arm of the woman next to her and pleaded. "I can't go back there. You can't let him in." Beneath her fingers, the soft fabric of the woman's dress caught Jane off guard. *Silk?* It couldn't be.

"I'm not kidding," the man behind the door continued. "Don't make me shoot you, Lou. I don't want no war."

"There won't be any war, Clarence Piedmont," the woman responded, "'cuz you're gonna walk away and forget any of this happened."

They know each other? Jane thought of the bartender at the Snug Harbor. "I have to go," she said. Only then did she notice the woman's arm wrapped around her waist.

"Be still," the woman whispered. Her arm tightened around Jane and she held out a tiny pistol, high enough for Jane to see but too low for the man to spy through the window. "Let me handle this."

"I'm gonna count to three, Lou, and you better hand her over." The man's features were coming into focus now as he peeked through the window. "One..."

"What do you want her for?" The woman asked, and her identity came flooding back to the forefront of Jane's memory.

Lou. From the restaurant.

"You know damn well what I want her for. Bunco'll have my hide if you don't turn her over." The man brought his gun to the window. "This is business and the count is at two."

To Jane's amazement, Lou snorted a laugh. "Bunco Kelly doesn't own this town any more than you or I do."

"But you'll be just as dead if you fuck with his money." He lowered the gun out of sight. "You wanna save the little slut? Fine. Pay me what I'm due and I'll stop counting. Eighty bucks."

"Fair enough," Lou said, and with one fluid motion, she brought her pistol to the window and fired a shot between Piedmont's eyes. His body dropped with a muffled thud behind the door. "She's worth three hundred you twisted bastard." Lou turned to Jane. "Did he hurt you, honey? Let me see."

With disbelief and immeasurable gratitude, Jane answered, "I'll be fine."

"Just look at you," Lou continued, scrutinizing Jane's face and rumpled clothing. "There's blood everywhere. And your hem—," the woman lifted Jane's dress to her calves, "Oh my God! We've got to get you off your feet." She turned her head to the ceiling. "Daniel!"

"Coming, Lou." Within seconds, a young man of maybe twenty came bounding down the stairs to the narrow stoop. Jane hadn't noticed the steep stairway until that moment.

"Take her to my private guest room upstairs," Lou instructed, "and send for the doctor."

"No," Jane gasped. "No doctor. The injuries aren't as bad as they seem."

"Nonsense," Lou replied. "Kelly and his insufferable lot sprinkle the tunnels with broken glass to keep their barefoot victims from escaping. Your feet must be shredded."

"I can see to them myself, really." Jane doubted she could stomach the task, knowing she might have to reopen the miraculously repaired skin to retrieve the shards, but she couldn't let anyone discover her secret. Not even a doctor who was sworn to keep his mouth shut.

Lou frowned. "Regardless, we need to get you cleaned up." She brought the pistol near her face, licked a finger on her opposite hand, and tested the temperature of the barrel. Then she tucked the tiny firearm between her breasts and turned to Daniel. "Carry her upstairs like I said, but hold off on the doctor for now. Oh, and get somebody to clear the tunnel. I don't want that man's stink fouling up my parlor."

"Yes, ma'am," the young man answered. "You ready, miss?" he asked Jane.

Jane looked at Lou, who smiled and nodded. "All right," she said to Daniel. He swept her into his arms and started up the stairs.

•

Lou's private guest room, as she called it, was appointed as luxuriously as an exclusive hotel. There was little furniture—an armoire, writing desk, wash basin and cabinet, and a feather bed—but the velvet draperies on the two tall windows, the landscape artwork, and the exquisite craftsmanship of everything within eyeshot made Jane feel as if she were in a palace suite. She snuggled under the goose down blanket wishing she could stay but fearing she'd been here too long already.

The door beyond the foot of the bed opened and Lou bounded in.

Her peach dress that had seemed so out of place at the restaurant earlier now blended in perfectly with its surroundings.

"How do you feel?" she asked, closing the door behind her.

Conscious of wearing nothing more than a nightdress, Jane sat up and adjusted the bedcovers around her. "I can't thank you enough for what you've done."

Lou plopped herself down on the bedside. "You're most welcome, but that's not what I asked."

Jane blushed. What was it about this woman that elicited such instant admiration and intrigue? "My feet will be in bandages for a few days, but the damage was nowhere near as bad as it looked."

In actuality, the damage had been quite extensive, and despite her body's efforts to repair itself, Jane would likely bear scars for the rest of her life. However long that may be.

"Good," Lou said, "I'm glad." The twinkle in her eyes convinced Jane she genuinely meant it. "And your face looks fine. I could swear I saw a cut there. He didn't hit you?"

"No," she lied. "Have you learned anything about my trunk?" Jane asked, changing the subject. Earlier, when Lou had insisted Jane bathe and rest, Daniel had been dispatched to check on the status of the ferry and to retrieve Jane's belongings at any cost.

"The ferry had already departed, I'm afraid," Lou reported. Jane's heart sank. "But no worries." Lou patted Jane's hand. "The men I sent after it will bring it back even if they have to steal it."

"And you trust them?" Jane grasped Lou's hand and squeezed.

Lou bent forward and stroked Jane's arm with her free hand. "Honey, any man can be trusted if he's played right."

"Beg pardon?"

"You know how they are." The vivacious woman with the blonde curls sat up. Jane reluctantly let go of her hand. "Satisfy their most primitive needs and they're loyal to the death."

Jane was embarrassed to ask. "And what exactly are their 'most primitive needs?'"

"Please," Lou's eyes grew wide, "you can't be serious. A beautiful girl like you doesn't know the secrets to a woman's success? 'Passion without commitment and commitment without strings,' I've always said. Have you never sweet-talked a man into doing your bidding knowing full well you'd give him nothing in return?"

"Never." At least not that she was aware. "Unless you count my father." She smiled at the recollection. "I could get him to do anything for me."

"Well, that's how it starts, now doesn't it? But excepting your father, have you ever loved a man?"

She thought of Oliver. "Yes, I think so, but we had only a short time together."

Lou shook her head. "Time makes no difference in affairs of the heart, dear girl. Did he love you in return?"

"I thought he did."

"And did you have occasion to, um, how shall I put this to such a cultured thing as yourself? Did you *consummate* your feelings?"

"Consummate? Oh." Jane blushed again. "Oh, no. I've never…um." She pretended to clear her throat.

Lou straightened her carriage, cocked her head, and spoke before Jane had a chance to formulate her next sentence. "So you're a virgin?"

Not able to look Lou in the eye as she answered—and not knowing why—Jane bowed her head. "Yes."

"And down in the tunnels, Piedmont didn't force you to do anything?"

"He tried, but no." Jane sensed Lou shift her weight on the bed before feeling Lou's warm fingers touch her chin and gently raise her face. Jane forced her gaze from her lap and felt instantly soothed by the care reflected in Lou's sparkling green eyes.

"There's no need to feel embarrassed with me."

"I know." A heaviness had fallen on Jane's chest and her breathing was short.

"Do you?"

"Yes," Jane breathed as Lou's fingers caressed her neck. Her pulse quickened and a tingling sensation ran up the length of her thighs as if someone had tickled the backs of her legs. When Lou again pulled her hand away, Jane thought the emptiness would overwhelm her.

"You showed great courage today escaping like you did. You've got guts." Lou stood, hoisted her skirts to her knees, and climbed upon the bed, finally coming to rest in a sitting position beside Jane. "But I knew that the second you walked into the restaurant this morning."

"You remembered me?"

Lou reached up and stroked Jane's cheek. "How could I forget a face like this?"

Jane fought the urge to reciprocate her touch, feeling simultaneously aroused and confused. "I was so impressed by the way you spoke to the busboy there."

"Ernest? He was nothing. It's his father that's the thorn in my side, but I don't want to talk about any of that now." Lou's fingers had moved around Jane's neck to the hairline behind her ears. She made no effort to stop her. "I want to talk about you. How is it that a prim and proper virgin of your obvious standing would land in the God-forsaken northwest territories? How old are you, anyway? If you don't mind my asking."

At this moment in time, Jane would answer any question Lou posed. And eagerly. "Thirty-two."

"That's impossible." She stopped caressing.

Jane wanted to beg her not to, but she restrained herself.

"You must be lying."

"No." Jane straightened, letting the bedcovers fall to her waist. "Please believe me. I wouldn't lie to you after all you've done." ...*And all I hope you will do*, her thoughts continued, but she couldn't think like that. She wasn't supposed to think like that. What a bizarre day this had turned out to be.

"You don't look older than twenty."

"My professor in San Francisco said it's genetics. A family trait passed to me by my parents."

"So you've been to college, too?"

"Six years. I would have attended longer, but there were no more classes to take."

"You took them all? How were your grades?"

"The highest in every class except advanced mathematics. I...

couldn't concentrate properly." In truth, her professor had propositioned her so many times that she felt uncomfortable in his classes.

"And you've never been married? Never been asked for your hand, even?"

"No." Jane fidgeted, but remained staunchly upright. "I met a man when my father died, but he disappeared. Then my brother died. Loneliness drove me to school. I wanted to be busy. I wanted to occupy my mind with thoughts apart from family and love and other dependencies. I wanted to need only me."

"And so you have," Lou stopped her rant. "But haven't you always known there was something else? Something more beyond the walls you've built around yourself?"

Jane's thoughts turned to the reasons for embarking on this journey in the first place. It had never been just the loss of her family and her curious affliction. Deep down she'd hoped to start fresh somewhere. And meet someone.

"Yes," she answered.

"Come work for me," Lou said, moving her hand to rest on Jane's thigh. The tingling sensation returned, but this time it was more powerful.

Jane's breath hitched. "What? I could never do what...you women do."

"You think I make my money on my back? Look around." Lou propped herself on one arm and moved her free hand up Jane's thigh to her waist. "Don't get me wrong. I spend plenty of time rustlin' the sheets, but it's at my discretion. Under my terms. And only when I want to."

Lou's hand gently squeezed and Jane's body shivered. Her skin broke out in goose flesh. She couldn't believe how much she craved the touch of this woman. The smell of her. The feel of her.

"Men may be foul, greedy bastards," Lou continued, "but if you play them right, their vices will keep you in jewels for the rest of your life." She leaned close to Jane's ear. Jane could smell her faint, sweet perfume. Her breath was warm against Jane's neck. "Men aren't the enemy, darlin'," she whispered, "they're the pawns."

Remembering she was clothed in only a thin nightdress, Jane felt suddenly vulnerable. But spectacularly alive. "What else can you teach me?" she asked, no longer believing that only a man could generate heat between her legs and not caring about the moral consequences of what she hoped was about to happen.

Lou pulled back, but not too far, and moved her hand delicately up the buttons of Jane's dress. "How much do you want to learn?"

"Everything."

Jane felt her top button unfasten. Lou's hand crept lower and started working on the second. "So you'll work for me?"

"I will. But if not as a whore, what will you have me do?"

Lou released the third button. "We can surely work something out. Are you comfortable?"

"Yes," but that wasn't entirely true, was it? Her stomach and nipples ached, her chest was heavy, her limbs felt limp, and the dampness between her legs had spread.

Lou's voice softened. "Now you know I can't technically deflower you."

"Yes."

With the last button unfastened, Lou traced the collar of the nightdress with her fingertips and pulled the gown free from Jane's shoulders. It cascaded to her waist, revealing her full breasts and erect nipples.

"You are beautiful."

Jane shook her arms free of the sleeves and brought her hands to Lou's face. Her skin was like satin. No longer able to resist, and relying on nothing more than instinct, Jane dove her fingers into Lou's blonde curls and pulled the woman's lips to her own. But the kiss didn't last nearly long enough. When their lips parted, Jane moaned and tried to pull her back.

"Not so fast," Lou said. "You need time to heal."

"But I'm f—"

"No," she interrupted, "I insist you rest today. Now lie back."

"But—"

"Ssshhh." Lou's finger touched Jane's lips. "Lie back."

She hesitated, trying hard not to look disappointed.

"Trust me."

Jane wiggled and positioned herself so her body could lie flat without her head hitting the headboard. She'd never felt so aroused in her life. How could she come so close to some type of release only to be told to rest? But, gazing up into Lou's face, Jane was encouraged by the devilish grin that looked back.

"*You* have to rest today," she said, removing the pistol she'd hidden in her cleavage, "but I don't." Lou dropped the weapon to the floor. Her hand fell upon Jane's breast at the same time their lips met for the second time. Jane returned the kiss hungrily, panting as she felt the woman's hand gently pinch and massage its way down her torso.

Her first release started before Lou's finger entered her.

Her last ended two hours later.

And Jane couldn't wait for more.

CHAPTER 15

The Sunset Limited slowed to a stop for the last time. At least, it was the last time for Jane. Shrugging off her memories of Portland, she picked up her shopping bag, exited the cabin, and slipped down the narrow hallway. She stepped through the electronic doors and planted her feet firmly on New Orleans soil for the first time since the birth of the twentieth century.

She breathed in. One-hundred years of hurricanes and Mardi Gras hadn't washed away the smell of refuse and river slime. But neither had they changed the dynamic energy of the city. It was early morning. Skyscrapers surrounding the passenger terminal reminded Jane that she was returning somewhere for the first time. Running *to* a place from her memory instead of *from* it.

A cab pulled to the curb in front of her. She climbed into the back seat. "1640 Royal, please."

Watching out the window, Jane noted how the business district had grown. Gray, nondescript hotels and office buildings towered above her where proud, elegant centers of enterprise once stood. She'd spent years here with Oliver, but a great deal of time had passed since then. Had she expected the city to remain as she'd left it?

The cab turned onto Carondelet. Traffic was heavy, but moving. She'd traveled this same road to the train station a century ago. Only it hadn't been a cab she'd ridden in. St. Charles would be running parallel. She could feel Oliver close by. Jane glanced down the side streets. Signs jutted out from buildings advertising restaurants and clubs. Most were unfamiliar, but some she could have sworn she'd seen before. Tourists, with their backpacks and white legs and cameras, ambled along the sidewalks. Asphalt gave way to cobblestone. Iron balconies of the past adorned buildings that had stood the test of time. The cab slowed and Jane saw that not all of New Orleans had changed.

Like her, the heart of the city—the Vieux Carré—had survived.

•

Standing at the base of the stairs, Oliver watched the front door and waited for sounds of Jane's arrival. His hands were clenched at his sides. Streaks of mid-morning sunlight cascaded around him through cracks in the window shutters above. How much longer would it be? Minutes? Seconds? Would she rush up to him? Should he rush to her?

Before any words passed between them, he wanted to gather her in his arms. Let her know right away he harbored no ill feelings for their long silence. *Water under the bridge*, as they say. Outside, the whirr of an approaching vehicle stole Oliver's attention. He hurried to the parlor and the circular area he'd cleared on the window. He peered out. A maroon van cruised past. It didn't stop.

Damn. It wasn't her.

According to Amtrak.com, her train was expected twenty-three minutes later than scheduled. Allowing for time to hail a cab and navigate the streets, she could be on his doorstep any time. Depending, of course, on the route the driver took. Carnival was long gone. Noise in the streets had subsided. Pedestrians were few. Oliver watched as a white taxi turned the corner off Prince Street. His heart beat faster. But the cab rolled on.

What if she'd chosen to walk? Or taken the streetcar to Canal? What if her train hadn't been late after all? He retreated into the foyer, following the path made by his boot prints on the dust-covered floorboards. His footfalls rebounded against the high ceiling. If she approached on foot, he might not see her before she reached the front door. He didn't want her to stand and wait for him to invite her in. But then, he didn't want to appear anxious, either. He stood again near the base of the stairs, waiting for a knock. Thirty seconds passed. Then thirty more.

He wondered if he would sense Jane's approach. He closed his eyes and thought of her. Her hair. Her eyes. Her fragrance. He'd been right to wait. His heart had told him she'd return, and he believed. Oliver heard another vehicle slowing outside. Would it be her? He dashed to the parlor window.

The cab was black, with white doors, hood, and trunk. It came to a stop. The back door opened. A woman in navy shorts and white sneakers and top stepped out and onto the sidewalk. Thick, dark hair fell past her shoulders.

He bolted to the foyer, paused to take in a deep breath, and grasped the front door's crystal knob. The cab drove away as he pulled the door open. She looked at him. There was weariness in her eyes. But she was still beautiful.

"Hello, Oliver." The sound of her voice brought a lump to his throat.

Oliver stepped down onto the sidewalk and politely kissed her hand. Then he rose and hugged her, pulling her head to his chest and grasping firmly around her shoulders. When her arms tightened around him, his heart soared.

It was Jane who broke the embrace. "A lot has happened since...we last spoke." She pulled his hands from her face and gripped them tightly. "I'm not the same person."

"Nor am I. But why are we standing here?" Dropping one of her hands, but holding fast to the other, he gestured for her to enter. "Come inside. We'll chat in the courtyard, or in the music room, if you'd prefer indoors." Then he motioned to the faded red shopping bag in her hand.

"Have you traveled with nothing more than that?"

She entered the foyer and let loose of his hand. "I left in a hurry." Looking around the room, she asked, "Oliver, what's happened here?"

"Beg pardon?" He followed and closed the door behind them. "What's happened to what?"

"This home was so beautiful." She walked into the shadows to the courtyard gates and looked out. "It's like a…tomb now."

"Oh. You know I hadn't noticed, but you're right. I admit the anticipation of your return had me…preoccupied for a time. But now that you're here, I'll see that these rooms are tidied-up immediately."

Jane turned away from the courtyard and walked toward him, into the light of the foyer. "But, Oliver, you've only known of my return for a few days. This house shows years of neglect."

"I suppose my priorities were elsewhere."

She didn't look like she believed him.

"Oh, good lord, where *are* my manners? Give me your bag and we'll go upstairs." He reached out, and she handed him her shopping bag. "I have to show you the website."

Jane followed him up the stairs. "Website?"

"It's what we've used to gather information. We applied a chat room concept with automatic translation."

"I'm sorry, a what? And who's 'we'?"

"'We' is myself, of course, and two assistants. And you've surely heard of chat rooms. Ours simply enable people to converse in different languages in real time."

"I have no idea what you just said."

Oliver reached the top of the stairs and turned to her, smiling. "It's easy. I'll show you."

She stopped on the last step and shook her head. "Aside from email and Google, computers are Greek to me."

"Oh, but you'll understand this. Did you know there are others, Jane?"

"Others?"

He touched her arm. "Like us. Immortals. Maybe hundreds of them."

Her eyes opened wide. "Why didn't you tell me?"

"I just did."

He felt her wanting to say something more, but she stood silent.

Oliver looked into her eyes and thought of their first meeting as immortals. He'd learned a great deal since then.

"Come with me." He took her hand. "There's so much to show you."

Leading Jane through the dim hallway, Oliver silently hoped that she was ready to understand and accept the Maltese Knight and the secrets of The Realm.

CHAPTER 16

SEATTLE, WASHINGTON TERRITORY – JUNE 5, 1889

Oliver sat alone at the bar in a parlor laced with bullshit and whores. He'd heard a rumor that the burgeoning mill town had a shortage of women, but all around him men indulged themselves, smoking, drinking, and forcing their opinions upon one another. Perhaps the rumor applied only to poor souls, because the wealthy seemed unaware.

The parlor was papered in rich violet and finished with pine floorboards and decorative trim. Framed mirrors reflected the candlelight from sconces and the room's single chandelier. There were no windows for ventilation and, paired with a low ceiling, smoke and perfume hung thick in the air. Anxious to get on with the night, Oliver nursed his scotch slowly, listening to the classical melodies played by a pianist in the corner. In ten minutes he'd accomplished nothing, except decline the company of a half dozen *hostesses*. It had been a shame turning them down. He'd promised to come back another time, but tonight... Tonight he was holding out for something special.

The front doors banged open, and a woman in burgundy silk burst into the room. "Lord God Almighty but this city has gone to hell." Her voice rose above all others.

Oliver watched from his seat near the entrance as she slammed the thick doors behind her. She hiked up the tail of her skirts with both hands as if she didn't notice the men in the room. "Does it ever stop rainin' in this rat-infested hole? Street's nothin' but potholes of mud. It's simply *impossible*... for a *lady*... to even *cross*... the Goddamned thing." She punctuated words with violent slaps to her dress. Blonde curls bounced across her face.

"I agree, Lou," spouted a man seated at the opposite end of the bar. He didn't look sober, but knew enough to hold his sloshing glass away from his tailored suit. "Somethin' oughtta be done. They ain't fit for man nor horse."

A stunning woman stood behind him giggling, her hand in his breast pocket, her lips on his ear.

"Stop with the flattery, Councilman," the boisterous woman replied, "and just fix the Goddamned street." She tossed her hat and coat onto the rack, revealing a flowing mane of golden curls and a low-cut corset trimmed in lavender that displayed her attributes well. She walked past Oliver, shooting a playful look in the councilman's direction. "Unless you'd like to start comin' in on Sundays to clean my laundry."

Men within earshot of the comment laughed.

Oliver didn't know who the woman was, but she obviously felt comfortable making a spectacle. She could be the Madame, but that wouldn't make any sense. The woman he searched for was reportedly in charge.

The vivacious woman stopped short of the full length of the bar, three stools down from Oliver. Brilliant jewels sparkled from her neck and ears. She winked at the bartender, who, in response, pushed a drink in front of her. "Thanks," she told him. It disappeared in one motion. She asked for another.

She pulled her skirts up again to mount the stool and tossed her handbag onto the bar. Then she glanced in Oliver's direction. Her eyes were shockingly blue. "Can I help you find something you like?"

"Ma'am?" He played the gentleman. "Were you addressing me?"

"Ha! I'm Lou, or Miss Lou, if you prefer the formality. Only my preacher calls me ma'am."

He laughed. "Then, Miss Lou, it's a pleasure. You're not a stranger here, I take it?"

"Oh, no. I own it. Which brings me to ask why you're unaccompanied. Have the ladies not greeted you?"

Oliver was confused, but didn't let on. "Yes, they have, and that's been my difficulty. Your hostesses are all very beautiful. Much like yourself."

"Don't even think about it. I'm *reserved*."

"Not if these past few moments are an indication."

She shook her head, chuckled, and took a strong sip of her drink. "Not that kind of reserved, dear boy, but I'll take the compliment just the same." She briefly surveyed the room, then asked, "What's your name, darlin'? I don't think I've seen you before."

"The name's Chatham. Oliver Chatham. And we haven't met because I just arrived."

"Came straight to the cathouse, then. I like you already. So what can I do to help you find a lady tonight, Mr. Chatham? Short of pulling them from the rooms, I can gather them up if you like."

"No, that won't be necessary."

"Well, as a lady, I'll invite you to stay as long as you like. You won't find women of this quality anywhere else in the territory." Miss Lou leaned in across the two empty seats between them. "But as a businesswoman, I must insist you decide on someone or take in the sights elsewhere. We don't make money on the booze." She sat upright, emptied her drink, then retrieved her handbag from the bar and hopped off the stool. "Enjoy your evening, Mr. Chatham." She moved through the crowd to a hallway opposite the front door and disappeared.

Although it was dark when he arrived in town, Oliver had easily located The Queen's Inn. Of course it helped knowing what to look for. The grandiose, three-story structure was noticeable from the carriage, off the main street by a block and well lit with a dozen gaslights. He'd wasted little time checking into the hotel before walking the few blocks back to the Inn.

He took another sip from his glass, then turned 'round from the bar.

Still not here, he thought, scanning the crowd. How long should he wait?

"I received my invitation to The Rainier Club dinner," someone to his right was saying. A redhead sat on the man's lap.

"They're fine dudes. Very influential." An associate sat across the table, as a hostess refreshed their drinks. "If not for the union meetings, I'd spend time there myself."

Opposite Oliver, where the councilman had been, a man with a well-groomed beard and gray suit was ordering a drink. Behind him, two men were leaving the parlor, accompanied by three giggling, buxom beauties. Oliver ordered another drink.

Movement in the center of the room caught his eye. He turned to look. His breath halted. Twenty years and a thousand women had passed since he'd first seen her. But he recognized her instantly. Her beauty hadn't faded. She stood in a floor-length gown of rich green with straps that fell loose on her shoulders. The cream color of her skin accentuated by cascading ringlets of dark hair. Two men who seemed familiar were speaking with her, and, as she conversed, smiling, her eyes seemed to dance. Her red lips glistened in the candlelight.

He finished his drink and stood up, then straightened his hat and lapel. His face had changed some since they first met, but Oliver knew he would still need charm and luck to keep her from recognizing him right away. Good thing he was skilled at both.

"Excuse me," he interrupted, "I'm sorry to impede your conversation, miss, but I wondered if I might speak to you alone?"

Her green eyes were intoxicating. "I don't believe we've properly met, sir."

Oliver had expected to see a woman of middle age, and he wondered if her youthful appearance this evening was a result of the lighting or simply his own imagination. "My apologies to the lady, and to the gentlemen," he acknowledged. "My name is..."

"It doesn't matter," one of the men jumped in, "the lady was speaking with us."

The other man concurred. "Wait your turn, boy. When we've ended our conversation satisfactorily, we'll gladly acquiesce our attentions."

"It's all right, gentlemen," she soothed. "No need for argument. Let him speak. He seems harmless enough."

"Thank you." He nodded to the men. "My name is Chaythum." He hoped the long "a" and lispy "th" would aid his deception. She appeared none the wiser. "I met earlier with your...governess, and she suggested I approach a dark-haired woman dressed in green. Forgive me if I'm mistaken, but may I please confirm your name?"

"My name is Marie, sir. Pleasure to meet you."

"The pleasure is mine." *Marie.*

She looked uncertain. "You're sure I'm the woman Lou suggested?"

"Oh, yes."

She seemed to consider the matter, then turned to the men. "I'm sorry, Cyrus, Judge Baker. It appears we must postpone our chat." She calmed their grumbling, then offered Oliver her elbow. "Shall we?"

Mesmerized, Oliver took her arm and followed her toward the doorway through which Lou and others earlier disappeared. She brought him to a set of broad, candlelit stairs. They ascended side-by-side.

"What kind of company interests you this evening, Mr. Chaythum? I don't know if Lou explained my particular contributions, but I don't provide the types of services men generally look for."

So she wasn't a hostess after all. Maybe his reports had been correct. "I thought we could talk for a while."

"My time is expensive, so it must be important. Unless you're hiding your true intentions," she looked back at him slyly, "but I'm afraid you're in the wrong place for that."

They stopped at the end of the short hall on the third floor, in front of an entrance marked PRIVATE. From a chain around her neck, she produced a key and opened the door.

"Do you have a match, Mr. Chaythum?"

"Yes." He found one in his trouser pocket and handed it over.

She struck it on the doorframe and lit a candle on a shelf to the right of the door. "This way. Lock the door behind you."

The echoes of his footfalls told him the room was big, but he could make out only shadows in the dark. He followed her silhouette past a cabinet on their right to an area just beyond it in the corner. She set the candle on a small table situated between two high-backed chairs.

"Won't you sit down?" She gestured that he take the chair facing the room. "May I take your hat and coat?"

"My hat, yes, thank you. I'll keep my coat."

She took his hat and stepped toward the cabinet they passed where a coat rack stood next to it a few feet to Oliver's left. "Are you cold? We can light a fire." She gestured toward the darkened corner opposite them.

"No, that won't be necessary. I'm fine." He'd grown accustomed to the warm, humid air of the southeast, but didn't want to get into a discussion of his travels as it would distract from his real purpose. He wondered what her reaction would be.

"Can I offer you a drink?" She stood now at the cabinet, having produced two glasses and an unmarked bottle.

"Yes, thank you."

She poured the drinks and, leaving the bottle on the cabinet, returned to the sitting area. "I believe you'll enjoy this. A friend on the northwest side of town started a distillery during the dry years here in Seattle. The ban was lifted last year, but he continues producing for pleasure. It's quite good."

Oliver sipped from his glass. "Yes, a bit stronger than I'd expected, but richly flavored."

Having grown accustomed to the low light, Oliver looked briefly about the room. It was large, as he'd guessed upon their arrival, and was simply furnished with a dressing area in the far left corner, a bed against the wall opposite the door, and an armoire directly ahead of him. Between the bed and the door they'd entered through, a large bouquet of wildflowers sat atop a small table. In the corner opposite him he could barely make out a fireplace to the left of the bed and a screened area that half concealed a large washtub. Walls were bare pine as were the furnishings, as far as he could tell. Two sets of double doors with paned glass, likely opening onto balconies, were placed opposite each other, one near the changing area to his far left and one on his immediate right.

"What is it you'd like to discuss this evening, Mr. Chaythum? Have you a business proposition?"

He smiled. "What I have...Miss *Marie*, is more of a confession." Again, he looked at her face and noted how young she appeared.

She sipped from her glass and set it on the table. Her hands folded in her lap. "You have my curiosity, sir, but shouldn't a church be a more appropriate venue for a confession?"

"Not one of this sort." He sat his glass on the table and reached for her hands. "May I?"

She looked fidgety, but unafraid. "This is quite mysterious, Mr. Chaythum. Your confession must be a grave one."

"It is." His hand lay atop hers. Would she remember him? "Look closely at my face. Do you know me?"

"Mr. Chaythum, I'm afraid I have no time for..."

"Please, 'Mr. Chaythum' is so formal," he braced himself for the shock, "call me Oliver."

"Very well, then, Oliver, I shall..." Her dark eyes widened with recognition. She pulled her hand free and bolted toward the door.

Oliver jumped after her. He grabbed her waist and held her tight.

"Let me go." She pounded on his arms, but he didn't let loose. "Let me go, I said. You can't hold me."

"Stop or you'll call attention." He'd expected surprise, but not this.

"Good!"

"I mean you no harm, Miss Dougharty."

"That's not my name." She twisted and struggled, still pounding at his arms.

"You *are* Jane Dougharty. We met in Sacramento."

"That's not true."

"You know it is," he managed to turn her body around to face him, and he backed her into the shadows against the door. He held her face to his. "Remember me."

Pounding erupted on the door from the hallway, "Miss Marie!" A man's voice. "You in there?"

"Yes and..." Oliver covered her mouth with one hand while he held her body firm with the other.

He whispered. "Don't. Talk to me." His eyes bore into hers as he slowly uncovered her mouth.

She paused before she spoke. "Yes, I'm here, Bertram. No cause for alarm."

"You sure?"

"Yes. I'll be out shortly."

"Okay, Ma'am. Call out if you need me."

She spoke after the man retreated down the stairs. "What are you doing here?"

He loosened his hold. "Come sit with me." He took her arm and guided her back to her chair. "You're not going to run again, are you?"

"No."

"Well, that's progress." He sat down again and picked up his drink.

She looked bewildered. "Your face is...you've changed, but... You didn't have the mustache and the patch on your chin before."

He chuckled. Forgotten memories of his first days with her were flooding back. "No. I'd only started shaving a year before we met."

"Why are you here, Oliver?" She seemed to be studying his face.

He thought a moment and phrased his words carefully, not wanting to let her know he'd come expressly for her. Not yet. "It's coincidence, really. I stopped at the Queen's Inn for the same reason as any man. Seeing you was a delightful surprise. My apologies if I frightened you."

Her breathing relaxed, but she remained guarded. "But why are you in Seattle? What made you leave Sacramento without word?" She continued to study him. "And why aren't you...older?"

Funny you should ask. "I could ask you the same."

Her chest rose and fell sharply. "Strange things have happened since we last spoke, Oliver."

His heart skipped a beat. Could it be true that this beautiful woman from his past had defied age and death as he had? "When you say 'strange,' do you hint at the inability to grow old?"

With both shock and relief, she whispered, "You're familiar with this condition?"

"A little."

"Are you responsible?"

"No."

"Are there others?"

"You're the first I've stumbled on."

"When did it happen to you? Do you remember?"

"Only fragments. I believe the onset forced my departure from Sacramento before you and I had a chance to..." He stopped, not wanting to tell too much. "What do you remember of the change?"

Jane stood. She circled the chair and stood before the set of French doors in the shadows. She pulled the draperies aside and let in the night. "I remember nothing of what happened to me. All I have are dreams and theories."

Oliver sipped at his drink. "What happened after I left?"

She was staring into the street below. "I never married, but that wasn't why people started to whisper."

"When did you leave?"

"Eight years after your disappearance."

"And you came here?"

"Not directly. I spent thirteen years in the Oregon Territory." She turned her head from the window. He saw sadness in her face. "Oliver, is there a way to stop it?"

"Stop it? You mean, is there some kind of cure?"

"Yes, so I can go home to Philadelphia and forget this dreadful corner of the world."

"Why not go now?"

Her hands were clenched at her sides. "To invite the whispering from uncles and aunts and cousins rather than strangers? What happens when they grow old and wither? How do I explain my obvious immunity?" She stepped into the candlelight. "Look at me, Oliver. I haven't changed in twenty years. Not one wrinkle. Not one scar. And it's not only that." She rushed to the chair and sat down, her skirt whirled about her. She leaned in close. "I've defied death on more than one occasion. Abrasions heal as I watch."

"Some would kill for that."

"This is no joke, Oliver. I didn't ask for this. I *don't* want this."

"Maybe it's temporary." He stroked the thin patch of hair on his chin. "It's a shame you're not enjoying it. I've become quite fond of the benefits to this 'condition.'"

"Benefits? What benefits are there to a life of hiding? Of being robbed of any lasting friendship?"

Heavy footsteps approached outside the door. A knock followed and Bertam's voice again flooded the room. "Miss Marie, Lou's wondering when she can expect you downstairs."

"Yes, um, I'm sorry." She dabbed at her eyes and cheeks with her sleeve.

"Will you be longer, then?"

"Tell Lou I'll rejoin her momentarily."

Bertram retreated and Jane looked somber. "I'm afraid we have to end this tonight."

He stood. "May I see you tomorrow? Say, after the noon hour, in the lobby of the Occidental?"

"Not in the lobby, but I'll meet you outside." She picked up the candle and stood.

"Can I help you with this?" He motioned to the glasses on the table.

"No. I'll see to them later."

Moving toward the door, Oliver retrieved his hat from the post and Jane returned the candlestick to its shelf near the door. They emerged into the hall with a pretended casualness and returned to the smoke-filled den of iniquity downstairs.

•

He hadn't planned to care for her again, but the powerful attraction wouldn't subside as he walked through the damp, dark Seattle streets to his hotel. His objective had been to simply find her and apologize. He'd wanted to for years, ever since his head cleared enough to realize what he'd done to her. But seeing her face had brought back old feelings. How could he have forgotten how much he'd cared for her? And how fortunate it was that she, too, had acquired the mysterious resistance to death. Maybe he could convince her to leave with him. Their love could be eternal.

Oliver passed under a gaslight. The soft breeze wafting in from Puget Sound made the glow flicker. A light rain hurried his steps as he plotted his strategy. He would talk to her the following day. Profess his devotion. Surely her feelings for him hadn't completely dulled, and hadn't she all but confessed her loneliness?

If she would have him, he would give up self-indulgence. In fact, to hold her in his arms—and to be the object of her affections—was worth any sacrifice. Oliver trotted through the rain and decided to do whatever it took to hold on to Jane Dougharty forever.

CHAPTER 17

Jane understood the neglect in the rest of the house the instant she stepped into the music room and saw what Oliver had done. Guarded by the ghosts of the orchestra, it was obvious he had built a hiding place where he'd proceeded to trade the real world for a virtual one. What had her absence done to him?

"Is this what you referred to as The Realm?" she asked.

"Oh, no," he laughed. "The Realm is the name of the website." He dropped her hand but continued walking, leading her toward the far corner and the computer bank situated there. "How did you know that name, anyway?"

"You told me in the hall just now."

At the back of the room, between two shuttered windows, four computer stations perched atop what Jane remembered as the dining room table downstairs. Two flat-screen monitors faced the wall, two faced the door through which they'd entered. Oliver placed her shopping bag gently on the floor under the window, then dropped into the chair facing her and started typing.

"I didn't tell you the name of the site."

"Yes you did." Of course he did.

He looked away from the screen to flash her a grin. Then he dropped his eyes to the keyboard. "No, I didn't." Then back at the screen. "I know because I was busy remembering how you looked in that green dress in Seattle. You were such a vision."

Jane pulled an office chair around the table to seat herself next to Oliver. "I don't know how you could remember Seattle so fondly. Your visit ended badly, if I'm not mistaken." A sudden and intense shiver radiated from the pit of Jane's stomach. A second later, the sensation was gone.

"You all right?" Oliver asked, still staring at the screen but no longer typing.

"Yes. I think so. Just a chill. A reaction to the change in temperature, maybe." Or maybe not. "Oliver, is anyone else in the house?"

"No."

"You're sure?"

"As sure as I am about not telling you the name of the website."

Seclusion, Jane thought, seemed not to be as detrimental to Oliver's psyche as she'd originally suspected. He hadn't really changed at all.

"Anyway," she shuffled about in her chair, getting comfortable, "you were saying earlier that there are others like us, and that you've found some Maltese knight?"

"Okay, that's it." He threw his hands up, mockingly. "Now, even *you* have to admit I never said anything about the knight."

It suddenly occurred to Jane how she'd discovered the information. "I read your mind, Oliver." She felt awkward, as if she'd trespassed. "I'd forgotten how easy it was."

"No harm. I expected you hadn't lost it."

"Still."

"Don't worry. To be honest, I sometimes miss the violation of my thoughts."

"Are you being crude?"

"Would you like me to be?"

God, but he hadn't changed. "Getting back to the knight and The

Realm, where you planning to show me something?"

"I thought you'd never ask." He returned his attention to the screen and his fingers to the keyboard. "First I should explain, though, that this man is not merely *some* knight, dear Jane, but *the* knight. It's my belief that he was the first immortal. He created all the others."

"How can you know this?" She rolled the chair closer for a better view of the screen. On a background of black, in small white letters, were the words:

"Until 1993," Oliver said, "the assistants I told you about earlier frequented an establishment on the Rue Bourbon. A café and club called The Thorned Rose. Ownership changed hands hundreds of times over the years, but the character of its clientele never did."

"I remember you mentioning it once, but what does the club have to do with the website?"

"Patience." He reached for the mouse and clicked on the center of the screen. As if sucked by a vacuum, the image disappeared into itself, revealing a list of *options* displayed cleanly in black on an antique ivory background.

"For most of the eighteenth and nineteenth centuries," Oliver continued, "the Rose was a gathering place for thieves and murderers. By the early-1900's, a sub-culture had developed there."

"Sub-culture?"

He nodded his head. "Vampires. Or so they called themselves. Some even claimed to be immortal, which is how my associates came to mention them to me. In the late 80's and on through the 90's, most of the vampires who spent their nights at the Rose were teenagers whose thirst for the world wide web grew as strong as their thirst for blood."

Jane was catching on. "So the owners of the café installed computers with Internet access?"

"Correct. They also recognized the need for a web presence of their own and, for whatever reason, charged my associates, then known by Frances and Dino, with the task of creating it. I purchased the equipment for them. They built the café's site here in the music room. Looking back, it was awful." Oliver laughed. "But I watched them and quickly understood the concept and potential of the Internet."

"So you built your own website?"

"Not right away." Oliver typed in a web address and a search page appeared. "I wanted to see what was already there, but locating information wasn't easy."

"What kind of information were you looking for?"

"Documents. Clues. Proof. You and I have conversed at great length on the subject of our condition. How we've managed to live so long. Who, or what, was responsible. To be honest, I didn't know what I was looking for then. It's hard to find answers when you're unsure of the questions. Then the Rose's site started bringing in all these emails. We set up a message board where, in their words, 'people could answer their own fucking questions,' and that's exactly what happened."

Oliver typed another address and the Rose's bulletin board appeared on the screen. He scrolled down revealing row after row of posted messages.

Jane understood. "Fans of the Rose started talking to one another."

"Yes. And we were watching. Vampires from all over the world found the message board. Some had elaborate life stories spanning decades. Most were obviously bogus, but some had threads of possibility. I started to wonder if any of them might be telling the truth." Oliver returned to his website and its list of options.

"When The Realm was launched, it originally gave visitors only two options: Mortal or Immortal. And only those who spoke English could make use of it. Now, the boards are translated automatically when a visitor enters."

"How?"

"It's technical, just think of it as a real-time translator."

"So conversations aren't limited by language."

"We also added options, which helped to funnel, or separate, the more useful information from the drivel."

Jane read the screen. *Tales of Re-Birth* and *Children of the Knight* were listed as third and fourth options, respectively.

"There are sub-groups in each category, but I won't go into that. And no one starts with access to all four categories. The original options of Mortal and Immortal are all a first-time visitor sees."

Jane was curious, but also impatient. "So tell me what you've found." The sudden tingle in her midsection returned. She felt a presence that was not entirely benign. "Oliver," she grasped his forearm, "are you sure there's no one else in the house?"

"Positive. Only two others are granted entry to this home, and they have been instructed to keep their distance."

Jane concentrated, trying to decipher the meaning of the odd sensation. "I don't think they listened."

"How can you know?"

Jane smirked. "It seems we both have secrets to share."

A rumbling in the hallway ended the silence and brought both Jane and Oliver to their feet. Two figures appeared in the doorway.

"O-man," greeted a short, pudgy man with unruly hair. Behind him, a taller, darker version stood, looking as if he'd been dragged along against his will.

Oliver was furious. "I told both of you to stay away."

"Didn't I tell you, fucknuts," the taller man said.

The fat one ignored him. "I know, O, but there was just one thing." The man froze with his arm extended, his finger pointing.

"I don't care," Oliver continued, "if the air in this house is the only thing keeping you from dying a long and painful death. You're not to set foot in it today."

Jane noticed the chubby man was still frozen in place. She stifled a laugh, hoping the events unfolding in front of her weren't serious.

"Did you hear me?" Oliver asked. "Get out, both of you, and come back tomorrow."

"Come on, Ozzy." The tall one grabbed his friend's jacket and tugged. "O wants us out, man. Come out of it."

"That's her, Coop," the frozen man whispered, finally lowering his arm. "The woman in the picture."

What picture? Jane wondered.

When the men in the doorway swiveled their heads to look at the wall behind them, Jane followed their line of vision and understood. A painting, with dimensions surely exceeding five-foot square, hung on the music room's opposite wall. She hadn't noticed it when she entered because it had been on the left when Oliver led her to the right.

"I'll not tell you again," Oliver said, now stomping away from the computer table toward the door.

"Let's go, Coop," muttered the short one, turning and shoving his friend through the doorway.

"Knock it off, Oz. I know the way out."

Jane watched Oliver usher the two strange visitors out into the hallway and close the door behind them. What kind of existence had Oliver carved out for himself here? And where had he found the painting above the fireplace?

"Oliver?"

He looked away from the door. "Yes, my dear."

"Who painted that picture?"

"I'm sure I don't remember." But he did remember.

Jane searched his thoughts. What was he hiding? "It's an extraordinary likeness," she said.

Winding her way through the room for a closer look, she stopped near Oliver and the door. The image was haunting.

It was a portrait of a woman—Jane—standing in front of the courtyard fountain as it looked in the days when the water was pure enough to drink. Flanked by her most treasured possessions, her figure stood in the foreground. The yellow antebellum dress and bright, blooming yellows, reds and purples of the courtyard brought back a thousand memories. Music. Literature. Theatre.

"Amazing." She turned to Oliver. "But I never posed for a portrait, or even a sketch. How is it that the features and details are so exact?"

Without offering a response, Oliver stepped away and returned to the chair in front of his computer.

That nineteenth-century woman in the painting is me, she thought. Could she really have lived so long? She pulled herself away from the portrait and walked back to the opposite side of the room.

He's not really looking at the screen, she thought. *He's thinking. Thinking hard about...not letting me know.*

Jane sat in the chair next to Oliver and placed her hand over the flat screen. "Until recently, no photographs of me existed, Oliver. How could someone paint such a likeness without aid of a print?"

He remained blankly focused on the screen. "From memory."

"*You* painted it." It wasn't a question. "But you were never a painter. You would have needed to learn and practice and...remember every detail."

"Yes." He looked at her with soft, brown eyes. His thoughts no longer hidden. "I didn't know when I would see you again. The painting holds all my memories of you. The yellow dress. The garden. Even your mother's antique box. I needed something..." He stopped. "What's wrong?"

"Your friends haven't left the grounds," Jane said without knowing how she knew. "Is that unusual?"

Oliver didn't question her certainty of their presence. "I'm not surprised. This has become their home as much as mine."

"But you told them to leave, and now they're..." she searched for the word, "hiding."

"They probably don't know where else to go. Their every moment of daylight is ordinarily spent here with me." He grinned and shook his head. "And if they're hiding, I'll bet it's to escape the sun."

"The sun? Why?"

"They think they're vampires."

"Vampires?"

"They're not really vampires, of course. Immortals, like us, yes, but not vampires. My theory has always been that they adopted the culture after spending too many years at the Rose."

Vampires. Paintings. Other immortals. Jane's head was swimming from overload.

"As ridiculous as it may seem," Oliver added, "I have to admit their delusions have been helpful where the website is concerned."

Jane wanted to know more about the painting and Oliver's vampiric associates, but her need to learn what news Oliver had gathered about their condition drove Jane to bring him back to the website.

"Let's forget about all this for now," she said, "and start over with your explanation."

"You sure?" Oliver poised his hands over the keyboard.

"Yes."

His eyes flashed to the screen, his fingers poked at the keys. His posture settled in. "Coop and Ozzy and I, we've had to be discerning in collecting data. Not everyone who visits The Realm tells the complete truth."

Jane thought he was putting it mildly. On the screen was what looked like an accounting spreadsheet.

"After a couple of years, we noticed that most of the older mortals reported to be from outside the U.S., so we started keeping records of certain information."

"But if you weren't sure they were telling the truth, how could you know for sure that someone really was immortal?"

"Well," he flushed, "our methods *were* a bit insensitive at first."

"Meaning what?" She was afraid to ask.

"There is only one way, after all, to prove one's immortality."

He didn't. "You killed them?"

"A few."

"Oh, Oliver."

His hands were in his lap. "We don't do that anymore. Well," the flush returned, "at least I don't. But moving on." He pointed at the top of a column on the screen.

"The entries in this column are the immortal's place of origin. The next column lists their date of birth, then the next their surname."

Jane read across the top of the table. *Occupations. Marriages.* The list went on.

"It's not much in its raw form, but when I started playing around with the information," Oliver brought a map to the screen, "this is one of the things I found."

It was a typical map of the world, with blue for the water and beige for the land. Colored dots, including two black ones in California, marked maybe two-hundred locations. The dots were connected by a series of red lines. "I assume the colored dots represent immortals?"

"Yes. Well, sort of." He clicked the computer's mouse and the picture zoomed in over North America and Europe. "Depending on the color, the dots represent locations where an immortal was born, was changed, or where he currently resides. The lines connect the three."

"It looks like a tangled mess, Oliver, why don't you tell me what you know and stop trying to show me how you did it."

"You're the one who asked."

He was right. "You're right."

"Thanks for admitting it." He pressed the power button on the monitor and the screen went blank.

"In the Mediterranean," Oliver began, "a legend dating back to the early sixteenth century tells of a man who grew to great power by slaying the members of a group known as the Knights of St. John, or the Knights Hospitalers, depending on what history book you subscribe to."

"You mean the Masons and Shriners?"

"No, you're thinking of the Templars. The group later emerged as the Knights of Malta, but centuries before they reestablished themselves, this man crowned himself King and demanded his subjects worship him by drinking the blood of the innocent. Those who refused his command were executed or, worse, made immortal and left naked and chained in the city streets for months as examples."

Jane wasn't liking any of this.

"It's assumed young maidens, or virgins, as well as children, were used in his ceremonial rituals."

Jane shivered. "What a horrible thought."

"It's only legend, remember. The likelihood that details have been enhanced over the years is high. Anyway, it's said the man ruled for two-hundred years from his palace in Malta. He was reputed to have preferred the painful cries of those unable to die more so than the screams of the dying. No one's entered the palace since the end of his reign, but it's believed he still walks the rooms and hallways, waiting for another victim to torture."

"And you think the man in the legend is the one who did this to us?" She wanted to believe, but it all sounded too fantastical. "How could you theorize that from information collected on an electronic message board used by people who believe they're vampires?"

"I'm not saying there aren't holes in the theory, but keep in mind not every immortal has contacted us. The data we have is incomplete." Oliver spoke in earnest.

Jane knew he believed what he was saying.

Oliver continued, "Every sixty years, give or take, a new immortal is created, and if you trace the pattern back far enough..."

"All the red lines led to the Mediterranean," Jane interrupted, having suddenly grasped the meaning of Oliver's map.

"I know it must sound bizarre, but..."

"'Bizarre' is an understatement. Especially after meeting your vampire friends." Jane got up from the chair and rubbed her eyes. "It's not that I don't believe you, Oliver, because I suppose I do." She glanced around the darkened room and wondered what time it was. "It's just a lot to take in."

"I understand." Oliver stood and pushed his chair away from the table. "Maybe it would help if you rested a while."

She was surprised to find she liked the idea. "Could I?"

"Of course. There's space in the library." Oliver stood up and offered his arm.

Jane considered refusing—she could get to the library on her own—but thought it best to acquiesce. They walked amid the abandoned instruments that once filled this room with melodies of another time. This was no longer the home she remembered.

Jane shot a quick, final glance at the portrait above the fireplace before she exited through the door Oliver held open. They walked around the hall overlooking the dimly-lit foyer and stepped through the arched passage into the library. Looking around, Jane thought it uncanny how the room appeared exactly as it had one-hundred years ago. The shelves of books, the red sofas, the area rug in the center of the hardwood floor. And it was clean.

"Is this the only other room you use now?"

"Yes. As these books once were for you, they are now my escape."

"Have you read them all?"

"At least once." He stood in the doorway. "I'll let you sleep. Take as long as you like."

"Thank you."

He left her. The sounds of his steps trailed down the hall and back to the computer.

There was more going on here than what Oliver shared. But Jane sensed even Oliver wasn't aware of it. It was like he was keeping secrets from himself, if that were possible. Jane looked down at the sofa and was relieved at its condition. She patted the cushions and pillows. There was dust, but not near what she expected. Her mind bursting with thoughts of other immortals, and vampires, and knights, and Oliver…and Rand, Jane laid down and propped her head and feet on the pillows. If she fell asleep, she was afraid she might not wake for days.

By scanning his mind, Jane knew Oliver's sincerity was genuine, but solitude must have had some effect on him. How long had he lived this way? How much of his story could be believed, and how much could be written off as the ramblings of an obsessed man? And what of the two immortals, Coop and Ozzy? Had they been *changed* by the same man? And for what purpose? What was the knight's motivation? How had he done this for so long without detection? And could it be undone? Were there consequences? Would she be able to return to Rand? What would life be like if she didn't have to run anymore?

Why haven't we all lost our minds?

Exhausted, Jane drifted off to sleep.

Chapter 18

Rand hadn't visited Dave and Karen Fristoe's Hutchinson Island home since the hurricanes of 2004, mostly because the couple had stayed with him and Jane for eight weeks while crews cleared the bridges. After two back-to-back storms and a case of bourbon, even the best of friends needed time apart.

He and Dave had just finished lunch in the kitchen. While Dave checked email, Rand walked to the front of the house to survey the noise outside the window. What was ordinarily a meticulously manicured, Mediterranean-style beach home, was now a construction zone. Parked in the driveway next to Karen's blue Porsche was a white van with a picture of a black and silver hammer and the name Weber & Co. General Contractors painted across the side. Another van, this one red and dented and advertising Tod's Plumbing Service, was parked along the road. On what had once been the front lawn sat a truck loaded with sod. Half a dozen sweaty men scattered the landscape, digging, trimming, and planting. An industrial-sized dumpster, filled with chunks of drywall, sat off to the left near the garage door.

"I'm so tired of rebuilding this house." Dave appeared behind him. "You know they haven't even started on the screened enclosure yet. We've had that contract for three months." He frowned, "By the way, man, you look like hell. I'm sure it's been rough for you, but when was the last time you showered?"

Rand continued to face the window. "I have something to tell you."

"Worse than you're skipping town to New Orleans because you're scared? I thought we talked it all out last night."

"Janie's alive, Dave."

"What?" Dave faced Rand. "But the accident...where did you find her?"

"I didn't. Not yet, but I know where she is."

"Don't tell me," Dave mocked, "New Orleans?"

"Yes."

"Maybe we should sit down." Dave pulled Rand's arm and coaxed him to sit on the sofa. Dave sat a reasonable distance away.

"I know it sounds crazy," Rand said, "and to be honest, I haven't been able to make complete sense of it all myself. I even lied to you to give me more time to sort it out."

"You're worrying me a bit, pal, you know that?"

"I can't explain it. Somehow I just know."

For a few seconds, Rand thought Dave might reach out and hold his hand. "What happened two days ago was a traumatic experience for you, Rand. For anybody. You lost your wife. It's a normal thing to want her back, but..."

"I'm not in denial, Dave. She's alive and she could be in trouble. I have to find her."

"So you're going to New Orleans? Even if you're right—and I'm not saying you are 'cuz this is really out there—but if you *are* right and she *is* there, I still can't see that it's a good idea for you to leave town right now. As your lawyer, I..."

"Fuck the lawyer shit, Dave. I'm sorry I strung you along last night, but I need a friend right now not a legal opinion."

Dave paused. "What do you need me to do?"

"On Sunday, Janie called somebody in New Orleans from a pay

phone. Find out who she called." He fished into his pocket and pulled out a business card. "This guy can tell you where and when. Find the pay phone she used and call your contact at the phone company."

"She's not always a sure thing."

"Do what you can, Dave. If I know who she called, I'd have somewhere to start looking."

"Of course. Do you need anything else?"

"Well, since you asked." Like it would have mattered. "Lend me your passport and a credit card."

Dave straightened. "You're not planning to leave the country?"

"No. Nothing like that. I need I.D. I can't use my own, and I can't ask you to give up your driver's license."

"But the picture...we don't look alike."

He was right. Dave's dark hair and Rand's light brown weren't exactly a match. "Let me worry about that."

"What are your plans?"

"It's best you don't know everything. Just that Janie's alive and I'm determined to find her. I'll check in."

"What about the police?"

"You do what you think you need to. Fill me in later on the cell phone. I'll check it for messages whenever I can."

"You're really serious about this?"

"Yeah. I am."

His friend stood up and returned to the window. "God, Rand. This is big. I'd like to say I'd do the same for Karen given the situation, but...I don't know, man. Is it love that's driving you to this, or something else?"

"There's no question it's love, but it's not that simple. I've learned things. Things that don't make sense."

"Like what?"

Rand wondered how much he should say. "For example, have you ever taken a good look at Janie, Dave?"

"Meaning what?"

"Meaning have you ever looked really close at her."

"Sure. Hundreds of times."

"Haven't you noticed she hasn't changed since Flagler? You and I, and even Karen, are aging, Dave. Look at our wrinkles. Your children could give you grandchildren any day."

"Bite your tongue," a woman's voice came floating in from the kitchen. "I heard you talking about gray hair and grandchildren." Karen's petite, familiar frame appeared in the doorway leading from the foyer. "I'll have you know, Jamie and Lee are happy bachelors who, at twenty-one and twenty-three, are in no hurry to start a family. Don't you dare jinx them."

Rand stood to greet her.

"You don't need to stand up, Rand. Once you've slept under our roof you're no longer a guest. Can I get you anything, honey?"

"No," Rand answered, "I'm fine."

Dave jumped in. "You never ask me if I want anything."

Karen smiled. "That's because I already know you want everything. You sure you don't want a soda or something, Rand?"

"No, thanks."

"Be careful, sweetheart," Dave said to Karen. "Don't forget the guy who nursed your hangover yesterday." He turned to Rand. "Forty years old and still thinking she can drink like a teenager."

Karen's hands flew to her hips. Her foot started tapping. "I'd be careful if I were *you*, mister."

"You know what? Speaking of hangovers, how about getting us a fresh pot of coffee, K?" Dave asked. "Rand, you up for coffee?"

"If it's no trouble."

"No trouble at all." Blowing a kiss to her husband, Karen turned her back to them and disappeared through the foyer.

Dave tapped Rand's arm. "Not a word about…you know," he whispered. "This is between you and me for now."

"Understood."

Dave leaned in close and whispered. "If the tables were turned, I know you'd be there for me. I want you to know I'll be there for you."

"I'm counting on it," Rand said, meaning every word.

•

Aside from calling the Coast Guard to report his wife had fallen overboard, saying goodbye to Dave and Karen was the hardest thing Rand had ever done. Not that he was afraid he'd never see them again, he just didn't want their next meeting to take place over the phone while sitting on opposite sides of a glass partition.

He'd chosen to fly from the Tampa airport, thinking if the police somehow got wind of his absence, they'd start their search on Florida's east coast. If nothing else, it would buy him time. And so far, so good. It was four o'clock and Rand was still a free man.

He slipped the credit-card-sized key into the slot on the hotel room door and anxiously watched for the red light to turn green. When it did, he let himself in, kicked the door closed and tossed a plastic Walgreen's bag onto the king-sized bed. It landed next to Jane's heirloom suitcase and the manila envelope containing the money he'd withdrawn from the bank. He had one thing to do before he left for the airport in the morning. After that, there'd be no bowing out. His hands were shaking. His breathing was worse.

Could he really go through with this?

His room at the Marriott wasn't bad. The way he saw it, he'd probably stare at the ceiling all night no matter where he stayed. Innocent or not, he looked guilty as hell by disappearing. The muscles in his neck stiffened. But he couldn't stop now. Not while there was hope of finding Jane and bringing her home. Yes, he was afraid, but his fear of being caught didn't drive him. Not like the fear of never seeing her again.

He'd called the airline and reserved a seat on the eleven-thirty flight, then he'd made a short trip to the drugstore. Now, standing in the barely-lit hotel room, staring at the items on the bed, he began to second-guess himself. What the fuck was he doing? He was a fifty-year-old photographer, not a thrill-seeker coaxing the police into a high-speed chase. As far as he knew, he hadn't been charged with anything.

The TV news and the papers were spewing the same crap as the day before. But he was sure the police had noticed his obvious absence. Eventually, if they found him, they'd arrest him on suspicion, or maybe they'd go straight for the Big Kahuna: murder.

Unless he could find her.

Rand opened the suitcase. The silk lining was rubbed thin, and the leather was cracked. He'd never seen Jane use it, so he assumed the extensive wear and tear happened long before the case fell into Jane's custody. Hopefully it wasn't priceless, and hopefully Jane would understand why he'd taken her luggage from the closet instead of a piece of his own.

Inside the case, lying helter-skelter on the bottom, were six of the framed photos from atop the desk in the bedroom on Palm Beach. Given the difficulty the police and media met with scrounging for photos, Rand snagged them believing they were the only pictures in existence of his wife. He'd always thought it ironic that Jane, being so acutely camera shy, had married a photographer. On the rare occasion she did allow him to snap a photo, she'd made him destroy the negative. He kidded her about it, and she was a good sport, but he was careful never to pry too deeply. Everyone, it seemed, had some phobia to live with. Rand's was spiders. Over the years, Jane's phobia about being photographed became simply another thing to love about her.

He tossed the envelope containing five-thousand dollars into the suitcase with the pictures, then upended the plastic Walgreen's bag and poured his drug store purchases on top. A toothbrush, a disposable razor, and travel-sized containers of toothpaste, shampoo, shaving cream, and mouthwash spilled into the case. The electric shaver, landing hard on the bare lining, made a muffled *thunk*.

His friend—his *lawyer*—said he was crazy to leave town. And that was *without* the knowledge of what Rand was about to do. But what option did he have? Dave's passport picture showed a man with salt and pepper hair that had receded beyond the crown of his head. Rand, with his light hair draped past his earlobes, wouldn't get beyond the ticket desk. Besides, there was always the chance someone would recognize him. He'd taken enough of a chance in leaving without telling the police. He couldn't run the risk of being caught.

Rand picked up the package and wrestled the shaver free from its thick, plastic wrapping. He gave a cursory glance at the directions, then pitched them into the suitcase with the mangled plastic. Carrying the shaver and its electrical cord, he walked into the bathroom and turned on the light. His reflection looked terrified.

He plugged-in the shaver, then sat it down next to the sink while he pulled his stuffy, white button-down up and over his head.

"Shouldn't have this in the bathroom," he muttered, and walked back to the bed and draped the shirt over the opened suitcase. In fact, he should probably cut back to his boxers, just in case.

As he kicked off his Oxfords and removed his jeans, Rand went over the plan again in his head. *In case anyone asks*, he thought, *I'm an accountant on my way to see a client*. No, he'd never been to New Orleans before and, no, he wouldn't have time for sightseeing during his visit. The money in the suitcase? For the client, of course. The gentleman was an eccentric who, for reasons known only to him, preferred his money be transported by personal escort than by more conventional means. The withdrawal slip from the bank—showing only an account number, not a name—would be in the suitcase should anyone question his legitimacy. Why wasn't the bag locked, or the money more secured? At the client's direction, the case must appear "average" and of little value. As should its escort. That would explain why Rand wasn't dressed like an accountant.

It had to work.

Wearing only blue silk boxer shorts, Rand returned to the bathroom and the Remington Titanium clippers. *Last chance*, he thought, challenging the distressed man in the mirror. He could explain the money. He could explain the hotel room. After shaving his head, though, he'd have no choice but to keep running until he found her.

He picked up the electric shaver. Its weight had tripled in the minutes since prying it from its wrapper. But that wasn't really the case, was it? Rand looked down at his right hand, the one that held the device too tight. His fingertips were a brilliant red. His palm was moist. Could he do this without carving his skull?

The Remington's tiny motor whirred to life as he slid the switch to ON. Taking a deep breath, he raised his hand level with his forehead, leaned over the sink, and brought the blades of the trimmer to his hairline. Then in one fluid motion, while locked in a stare with his reflection and holding his breath, he buzzed a two-inch-wide swath up and over his head to the base of his neck. Strands of hair brushed the backs of his hand as it fell to the counter and into the sink. The air in his lungs escaped. He brought the shaver back to his forehead and made the motion again, this time further to the right. Like mowing the lawn. He buzzed another row. And another. Then he moved to the left side. It hadn't been as dangerous an activity as he'd expected.

When it was done, hair carpeted the base of the sink and clung to Rand's perspiring skin. He cleared the counter, sink, and floor and stuffed the remains in the bag-lined garbage can. He was thorough, but not obsessive. A few strays wouldn't matter. It wasn't unusual, after all, to encounter a hair or two in a hotel bathroom. He unplugged the shaver and wrapped the cord around it like a cocoon, then reached down and removed the lining from the garbage can. Returning to the foot of the bed, Rand tossed the shaver into the suitcase and stuffed the bathroom garbage and the mangled plastic packaging into the empty Walgreen's bag. He'd throw it into the trashcan near the rental car before he left. But first, he'd take a quick shower to rinse off the stray hair.

Rand removed his boxers and shook them out. He tossed them onto the back of the suitcase with his other clothes and grabbed the disposable razor and mini shaving cream. But something seemed out of place. A stinging sensation climbed up the back of Rand's legs and through his spine. What had he forgotten? Or maybe that wasn't it at all. Maybe the police were finally out there. In the lobby. Riding up the elevator. Within sight of the door.

No, he thought, shaking himself free of the paranoia. It was something else. Standing barefoot, naked and shorn, and holding a razor and shaving cream in his hand, he scanned the contents of the suitcase—money, pictures, toiletries—and it hit him. Despite the hours of imagining every detail. Despite covering his tracks. Despite his plan. How could he have been so absent-minded?

He'd bought shampoo.

Along with the clippers and razor with which he planned to cut his hair *off*, he had also thrown into the shopping basket a bottle of shampoo to…to what? Wash the hair on his balls? What the hell was he thinking? But that's precisely the point: he hadn't been thinking. Force of habit—instinct—had taken over. Instinct he desperately needed to trust right now. Was he overreacting? It was only shampoo.

He hurried back into the bathroom to use the shaving cream and razor on what was left of his hair. *After that*, he recited, *I'll rinse off, throw some clothes on, and find dinner*. Then he'd try to get some sleep, wake up in the morning, and drive to the airport.

One foot in front of the other.

There could be a lot of ground to cover in New Orleans. He'd gain an hour because of the time difference, so if they landed on time at three o'clock, a cab could get him to the other side of the river long before dark. He'd start at the train station and work his way out. Show Jane's picture to everyone. Someone had to have seen her. Noticed which direction she was going. Hopefully Dave would get lucky with the phone records. Beyond that, Rand would have to rely on his instinct.

The same one, he reminded himself, that bought shampoo.

CHAPTER 19

Behind a thick bougainvillea curtain in the shadows of the courtyard, the would-be vampires huddled, watching lizards jump from palm leaves and scurry under vines. Their backs were propped against the brick wall, their legs chilled on the cobblestones. It was uncomfortable, but Ozzy was a long-time acquaintance of discomfort. He'd get through it. The important thing was not to lose sight of the objective. And so far, he and Coop had been dead on.

"Isn't this trespassing or something?" Coop whispered.

Here we go again, Ozzy thought. "It's only trespassing if we get caught."

"Well, how much longer do we have to stay?"

"Jesus," he said too loud, "the stupid fucking questions don't stop with you, do they? *Ojos y oídos, amigo*. Eyes and ears. Remember the agreement?" Ozzy pointed to his eyes and ears, respectively, and lowered his voice. "When the man says stay, we stay. Trespassing or no." He rested his case.

Ozzy stole a quick glance at his sorry-ass companion. As always,

Coop was gnawing on his fingernails. *Deep down in that empty head of his,* Ozzy thought, *he has to understand our indebtedness to the Creator. If not for our immortality, we would never have survived the Atlantic for three days after our ship plunged to the ocean floor.* He'd given them skills and the opportunity to matter in an otherwise fucked up existence.

"What's with the woman in the painting, Oz?" Coop had never done well with silence.

"A friend of Oliver's is my guess. Maybe the one he used to talk to on the phone every week."

Coop didn't sound satisfied. "But that was maybe ten, twenty years ago. Oliver hung that painting in the thirties. I remember, 'cuz the Rose went underground 'bout the same time."

"What part of 'The Woman Is Obviously Immortal' do you not get?" Ozzy couldn't believe how Coop managed being to be so fucking stupid. "You mean to say you never noticed Oliver's weekly conversations with the same person for forty years?"

"How was I supposed to know it was the same person?"

"The guy gets one call a week, and at the same time on the same day of the week, for forty years and you can't make the connection?" Ozzy shook his head and pulled his knees to his chest.

After two centuries, Ozzy was used to his companion's lack of sense. He often wondered how they'd remained together so long. How he and Coop became an immortal duo could have been a story for the ages had it not been so dull. Ozzy didn't remember as much as he used to, but they'd started their lives as Antony (Ozzy) and Miguel (Coop). A man in a bar near the docks offered them immortality. They were new fathers living on the coast of eighteenth century Spain, which meant they'd be penniless drunks before the age of thirty like their fathers before them. Facing an undesirable future, immortality seemed like a good idea at the time.

The cellular phone in Ozzy's denim jacket pocket started vibrating. He fumbled it out and brought it to his ear.

"What is it?" he heard Coop asking.

Ozzy flapped his free hand in the air and mouthed "Shut up."

The voice on the other end of the connection was dry. "Is she there?"

"She's here," Ozzy answered, nodding. "Same as the painting, just like you said."

"Excellent. You know what to do?"

"Yes," he nodded again.

"Don't leave the airport until they're off the ground. Understood?"

"Understood." He heard the click of a severed connection, hung up, and shoved the phone back into his pocket.

"Well?" Coop asked.

"We're staying here."

"Here? With the lizards? But Oliver told us to go."

All Ozzy could do to keep from slapping him was hide his face in his hands. The stupid fucking questions never stopped.

•

Had he not foregone the buying trip, DeSain would have been standing on the grand terrace in Rockefeller Center overlooking the gleaming bronze of Prometheus. Instead, he was home in his study, his gaze riveted to the silent telephone on the desk. *From the line of LaCassiere.* The old seer's words ran through his mind as if on a string. *Your heir will be born.* Given the choice between Christie's in New York and fulfilling his destiny, DeSain would take the study of his sixteenth-century *casa* every time.

Two days earlier, his intuition—his *inner eye*—launched flares as the Dougharty woman began her journey to Oliver. With emotion bleeding through the defenses of her mind, her movements were clear. DeSain smiled to himself, knowing what awaited her in Oliver's care would lead her here. As with the telephone confirmation from the Spaniards, he'd taken no chances.

"The time of the prophecy has come," he whispered, rising from the desk. He summoned his servants telepathically and exited the study to prepare for her coming.

CHAPTER 20

"Jesus, Janson," Sergeant Benson was spitting, "*Entertainment-fucking-Tonight* knows more than we do!"

Janson flinched, feeling the tremors in the air. For a small, bald guy, the Sarge could belt shit out when he wanted.

It was Wednesday evening, the incident in question had occurred on Monday, and they were no closer to answers. Janson and Griffiths stood in Benson's office deserving every bit of the verbal lashing.

Janson tried to remain calm. "There is no evidence of foul play anywhere, sir. We searched the boat, the marina, the docks..."

"Did you search the house?"

Janson pretended not to hear. "We've been waiting for a positive ID on the body in Juno. Coroner's still not able to match Jane Doe to Mrs. Ackerton because medical records on the Ackerton woman haven't arrived."

"What about dental records?"

"Wouldn't matter, sir. No head on the remains."

"Oh, but how does that keep you from searching the house?"

With forty-eight hours of work and only more questions to show for it, Janson hated to tell the Sarge what else had gone wrong. "We can't search the house 'til morning."

"Why not go now?"

"We're waiting for a warrant, sir." The truth was sure to come out now.

"Why would you need a warrant? Won't the guy let you in?"

Janson tried not to fidget. "We've been calling for a couple hours now. No answer. One of our guys drove by and knocked, but no one's answering."

"You think the guy skipped town?"

"It's possible. None of his friends have heard from him."

"Sounds like probable cause to me. Men don't run unless they're guilty. Bring him in." The boss made it sound so simple.

"We're working on that."

"Work faster. And get into that house." Benson waved a shoo-fly gesture in their direction and picked up his telephone.

Janson about-faced, held the door for Griffiths, and the two detectives stepped quietly into the hall.

"Maybe Davis got something from records," Griffiths suggested after the door shut securely behind them. "He should be here in a couple hours." The fluorescent lights highlighted the gray in her hair and Janson was reminded how long they'd had each others' backs.

"I'll call again about the warrant," Janson agreed. Their shoes scuffed across the industrial carpet as they vacated Benson's office, bound for the cube farms around the corner.

"You're here early," Janson said when they found Davis sitting in his cube.

"Thought I'd follow your example, Janson," Davis greeted. "It's amazing how much you can get done when you give up sleeping."

"Very funny. Hope you've got something good. We all know how much better life is when the fat man next door is happy." Janson sat in the chair opposite Davis. Griffiths sat in her own.

"Don't know that I've got anything useful, but I found something interesting."

Janson frowned. "Why don't I like the sound of that?"

"Ignore him," Griffiths said to Davis. "We just saw the Sarge, so he's a little bitchy."

"Gotcha," Davis said, but Janson got the impression the young black detective had no clue what the Sarge's wrath was like when the man got really mad.

"Show us what you got," Janson said, propping his hands in his lap.

"In addition to public records, I've been scanning messages from the Florida Tips line. Ever since the woman's picture hit the news, the crazies have come out of the woodwork."

"People have seen her?" Adrianne asked.

"Believe it or not, there have been two recent sightings worth following up on, but most have been pranks. It's the calls from up north that caught my attention. Seventeen of them. Six of them veterans of World War II. All claiming they knew the woman years ago."

Griffiths said what Janson was thinking. "What's so crazy about that?"

"Here," Davis pulled a pink message slip off his desk and held it up. Janson and Griffiths leaned forward. "This guy says he used to dance with her at the clubs in Chicago pretty regular—in the 1930's. Said he'd never forget her face." J. B. added another slip. "This one says she was a vocalist with a band he played with back in '56 and '57 in Detroit." And another. "This is a woman who rented a room to her in Boston from '62 to '69."

Janson wasn't buying it. "We get bullshit calls on the tip line every day. It's a high profile case. A lot of nuts are gonna roll out."

"I'm not saying I believe she's the same woman," J. B. argued, sitting straight in his chair, "all I'm saying is that these messages are too coincidental to dismiss as pranks."

"So she looks like somebody, what's the big deal?"

"Look at the facts." Davis leaned sideways, propped an elbow on his desk and counted with his fingers. "There are no medical records, no history before she started teaching at Flagler College, her bogus birth certificate, now these tips, all from people who said one day they knew her and the next day—bam—she was gone."

"She can't be the same woman these people say they knew. She's not old enough."

"But I think there's a link and a strong possibility this woman didn't drown at all."

"The Sergeant's right," Janson slammed his fist on the arm of the chair. "We've been at this for days and still can't decide whether it's a missing persons case or a murder."

"We'll get it," Adrianne's voice was calming, "we just need a little more time. Why don't you check on the warrant to search the house while I call the friends again and start combing the neighborhood? Maybe they'll have some idea where Mr. Ackerton might have gone."

Janson was glad he had backup with more of a level head than his own. "Sounds good. We doin' take-out, or did you bring yogurt or a carrot stick or something?"

Griffiths smiled. "Take-out's fine." Opening a desk drawer, she retrieved her purse. "I'll go."

"What can I work on?" Davis asked.

Janson stood up and walked to his own desk chair. "Why don't you find something in those tips we can actually use?"

"Already started."

"Good." Janson sat down, picked up the phone, and hit the speed dial button for the courthouse, hoping tonight would reveal more answers than questions and justify another dinner apart from his wife.

DAY 4

CHAPTER 21

Just as Janson expected, the warrant to search Ackerton's house didn't come through until morning, but at least that meant he was able to get some rest. He'd sent Griffiths home, too, and even let her sit it out this morning while he and Davis searched the Ackerton house.

Standing in the spacious living room at eight o'clock in the morning, he heard Davis's footsteps descending the stairs. "You find anything?"

"Somebody did a job on the closet, mainly her side. Clothes, boxes, stuff off the shelves, thrown in a pile on the floor."

"Ackerton looking for something?"

"That was my take. The guy lost his wife. It could have been rage, denial, whatever. Maybe he wanted some keepsake to take with him."

"Or maybe there was something he didn't want us to find. He'd been through the file drawers down here, too. Couple of folders in the kitchen, but no medical files on the wife. You find a safe?"

"No, you?"

"No."

He and Davis had searched the house for two hours. They'd found nothing to further the case. What they *had* uncovered was that the Ackertons were a wealthy, happy, civic-minded couple with no prenuptial agreement, no insurance policies, and no clear motive to put an end to any of it.

Detective Davis was taking in the residence like the patron of an art museum. "There was a spectacular sunrise, though. Bedroom window was open. They had a great view."

Janson pulled off the rubber gloves he'd used to search the living room and kitchen. "Yeah, I saw it too," he said sarcastically, "while I had my head stuffed under the dash of the car in the garage. Spectacular." He could see Davis got the hint that he hadn't appreciated the commentary. "So we can rule this place out as a possible crime scene, don't you agree?"

"I think so." Davis looked chastised, but Janson had expected hints of intimidation and awe. After twenty-five years of one mansion after the next, a guy stopped noticing, but the young detective had only been in Palm Beach for six months.

"Let's take inventory," Janson said. "With the house, the boat, and the cars clean, what are we left with?"

"Um..." Detective Davis was thinking.

Janson waved the gloves in the air. They looked like spent condoms. "Somewhere between South Florida and the Atlantic Ocean is our crime scene. Either that or there's no crime scene at all. But then, there's the body and the fact that the husband bolted..." He trailed off, wishing he could close this case as accidental drowning, but wanting for the wife's sake to uncover the truth.

Davis held out his hand. "Here, let me take those."

Janson passed the latex gloves to J. B.

"I assume there's a garbage bin in the kitchen?"

"Yeah. Under the sink. Thanks."

Davis stepped into the open kitchen, around the island, and tossed the gloves in the garbage bin. "You know," Davis shut the cabinet door, "I'm not convinced, Detective, that there's been a crime committed at all."

"What?" Had Davis missed the events of the past few days? "We get a Coast Guard report that some rich guy's wife has fallen overboard, he gets bitchy when we ask him questions, and when a body washes up, he scoots. Ackerton's got something to hide."

"Maybe something to hide, yes, but it might not have been murder."

What else could it be? Janson wondered. "Before I hear this theory you're probably going to tell me, we should think about getting out of here. You hungry?"

"I could eat." Davis stepped around the kitchen island and joined Janson in the living room. "But we're not doing drive-through. Did you see that fast food movie?"

"No." Janson strode through the foyer and to the front door. "How 'bout Havana? They don't have a drive-through."

"Cuba?" The look on Davis's face, Janson thought, was priceless.

Janson turned the knob on the front door and stepped out into the twilight. "It's a restaurant south of here on Dixie Highway." Davis joined him on the stoop and Janson secured the door behind them. "You like Cuban food?"

"It's all right."

"Then let's change your opinion." Janson led the way to the tan Saturn in the gravel, U-shaped drive. The manicured hedge along the street was trimmed short, so Janson could see there were no reporters lying in wait. *They must know Ackerton's not home*, he thought. He walked around to the driver's side as Davis opened the door on the passenger side. Retrieving his keys from his jacket pocket, Janson opened the door, slid in behind the wheel, and started the engine.

Getting comfortable and fastening his seatbelt, Davis asked, "What about this man makes you think he's guilty?"

"I didn't at first." Janson shut his door and shifted the car into drive. "He came across as being really sick over the loss of his wife."

"What changed your mind?"

"Besides the fact that our grieving husband is gone? Those accounts you found last night. The woman was loaded." The car rolled out of the drive.

"I agree money's always a motive to consider," Davis continued, "but aside from the three-point-five mill in New York, the rest were trust funds and deposit boxes that hadn't been accessed within the past forty years. There's no evidence to suggest she even knew the money existed."

"Who accessed the accounts before that?"

"Forty years ago, Mrs. Ackerton would have been thirteen years old. It couldn't have been her."

"Still," Janson turned the car south onto Ocean Drive, "money makes people do things you wouldn't expect them to do."

Davis seemed to consider it. "But Ackerton had his own money. He didn't need hers."

"Ackerton was rich, but you said there could be as much as a billion dollars in those accounts. Can you conceptualize that amount of money? I can't. From my perspective, that bumps his missus from just rich to wealthy. There's a difference, you know."

"The boxes could be empty, and they might not even be hers."

"But you found them, right? There must be some link or you wouldn't have run across anything." Janson started to wonder. "How did you find those accounts, anyway?"

"That's where the gray area comes in."

"Gray area?" The road curved ahead onto Southern Boulevard. Janson followed it over the intracoastal bridge.

"You remember the crank calls on the tip line?" Davis's body language was screaming discomfort.

Janson braced himself for the rest. "Yeah."

"Using the alias I found in New York yesterday, and after checking the more reasonable leads first, of course..."

"Yeah," he repeated.

"I did a few bank searches in the cities the people claimed they'd seen her in."

"So if some geriatric said he saw her once at a night club in Chicago in the fifties, you checked area banks for her name?"

"Actually, it was Detroit in the fifties."

Janson shot him an irritated look.

Davis responded quietly, but with conviction. "There was at least one account in each city, under some combination of the names Jane, Catherine, and Marie with the last name of Williams or Dougharty."

"Marie Dougharty was the alias you found through DMV in New York, right?"

"Yeah. I assumed at first she'd probably gotten the license for the same reason most teenagers get fake IDs."

"To drink."

"Right, but think about it. She would have had to walk in and take the driver's test personally for DMV to have her picture archived. The license was issued in 1963, showing a birth date of 1938."

"So she lied about her age."

"No way can I believe an eleven-year-old could pass herself off as twenty-five."

"Good genes, maybe? Hell, I don't know. Everyone we've spoken to said the woman didn't look a day over thirty."

"Yeah, and she could probably get away with that at fifty-three, like her birth certificate says, but at sixty-three? No way she could pull off thirty in her sixties. And then, there's the pictures."

There was more? "What pictures?"

"Tell me something, Janson, how long you been married?" Davis shifted in his seat as Janson turned left onto Dixie Highway.

"Me? Almost thirty years. Why?"

"You got photo albums? You know, scrapbooks, family pictures?"

"Yeah," where was he going with this? "The wife is always snappin' pictures of the kids. I imagine she's got a ton of them. What's on your mind?"

"Twenty years together and the Ackertons have nothing like that. A few pictures on the desk in the master bedroom—and I believe some of them are missing—but no albums, no family scrapbooks, nothing."

"Well, they had no children. Plus, the walls of that house were covered with photographs."

"But none are portraits. Ackerton's a portrait photographer. Wouldn't you think he'd take a few pictures of his wife?"

"You said a few of the pictures upstairs are missing, right?"

"Right, but I'm not really sure. They had a helluva cleaning lady. Barely dust anywhere. But, even if the missing pictures were of the wife, and let's say there were three of them, that brings the total existing photo count all the way to eight."

"Eight?"

"The pictures we got from Palm Beach and Westchester DMVs, the photos of the happy couple we got from Ackerton, and I assume she had a passport?"

"Yeah, it was in the file on the kitchen counter."

"And the three missing pictures. That makes eight known photographs of someone who claims to be at least fifty-three years old."

The phone in Janson's pocket vibrated. "Hold on a minute," he said to Davis as he maneuvered into a parking spot and flipped the phone open. "Janson."

It was Griffiths. "You sitting down?"

"Yeah. You're not telling me you're quitting, are you?"

"No," she chuckled, "this is better."

Janson smiled.

The female detective continued. "I've got an Amtrak passenger list in front of me. Tuesday morning departure."

"The day after the boat trip. But Ackerton didn't bail until yesterday. Why go that far back?"

"I wasn't looking for *Mister* Ackerton."

"Oh." He looked over at Detective Davis. "What did you find?"

"A Catherine Jane Williams reportedly climbed on board at Tamarind Street downtown. She reportedly got off in New Orleans."

No fuckin' way, Janson thought. *Too much of a coincidence*. But maybe J. B. was right, or at least partially. Maybe the woman wasn't dead and the husband was tracking her.

"New Orleans?" he repeated. "Have we got a witness?"

"No, but I've got a call into the conductor on duty at the time. A Sampson Delano."

"Hang on a sec, Adrianne." Janson moved the phone away from his ear and looked at Davis. "J. B., any of the calls we get on the tip line mention a train or any of the stations?"

"Recently, or ever?"

Now there was a question. "Past couple of days."

"No." He looked decisive.

Janson brought the phone back to his ear. "Find a way to get a positive ID from Delano. I'm not jumping up and down yet. Until proven otherwise, this woman is missing, presumed drowned."

"If he's got access to the Internet or a fax machine, I'll get a picture to him."

Janson turned the key in the ignition and the engine stopped. "Good work, Griffiths."

"Thanks."

Janson opened the door and crawled out of the car. "Any news on the husband?"

"No, but I'm running his name in all the usual places."

"Can you narrow the search to look for only travel to New Orleans?"

"I'm one step ahead of you."

He couldn't have asked for a better assist on this case. "One last thing, Griffiths."

"Yeah?"

"You want a sandwich?"

"You at Havana?"

She knew him too well. He said, "Give us half an hour."

"I'm watching the clock."

He knew she would. Janson hung up his phone and shoved it into his front pants pocket.

"We goin' in?" J. B. walked around the back of the car.

"Nah, they got a walk-up window."

Davis sighed.

"Relax, it's not drive-through. This place has been a staple for a while. I'm surprised you never heard of it."

They walked through the gravel parking lot toward the sidewalk.

"What'd you hear from Griffiths?" J. B. asked.

"She said someone named Catherine Jane Williams boarded Amtrak Tuesday morning bound for New Orleans. Were any of those accounts you found in Louisiana, by any chance?"

"Um, yeah. Cash and a safe deposit box."

As they rounded the corner and approached the order window, Janson glanced at the bright detective who was at least fifteen years his junior. Could Davis be on the right track? The Ackertons were definitely up to something. Why would they change identities? Was it fraud?

"Do you happen to recall how much money was in that particular account?"

"Not the exact number, no."

That was disappointing.

"But there were only six accounts, plus the joint account she had with Ackerton in Palm Beach, all of them valued between three and forty million each."

Bingo! They'd hopefully get the truth out of the husband once they found him—and if anybody could find a needle in a haystack, Griffiths could—but in the meantime, Janson was curious as hell.

"So, Detective Davis," he threw an arm around J. B.'s shoulders as the two stepped up to the take-out window, "why don't you tell me more about this theory of yours."

CHAPTER 22

Jane is with Oliver in the courtyard. He pulls her into his arms. Kisses her. Makes love to her beneath the trickling fountain.

But they're falling. She sees him reach, but their bodies move too fast toward the ground.

And then silence.

Jane awoke wondering if she'd done the right thing in coming to New Orleans. Maybe she'd given Oliver the wrong impression by responding so quickly. Maybe she shouldn't have left so abruptly all those years ago. Maybe she should have stayed in touch after her wedding. Her reasons for leaving Oliver were selfish and immature, considering her age at the time. But what could she have done differently? What would she have become if she'd stayed here?

Daylight was streaming through the French doors overlooking the courtyard, but the angles of light, along with the aches in her back and neck, told her she'd slept longer than a few hours. As she pushed herself up to a sitting position on the comfortable sofa, she was overcome with a sense of confusion. So much was on her mind—Rand, Oliver, the knight—yet she felt a need for both rest and immediacy, as if her intuition were telling her to be relaxed and alarmed at the same time. Maybe after the grogginess wore off she'd interpret her senses more clearly.

She stood up and, locking her fingers over her head, stretched her arms and arched her back. In one deep breath, the aromas of the old city sent her back a hundred years. She smelled the produce in the markets down the street. The whiskey spilled on the floors of the saloons around the corner. The food simmering in the kitchens of the cafés filled the air with the scents of Creole and French and Spanish and Cajun fare. And the centuries of trodden earth and cobblestones that made up the wandering, ancient pathways of the Vieux Carré. It felt unreal to be here again. She retrieved a band from her pocket and gathered her hair in a ponytail. Retracing her steps from the music room, she exited the library and stumbled off to find Oliver.

He's at the computer, her mind whispered. *You remember the way.*

More French doors to the courtyard balcony were on her left as she walked gingerly along the hardwood floor of the hall. She turned left into the shadows and entered the door on her right. Oliver sat before the same computer, at the far table near the shuttered windows.

"How long did I sleep?" she called out.

"Ah, I didn't notice you come in, my dear. Let's see. You've been asleep for," he squinted at the computer screen, "twenty-two hours, eleven minutes."

"Good lord. Why didn't you wake me?" She followed the worn path on the floorboards through the rows of empty orchestra chairs.

"You were obviously weary."

"I suppose that's true, but still." Jane stood at the edge of the table near Oliver and wondered how she'd slept so long.

"You look lovely, my darling." Oliver stood and kissed her cheeks, greeting her as if she'd come for tea. "These are exciting times. I almost woke you, but I told myself there would be plenty of time for training on the airplane."

"Airplane?"

He acted like he didn't hear. "And you'll need your strength, so I let you sleep."

"My strength?" Jane's hands flew to her hips. "What are you talking about?"

"It's a lengthy journey, although nothing like the earlier days. Do you remember? Six months by sea or land from New York to San Francisco. Now, one can fly from the state of Louisiana to the coast of Italy in fewer than sixteen hours."

Not that it mattered, but Jane was sure Oliver had told her they were leaving Friday. She'd hoped to learn more about the knight before standing on his doorstep.

"We're flying out today? But you said..."

"I said we *arrive* Friday, my dear, we *leave* today. Four o'clock." He reached out and took both her hands in his. "You must be overdosed with excitement."

Was he kidding? "Are you mad?" She felt as if she were being led blindfolded into a lion's den.

"I've thought everything out already," he assured. "I could have made the trip a decade ago, when I first suspected, but I..."

...did it for you. She finished his thought.

He tightened his grip around her hands. "From the moment I met you, all my heart wanted was your happiness."

Jane gave a light tug to pull away.

Oliver held firm. "Don't pretend my confession surprises you."

"It's not surprise that draws me away."

"Then what?"

She considered her answer. Should she tell him about the hidden corners in his mind? "I feel unprepared, that's all." She decided to keep his secrets secret.

"You need to trust me. You're more prepared than you think." He released her hands and returned to his chair.

Jane knew he wanted to say more. Oliver always needed to prove himself, justify his opinion. But Jane wasn't playing that game today. "How much do you know about the knight, and how do you propose we approach him? Do you expect he'll receive us on friendly terms?"

"We mean him no ill. He'll sense that. And there's no evidence to suggest he's still the barbarian who terrorized sixteenth century Europe.

I've detected a more refined and sophisticated manner in him."

"Detected? You speak as if you know him intimately."

"I feel I do." Oliver pushed away from the computer, no longer feigning preoccupation. "I don't believe we were chosen at random. We're not strangers to him. We are more like his children."

"Children? So you're suggesting we approach him as a child would approach his father? Should we ask for a raise in our allowance or to borrow the keys to the car?"

"I'm not pretending it will be that simple. I have solid perceptions of the man, but there are still a good many things I'm uncertain of."

Jane dropped onto an office chair and wheeled up to the man who planned to lead her into the unknown. "Like what?"

"Like security, for example. The location and appearance of the knight's home in Malta is well documented, but there have never been firsthand accounts of what's inside."

"Have you considered that maybe there are no firsthand accounts because no one's lived to tell?"

"I have considered that, yes, but what is there to fear? We're immortal. If we're successful, we'll be freed from the uncertainty. We'll move forward with renewed purpose and live, as they say in children's tales, happily ever after."

"And if we fail?"

"Our sorrows will be erased either way."

Yes, Jane thought after a pause, she supposed they would.

Oliver ran his hands through his hair. "What do you cry for most in this life, sweet Jane?"

How many times had she asked herself that question? "How many answers do I get?"

"Ha, I'm afraid only one, my dear." He swung his feet onto the table and crossed his ankles. "Maybe your weariness comes from the fact that you expect too much."

"First and foremost, Oliver, I want to know who I am. *Why* I am. That alone could make the running bearable."

Oliver tightened his grasp on her folded hands. "And what if the knight were able to do more than explain? What if he could change the physiology of things? I have to assume if he can create, he can *re*-create."

If Oliver was right and the spell could be broken, what might be the consequences? How much time would they have before death caught up? Would the clock begin where it ended? Or would nature somehow make allowances for time served?

But what was she thinking? "Forgive me, Oliver, but I'm still finding this hard to believe." She scooted her chair back an inch. "I know you believe it, but you've based your entire profile of this knight on information compiled from supposed vampires, who communicate with each other on Internet message boards."

"That's how it started, yes, but my certainty is derived from more than what I've found on the computer screen."

"What do you mean?"

"I *feel* he's there. I'm sure you can, too, if you try. Close your eyes and relax."

"Why?"

"Just close your eyes. You need to believe."

"This is silly." But still, she closed her eyes and lay back in the chair.

"Picture a man with dark hair and olive skin."

Antonio Banderas. "Got it." This was easy.

"Jane, dear, you have to be silent. Concentrate."

"Sorry." *Being silent.*

"This man stands on the hill of battle. He wears a chest plate and helmet. His cape is crimson red."

A man with olive skin on the hill of battle.

"He holds his sword high as a sign of victory."

It's easier, Oliver, if I look in your mind.

"Malta's enemies have been defeated again."

Blood drips from his sword into puddles at his feet.

"Now he is in America."

In our time.

"There are no more battles to fight. His armor is gone."

He wears black to mimic the undertakers. The sidewalk creaks from the weight under his boots.

"He wouldn't be a tall man."

Unless he possessed the ability to appear otherwise.

"Yet his presence casts a shadow…"

…of fear…

"over every living thing."

They want to cry out, but the feeling has left them, and they can't remember what happened. What had happened to her? *But, he's not there in our time he's here in this time. Wearing white—his face is the same—preparing Casa Vienna for the arrival of his queen.*

He's in Malta.

Jane snapped to and screamed. "How do I know that?" She reached out and grasped Oliver by the shoulders. "How do I know where he is?"

"Then you believe?"

"Not so much in the hills of battle and all that, but I saw him, Oliver. How did you know that would happen?"

"I didn't. Not for certain. I only remembered how keen your focus was. How strong your intuition. I was sure you would get a sense of him as I had." *But I also hoped you would see more than I.*

"What did *you* see?"

"A figure." Oliver's face went pale. "His face was unclear, but I felt I'd seen him before."

Jane understood. "How did you know he was in Malta?"

"I saw a castle." His color was returning. "When I noticed that the pattern of immortals pointed to the Mediterranean, I scoured resource books and the Internet until I came across a thirteenth-century estate built for Count Gerard II of Armagnac…"

"Casa Vienna," Jane finished.

Oliver looked confused. "Did you get that from me just now, or did you see it in your vision of him?"

"I didn't hear it from you."

"I knew it." Oliver stood and skirted Jane's chair to stand near the window. He looked toward it, as if he were watching the street below. "Some immortals are stronger in telepathic ability than others, and I knew you were one of the more gifted." He continued, intentionally not speaking aloud. *What else did you see?*

"Nothing." She wasn't ready to surrender all her cards to an obsessed man.

"We'll work on that, but first," Oliver spun on his heel and clapped his hands together. "I'll need to get your photograph before we leave."

"Oliver, this immortal may not be as accommodating as you've made him out to be. There is evil in him." She couldn't hide everything.

"Of course there is. There is evil in all of us." Oliver paced to a large wooden hutch against the wall and opened the cabinet door. "He is powerful enough to grant immortality. One doesn't wield that kind of power without consequence."

"But if we have to fight him..."

"Fight him?" he interrupted, removing a Polaroid camera from the shelf and closing the cabinet door. "One doesn't fight the Maltese Knight. He's survived for five centuries, and likely for good reason."

"So you would rather die than defend yourself?"

"Why would I defend myself from death? Nothing alive is guaranteed eternity, my dear. Everything dies. Would you step over here, please?" Oliver pulled a string hanging from a tube-like case attached to the wall and produced a white screen. He motioned for Jane to step in front of it.

She stood and moved toward him. "What is this for?"

"Your passport. It may be faster to travel in these times, but it's considerably more complicated."

"Under what identities will we travel? Mr. and Mrs. Oliver Chatham?"

"However did you guess?" He smiled and pulled her elbow. "Stand here."

"Isn't this dangerous?"

He stood five feet away and brought the camera's viewfinder to his eye. "How dare you doubt me. Who did you think was supplying your identification all those years?" He pressed the button—*flash!*—and an undeveloped photograph slid out from the bottom of the camera.

"I know, but a passport? This is serious, Oliver. I can't be detained now. A passport is delicate work. You can't slap one together in an afternoon."

"An afternoon? Ha! Five minutes, tops."

"What if we're caught by airport security? Wouldn't it be better to simply stow away?"

Oliver waved the Polaroid image in the air. "We've been doing this for years."

"So let's say we make it to Malta and find DeSain. What happens after..."

"You said his name." Oliver's face was whiter than before. The camera hung loose from his fingertips.

"His name? You must have told me." *He did. In his mind.*

"I didn't. His name was never clear. Not to anyone."

He told the truth, but yet...he knew more. Something guarded that part of his mind. She had an idea. "I need to know how you hide your thoughts from me."

"But I do no such thing."

"You do, Oliver, you always have, and I feel it's important I learn how, too."

"For what purpose? Not to hide anything from me, I can't read minds as you do."

"I can't see every mind, only those who've grown familiar, like you and..." *Like Rand.* But that doesn't apply in this case, does it?

"How then," he challenged her, "if you're not able to read minds, do you explain your sudden knowledge of the Maltese Knight?"

"I can't." And she couldn't. "Which makes it that much more important for me to learn to hide my mind. I'll not face this man defenseless."

"As I said before," Oliver, regaining his composure, placed the camera back in the cabinet, "we'll have plenty of time to discuss this on the plane." He regarded the spit-out photograph in his hand, declaring it, "Perfect!"

"Do you feel like Dorothy in *The Wizard of Oz?*" she asked.

"Huh? Oh, yes, I remember," he replied. "You mean the part where she starts her journey down the yellow brick road?"

"No." Jane walked to the shuttered window and wished she could see what Oliver had seen through it earlier. "Dorothy was singing and skipping, free of care when she began her journey. I feel, instead, as Dorothy felt when she and her friends were trapped by castle soldiers in the guardhouse atop the fortress wall. With nowhere to go but to stand face-to-face with the inevitable."

"We've overcome adversity before." Oliver crept behind her and slid his arm across her shoulders. "Think of Seattle."

"The city burned to the ground!"

"But you and I were okay."

"That's not the point, Oliver." Jane squirmed from his arm.

"You and I will go before this man and ask what our hearts desire. What happens after that can only be better than the lives we have now."

As fantastical as it all seemed, Jane knew there was no other path to follow at this juncture. It had been predetermined long ago. She could feel it now, as she would an undeniable itch.

"Besides," Oliver continued, "if you feel so much like Dorothy, my love, it might be good to remember Dorothy won."

Jane slumped into the chair near Oliver's computer. "When you and I come face-to-face with the inevitable, Oliver," she paused, thinking of an evil knight in a Maltese castle, "I don't imagine a pail of water will be enough."

CHAPTER 23

SEATTLE, WASHINGTON TERRITORY – JUNE 6, 1889

"I used to hate being near the water," Jane told Oliver as she guided him along the boardwalk of Commercial Street's east side. "The smell of the river scum and vulgarity of the dock workers made my stomach turn."

"Then why suggest we walk this direction?" Oliver asked.

She smiled, thinking about the walks with Eddie to see her father. "I don't hate it anymore."

She'd questioned herself about her decision to meet him at his hotel, but she enjoyed his company. Even the Seattle weather was dry and agreeable. Remnants of the previous night's rain were evident in the dirt streets and along the shaded storefronts, but the sun had shone bright all morning. A blue sky hovered above. Around them, women and businessmen took advantage of the break in the weather. Before them, the waters of Puget Sound shimmered. With snow-covered Mount Rainier standing tall in the distance beyond the misty foothills, the city looked as serene as an Old Master's painting.

"I assume your hatred of the water stems from Sacramento. Didn't you like it there?"

"No." No hesitation. "I never wanted to leave Philadelphia. Of course, I hadn't a choice at the time. Eddie liked it, though."

"Your brother?"

"Yes. He liked everything about the river, but especially its access to the sea. He told me once he dreamed of sailing away. Before he died."

"Oh, I'm sorry." Oliver stopped and grabbed for her hand. "How...I mean, what happened?"

She thought about pulling her hand away, but didn't. Instead, she let herself look at him. His soft brown eyes and hair. The dimples she knew lay in hiding, waiting for his smile. In the midday sun, she could almost remember how much he'd stirred her heart. Once upon a time.

"Smallpox," she said, and then she did pull her hand away. "He was seventeen and one of the last cases in the city."

"But there was vaccine."

Jane resumed her pace along the walk. "Supplies had run out. A shipment from San Francisco was delayed. Eddie was dead by the time it arrived."

"I...I'm so sorry."

Commercial Street ended at the rail yards, flanked by manufacturing warehouses and mills. It was June, prime building season, and the district was a blur with activity. Jane stopped on the edge of the last boarded walk and breathed in deep. With the brackish waters of the port to their right, the air reminded her of Sacramento. And Eddie. And her father. She'd hated it there, that much was true, but it had also been the last place where she'd felt whole. Maybe under different circumstances—if she'd not lost her family or if she'd gotten married—she could have grown to love California. Maybe she only hated it because she'd been left alone.

"Oliver?"

"Yes."

She turned to face him. "What made you leave Sacramento without telling anyone?"

"Oh. I was called away. Family emergency back east."

"So suddenly?"

"I received a letter requesting my immediate departure. I packed quickly and left the next morning. There was no time."

Something didn't sound right about his explanation, and Jane couldn't shake the feeling that Oliver was knowingly deceiving her. "You couldn't send word after you'd arrived in the east?"

He adjusted his hat and fumbled with the buttons on his coat. "I wouldn't have known what to say. We'd only just met. I didn't want to presume that you felt… Anyway, the longer I waited, the more difficult it got." Was it shyness, or was he hiding something?

"I would like to have heard from you."

"You're hearing from me now." He smiled. And there were the dimples she'd remembered. He removed his hat and held it with both hands at his waist. "Is it too late to pick up where we left off?"

"That's absurd," she laughed and turned to walk back toward the city center and Oliver's hotel.

"Is it?" He followed her.

"A great many things have changed since I was a teenager being courted by a young accountant."

"Things have changed for both of us."

"Indeed. Lou told me this morning how you made the Inn your first stop in Seattle." She speeded her pace.

"It wasn't like that. I thought it was a saloon."

"Bad directions from the hotel?" She looked back as he kept up behind her. "Last night, you made it sound as if you were accustomed to patronizing establishments such as the Inn."

"Please, Miss Dougharty…I mean, Jane."

"Shush!" She stopped and turned, her finger pointed at him. "Don't say that name again."

"You're right…Marie…my apologies."

She looked around briefly. Thankfully, no one familiar was within earshot. "No harm done. But tread carefully, Mr. *Chay-thum*."

Oliver replaced his hat and bowed his head sheepishly. Jane thought of how much he looked like an adolescent who'd just spoken out of turn amid a group of adults.

They walked the remaining two blocks in silence, through the bank district and back to Mill Street and the hotel. Jane still had so many questions, mostly concerning the *condition* she and Oliver appeared to share. After his comment the previous night about "benefits," she was anxious to learn what more he knew. However, the open streets of downtown Seattle didn't seem the place to discuss the matter.

"Would you like to come inside?" Oliver asked, standing near the front step of the entrance to the Occidental.

"I shouldn't. We might be seen."

He broke into his sheepish look again. "Pardon my confusion, but why would you be concerned with what people think when you operate a house of prostitution?"

A group of men in dark suits exited the hotel. "Good afternoon, Ma'am," a portly man with a cane nodded his head and winked. "Fine day for a stroll."

"It is indeed, Mayor, gentlemen," Jane answered. She nodded to each of the men as they tipped their hats. They walked around the corner up Mill Street and out of sight. She returned her attention to Oliver. "The clientele of the Queen's Inn is exclusive. There's a certain propriety that must be maintained."

"But that shouldn't interfere with your personal life."

"The Inn *is* my life."

"Then it's still unclear to me why'd you'd worry about others' perceptions when they already know you're a whore."

"I am *not* a whore, nor have I ever been." Her heart rate quickened. "If a whore is all you believe me to be, then our business here is finished." She stormed away in the direction opposite from where they'd come.

She heard him call after her to wait, but didn't look back.

The favorable weather, with its cool breeze and uncharacteristic sunshine, likely played a part in the increased traffic along Front Street. Mothers with small children weaved through the merchants along the boardwalk. Horses and loaded carts lined the street. Jane bore through without regard for familiarity, her mind racing with the issues of her situation.

Oliver caught up as she crossed Columbia Street. "Forgive me." He was close behind her. She didn't stop. "I meant no offense."

As a young man, Oliver had been kind. Jane had cared for him, even believed that she loved him.

"Marie, please wait."

But the man he'd become was different. Beyond self-assured. He had stepped into her life after twenty years of absence and made judgments based on who he *thought* she was.

"Don't let me lose you again."

She stopped. He had nerve. "You may think I'm a rich daddy's girl turned whore, but you do so with no idea of who I am." People skirted by as they stood in the center of the boardwalk.

"I don't think that at all. It was insensitive of me to..."

"When my father died, you made me believe you would be there for me. Your promises filled my despair with hope. And then you disappeared as though I meant nothing to you."

"You're wrong. You meant everything to me."

"I've done well without you."

"You've survived."

"I've earned respect and friendship."

"But you're not happy."

"What would you know of my happiness?" Jane sensed their conversation was calling attention as pedestrians gave them a wide berth. She resumed her course north along the shops and hotels.

"I know you live in hiding. A woman with spirit such as yours can't find that satisfying."

Spirit such as mine. Does his cockiness never cease?

"If nothing else, we could learn from one another. Explore the benefits of our shared condition."

Jane was about to step onto the boarded walk in front of the Opera House, but she changed her mind. Her pale blue dress twirled about her in the sunlight as she turned to face Oliver. "We may share the same disease, but that alone does not make us allies."

"Then rid me of my ignorance and tell me all there is to know about you." As he had earlier, he removed his hat and held it to his waist. His eyes squinted against the sun. "The first time I saw you, you were...unlike any other. I was speechless."

The doors opened to the Opera House and attendees of the matinee filtered out onto the streets. Oliver took Jane's arm and led her away from the crowd into the shade of the building.

"We can't change what's done," he said.

Why was she still listening to him?

"Don't you think we've been reunited for a reason?"

It did seem coincidental, but these things happened.

"I can show you how to live without fear and you can teach me how not to insult beautiful women."

She refused to even hint at a smile.

As the matinee crowd dwindled, Jane noticed an older gentleman who'd stepped outside the general flow of traffic. He stood facing in their direction, a quizzical look on his face.

"That man there," she nodded, "is staring at us."

Oliver turned. "What can we do for you, sir?"

Sunlight reflected off the white of his beard. His head straightened, but the old man said nothing.

"I said, is there anything we can do for you, sir?" Oliver walked toward the man in the center of the street.

"I know her," the man said, pointing at Jane. Oliver halted. "I know you." The old man took several steps closer. "Dougharty was your father. You're that witch woman."

Jane consciously held her expression. "Beg pardon, sir, but I believe you've mistaken me for someone else."

The old man squinted. "No mistake. I know you. I worked with your father on the rails. Sacramento. Sixty-seven or sixty-eight."

"My father was a Frenchman, sir, who never saw America." Jane had been recognized in the territories before, but she was beginning to believe this man wasn't going to be deterred.

"Mister," Oliver interjected, taking the old man's arm, "I believe the lady wishes to be left alone." He attempted to lead the man away, but the man shook free.

"Oh, I know you. You're the one they said found a potion to keep from gettin' sick or dyin.' Holed up in that house alone. Never came out. A witch, they said you were."

"That's enough, mister," Oliver grabbed him again.

The old man looked up at his captor. "You let loose, boy, or... Wait. I remember you, too." His finger pointed accusingly at Oliver's face.

"I don't know what you're up to, old man, but I suggest you get back on your way."

"You're that kid from the bank. The one they sent with Stanford that day to the Dougharty house."

Oliver looked at Jane. "Miss Marie, why don't you run on ahead. I'll catch up." He nodded toward the boardwalk. Jane shook her head, determined to stay.

"You're like her, aren't ye?" The old man was persistent. "Don't remember me, do ye? Norton's the name. I rode in from camp the day Dougharty died. I went with you and the chiefs to inform the children. I may be knockin' on sixty, but a man never forgets faces like that." The old man looked at each of them. "You're both the same now as you were then."

Oliver let go of the man. "The lady and I are taking leave of you and your delusions." He walked to Jane and offered his arm. "We need to get out of here."

She took his arm and turned away from the old man.

"Demons." He called out from behind them. "You don't belong here."

Jane and Oliver stepped onto the Opera House boardwalk. The sound of a gunshot startled them. Screams erupted from the afternoon crowds.

"Run," Oliver commanded.

Jane grabbed the hem of her dress and, clutching her handbag with the other hand, bolted across the boarded walk, dodging people who now scurried in every direction. Beyond the Opera House, she ducked into one of the shops. Oliver followed close behind and shut the door.

"Hey," came a voice from the rear of the room. "What in hell's goin' on out there?"

"There's a madman in the streets," Oliver told him. Potent smells of turpentine and paint filled the air. "Is there a back door?"

"Uh, yeah." The man in the smudged apron pointed. "Down that hall."

"Much obliged." Oliver grabbed Jane's arm and hurried past the small shop's work benches and desk. The hallway turned left. Doors opened onto both sides. "It must be this one," he said, grabbing for a knob on the right.

"Oliver," Jane gasped, "you've been shot." A hole, bordered in crimson, had appeared in Oliver's coat below his right shoulder blade.

Oliver craned his neck to look. "It's not the first time."

The door of the paint shop opened behind them. "Demons! I saw you run in here," the man's voice bellowed.

Oliver turned the knob and opened the door. Steps leading down into semi-darkness appeared before them. The door wasn't an exit. "No choice," Oliver whispered. "Hurry."

Jane descended quietly, careful to avoid each step's center, the areas most likely to creak. Her eyes adjusted as she reached solid ground. They found another hallway, this one lit by small windows set close to the ceiling.

"Which one?" She whispered to Oliver when he'd joined her. As above, doors lined both sides of the long hall.

"The one at the end." Oliver pointed.

Her sense of direction now impaired, Jane hurried along the dank hallway toward the door. Footsteps and shouts overhead told them the old man had not given up the chase.

Oliver opened the door. Light from the high open windows flooded the room, as did the pungent odor of wood shavings and varnish. A half-dozen men looked up from their work.

"Who are you?" one of the men asked. Wood cabinetry of all sizes and degrees of completion filled the space.

"And what's a woman doin' here?" another added.

"Please," Oliver's voice was low, his finger placed over his lips, "keep quiet and don't call attention. We're attempting to flee from a lunatic."

"Lunatic, huh?" The first man spoke again with no attempt to quiet himself. "Was that the shot I heard a minute ago?"

"Yes," Oliver pleaded, "and we don't want him to follow us, so please. Sshhh."

"But you can't..."

The worker's statement was cut short by the distant sound of a banging door. The old man's voice echoed down the stairs and along the hallway walls. "Nowhere to hide, Demons. Get out or I'll send you back to Hell."

"What do we do?" Jane whispered, clutching Oliver's arm with both hands.

"He can't hurt us, but the others..." Oliver looked around the room. "Quick, hide here behind the door." Oliver ushered her behind the open door of the shop. The sounds of heavy footfalls traveled down the steps at the end of the hall. "Just sit tight. We'll be fine." She wasn't sure if he was right, but she obeyed.

Oliver scattered the men about the perimeter of the room, then placed himself in a position of full view from the doorway. "Old fool," he called out. "Your demon awaits."

Shuffling noises came from the hall. Then something like the sound of snickering. "Ah ha! You admit what you are, then."

"If I am a demon, then why should I be afraid of the likes of you?"

The man reached the open door. Jane looked at Oliver. His eyes were cold and fixed on the doorway. From the opposite side of the door, she could hear the deep rasp in the old man's throat with each breath.

"I am a Christian who walks the holy path of righteousness. God has no place in His kingdom for you or your witch. And where is she, anyway? Did she conjure up a smoke screen and leave you behind?"

"Jesus Christ," Jane heard one of the cabinet workers say. "The man *is* a lunatic."

"If you men there are cavorting with these unholy creatures, I'll be sending you to Hell with them."

"They're innocents in this." Oliver stood firm. Unafraid. "What does your almighty have to say about murdering innocent people?"

"You're a smooth talker, you are. Devil's talk. I'll bet they've got that witch over there with them. Hidin' her. Doin' her biddin.'" The man stepped forward. Jane could see now that his pistol was raised at Oliver.

"You ain't right in the head, ol' timer," a worker spoke up.

"It's *them* that ain't right. That demon and his witch." He was gesturing with the gun. "You men watch. When he falls, he'll turn into the dark soul he really is. Right before your eyes." The man cocked the gun. Jane couldn't watch any more.

She shoved the door with both hands. The gun went off. Norton went sprawling into a nearby work bench. Oliver lunged for him. Jane searched quickly for something heavy. Spotting a long carpenter's lathe leaning against the wall, she grabbed it and turned. Oliver's hand was wrapped around the old man's wrist. He was struggling to remove the gun. The shop workers backed away, stunned. She swung the lathe over her shoulder and pulled it forward quickly, landing the strike across the old man's back. Oliver jumped aside. The gun dropped. The old man swayed, took two steps sideways, and fell against the stove at the center of the room. He clutched his chest with one hand as his body slid to the floor. The other hand brushed a pot simmering on the stove. His hand fell. The pot teetered. Then tipped. Flames shot out through the small opening in the wood-burning stove.

"Quick," shouted one of the men, "put it out. The glue pot's burnin.'" He rushed to smother the flame with shavings and chips from the floor.

Oliver hurried to Jane's side. "We need to go."

"And leave these people like this?"

"They've got things under control. When the old man wakes up, they'll see that he's taken to jail."

"Move," shouted a stocky blonde man who pushed past them. He hoisted a pail over the flames.

"No!" Jane didn't know whose voice rose above the scuttle.

Flames jumped into the air and cascaded down the sides of the stove and onto the woodchip-covered floor.

"Oliver!" She couldn't believe her eyes.

"We've got to go now."

"But we can't leave him."

"He's already gone." Jane looked down and saw Norton's body was now engulfed in flames. "The wind through those open windows will spread this faster than we can run."

Oliver grabbed her arm and ran to the door. The men who had tried so desperately to put out the small fire fled past them. Smoke filled the hallway and staircase. It billowed out around them as they exited through the alley door behind the workers.

"This way." Oliver clasped her hand. They hurried behind the Opera House and didn't stop until they'd put three blocks behind them. At Cherry, they slipped back onto the main street and crossed to the west side.

The crowds of people who had filled the boardwalks of Front Street were now slowly gathering near the north end of the area locals referred to as the Denny Block. Smoke poured from the basement and first floor windows. Through breaks in the crowd, Jane saw flames licking at the outside of the wood-framed building. Shouts of "Fire!" and "Get the fire department!" rose from the chaos.

"What do we do now?" Jane asked.

"There's nothing we can do. Unless you've a water hose under that dress."

"This is no time for jokes. A man just died in there and we're responsible."

"He was close to death, anyway, and obviously a danger to society."

"He knew us, Oliver."

"You're wrong there. He didn't know us. He thought we were demons. The man was out of his self-righteous mind."

"But that was no reason to kill him."

"I'm not the one who knocked him into the stove."

That was an accident, Jane thought. "I was protecting you."

Oliver remained unaffected. "He couldn't hurt me."

"But he shot you." She grabbed his shoulders and spun him around. "The hole is right here in your coat. You've been wounded."

"It will heal."

"This is the exact kind of thing I left California to avoid. Is there nowhere in this infernal west where a person can hide?"

Oliver was without emotion.

"How can you be so nonchalant?" she demanded.

"Because I know it will heal." It was Oliver's turn to grab Jane by the shoulders. "Listen, his bullets won't harm me. Nor will they harm you, if we indeed share the same condition." He spoke slowly, as if to a child. "The wound will disappear. It's happened before."

"Oh!" Jane clenched her fists and paced in a circle. "What am I to do? I can't stay here now that an army of cabinetmakers can identify me as a murderer."

"It wasn't exactly an army."

"Shut up! You with your high-headedness and disregard for human life."

"What would you do, then, turn yourself in and risk hanging? Have you learned nothing about your condition in the past twenty years?" Oliver finally appeared anxious about something. "You can't die!"

"I could argue self-defense, like they write in the papers and avoid the gallows completely."

"And if that doesn't work, how will you explain your failure to die to your executioner?"

The clanging of a bell sounded. Firemen were on their way. Jane looked again down the street. Thick smoke filled the air. The fire had spread to the upper floors as well as to the adjacent Opera House. "Oh my God. Oliver, look."

Oliver turned. "This isn't good."

The curious remained standing near the blaze. The rest of the afternoon crowd hurried away, shepherded by a young man in a shirt, suspenders, and fireman cap who was obviously yelling something to them.

Jane looked at Oliver. "That boy there. I can't make out what he's saying."

"He's coming this direction, so we'll know soon enough."

The young fireman walked purposefully through the center of the street. His hands were held up to the sides of his mouth to better project his words. As he neared, he grew more audible. "...spreading. I repeat, the fire is spreading. Gather your valuables and move quickly out of the city. The fire is spreading. I repeat, the fire is spreading…"

"Boy!" Oliver took Jane's hand again and pulled her to the street's center. "How far has it spread?"

"It's jumped over Marion, sir, toward Columbia. The city is being evacuated as a precaution. I'm sorry I can't say more, sir." The boy continued on his mission to warn the city. "The fire is spreading. I repeat, the fire is spreading…"

"I have to warn Lou." Jane turned to run.

Oliver wouldn't let go. "I'll get my things from the hotel and pick you up at the Inn."

"What?"

"Warn Lou, then be ready for me at the door."

"Are you suggesting we travel together?"

"I'm suggesting there's no better time to put this city behind us."

People clutching suitcases and dragging trunks were leaving the hotels surrounding them. The city was in a state of emergency.

"But…" She couldn't leave. Not for good. There were official matters to consider. "I…" She couldn't desert Lou, her partner and friend.

His grip on her hand tightened. The fire was spreading. At its heart, a man named Norton lay dead.

Oliver was hiding something. Jane knew that for sure, but what was worse? Following a man—an immortal—into the unknown, or staying to watch everything she'd built for herself here be destroyed?

"If I go with you, it must be understood that I go as a traveling companion and not a…"

"I'm not asking you to marry me," Oliver said desperately. "I only want to help you."

Did he speak the truth? Above the Seattle skyline, smoke rose to the clouds. "Fine." Jane relented.

Oliver was right. There was no better time.

CHAPTER 24

Jane stood at the top of the stairs dressed in a tan, calf-length skirt and a white, sleeveless shirt Oliver had produced earlier. "Where did you get these things?" She was speaking to the back of his head as he descended ahead of her. "Or should I ask *when*? I look like Audrey Hepburn in *Roman Holiday*."

"I have no idea to what you're referring," he said without turning around, "but you, my dear, look beautiful. Not bad for online shopping, if I say so myself. I even guessed your size correctly."

She followed him down the stairs. "You got lucky on the fit, but your sense of style is behind by fifty years." Reaching the foyer, she found Oliver standing patiently near the courtyard doors. "I mean really," she continued, "look at these shoes. And what's with the bobby socks? All I'm missing is the poodle and the look's complete."

"The what?"

"Never mind. Let's just go." She watched Oliver open one of the French doors. "Wait. Are you sure my heirlooms are safe here?"

"Perfectly."

Jane had few things to call her own. If fate allowed her to return, she hated the thought of going on without her most precious possessions. "Where did you put the shopping bag?"

"In the library. I cleared a shelf."

"What about your friends?"

Oliver's foot tapped on the hardwood floor. "They never go in there. Trust me. Can we leave now?"

"Shouldn't we call a cab?"

"Certainly not. We'll drive to the airport."

"In what?"

"The Dodge. Stop worrying and follow me."

Jane didn't stop worrying, but she did follow Oliver into the courtyard. The neglect she'd noticed throughout the house seemed to have been applied to the courtyard as well. And there was something else, too. A presence. Or maybe more than one.

"Oliver?"

"Yes?" He'd stopped to open the door to the carriage house.

"I think your friends are still here."

"My friends? Oh, you mean the boys. I'm not surprised." Oliver looked around. "Boys!" he called out. "Ozzy! Coop! We're leaving."

"Hold up," a muffled voice rang out from the furthest corner from them, under the second-floor awning.

Two images popped up from the overgrowth and made their way through the shadows toward Oliver and Jane. She could hear them arguing.

"Go that way," one said.

"No, that way," piped in the other one.

Quite the pair of clowns. The chubby one with scruffy, brown hair approached first. "Whoa, Oliver, my man, you ditched the button-flies. Where are you going in the new threads?"

Jane had been so preoccupied with her own costume she hadn't noticed Oliver until the vampire spoke. He did look rather handsome in his beige linen suit.

"We're going away," Oliver answered. "I've left instructions for both of you upstairs."

"Can we go with you?" the lean, dark-haired vampire bringing up the rear asked.

"Yeah," his friend agreed. "Are you taking the car? Why not let us drive you?"

"You're not driving," the dark-haired one said. "The last time you did we got stuck in the Arizona desert for a month."

"That was like eighty years ago."

"Don't exaggerate."

"Don't be a jackass."

Oliver stopped them. "Neither of you will be joining us. You're staying here. I need you to take care of the house."

"But, O," the chubby one objected, "can you even remember how to drive? And how will you know where to go? It's been a while, man."

"It's only the other side of the river," Oliver argued with the single-fanged immortal, "and I'm sure east and west haven't changed."

"Let Coop do it. We'll take you wherever you're going, then come straight back here."

Jane was gathering from everyone's thoughts that Oliver's last spin behind the wheel had occurred not long after the Depression.

"I'm sorry, boys," Oliver wasn't changing his mind. "This is a journey Jane and I must make alone."

"Oliver, if I might interject," Jane interrupted, "I think your friends have a point, especially if it's been a while since you've driven. Unless you'd like me to drive."

"No," Oliver said quickly, "you're my guest." He turned to the boys. "You can drive us on one condition."

"Name it," one said.

"You got it, O," said the other.

Oliver pointed his finger as if he were talking to children. "Neither one of you is to utter a word while we're in the car. Is that understood?"

"We can do that, can't we Ozzy?"

"Sure."

Jane doubted it.

"Good." Oliver said, tossing a ring of keys to the skinny, dark-haired one. "Then let's go."

Oliver opened the wooden door and motioned for the vampires to step ahead into the dark carriage house. "Ah, wait a minute," the skinny one—Coop—stopped. "What about the sun, Oz?"

"We'll be inside the car, fucknuts," Ozzy answered with obvious impatience.

"Oh, yeah."

Oliver ushered them both forward with a push. "Get in the car."

They stumbled ahead. Jane followed.

Afternoon light poured into the carriage house from the open door and through thin cracks in the walls. Jane half-expected to see an actual carriage, which had been, after all, the last vehicle she'd seen parked here. But that's not what she saw.

"This is the Dodge?" she asked.

"Yes, ma'am," Oliver said from her left. She watched as he approached the wide wooden doors leading to the street. Sliding the bar out of its locking position, Oliver shoved the double doors open, and light flooded into the carriage house and washed over the ancient automobile.

"It's a 1941 Lincoln," Oliver said as he tossed the iron bar to one side and approached her. She stepped back to admire its flawless, deep maroon finish. Obviously, it had been well cared-for, and the shape of it took her mind back. If she didn't know better, she'd swear she could hear Tommy Dorsey's orchestra playing.

Ozzy rolled down the passenger-side window and brought her back to the present. "And it's a Zephyr. Like the roller coaster at Pontchartrain."

"Does it still run?" Jane asked.

"Sure does," Coop called out from the driver seat, and the engine roared to life. "Oliver didn't want it at first, but..."

"We've told enough old stories," Oliver interrupted him, as he opened the back door and gestured for Jane to climb in. "It's twelve-thirty and we have a plane to catch." Jane crawled into the back seat, and Oliver shut the door behind her.

The black interior had an old, but not unpleasant smell. Everything inside seemed original.

"I'm impressed," she said when Oliver sat down in the seat beside her. She could tell he liked the compliment. "The computer, the phone, the television, the car. I thought for a while yesterday that you might have lost...some of your edge, Oliver." Actually, she'd worried he'd lost his mind. "Besides the Internet, of course, I was afraid you had let the world go by."

"I'm not as out of touch as you might think."

"Obviously."

Coop pulled the column shift into reverse and backed the Lincoln—or the Dodge, as Oliver had referred to it—onto Royal Street and, to Jane's amazement, parked it neatly parallel to the curb in front of the house.

"Get the doors," he said to Ozzy. "Oliver ain't got all day."

"Don't tell me what to do," Ozzy replied, stepping out of the car and into the carriage house.

"So we're going to the airport, huh, O?" Coop asked, turning in the driver's seat.

"Yes."

"Flying somewhere, you said?"

"Yes."

"Vacation?"

"If it satisfies your curiosity, then yes, vacation."

"No luggage?"

"Don't need it."

For a moment, Jane thought the intellectually-challenged man was finished. But then he asked, "Where you going?"

Oliver was obviously ruffled. "Nowhere that concerns you, now stop talking."

Jane thought Oliver's secrecy a bit strange, considering he'd professed to spend most of the past century with the two men.

"Actually," Jane jumped into the conversation, "why wouldn't our trip concern them? They're like us, are they not?"

Oliver turned to look at her. *We won't discuss it here, in front of them*, his mind was telling her.

She looked at him inquisitively, knowing he couldn't read her thoughts as she could his.

Later, his mind responded.

"Wherever it is, it must be an important trip," Coop said as Ozzy, having locked up the carriage house, climbed back into the car. "I don't think we've seen you leave the house since..."

"Never you mind," Oliver interrupted. "The agreement was that you would drive without saying a word. Now, drive."

"Okay," Coop said, shifting into first and pulling forward, "but I had to ask where you were going or I couldn't have driven you there."

"That's true," Ozzy said. "So where are we going?"

"To the airport," Coop answered.

"Across the river?"

"What other airports are there?"

"I don't know, I was just making sure you knew where you were going."

"I know where I'm going."

"Oh for Christ's sake," Oliver interjected, "would you please stop the banter?"

Part of her wanted Oliver to let the boys continue. The comic relief of their chatter was better than battling the silent fear that clouded her thoughts. As they proceeded slowly down Royal Street, Jane settled in and watched the French Quarter roll by through the Lincoln's narrow windows. A year ago, she'd shared the country's concern when New Orleans flooded in the wake of Hurricane Katrina. She'd been relieved to learn the Quarter—the Vieux Carré—had survived. It was sad that, after all the courage she had summoned to return, she was already leaving. And, depending on what awaited them in Malta, she might not get a second chance to come back.

But isn't this what she'd always expected from Oliver? She hadn't come to him for a shoulder to cry on, she was counting on him to make things better. To bail her out, like he did in Seattle when the fire started. Like he'd done in Sacramento when her father died. Oliver was her safety net. She'd gone flitting about the country, pretending she was fine and in control, when, in reality, she was still the willful and stubborn girl who expected the dirty jobs to be handled by someone else.

It was a pity it took one-hundred and fifty years to realize she'd been acting like a spoiled child.

"What troubles you, my love?" The sudden and ancient familiarity of Oliver's voice startled her.

"I'm sorry. I was just thinking."

"Are you anxious about our flight?"

"Of course, but, what waits for us at the other end is more worrisome."

"We won't let that ruin our drive, though." His eyes reminded her to keep the purpose of their trip to themselves.

"So what shall we talk about, then?"

"I think I have the perfect topic. Something I came across while answering email this morning."

"What is it?"

"Well," he scooted closer on the seat, "it seems a certain photographer in Palm Beach misplaced his wife a few days ago. I thought you might know more of the story since that's your neck of the woods." As Oliver released the bond he held over his thoughts, his knowledge of Rand and the "accident" became clear. *How did he do that?*

"What do you want to know?"

"For starters, are you sure you covered your tracks well?"

"Of course." Did he think she was stupid? "This isn't the first time I've had to disappear, Oliver."

"Yes, my dear, but it's a new age, with new technologies."

"I didn't leave a trace."

"You're sure?"

"Yes." But was she really? Oliver's persistence was forming a cloud of uncertainty above her head.

"From what I gathered on email, your picture has been broadcast on national television. You run a great risk of being identified."

Her doubt was growing. How had she not considered changing her appearance before leaving Palm Beach? "What do you suggest I do about it now, Oliver. Had you mentioned it before, I could have changed something."

It would be disastrous to come this far, to be this close, only to be discovered and denied the opportunity to find the truth. "You don't think we'll be stopped, do you?"

Outside, the steel bridge spanning the Mississippi River loomed before them. "I have an idea," Oliver said with a wry smile.

Jane hoped it was a good one.

CHAPTER 25

"We've got him." Adrianne Griffiths hung up the phone on her desk.

Janson leaned against the cubicle frame and sighed with relief. "Where?"

"I'll give you three guesses."

"New Orleans?"

His fellow detective grinned. "You got it in the first guess, Detective. I guess that's why they pay you the big bucks."

"Sure," Janson said, "and I've got the Rolex to prove it." It was after lunchtime, and Janson had just stood up from his desk to get coffee. The news she'd just given him, however, made him consider upping the ante to a bottle of Dom. "How'd you find him? And have we got someone picking him up?"

"I was browsing the manifests from Florida's major airports, specifically flights that stopped in New Orleans. The name of one of the passengers caught my eye."

"You mean Ackerton used his own name?"

"No. The one I found was David Fristoe."

Janson thought a second. "Isn't that the lawyer?"

"Uh huh." His partner's short, brown hair bounced as she nodded her head. "Turns out David Fristoe not only booked a flight from Tampa to New Orleans, he rented a car yesterday from an agency up north near Hutchinson Island."

"You spoken to Fristoe?"

"That was him on the phone just now. Safe and sound at the office. I didn't let on that I knew about the flight and the car. I figured we'd get a chance to ask him about that after we picked up his boy."

For an innocent man, Janson thought, Ackerton was doing a helluva job acting guilty. "What time's his plane get in?"

"About twenty minutes. N.O.P.D. has his picture. They're sending two plainclothes to meet him."

Janson pounded his fist against the cubicle frame. "God*damn*, it's gonna be good to get some answers." He winked at Griffiths, feeling satisfied for the first time in three days.

CHAPTER 26

Ozzy walked casually into the airport terminal with Coop, Oliver, and Jane, but he didn't let the camaraderie fool him. Oliver thought he was being clever, but Ozzy understood what was happening. Oliver was going to Malta to see the knight, and Coop and Ozzy would be left behind. Again.

Things had been this way since the beginning, when they first met DeSain. The knight paid them well and taught them much, but the Spaniards were never commissioned to do anything of importance. Never allowed to prove how valuable they could be. Oliver might have been their longest charge, but the fact remained he was only the most recent in what had become a very long chain.

"These are e-tickets," Oliver was walking ahead of them and speaking to the woman. "We can go straight to the gate."

"And you're sure these passports will get us through?"

"Absolutely." He padded alongside her as if he were a puppy.

"And I won't be recognized?"

"If you believe someone has seen you, remember what I said in the car: Use your mind to convince them otherwise."

"Oliver, I can read thoughts, but I can't produce them."

"Have you tried?"

Ozzy let the lovebirds carry-on while he used the opportunity to think more on the situation. As long as the woman was distracted, Ozzy didn't have to concentrate so much on hiding his thoughts.

It was obvious the knight considered her precious. Otherwise, Oliver wouldn't be delivering her personally and Ozzy and Coop wouldn't be here making sure he did. But why did Oliver get to deliver the prize? Why not Ozzy and Coop? They'd been loyal to the knight. Why not trust *them* with the beautiful cargo?

Coop didn't get it, but he was a moron who'd forever be shy a few cards from a full deck. Ozzy had long-ago accepted the burden of being the brains of the two, and he knew the end when he saw it. Oliver was leaving. The website would end. Another charge would come along that the knight would ask them to "look after." Round and round it went. Ozzy was tired of it.

Up ahead, Oliver stopped at a sign marked FOLLOW ARROWS TO SECURITY and turned to face his companions. "This is us, boys."

"You know your way around pretty good," Ozzy said, "for a guy who doesn't get out of the house much."

"I spent time on the website this morning. It's amazing how much you can find out on the Internet."

"You got that right, O," Coop snorted, biting his nails.

"Quit suckin' up, idiot." Ozzy slapped him on the arm.

"God, why do you have to hit me?"

"Why do you have to breathe?"

"On that note, boys," Oliver said, holding out his hand, "we'll bid you farewell."

Coop shook his hand first. "Take care, O-man. Call us when you get back and we'll pick you up."

"You've got a deal." He offered his hand to Ozzy, who knew better than to think Oliver would be back. "Come on, Oz, we had a good time, right?"

"Right." *Sure.* He shook Oliver's hand.

"I owe you both a great deal of thanks for the website and for the work you've done for me."

"Pleasure to be of service, O," Coop said. Ignorance must be bliss.

"Enjoy your trip." It was the only thing Ozzy could come up with. "And it was nice meeting you, Jane."

"Yeah," Coop added, "me, too."

They watched Oliver and Jane step into the line that led to the security area.

"Has O ever flown before?" Coop asked.

"You've known him as long as I have dumbass. No. He's never been on an airplane."

"You think he'll be okay?"

"Yeah." Oliver was going to be fine. More than Ozzy could say for Coop and himself.

"Hey, Oz, there's a Ben & Jerry's." He was pointing down the long, sky-lit corridor. "Can we get some ice cream?"

"Don't you ever get sick of that shit?"

"No fuckin' way, man. It's awesome. Can we?"

"Might as fuckin' well." They couldn't leave until they verified the plane had taken off, anyway.

Coop would have run if Ozzy let him, but they looked out of place enough without throwing up a neon sign. That was the only problem leaving the Vieux Carré. Vampires didn't blend so well on the outside.

The airport was crowded with white bread business people and families. Friday afternoon fare. Lawyers with briefcases. Corporate guys with laptops. And spoiled brat kids in designer clothes screaming at their parents to buy them something else.

"Hurry up, man, there's no line."

"I'm coming." Jesus, so much fuss over fuckin' ice cream.

"You got cash?"

"Yeah." Ozzy dug into his front jeans pocket and pulled out a roll of bills. "Here."

"A five? I'm not ordering off the kiddie menu. What the fuck?"

"You sure? You've got the act down to a tee." He shoved another bill in Coop's hand.

"That's better." He looked up at the menu. "Whaddya' think? Gobfather or Dublin Mudslide?"

"Who the hell cares?"

"Ain't you gettin' any?"

"Nah. It'll just give me the shits."

A gray-haired man standing in line ahead of them turned his head around.

"What are you looking at?" Ozzy snapped. "Go back to your paper."

The man did as he was told.

"Hey, Oz, isn't that the chick we just brung to the airport?" Coop was pointing at a television screen affixed to the ceiling in a nearby seating area.

"It's hard to tell. You stay here."

"I ain't movin'."

The vampire shuffled toward the screen, straining to hear the audio. "Where's the sound for this TV?" he asked a black woman seated near the screen.

"There." She pointed to the ceiling about twenty feet away.

"I see it." If the woman pictured on the television was Jane, and he was sure it was, that must mean the guy pictured next to her was the husband she and Oliver were talking about on the ride here. He had the face of a guy who couldn't swat at a mosquito. "Dumb mortal bastard," Ozzy muttered to himself as he stood under the speaker and watched the news broadcast.

"...after the disappearance of his wife," the woman's voice from the speaker was saying. The pictures changed from a snapshot of the couple to a headshot of just the man. "Authorities have issued a warrant for Mr. Ackerton's arrest, but they're stressing he's wanted only for questioning."

The picture had switched again, this time showing a woman in heavy makeup who looked like she enjoyed passing along bad news. "If you have information concerning this case, police are urging you to call their toll-free tip line." The number 1-800-FLA-TIPS appeared at the bottom of the screen.

"I got your tip line," Ozzy muttered, grabbing his crotch.

The newswoman moved on to another story.

Ozzy walked back to Ben & Jerry's and Coop. "You finished?"

"Hold on." Coop was standing at the counter with his hand out, waiting for the clerk to count back change. He stuffed the cash in his pocket and turned away from the ice cream shop. "What's your hurry, anyway? Oliver and the woman aren't even through security." Coop bit off a chunk from his giant waffle cone and swallowed. "Ah," he said, wincing and shaking his head, "that's such a rush."

Ozzy looked back at the spot where they'd left Oliver and Jane. There were a hundred people or more crowded into the weaving security line. Coop and Ozzy were too far away to identify faces, but Ozzy knew Coop was right. Oliver and Jane were still in the line.

Coop swallowed another bite. "Mmm, damn this is good. Want a bite?"

"No."

"Sure?"

"Yes."

"So, you wanna head out now?"

"No. Our instructions were to be certain they got on the plane and verify the plane left the ground."

"Oh. So you wanna go down to the gate then, Oz?"

"Not yet. They might see us."

"Who?"

"Oliver and the woman."

Coop stopped licking his treat and cocked his head. "But don't they already know we're here?"

"Of course they know we're here." Ozzy restrained the urge to choke him. "We don't want them to know we're watching them."

Coop had a confused look as he bit into the waffle cone. "Why don't we go downstairs or something?" He still had ice cream in his mouth. "I know, let's fuck with the guys in the passenger vans. Jump in front of 'em and stuff."

"Not today." Ozzy started meandering toward the escalator leading down to baggage claim.

"Where you going?"

"Goin' outside for a smoke."

"After that, then, you wanna go to the gate?"

"Sure."

Coop slurped at his ice cream while he struggled to keep up. "Hey, Oz?"

"Yeah."

"Why do you think he wants her?"

Ozzy stopped cold. He spun around and grabbed Coop by the neck of his t-shirt. Being taller than Ozzy, Coop stumbled as Ozzy pulled his face close. "Not here. Not now."

"Watch the Ben & Jerry's, man."

"I'm serious, you fuckin' retard, shut your mouth and mind your thoughts. She can hear us."

"All right, Jesus. Let loose, okay?"

Summoning all the bitterness and hate Ozzy felt it safe to reveal, he stared into Coop's eyes and tightened his grip. "Do you understand me?"

Coop tried to answer, but all that escaped was a strangled *quack*.

Around the pair, people were noticing the altercation.

"Leave us be," Ozzy hissed, and he watched the mortals skitter on about their business. Turning back to Coop, he asked again, "Do you understand me?" The vampire holding the waffle cone attempted to nod. It was enough. Ozzy let go and marched on toward the escalator.

•

When the plane from Tampa landed in New Orleans, Rand didn't know whether to give thanks for his hours of preparation or his luck. He decided to be grateful for both. Until he stepped outside. It had been unusually cold in South Florida, but it was nothing like the brisk fifties that chilled the air outside Louis Armstrong Airport. And Rand hadn't brought along a jacket.

"Taxi," he called, trying to flag down a car quickly to get away from the cold.

Everything had gone well in Palm Beach, except for one near setback when security asked to see the contents of his suitcase. He'd shown the man the withdrawal slip from the bank and given him his story, but the man didn't seem to buy it. Then Rand mentioned he was hoping to see a Hornets game while he was in town.

"Hornets?" the security officer had asked. "Isn't that where Jamal Mashburn and P. J. Brown went?"

"Yes," Rand had said.

"I sure miss watchin' them play with the Heat," the officer continued. "At least Mourning's back."

Rand said, "and don't forget we got The Diesel."

The two made small talk and the camaraderie got Rand through security and into the friendly skies to Louisiana. *With an ounce of preparation and seventeen tons of luck*, he thought.

"Taxi," he called again. This time, a black and white cab pulled up in front of him. He reached out his hand to open the back door.

•

"Wait up," Coop shouted behind him.

Ozzy half-listened to his companion's shuffling and complaining as they rode the escalator to the ground floor. When he stepped off the conveyor, Ozzy marched to the sliding door leading out to the pick-up area. He found a bench and sat down.

When Coop sat down beside him, Ozzy barked, "Gimme a smoke."

Coop was wiping his hand on his worn jeans. "You know you made me crush my ice cream."

"Who gives a fuck? Give me a smoke."

"What crawled up your ass today?" He was using his shirt now to clean between his fingers. "You want hand-rolled or Pall Mall?"

Now there was an idea. "Hand-rolled. Let's see if we can stop the voices in my head."

Coop dug into the pocket of his beat-up leather jacket. "Here."

"Thanks."

"You got fire?"

"Yeah." Ozzy reached into his pants pocket and retrieved a lighter.

He popped the smoke in his mouth and lit it.

"I knew the woman could hear us." Coop fidgeted on the bench beside him. "I'm not stupid, Antony."

"It's *Ozzy*, dumbfuck." Ozzy held in as much smoke as he could, but exasperation got the best of him. "Call me Ozzy." He took another hard drag and held it.

"Sorry." He was still fidgeting. "I'm just saying, I had my guard up back there. You didn't need to strangle me."

"I didn't strangle you." Ozzy blew out the smoke in rings above his head. "You want some?"

"Okay." Coop took the hand-rolled joint from Ozzy.

"I've had a lot on my mind. I don't mean to take it out on you."

Coop held his breath a few seconds. Then a few more. "You don't think I know that, either?" he said once he'd exhaled. "You're wondering the same things I am."

"That could be true, but we're not talking about it here."

Coop passed the joint back to Ozzy. "But, Oz, the woman and Oliver are getting on the plane right now. She can't read us from there. Especially not without a defense."

"We don't know that."

"Oliver's mind doesn't believe she's strong enough."

"Yeah?" Ozzy exhaled. "Oliver doesn't know half of what we know."

"Who do you think she is?"

Ozzy genuinely wondered.

"Oz? Do you think Oliver is really taking her to the knight?"

Ozzy was gazing blankly ahead and over the lanes of traffic thinking about everything and nothing in particular. Afternoon travelers were dodging taxicabs and climbing into buses. Throwing suitcases into trunks. Calling husbands and wives and children and mistresses on cell phones to come pick them up.

"Hey, Coop."

"Yeah."

"Check out the dumbfuck skinhead with the gay suitcase." Ozzy pointed with the hand in which he held the joint.

"Oh, man." Coop stood up for a better look. "Bet he's going to some fag white supremacist homo convention downtown."

Ozzy grinned, not sure which was more amusing, the skinhead or Coop's remarkable lack of intelligence. "You mean the fag fair?"

Coop bent over and laughed.

Out of curiosity, Ozzy touched the skinhead's mind. *You goin' to the supremacist homo convention, buddy?* No? Damn. But there was something else. Ozzy patted Coop on the ass. "That guy look familiar to you, man? I've seen him somewhere."

"No." Coop moved a few steps closer to the stranger. "But, now that you got me looking, I think I've seen that suitcase."

Suitcase? *Fuck me.*

"What is it, Oz?" Coop was rubbing his ear. "I got ya' too loud and clear on that one."

Ozzy jumped up off the bench and stood beside Coop. "Think of Oliver's painting, *Miguelito.* That's her suitcase. He's the fuckin' husband, man."

Hesitant to take his eyes off the man hailing the cab, Ozzy turned quickly to look up at his companion. Maybe Coop would have an idea as to what they should do next.

Coop pried his own gaze from the man and looked down at Ozzy. "We can't let him go, can we?"

"No. The police are looking for him. But, what would we do with him?"

"Maybe we should ask the knight."

The phone in Ozzy's pocket started to ring.

Coop summed up the moment in two words: "Fuck me."

CHAPTER 27

Having anticipated capture at every step, Rand grasped the cab's rear door knob, relieved to climb in and put some distance between himself and the New Orleans Airport.

"Sir!" A voice boomed over the sounds of traffic.

Is he talking to me? Rand wondered. Where was the voice coming from?

"Step away from the car, Ackerton." It came from his left.

Don't stop now, Ackerton, Rand told himself. *They'll keep you from finding Jane.* Clutching his wife's bag in one hand and pulling the taxi door open with the other, Rand noticed a tall, burly man in jeans and a tee-shirt approaching. In his left hand was a badge. In his right was a handgun pointed at Rand's head. Rand swung his arm backward, preparing to toss the bag into the seat and jump in after it.

"I'll get that, man." Someone grabbed Rand's wrist from behind and spun him around. A punk in a denim jacket and greasy hair slapped Rand's hand away from the door knob and slammed the door. The punk pounded on the cab window. "Never mind, jerk-off. Get the next one."

"Mr. Ackerton, you're under arrest." The policeman was upon them. "Get out of the way, scumbag. This man's coming with me."

Another punk, this one taller, gripped Rand's shoulder. "Sorry, officer." He spoke with authority. "The skinhead's comin' with us."

Rand watched in disbelief as the huge man holstered his gun and turned timidly away. "Who the fuck are you?" he asked the punks.

"Never mind."

"I'm not a skinhead, you know. I'm a pho...an accountant." In the skirmish, Rand nearly forgot his cover story.

"Well," the shorter, fatter one said, "which is it? A faggoty 'fo'—whatever the fuck that is—or an asshole accountant?" His breath could halt the progress of time. "And what you got there?" The punk reached for Jane's suitcase.

"Stop," Rand shouted, "I'll call the policeman back."

"Call 'im." The punk stepped back and extended his arms in a nothing-up-my-sleeve fashion. "Go ahead. Let him go, Coop." The taller one released Rand's shoulder. "Call for the police, Mr. Pansy-Ass Suitcase."

Rand did the best he could not to show his aggressors he was afraid. But his breathing was hitched. His hands were shaking.

"Call 'em. Oh, better yet, I'll do it for you." The short, fat one in the denim jacket turned around and cupped his hands around his mouth. "Hey, police! Yo, police over here."

"Stop it, asshole. That's enough. What do you want?"

"What'd you call me?" he stepped close. His friend brought an iron grip back onto Rand's shoulder. "Don't think I can't kill you, motherfucker, because I can." The tall one made some kind of hissing noise and bared his teeth.

"Jesus," Rand tried to move back, but the man's hold was firm. "Who the fuck are you people? Is it money you want?"

"Oh, you've got what we want." The short one's face was inches from Rand's.

"I'll give you a hundred dollars to move the fuck on and leave me alone."

The short one laughed. Seemingly on cue, the taller one snorted along. "A hundred dollars, he says, Coop. What do you make of that?"

"I'd say he's stiffin' us, Oz."

"Coop says you're stiffin' us offerin' only a hundred bucks." His breath was foul, but Rand was unable to pull away. "We think you got more."

"Three-hundred then. Take it or leave it." Were they buying this? He looked into their criminal faces. "That's all I have."

"You're full of shit. There's close to five grand in that case."

How would he know that? "Three hundred is my offer." Rand almost wished the police would come. And why wouldn't they? The fat fucker had screamed loud enough.

"Nobody's comin' to save you, if that's what you're thinking."

"How the hell would you know what I'm thinking?" How the hell *did* he know?

"You don't want the police."

"Why wouldn't I? Isn't this attempted robbery?"

"Actually, no. More like, um, robbery in progress, I think. Don't you think, Coop?"

"Yep. 'In progress' sounds better."

"Yeah, anyway," the short one grabbed Rand's other shoulder and snatched the suitcase from his hand. Rand hadn't even felt a tug. Before he knew what was happening, the punks shoved him hard onto a concrete bench. "Let's cut the bullshit, okay?"

"Don't damage the case. I'll give you anything you want, just please don't damage the suitcase. It belongs to my wife."

"Wife? Did you hear that, Coop? Now we're getting somewhere."

Rand was amazed no one was running to his aid. Surely someone had seen the assault. And this was Louisiana. The Deep South. America's hospitality belt.

"I told you already, mister, there ain't nobody coming to help you. You're under our protection."

"Your protection?" What the fuck was going on?

"I know all about your money and all about your wife and I'm not gonna bust up your fuckin' suitcase. Although," he stepped a few feet from the bench and rubbed his chin as if he were thinking, "it's not like you can take it with you where you're going."

"What are you talking about?" Rand sat up and rubbed his shoulder. "What do you know about my wife?"

"I know you lost her. I know you're lookin' for her."

"Do you know where she is?"

"Oz?" The tall one spoke from behind the bench.

"What?" the short one answered.

"I think the plane's ready to take off."

"I know what the plane's doin', don't you think I can do two things at fuckin' once?"

"We were supposed to call, right?"

"Yeah, and I'm gonna get to that when I'm finished talkin' to the guy here, okay?"

"Where are we takin' him, Oz?" the tall one asked from behind the bench.

"Don't worry about it, Coop, I got instructions."

Rand wished he knew what the hell was going on.

•

A lovely flight attendant was walking up the aisle collecting trash when Oliver's seatmate blurted, "I've got to get off the plane, Oliver." Jane sat suddenly upright in her window seat. Her eyes appeared desperate. "Now."

Oliver patted her arm. "The safety check's finished and I believe we're readying for take-off, my dear. It's too late, but I assure you, air travel is the safest method of all..."

"No, Oliver, I'm not afraid to fly." She was looking every which way. Oliver couldn't remember the last time he'd seen Jane so panicked. "It's Rand. He's here. In the airport. We've got to get off the plane."

Oliver's briefly-quickened pulse relaxed. "Now, sweetheart, you can't believe that."

"I do, Oliver. I can't explain it, but I do."

He believed she did, but still... "How on earth would this mortal husband of yours find his way to New Orleans?"

"I know it seems impossible, but..."

"It *is* impossible," he covered her hand as it clenched the armrest, "which is why you should just sit back and..."

"I'm not sitting back." She reached down and unbuckled her seat belt and stood up. "I need to get off." Oliver pulled her down as the engines at the back of the 767 roared and the aircraft bolted forward. Gravity held Jane in the seat as the plane lifted off the ground and launched skyward.

"You see, my dear," Oliver whispered, "it's too late."

Jane sat quietly while Oliver surveyed the heads in the plane. Finally, after several gravity-filled minutes, the aircraft's PA system clicked on.

"Good afternoon ladies and gentlemen, this is your captain speaking." Oliver thought the man's voice sounded a bit tinny, but there was enough confidence in his tone to assure Oliver they were in good hands. "We have arrived at our cruising altitude of thirty-thousand feet, so I've turned off the seat belt sign."

Thank goodness, Oliver thought, and unbuckled the snug harness across his lap.

"However," the pilot continued, "I must ask that you keep your seat belts fastened as long as you're in your seat and thanks for flying Delta with us today."

Oliver grudgingly refastened his seat belt.

"Thank you," Jane said.

Oliver wasn't sure she was speaking to him. But who else would she have been speaking to? "For what?"

"For saving me the embarrassment of toppling end-over-teakettle down the aisle. I don't know what came over me."

"You've had a difficult week."

"I've had a difficult life, Oliver."

Oliver remembered how he'd once thought her self-pity charming. "And you think you're alone in this?"

"Of course not."

A flight attendant interrupted them. "Ma'am?"

"Do you mean me?" Jane asked the woman.

"Yes, ma'am. I have to ask that you keep your safety belt on as long as you're seated."

"Oh, certainly," Jane responded. "I'm sorry." She shifted in her seat and re-attached the buckle.

Oliver watched the attendant walk forward and around the thin wall into the galley behind the cockpit. A long time ago, he would have enjoyed spending *quality time* with someone like that. But soon—he looked at Jane—he would have all he ever wanted.

She smiled at him.

Things were working out better than he could have imagined.

•

Rand's captors had been arguing for several minutes while Rand sat on the bench rubbing his sore shoulder.

The thinner man, now seated next to Rand, seemed uneasy with something his partner had said earlier. "You still haven't explained what you meant, Oz, when you said we had instructions. Did the knight know we'd find this guy? You said the phone connection was bad."

"No I didn't." The fat, dirty blonde stood several feet away puffing on a joint.

"Yes, you did, man. Right after it rang, remember? Before we grabbed the husband. You said the connection was bad and you couldn't hear what he said."

The fat one lurched toward the bench and shouted at his friend. "Just shut up for now, okay? I know what to do. Christ on a fuckin' cracker."

Rand grew more confused than frightened. "Could someone please tell me what the fuck is going on here?"

"Your wife just left," the fat one said.

"How do you know that?" Who the fuck were these people? "What do you mean 'just left?'"

"Her plane took off a few minutes ago. It's right there." He pointed up, but Rand saw nothing. "And I know because I know."

"What kind of cryptic bullshit is that?" Rand stood, aware of the pain surging down the back of his leg from the spot where he'd connected after being thrown onto the bench earlier. "How do you know my wife? How do you know she's on that plane? And where is it going?"

"All in due time, my boy. Patience is a virtue, you know."

"Fuck your patience," Rand shoved the punk in the chest, "and I'm old enough to be your father, so take your 'my boy' shit and shove it up your doughboy ass."

The punk's round face grew dark. "You wanna throw down? Is that it, mortal?" With lightning speed, he grabbed Rand by the throat and squeezed. "All full of piss over some fuckin' woman you can't ever have."

She's my wife, Rand wanted to say, but it was impossible to breathe, let alone speak.

"You belong to me now, and you know why? Because you've become a liability." He squeezed tighter. Rand's consciousness was wavering. The punk's lips were close enough to Rand's to kiss. "I am old enough to be your great-grandfather's great-grandfather, you worthless piece of mortal shit." *And whether I kill you here and now or feed on you later makes no difference to me.*

Rand wasn't sure he'd heard the last part clearly. He was busy praying for air as his confusion came full circle back to fear.

•

"You were saying, my love, that you do *not* consider yourself the only one who's had a difficult life."

"Of course not. That's ridiculous." Jane said it with conviction, but Oliver sensed she hadn't had the opinion long.

"Maybe you've set your expectations too high."

She turned in her window seat to face him. "Expectations for what?"

"Life."

"What would you know of life?"

"I've been 'round as long as you."

"But when was the last time you traveled beyond your front door? The last time you made love to a woman?"

He considered her questions, but Oliver had long ago come to terms with his reclusive tendencies. "If you define life by accounting for the frequency of sex and vacations, I think you're missing the point."

"Excuse me." A woman seated behind them leaned forward and called through the seats. "I can't hear the news report on the screen."

"Our most sincere apologies, madame," Oliver crooned through the seats. "Jane, dear," he smiled, sensing an opening, "why not give your mind a stretch and convince the passengers on this aircraft to ignore us."

She glared at him questioningly. "There are three-hundred people on this airplane."

"Go for the surrounding rows, then. Come on, I know you can do it."

"You're talking mass mind control."

"And you, with your college education, can't tell me there weren't others with that ability?"

A harsh *SSSHHHHH* came from behind them.

"Please?" Oliver smiled wider. "Relax your mind and send out a suggestion. Like we talked about in the car."

"Oh, for crying out loud." Jane looked around the first class cabin. Then she closed her eyes.

Oliver unbuckled his seat belt.

Jane opened her eyes. "What are you doing?"

"Don't mind me. Keep going." Oliver stood up.

She closed her eyes again. He spun around and climbed onto his knees in the seat so he could see the woman with the gray hair seated behind them.

"Boo!" he said.

The woman offered no visible response. He climbed over the couple who sat in the seats next to his and Jane's and jumped into the aisle.

"Hey, motherfuckers!" he called out to the surrounding passengers.

"Oliver!"

He didn't look to see if her eyes were open. "Hang on to it, Jane. Don't freeze them, just tell them to ignore us."

"I've got it, but you don't need to insult them."

"I'm trying to distract you."

"It's working."

"Are you still holding on?"

"Yes, but..."

"Good." He ambled toward the drape between first class and coach, but stopped short. "Oh, and Janie, dear."

"Yeah."

"Leave the pilot alone."

"How do I do that?"

"I don't know. I've never done this myself. But it might not be good to practice on the pilot's mind while he's flying the plane." Oliver resumed his progression down the aisle toward the drape.

"Oliver, this is stupid."

"You're the one who wanted to learn." He opened the drape and secured it with the Velcro strap.

"Learn what?"

"Okay," he ignored her, "I'm going to strip down, so don't look."

"Are you crazy? What are you doing?"

"Strengthening your mind." He scanned the sea of faces going about their business in their cramped airline seats. "Ladies and Gentlemen," he called out, slipping off his linen jacket and draping it on the back of the seat to his left. No eyes in the cabin were upon him. "What you are about to witness, is a demonstration of the *raw power* of the human mind." He had to emphasize something to add a pinch of the dramatic.

From her first class seat, Jane continued her opposition. "You've got to be kidding me. Oliver, this isn't necessary."

"Oh, but it is." Moving his hands to his shirt, he undid the top button. Half of the passengers stared forward, watching electronic monitors that flipped down from the ceiling. A child was reading a comic book in the first row ahead. He undid the next button. A man in the third row stood up to let a young woman out of her seat. She crept past him and into the aisle, then walked to the rear of the plane and into the lavatory.

Oliver slowly pulled at the cuff of his shirt. "Sing with me, Janie. Da da da, di da da da. Come on."

"You've gone mad."

"You better hang on or you'll have to explain to these people why I'm undressing in the middle of a crowded airplane."

"Don't do this. Oh, my God."

"Da da da," Oliver pulled one arm out of a sleeve, then started on the other, "di da da da."

The young woman emerged from the lavatory. Another passenger stepped in. Oliver removed his shirt and laid it on top of his jacket. "Some of you may think, Ladies and Gentlemen, that this woman here can't pull this off." He kicked off his shoes. He unbuttoned and unzipped his suit pants and let them fall to his ankles. "Even the woman herself has doubts she can stave off all your attentions." He stepped out of the pants and added them to the pile on the chair.

"This is one for the books, Oliver."

"You're not peeking, are you?" He turned to look back at her. She'd spun in her chair, facing the rear of the first class cabin, but her eyes were clenched shut.

"No," she said.

"You're dying to peek, though, aren't you?" Oliver slid his boxer briefs down past his knees and kicked them off. They landed on the laptop of a man seated in the back row of first class.

Jane started laughing.

"You *were* peeking. I knew it." Oliver watched the man pick up the briefs and absent-mindedly toss them into the aisle. Oliver's laughter joined Jane's.

"How could I not watch you make such a fool of yourself."

"Then you'll love this." Oliver skipped down the aisle toward the rear of the plane.

"You really are crazy," he heard her screaming.

He made a loop through the rear kitchen where the flight attendants were preparing to serve what looked to be sandwiches. As he re-entered the main cabin, he could see Jane far ahead, leaning on the back of her seat and laughing. Oliver skipped up the left-side aisle and back into the first class cabin.

"So," he said, standing in front of the cockpit door, "do you believe now?"

"Believe in what?" Jane fell into her seat and looked forward at Oliver in his naked glory. "That you're wild and untamed?"

"No." He waved his hands over the heads of the indifferent passengers. "That you are capable of more than you think."

"I wouldn't have believed it if you hadn't…" She stopped.

Oliver took it as a sign that she was overcome with gratitude.

"I don't possess near the capability you do, Jane. I've known it since…since… Jane?" Something was wrong. Her face had gone white. He started to approach her.

"Hey," a man seated at Oliver's right shouted, "what the hell are you doing?"

"Jane? Janie?" Oliver looked down at the man who had pushed his attendant call button. "This is no time to lose concentration."

"Rand's in trouble," Jane said, her eyes were wide and fixed forward.

"Not this again."

"Aaaahh." A woman to his left shrieked and covered her face.

"Uh, Janie. Snap out of it. Get 'em back, sweetie, or we've got a situation here." He ran forward and lunged across the couple between Jane and the aisle. "Snap out of it," he pleaded.

"He's on the screen, Oliver, look."

"I'd love to, darling, but first you need to focus on a few of our friends here."

"Get off my wife," the man under Oliver was screaming.

"So sorry, sir," Oliver scrambled to separate himself from the couple and return to the aisle.

The man stood up. "You put some fucking clothes on freak or I'll rip your dick off and shove it down your throat."

"How original," Oliver said. "Janie? Oh, Jane!" he screamed, "you wanna help out here, please?"

"Oh my God, Oliver." She'd come to. "Oh, shit. I'm so sorry."

The flight attendant he'd noticed earlier was standing behind him now. "Sir," her voice was stern as she tapped on his shoulder, "please walk calmly to the rear of the plane, sir." And then she turned away.

Oliver watched as she bent over the man who'd asked Oliver what the hell he was doing.

"Can I get you anything sir?" she asked him. The man ordered a gin and tonic.

Just like that, it was over.

Oliver walked humbly to the seat where he'd left his clothes, then he retrieved his underwear from the opposite aisle. "You scared the shit out of me. You got everyone back in check?"

"Yes. I'm so sorry, Oliver, but look."

As he dressed in the aisle, he watched the screen protruding from the ceiling. "So that's him, huh? Your husband?"

"Yes. The reporter said the police were looking for him. He's not in Palm Beach."

The report was over and Oliver was dressed. He climbed back into his seat and fastened his belt. "So he skipped town, huh? That's not going to look good to the police."

"But he didn't do anything wrong."

"The police don't know that. And what do you care, anyway? You left him, right?"

"I suppose."

"Fuck suppose. You're here, aren't you?"

"Really, Oliver, that language isn't necessary."

"Why? Does *fuck* offend your delicate ears?"

"No. It's just not necessary. I think you spent too much time locked in a room with your vampire friends."

"See, now, you're taking us back to where we started. You're insinuating that I've had no life." He pretended to be angry. "And for the record, that door was never locked."

"Still." Although the report had ended, she continued watching the screen. "Rand and I had a great life together. He should have mourned and let it go. He's jeopardized everything by running."

"Stop right there." He swiveled his torso to face her. "First, you were living Rand's life, not yours, and second, you're the one who put him in peril when you jumped in the water."

"It wasn't only Rand's life, it was mine, too." Was she starting to cry? "And he would have been safe if he'd stayed home. My death was an accident."

"Your death wasn't real."

"Right, and without a body, they can't charge him with anything."

"Good lord, Janie, where have you been? Being charged with a crime has nothing to do with whether or not there was an actual crime. It's not even about guilt or innocence. It's about evidence. And they do have a body, you know. I read about it on the Internet."

Her eyes grew wide. "That's impossible."

"They haven't identified the remains, but it's coincidental and therefore suspicious. That's all they need."

Jane hung her head. "How did it all get so complicated?"

Oliver faced the front, stretched his legs, and wiggled into a comfortable position. "What you interpret as complicated, I regard as progress."

He heard her settle into her own seat. "That's where you and I differ."

She had that right, Oliver thought.

The travelers sat in silence for several minutes, until a flight attendant interrupted them. "Would you two care for dinner?"

"I'm fine," Oliver told her. Not requiring food was something Oliver had always seen as a benefit of immortality.

"No thanks," Jane seconded it. While the attendant served the couple beside them, Jane turned to Oliver. "How did you know about the mind tricks, anyway?"

He knew the question would come. "Other immortals have similar abilities. Coop and Ozzy communicate telepathically on occasion, though I suspect a degree of their intuition comes from being together so long."

"How, for all these years, have I not been aware of this gift?"

Oliver couldn't imagine. "You always have, at least on some level. You were reading my mind a hundred years ago."

"But that wasn't control. It was more like, I don't know, maybe eavesdropping." She paused, seeming to choose her words carefully. "Manipulating the minds of others is powerful stuff, Oliver. Why do I have this ability?"

"To be honest, I don't know." He unbuckled his seat belt—*damn the pilot's warning!*—and twisted to face her. "Can you mask our conversation?"

"You don't hear that woman behind us bitching, do you?"

"You always were too quick for me."

Jane unfastened her own belt, adjusted her skirt, and turned her back to the window.

"Every immortal has some degree of mental control," Oliver said.

Jane nodded, as an alert pupil would nod to her professor. Sitting there in her sleeveless shirt with her hair pulled back, Oliver thought she could easily pass for a college student.

"Some, like me," he continued, "have only the power to block our own thoughts. Others, like you, can influence the thoughts of people around you."

"Does that mean I can touch the mind of every person on earth?"

"Oh, no. There are limitations. An airplane is one thing. An entire town is another. Plus, there are consequences to consider. For example, you could easily tell the pilot to turn the plane right now."

"Wouldn't someone on the ground notice the change in the flight path?"

"Exactly."

She seemed unsatisfied, fidgeting with her hands in her lap. "If you don't know why I have these abilities, why have you been insistent that I strengthen them?"

Another question he'd expected, but this time he'd hide the truth. "I thought you'd want to know."

"Come on, Oliver. Don't play with me." She reached into his mind.

He didn't let her in. "I believe, and it's just a theory, that we each have a purpose."

"How very theological of you," she mocked.

"I mean it. I've studied the movements of immortals for a decade, and their placement doesn't appear random."

"So what's my purpose? Do you know?"

"No." But he did, didn't he? He just couldn't reach it. "No one's purpose is clear, not even my own."

"How can that be?" She probed deeper, still trying to override the defenses of his mind. "If we do serve a purpose, how can we know what to do without being aware of it?"

Oliver stiffened. He could feel a faint pulse in his head. She was breaking through.

"What's the big secret, Oliver? What aren't you telling me?" She blinked her bright green eyes at him and cocked her head. "I'll show you mine if you show me yours." *You can't hide your thoughts from me.*

"Yes I can. I always have." He shook his head. His skull felt as if it held a million tiny bees. "Stop." Could she really dig deep enough? Should he let her? "What did you do?"

She peered seductively, like a leopard ready to pounce. "This mind thing is easy once you get the hang of it." *What is our purpose, Oliver?*

I won't tell you. He brought his palms to his ears and tried not to think.

"Come on." *It's easy. Just let me see.* She brought her fingertip to his forehead.

"I won't." *Stop.* What had he created? *What are you doing?*

Her fingertip traced an imaginary circle on his brow. "Distracting you." *Where have I heard that before?*

"Why?"

"It's me, isn't it? I'm your purpose." *At least that's what you think.*

"You're wrong."

"Wrong that it's me or wrong that you only think it is?"

I don't know. "It's not clear."

Then I'll dig deeper.

"No." The bees had become dragonflies. The sensation wasn't painful, but it made concentration impossible. Giving up, he lowered his arms, slumped in his chair, and closed his eyes.

"Is this what you wanted when you set out to teach me what I was capable of?"

I know what you're capable of. But the knight is…

"He's dangerous, isn't he Oliver? Tell me, or take down the barriers and let me see."

"There are no barriers." *I'm not strong enough now.*

"But there's more. I feel it."

"No." The flutter in his head tapered out, but he felt her probing continue as if the fingers of her mind were blazing trails. He returned to his upright position, facing forward, and opened his eyes.

"Am I your purpose?" she asked.

Oliver was silent, but it didn't matter.

"There are fragments of your mind, Oliver, that are hiding from me. Did you lock them in somehow?"

"I don't remember."

She grasped his hand and lightly squeezed. "How long have they been there?"

"Always." But she already knew that, and he didn't need to read her mind to know.

Jane sat back in her seat and turned her face to the window. "I know you would never willfully cause me harm or misfortune." When she removed her hand from his, he suddenly wished he could touch her and never let go.

"No. I'd never hurt you." He reached for the hand in her lap. Her skin was soft, just as it had been in the days when she'd returned his affections. For a second, he thought she'd pull away. But she didn't.

She continued, gazing through the window at the cloud-filled sky. "The fact remains there are thoughts tucked away in the deepest corners of your mind. Thoughts hidden even from you." She faced him again. "And they're not the same as any of the others."

"How would I ever hide thoughts from myself?"

"Maybe they aren't your thoughts."

Oliver let her comment sink in as a flight attendant rumbled a beverage cart past them. He knew the part of his mind Jane referred to, and he thought of Jane's earlier question about how immortals carried out orders without knowing what they were. *Could the knight have planted something there?*

"I don't know," Jane answered aloud, "but it might be to our advantage to decipher the information locked inside your head before we get off the plane in Malta."

As the 767 shot through the clouds toward the Mediterranean, Oliver knew in his heart she was right. Unfortunately, he felt in his bones he had made a big mistake.

DAY 5

CHAPTER 28

Standing at the foot of the Y-shaped stone staircase, DeSain gazed upward at the landing where a blood-red tapestry hung from twelve iron hooks. The coat of arms of LaCassiere. The immortal's heart stirred with melancholy as he was reminded of loyalties won and lost.

Woven into the tapestry was a golden griffin, the standard for strength and vigilance, sitting atop a soldier's helmet. Below was the family's battle shield bearing a red, ancient Maltese cross on a yellow background and bordered above by the blue and white stripes of Normandy. The symbols were supported by a dragon on the left and a lion on the right in homage to the ancestral allegiances to Gerald of Aquitaine and King Richard the Lionhearted.

DeSain knew these things because they were important in his time. As descendent of Baron Frederic LaCassiere, he had borne the family's coat of arms proudly into battle more than a dozen times, fighting first against the Knights of St. John, then fighting beside them, but always in defense of the inhabitants of Malta. Peace had taken hold in the twentieth century, but only after centuries of bloodshed. The immortal knight bowed low, both to honor his ancestors' struggle and to request their blessing. The time of the prophecy was upon them. The LaCassiere legacy would soon come full circle. DeSain stood and breathed in hard, summoning strength.

He was ready.

Casa Vienna, the medieval palace in which DeSain resided, had been his home since childhood. Its walls had grown womblike in their comfort. Its portraits and tapestries were companions. Built of native stone in the mid-fourteenth century, the fortress stood on the site of a first-century estate destroyed by war. Five-hundred years earlier, the prophecy had been spoken here. Upstairs in the Terrace Room. DeSain could not imagine a better place to witness its fulfillment.

"Forgive me, my lord." Across the vast foyer, a young man in a black tunic appeared, nervous as he stood beneath the pillared archway.

"Approach." DeSain turned to receive him, already knowing the boy had come from the kitchens to ask a favor.

The boy shuffled quickly across the floor, trying not to make noise but failing as the sound of his footfalls clicked against the walls in the massive baroque chamber. He stopped several feet from the immortal and, looking down so that his shoulder length hair obscured his handsome face, he cleared his throat.

"Yes, Carlos," DeSain said, not waiting for the boy to ask his question, "you may escort Francesca to the festival tonight."

Accustomed to his master's clairvoyance, the relieved boy merely raised his head and smiled. "Thank you, my lord." He bowed quickly but respectfully and retreated, returning to the kitchen where he worked as an assistant to the chef.

Before a family dispute in the 1700's prompted DeSain to use immortals as sentinels, he had created them as personal servants. In time he learned that if he held their minds too tightly, however, their usefulness was temporary. On the other hand, if he didn't grip tightly enough, their loyalty was compromised. So young Carlos was mortal, as were all members of DeSain's staff, including Francesca, who, DeSain imagined, would later take Carlos into her arms and between her legs. DeSain had not been blind to their yearnings. *Lucky for them both*, he thought. Sex with either was extraordinary.

DeSain glanced one final time at the tapestry, then walked rhythmically, purposefully, across the foyer in the opposite direction toward the sitting room. The echo of his boots on the smooth, stone floor reached the frescoes on the three-stories-high ceiling.

Once through the arched doorway, flanked with pillars matching those across the foyer, DeSain surveyed the room where his guests would be escorted upon arrival. It was well lit, but not too brightly, by a small blaze in the stone mosaic fireplace that dominated the far wall and a silver and crystal chandelier whose candle holders had been replaced with electronic bulbs decades earlier. DeSain stepped to the wall and slid the dimmer switch up and down.

"Perfect," he said to himself, finding the right brightness. The temperature was warmer than he would have liked, but it was comfortable. He swept his gaze around the room and across the faces in the portraits displayed on all four walls. It was good that his ancestors would be watching over the day's proceedings.

Besides the foyer, the only two downstairs rooms that were used by DeSain and his guests were the library near the hall to the kitchen and the sitting room. For reasons that were practical centuries ago, neither space had windows. But DeSain liked it that way. The soft glow in the room added warmth to the antique Italian furniture and eclectic collection of ancient statues and relics. The corners of DeSain's mouth curled upward as he thought of a children's story. *Come to my parlor, said the spider to the fly.* Hearing footsteps descending the grand staircase, the immortal softened his smile and about-faced.

"Is the room set to your liking, my lord?" Another servant, this one a slight gentleman in his fifties, addressed the knight as he crossed the foyer, clothed as Carlos had been in a tailored black tunic and pants.

"Yes, thank you, Dominic. I believe our guests will be quite comfortable here."

The servant halted, his hands clasped in front of him. "The Terrace Room is ready as well, my lord." He was careful not to make direct eye contact. "I will accompany you if you would care to see."

"I would."

Dominic turned on his heels, but waited, allowing DeSain to take the lead.

The Terrace Room, DeSain thought. *Where it began, it now ends.*

He crossed to the carved stone staircase and climbed, remembering the stormy night he had become an immortal. The night he learned his future. Arriving at the fork in the stairs, he shot a quick glance at the red crest tapestry again before ascending further to his left.

From the line of LaCassiere.

Fate could not have brought him a better woman, nor chosen a better time, DeSain thought as he reached the second floor. A long hallway, lined with marble busts and suits of armor, stretched out ahead of him. DeSain's pace quickened as he drew ever closer to the last door on the right.

Dominic's voice rang out from behind. "Will your guests be arriving on time, my lord?"

"Yes," DeSain answered, passing the first suit of armor Baron LaCassiere had worn. "I expect they'll be here within the hour."

"And the Spaniards, sir?"

The Spaniards. *Yes.* DeSain felt for their immortal minds. They were still coming. "Bring them directly here." The tall, wooden doors to the Terrace Room loomed ominously before them. DeSain's march ceased. "Plan for them to arrive approximately four hours later than our first guests."

"Yes, my lord." Dominic skirted past DeSain. "Shall I get the doors?" he asked, grasping the forged steel rings.

"Please. Oh, and Dominic,"

"Yes, sir?" He was pulling with great difficulty.

"When they arrive, show the Spaniards no hospitality. I want them uncomfortable." The ancient ghosts of the room behind the medieval doors called to him. "They're to be punished for what they've done."

"Of course."

It had been the Spaniards' simple and ignorant natures, DeSain believed, that had allowed the watchmen to serve so effectively for so long. But they were hiding something from him and, faithful servants or not, the knight had no tolerance for deception.

DeSain watched as Dominic's efforts were rewarded and the heavy doors swung open onto the Terrace Room. DeSain closed his eyes, feeling the souls of his ancestors rushing to greet him.

No better place, no better time, the ghosts whispered.

The knight took in a deep breath and smiled. Even the dead, it seemed, were anxious to finish the day.

CHAPTER 29

Standing impatiently on the curb outside Malta International Airport, Jane watched Oliver argue with a third cab driver and began to wonder if they were ever going to put the smell of jet fuel behind them.

After Oliver's brief streak of indecency, the first leg of their journey had continued for thirteen hours without incident to Barcelona. From there, Jane used her powers of persuasion to guide them through security checkpoints and onto the stiflingly hot, but thankfully brief, flight onto the island. They had arrived in Luqa at nine-fifteen that morning local time, stiff from sitting for sixteen hours but none the worse for wear, and walked directly to the taxi area. Now, bending to peer through the open window of a beaten 1970's Ford, Jane thought it surely must be past ten.

"I told you," the cab driver was hollering above the noise of traffic. "I go to Casa Vienna for no less than two-hundred dollars."

Jane straightened and tapped her traveling companion on the shoulder. "Just pay the guy, Oliver. At least he didn't say no like the others."

Oliver was fanning himself with a straw hat he'd purchased at the airport in Spain, although he wasn't perspiring as far as Jane could tell.

"I read on the Internet," he said, "that a cab ride across the main island could cost up to eighty US dollars. Two-hundred is robbery."

"Pay the man."

Reluctantly, Oliver reached into the pocket of his linen pants and produced a money clip straining to hold the wad of bills. "We're being taken advantage of, here." He counted out fifties.

"It's only money, Oliver, and we need transportation. Would you rather find a bus?"

Oliver reached through the passenger side window and handed the man four fifties. Originally, Oliver had suggested Jane manipulate the man to escape paying any fee at all, but she refused to unnecessarily rob someone of an honest wage. Even though it would have been good practice.

She grasped the yellow cab's rear door handle and jumped in, then slid across the torn vinyl seat to give Oliver room. The warm air inside the car smelled like sweat, stale smoke, and upholstery cleaner. Jane's body tingled as cells worked to recover from jet lag. It was a feeling she knew well, having traveled extensively with Rand.

Rand.

God, she missed him. He appeared in her mind, looking as he had the last day on the boat. His broad shoulders dusted with fading daylight. His quiet hazel eyes professing devotion.

"This better be a spectacular fucking ride." Oliver's rant continued as he climbed into the car. "Two-hundred dollars," he muttered and slammed the door. "You should be reported."

The driver turned to face the back seat. "You want to walk, *sinjur?*"

"Don't listen to this man," Jane instructed the driver, nudging him with her newly-discovered talent. "His social skills are rusty." Without further exchange, the man shifted the Ford into drive and pulled away from the curb.

Oliver was still ruffled, turning his hat in his hands, nervously scrunching the rim, and sneering at the back of the driver's head. "My social skills aren't in question here."

Jane tried to calm him. "This is a silly thing to get worked up over, Oliver. Besides, you've never been here before. Maybe it's a long drive to Casa Vienna."

"Long drive?" Oliver responded. "Malta's largest island doesn't exceed fifty miles across from its widest points, and we started from the center."

"Still," she said, suddenly curious as to why the driver had charged so much. "We could ask him," Jane said. "Maybe there's a logical explanation for the inflated fare."

Oliver shrugged.

The cab turned left and merged onto a cobblestone street where medieval stone churches were dwarfed by towering marble cathedrals. Side streets with shuttered windows, high balconies, and protruding business signs reminded her of New Orleans and St. Augustine, but they were narrower here, like in San Juan, Puerto Rico. And more weathered.

They're ancient, she reminded herself.

The varying architecture was stunning. Row upon row of buildings made of brick and stone were crammed together, some veiled in trailing ivy, others guarded by palm trees. She imagined this would be what ancient Alexandria would have looked like. But, Jane remembered, they weren't on a sightseeing tour.

She released her light hold on the driver's mind and asked, "Excuse, me, sir?"

"*Iva, sinjura.*"

"Why is the fee to Casa Vienna so high?"

"You're lucky I drive you at all," he said, his eyes never leaving the road. Jane couldn't place his accent, but then she'd never spoken to a Maltese local. "Casa Vienna is a *dar iswed*, a black house, *sinjura*."

Jane flashed a look at Oliver. "Does that mean it's haunted?"

The driver answered. "Haunted yes, but Malta is old. There are many spirits here." He paused, signaling another left turn. "Casa Vienna, she is evil."

"That's a lie," Oliver charged. "The Internet said nothing about evil spirits at Casa Vienna."

"Your Internet is mistaken," the driver said.

Jane could see the driver's dark eyes reflected in the rearview mirror.

He added, "The people of Malta have known the castle's secret for centuries."

"But if it's such a bad place," Jane interjected, "why aren't *you* afraid to take us there?"

The man laughed. "For two-hundred American dollars, I can forget fear long enough to drive you to the gate."

Jane considered asking the man more questions, but wondered how much truth there could be in a centuries-old legend. "Thank you, sir."

Oliver asked smugly, "Satisfied?"

Far from it, she thought. "What else haven't you told me, Oliver? How much do you really know about this man we've come to see?"

"I never said there wouldn't be danger."

"You said the man was cultured and refined."

"What did you expect?"

Now there's a question, she thought. After speaking with Oliver a week ago, what *had* she expected from this pilgrimage? Had she really believed they could simply waltz in unannounced, uninvited, and ask for the return of their mortality? Oliver had said on the plane every immortal had a purpose, so there was obviously something bigger going on. Some grand plan in which they all played a part.

They had driven ten miles from the airport, but outside, the mixed architecture continued as ancient and modern buildings crowded one another along both sides of the two-lane road.

Jane turned to Oliver and asked, "How much farther do you think we have to go?"

"My guess," he said, looking out the window, "is maybe twenty minutes. It's supposed to be on the west coast. Fifteen miles from the airport." He turned to her and smiled. "If we were crows, we'd already be there."

How clever, she thought. "If we were crows, Oliver, we wouldn't be here at all."

"True," he conceded. "You have to admit, though, Jane, that there is a growing excitement. Can't you feel the energy?"

She felt an energy, yes, but it had little to do with excitement. Fear, maybe, and definitely unease, but...

"I'm not as mentally intuitive as you," Oliver continued, "but I can't help feeling we are exactly where we're supposed to be. As if it were our destiny."

If it were, indeed, their destiny to enter Casa Vienna, Jane was completely unprepared. There was still so much she didn't know. She wished she'd been able to tap into the hidden thoughts in Oliver's mind, but she'd tried for hours on the plane with no results. All she knew for sure was that the information stored there was important. And Oliver hadn't put it there.

"I take you only to the gate," the cab driver reminded them.

Jane glanced outside and noticed that towering greenery had replaced the man-made structures along the roadsides. A row of old-growth trees that resembled oaks lined the road ahead. Behind them, Jane recognized apple and citrus trees. "Are we here?"

"*Iva*, yes. Hundreds of years ago, these were gardens and hunting grounds. Now, the *werak*, the plants, have taken over. No one ventures into the forest."

"I suppose the forest's haunted, too," Oliver scoffed.

Jane nudged him.

The car slowed, turned a half circle, and came to rest in front of a solid iron gate. Reluctantly, Jane opened the door and stepped outside. Oliver did the same. Before either could shut their doors, the cab peeled away.

"Wait!" Jane yelled. She waved her arms frantically. "Stop!" The dented Ford disappeared in a cloud of gravel and dust. "This is great, Oliver. How do we get back?"

"Walk, I guess." Surprisingly, he didn't seem troubled. "Come on," he waved for her to follow. "This way." He stepped through the gravel to the right side of the formidable gate.

"Is it locked?" she asked.

"I don't know, but it doesn't matter. There's only a hedge. No fence. We can squeeze around the gate."

Seeing he was right, she followed as he skirted the twenty-foot-high iron roadblock. On the other side, tire tracks revealed Jane and Oliver hadn't been Casa Vienna's only visitors.

"You see," Oliver said, puffing himself up triumphantly, "no ghosts here. The road's still used."

She saw the tracks, but there was no comfort in his assurance. "You said yourself that every legend has elements of truth." *How far did the single-lane road stretch into the forest?* she wondered. Wearing a skirt and penny loafers, Jane hoped the trek would be free of obstacles. But at least they had no bags to carry.

Oliver squinted, shielding his eyes with his hat. "I think there's a curve to the right. Maybe a quarter mile. Maybe less. Hard to tell where it goes from there." He plopped the white straw hat on his head and started striding along the dirt and gravel drive.

Can't you feel the energy? he'd asked her. She hadn't then, now it was undeniable. Something hovered over the forest like a current of electricity. She understood why the locals avoided Casa Vienna. In the distance, an animal howled.

Jane hurried to catch up with Oliver. "If we make it through this alive, remind me to kill you."

"If only you could," he laughed and quickened his pace.

•

They're almost here.

DeSain used his third eye to watch Jane and Oliver as the pair, joking and squabbling, as they made their way along the forest road. Soon they would be in view of the house and DeSain would see them through the glass. He stood up from his desk and walked to the last of three oversized, stained-glass windows overlooking the home's main entrance. Peering through a clear pane, he surveyed the empty road and the circular drive below.

Almost here.

DeSain stretched and straightened his collar.

The room the immortal called his study had not been originally constructed as a chapel, but during the reign of the Knights of St. John it served as such for a century. Eight windows, two feet wide by twenty feet high from floor to ceiling, had been installed, each one depicting an event in the life of John the Baptist. The furthest window to the right, where DeSain stood, portrayed his death. Salome', in a flowing purple gown, receives the head of John the Baptist, which rests on a tray held by a kneeling servant. Through the clear glass of the Saint's severed head, DeSain peered, poised to witness the return of LaCassiere blood to Casa Vienna.

Dominic could have been instructed to pick them up at the airport, but, in adherence to the oath he'd made centuries earlier, DeSain hadn't interfered. Instead, he'd told his servants to wait for the knock at the door. Tension grew in DeSain's muscles, as if his entire body were bracing for the fulfillment of the prophecy.

It won't be long, he reminded himself, looking out across the forest that had been both playground and sanctuary. *They're so close. They're so...*

And there they were.

•

Oliver halted as he rounded the corner and spied the castle, now only two- or three-hundred yards away, framed on either side by the edges of the pine forest. The gravel road leading to the entrance widened, and to the left and right tall grass replaced dense underbrush. In his research, he'd only viewed centuries-old sketches and prints of the fortress. Now, before him in full color against a blue sky, the stone façade of the grand structure glowed a faint pink-orange in the late morning sun. Oliver couldn't wait to get closer and see more detail.

Behind him, Jane stopped walking. "Oh my God, Oliver. He's watching us."

"That's not possible, my dear." Her paranoia had been charming in the beginning, providing Oliver the opportunity to be chivalrous. But his tolerance had since run low. "He doesn't even know we're coming."

"But he does. Can't you feel him?" Her tone was insistent. She looked terrified.

"Calm down, love." He touched her arm. "There's nothing to be afraid of. We can't be hurt, remember?"

"Isn't that smoke rising there?" She pointed to an ascending cloud on the far right of the building.

"Yes, I think it is, and that's good. Means there's someone home." He cupped his hand under her elbow. "Shall we proceed?"

She looked to him, then to the castle, then back. "Now or never, right?"

"Right."

She pulled his hand from her elbow and interlaced her fingers with his. Hand in hand, they resumed their march to the castle doors.

•

Easily larger than any plantation house or mansion Oliver had seen, Casa Vienna was an imposing fortress situated squarely at the end of what remained of the road. Ominous medieval bastions with narrow windows guarded its corners, reminding Oliver of the age of the immortal they had come to confront. At the center of the parapet roof and overlooking the entrance was a coat of arms. Skillfully carved from a darker stone than the rest of the structure, the symbol appeared almost red in contrast.

At the castle's base, Oliver and Jane walked beneath an arched entryway into a circular, walled drive. At its center was a ten-foot high sculpture of a lion and a dragon. Water shot up between the two figures and cascaded into the stone pond below them. Whether they were fighting or embracing, Oliver didn't know for sure.

"I think we enter there," he said to Jane, pointing. As far as he could tell, the only windows were on the second floor. And some, he noticed on the right, appeared religious in nature. He found that intriguing.

Jane squeezed his hand as they rounded the fountain toward the door. "This looks like the home of a very important person, Oliver. Not just anybody lives like this. Are you sure we're in the right place?"

"It was you who said he was at Casa Vienna, remember? If we're in the wrong place, it's your fault." But this wasn't the wrong place.

Oliver knew.

Within the walled entryway, the drive resembled a courtyard, decorated with blossoming citrus trees and wandering vines with small yellow and white blooms. For the first time, Oliver noticed the air had a sweet smell. Ahead, a stone staircase measuring maybe six foot wide led to a set of two weathered, wooden doors. An intricate border of carved reddish stone decorated the door frame.

"There's our way in," Oliver said.

"I'm scared," Jane replied, but she kept up.

"We'll be all right." Oliver's gait slowed as they drew closer to the door. *But just in case, I'm blocking my mind*, he thought.

"Oliver," Jane stopped and squeezed his hand, "I never properly learned how to guard my thoughts."

Since she held his hand, he had to stop with her. "How would you have learned without a way to practice? I can't tap in like you." He pulled her on.

"True," she continued as they mounted the worn stone steps. "I'd feel better if I knew, though. Just as a precaution."

"We won't even need to worry about that." He mounted the stairs.

She stepped up next to him.

"Now or never." He reached up and rapped three times on the door.

She straightened the waistband of her skirt as footsteps became audible behind the oversized doors. Without barely a sound, the left door swung open.

A small-framed man in black greeted them in a thick Italian accent. "Good morning. Who may I say is calling?"

Tipping his hat, Oliver replied, "You may say Miss Jane Dougharty and Mr. Oliver Chatham are here."

"To request an audience with Sir DeSain," Jane added, and Oliver assumed, to let him know she wouldn't play silent partner.

"Please come in." The man waved them inside.

"After you." Oliver bowed for Jane to enter first, following on her heels through the door.

•

Had someone told Jane a week earlier that she would be standing in a palace on the island of Malta waiting to speak to the creator of all immortals, she'd have thought that person insane. What a difference five days can make in a life.

She couldn't help but gawk at Casa Vienna's grand foyer as they followed the man from the doorway. The vast room was carved entirely of pale-colored stone and polished to a gleaming finish. Three stunning chandeliers, ten foot in diameter each, cast a bright glow, even into the hollowed recessions along the walls where marble busts were displayed. Some thirty feet above them, the arched ceiling was a work of art itself, bearing frescoes that could arguably be compared to the greatest cathedrals in Europe.

"This way, please," the Italian man directed, ushering them into a parlor on the right that could have doubled for a fine antiques showroom.

"The place is exquisite," she heard Oliver say as he entered the room behind her. "Doesn't this room remind you, Jane, of the parlor in New Orleans?"

"Maybe before the dust truck arrived," she replied, looking about. "And this furniture is Italian if I'm not mistaken. Yours is French."

The man who'd met them at the front door gestured toward a white sofa facing the entrance from the foyer. "If you would have a seat here, I will inform the master of your arrival."

The master, Jane's mind echoed. "Thank you," she said to the doorman as she and Oliver moved toward the sofa. What must it be like, she wondered, to have servants who refer to you as The Master? How much respect would a man like that command?

Jane sat down gingerly on the antique sofa. "We can't even be sure yet, Oliver, that we're in the right place." But she could feel it, couldn't she?

"How can you say that?" He sat beside her.

"The man who brought us to this room didn't confirm the knight is here."

"He didn't deny it, either, but we didn't ask." He grabbed her arm. "And you can't tell me you don't already know."

He was right. She knew. "All I'm saying, Oliver, is that it's possible we've made a mistake."

He shook his head. "All these years and you still doubt yourself. What will it take for you to trust your intuition?"

"If I might interject," a voice from the corner behind them brought Jane and Oliver to their feet.

Jane spun around and recognized him immediately, although where she recognized him from momentarily escaped her.

"Perhaps," he continued, moving leisurely from the shadows behind the fireplace, "the lady would be more inclined to trust her intuition if she knew who she was."

Jane wanted to speak, but awe stilled her tongue. Oliver remained next to her, frozen in place as well.

"You have come a long way, both of you." His voice was quiet, but commanding. Stepping from the marble onto the rug, his shoes made no sound as he rounded the corner of the sofa.

Jane followed his progress with her body, almost subconsciously, not wanting him at her back.

"I admire people who are willing to go the distance for what they believe." He stopped before an antique armchair and sat down. "Please sit," he offered.

They dropped as if pushed.

"I don't receive many visitors, as you can understand." He sat up straight in the chair.

Was he trying to make small talk? Jane wondered. Was he playing with them, or was his charm sincere?

"What I'm trying to say is that it's a pleasure to welcome you both, although from the frightened expressions on your faces I've done a poor job."

Had she shown her fright? Was Oliver afraid, too? Jane suddenly felt overcome with embarrassment. "I'm so sorry, um..." *Your lordship? Your highness? Master?* What should she call him?

Oliver kept it simple. "Forgive us, sir, for our shock. Your appearance from behind caught us off guard."

"Oh, of course. My apologies."

After an awkward pause, the man seated in the chair before them continued, "You have many questions." He made more of a statement than a query.

Jane noted his fluid movement as he rested his elbows on the upholstered armrest and linked his index fingers at his waist. His beige shirt hung loose at his waist, its bottom button undone. As if to give her a better view of his lap, the knight stretched out his legs and crossed his ankles. Jane's gaze flew quickly up and met his eyes.

"Do you like what you see, Miss Dougharty?" His dark hair, pulled back from his face, hung loosely to his shoulders and over his collar. The unfastened buttons below his neck exposed a sliver of sculpted chest. The only word Jane could think of to describe him was *elegant*.

"Your home *is* extraordinary," she said, being coy. But why, if she feared this man, was she allowing him to seduce her?

"I'll admit I never grow bored here. No matter how long I stay."

Jane had difficulty prying her eyes from his. Why was his face so familiar? "But surely you go out from time to time." *Maybe visited Sacramento once or twice?*

"Oh, of course. I wouldn't dream of spending my entire life confined within the walls of even the most desirable of estates. There's too much of the world to see." He broke his gaze and glanced at Oliver. "Don't you agree, Mr. Chatham?"

Jane turned to Oliver.

"Absolutely," Oliver said, twisting the corners of his hat as if it was a strand of rosary beads. Jane sensed that her friend had lost track of the conversation.

Are you all right, Oliver? she asked telepathically. She shouldn't have been surprised when the answer came from the knight.

"I assure you he's all right, Miss Dougharty. A little shell-shocked perhaps, but perfectly fine. Aren't you, Oliver?"

"Never better," he said, but Jane felt something was amiss.

She straightened on the sofa and again faced the knight. "You said when you first...*appeared,* that I would trust my intuition better if I knew who I was. What did you mean?"

He smiled. "It's a fascinating story, but I believe," he pulled in his legs and stood, "it's one best told over lunch. Would you join me?" He turned and offered her his arm. "My staff has prepared a room upstairs for us."

"Us?" Despite her surprise that the master of the house had been expecting them, Jane discovered she had stood without thinking and had taken his arm.

"Yes. The three of us." He called over his shoulder. "Come, Oliver. Keep up."

"Right behind you," he said.

Jane let their host lead her away from the warmth of the fireplace into the spaciousness of the opulent foyer. Walking with him beneath the vaulted, arched ceiling made Jane feel like a princess in a fairy tale. She almost forgot Oliver walked behind.

"This way," he pointed, and escorted her to a wide, stone staircase draped with red carpet. At the center of the incline, the stairs split. An ancient red tapestry decorated the landing.

Jane recognized the symbols from the rooftop above the entryway.

"My family crest," he said as they ascended the left stairs. "I'll tell you about it when we've settled in."

Was he outwardly reading Jane's mind, she wondered, or was she only imagining?

They crested the staircase and proceeded down a long hallway flanked by portraits, sculptures, and artifacts of war.

"Are these your ancestors?" she asked, referring to the paintings.

"Yes, mostly. But some like this one," he pointed to a portrait of a bearded man on a horse, "were also leaders of battles. Gerard of Aquitaine, the original builder and owner of Casa Vienna. He was given the grounds a millennia ago as a gift from his friend," he pointed to a marble bust atop a pillar on the opposite wall, "Roger the Norman, the first in recorded history to conquer Malta."

They passed whole suits of armor, maces, shields, and swords. "You seem to have an extensive collection of weapons and armor. Is there any particular battle that interests you?"

"Only the battles for Malta."

"Were there many?"

He urged her to a stop before a set of double doors. "The people of Malta fought for centuries for freedom and sovereignty. Peace has only come within the last hundred years." He pulled his arm free of her hand and positioned himself at the center of the two wooden doors. Grasping two dark iron rings, he tugged. The hinges cried as the heavy doors swung open.

"After you, my dear." DeSain tipped his head.

At first, she thought the room was bigger than it actually was. Much bigger. Until she stepped inside and realized that two exterior walls were transparent glass. The vastness she felt was a result of the blue skies outside, that and the fact that a table and three chairs was the only furniture. *The Terrace Room*, she remembered. But how? Had their host mentioned it earlier?

Suspended from chains were two wooden chandeliers, stark in contrast to the detailed craftsmanship found downstairs. The two remaining walls and ten-foot-high ceiling appeared to have been painted dark gray to match a rough stone floor unlike any other she had seen in the castle, or anywhere else for that matter. Her shoes made little noise on its surface and, like concrete, there were no visible seams. The air was thick with the smell of earth and the temperature seemed to drop. Rather than a large room, it suddenly felt more like a cave with a view. She stopped and turned, wanting to know how closely DeSain followed her. She saw Oliver stepping through the doorway.

Why do I keep forgetting he's with me? she wondered, but the Maltese Knight approached her and again offered his arm.

"I hope you find the accommodations to your liking."

Her eyes left Oliver as she took DeSain's arm and walked with him farther into the room, finding it hard to shake the gnawing familiarity of his touch. On the wall to their left were two swords mounted on a shield.

More military relics, she thought.

However, at the center of the room, upon the long table, sat something unexpected: a stunning floral bouquet, dominated by brilliant violet and orange flowers as large as lilies set against sparks of yellow and red. Arranged in an aged pottery urn, and reaching three feet high from its base, the shock of color was mesmerizing and reminded Jane of flames in a fire.

The flowers must be native, she thought.

"They are," the knight said as they neared the three place settings at the far right end of the table. "The purple are *fjurdulis salvagg*, a member of the iris family. The deep red-orange blooms are *lathyrus clymenum* or crimson pea."

So he *had* read her mind earlier. He wasn't even pretending. Jane wished she'd learned to keep her thoughts to herself.

"We have nothing to hide from one another, Miss Dougharty. I know all your secrets, and soon you'll know mine."

"What is this place?"

Oliver's voice startled her. "It's a cliff." He was standing at the far wall, facing out toward the sky.

The knight's voice was close to her ear. "The view is breathtaking, Jane Marie." When had he grasped her hand? "Go to him and see."

She obeyed, but not without noticing he'd called her Jane Marie. She hadn't heard that name since her father died.

Dominant in her line of sight was the clear blue Mediterranean sky, but as she got closer, expecting to see the green tops of trees, she was surprised to discover a wandering line of cliffs extending out ten to twenty miles in either direction. Walking to the corner of the room, where the thick glass walls intersected, Jane guessed the ocean to be about five-hundred feet below. It was amazing the terrain had been so well hidden from the road outside.

"Takes your breath away, doesn't it?" The knight whispered again in her ear.

Jane tried to step back, but his body was too close.

"You stand in the footprints of a million soldiers, watching the seas to protect their homeland. When the sun sets on the horizon there," he placed his hand on the glass beside her head, "the whole of the sky blazes burnt orange and violet in their memory."

Like the flowers, she thought.

"Yes, like the flowers." His accent, rich with cultures not his own, was melodic. He pressed closer. His other hand slapped against the other glass, penning her in. She felt his breath on her neck.

Jane looked down and realized she perched at the tip of a rock jutting out from the cliff face. She brought her hands up and pushed against the glass. The knight stood firm.

"What do you want from me?" she asked.

"Everything," he whispered. "But first," he backed away from her suddenly and clapped his hands twice, "we eat."

Jane pushed herself away from the corner. She was out of breath. But where was Oliver? She scanned the room. He and the knight were standing patiently near the banquet table.

"Are you ready, my dear?" Her host pulled out the chair opposite Oliver. Servers—a total of six—began filing in through the door, carrying platters and tureens. Overcoming her vertigo, Jane took her seat at the table.

"Wine?" a woman standing at her left offered.

"Please." The effects of alcohol never lasted long, but, glancing from Oliver to the knight, Jane believed she could use a drink about now.

CHAPTER 30

Jane watched DeSain wipe his lips for the last time and toss his linen napkin onto the empty plate in front of him.

"I cannot eat another bite," he announced.

"It was splendid," Jane said, and she meant it.

Everything had been a delight to the palate, from the *minestra* soup to the *fenek*—or rabbit—with rich wine sauce and the heavenly dessert pastries filled with ricotta, almonds, and figs.

"I haven't enjoyed a meal like that in years." She placed her own napkin on her plate.

"I don't think I've eaten at all in years," Oliver said, his spirits revived since they'd started lunch. His dinner companions laughed with him at the joke.

"The secret to the perfect meal," their host said, "is to spread them out. Don't make them menial by eating every day. As you know, we have the privilege of suspending our hunger."

No longer afraid of their host, Jane and Oliver nodded. *We could learn so much from him*, Jane thought. But that wasn't why they were here, she reminded herself. There was the matter of immortality.

And the matter of your destiny. The voice that whispered in Jane's mind was feminine and, though she hadn't heard it for more than a century, Jane could swear it belonged to her mother. *But you mustn't let him know.*

"Sir," she began, "I hate to interrupt your dining lesson, but..."

"You want to return to business? We've broken bread together now, my dear, please call me Moncado."

"Moncado," she repeated. It was awkward, but something she could get used to since, as he'd said, they'd broken bread together. "You said you'd tell my story over lunch, but we've sat and laughed the time away for hours and I still know nothing more than when we arrived."

"That's not entirely true, Jane," Oliver chimed in, "we've learned that Sir DeSain is an intellectual and entertaining host. That counts for something."

"The lady is insistent, my boy," DeSain said, leaning back to allow a servant to pick up his plate and silver. "Leave the glasses, please, and bring more wine."

"Yes, my lord," the servant girl curtsied, gathered the other guests' dishes, and left the room.

"Are they immortal, too?" Oliver asked. "The staff, I mean."

"Oh, no," DeSain chuckled. "That's an honor reserved for only the chosen."

Oliver sat up in his seat. "So immortals are not created at random?"

"Of course not." The knight took a sip from his wine glass. "But you knew that already, Oliver. In fact, you have a number of theories, and I can tell you no one apart from myself is more knowledgeable than you where immortals are concerned."

Jane was impressed, but she could feel the mood at the table had changed with the conversation. Or was it only her perceptions that had changed?

Oliver blushed. "I must admit, sir, your compliment confuses me." He rested his arms on the table and looked briefly at Jane before returning his gaze to the knight.

What is he doing? Jane wondered.

"How could you know of my knowledge of immortals?" Oliver continued. "I live thousands of miles away and have never told a soul what I've learned about you, or any other immortal."

"You told Jane."

"What difference does that make?"

The knight leaned back in his chair, his hands lay in his lap. "Did you know, Oliver, that when a person speaks, the words are imprinted on his mind?"

"No."

"I do, and so does Jane," he nodded in her direction, but remained focused on Oliver.

What point is he making? Jane wondered.

"My point is," and this time he did look at Jane, but quickly, "I know everything in your head. Everything you've ever put there."

"And the things he didn't put there?" Jane asked. "Do you know those things, too?"

You're a brave one, aren't you? his mind caressed hers. "But we shouldn't start the story from the middle."

From behind her, a woman appeared with more wine. Jane pushed her glass down the table for the servant to fill. When she was finished, Jane hoisted the glass as if making a toast. "From the beginning, then." She downed the wine completely, although she was sure it was old and expensive, and waited for the servant woman to fill her glass again.

"Your mother was one of the most beautiful women I'd ever seen."

"You knew my mother?" *Of course, he did*, she thought. *He was the man in the parlor.* Jane's stomach tightened. She was afraid she might vomit. How could she not recognize him? But she had, hadn't she? *You are the one who killed my mother.*

"I didn't kill her," he said, resting his elbows on the table and tracing the top of his wine glass with his finger. "But I understand how it could have looked that way to you. A child losing a mother is a traumatic event."

Lies. He was toying with her, holding back, but she didn't dare give into her fear. With the truth revealed, DeSain had instantly become more dangerous. But his ability to read her thoughts gave her an idea.

"Catherine had a powerful mind," he continued, staring at his fingertip as it circled the glass, "which is to say she had visions outside the realm of ordinary telepathy."

"Visions?" Jane leaned in, feigning interest. "Could she tell the future?"

"On occasion, but your mother wasn't a seer." He'd stopped caressing his wine glass. "Her gift was her ability to know a man for what he really was. All she had to do was touch," DeSain's arm stretched out to her, his fingertip touched her shoulder, "and she saw the truth."

"My mother saw who you really were..."

"And ended her life to protect you," he finished.

Jane didn't believe him. "That's not what I see in you."

"You see nothing in me."

But I do, she thought, knowing he would hear.

"Your mother knew if she were dead, her mind would be forever closed to me." *The truth about you would be safe*, she heard his mind say.

That I believe, she admitted.

Get out of my head. I'm warning you.

Jane was determined. *What truth was my mother hiding about me?*

"What's going on with you two?" Oliver interjected.

GET OUT! Jane felt the knight scream along with her as they mentally pushed Oliver away from their conversation.

Oliver's chair toppled backward. He fell to the floor.

"Oh my God, Oliver." Jane leapt from her chair and rushed around DeSain to see what happened.

Oliver's eyes were closed. He wasn't moving. She knelt by his side.

"Oliver," she shook him, "are you okay?" She leaned in near his face. His eyes flew open. What they said came through in a split second.

Itwasloudreallyloudanditknockedmebut...

She disposed of it as quickly. "Oliver, oh my God, you scared me." She backed away slightly and stood, then offered her hand.

Oliver rubbed his head as he stumbled to his feet. "I think I knocked myself good on the floor. It'll be gone in a minute or two."

"Are you sure that's all that happened?" DeSain asked, never leaving his chair.

"Can't fool a pro, right?" Oliver laughed.

Jane felt the back of Oliver's head. "There is a knot here."

"I'm not surprised," he agreed. "But finish your story." Oliver straightened his shirt and repositioned his seat. He retrieved his jacket from the floor, returned it to the back of his chair and sat down. "You were saying, Sir DeSain, how Jane's mother could see the truth in people." He reached for his wine glass.

"Yes," Jane agreed, returning to her own seat and pretending the mental discourse hadn't happened. "About this gift my mother had, why was it of interest to you?"

"I had an obligation to protect her, with or without her gift."

That wasn't his only obligation. Jane heard another female voice. But she wouldn't flinch. There would be a time to act, but not until she had answers.

DeSain continued, appearing not to notice Jane's inner dialogue. "But witches of the time were not safe in Europe."

"So you moved her to America?" Jane asked.

"I didn't move her, she ran. First to Ireland, where she married. Then to America."

"And you followed her?"

"Had her followed, to be precise. I can't personally attend to every steward in my charge."

"Why, then, were you at the house that day in Philadelphia? What was your obligation to my mother and these other *stewards*? You said you had to protect her, regardless of her gift."

"I took an oath five-hundred years ago to protect the bloodline of LaCassiere."

"For what purpose?"

DeSain didn't answer.

For what purpose? Jane taunted him.

His mind was blank.

Oliver sat straight up in his chair. "I get it! It all makes sense now. He employed immortals to watch over the descendents of LaCassiere. That explains the geographic pattern. As generations branched off into other parts of the world, immortals were assigned to follow them."

"That's correct," the knight acknowledged.

"But if my mother was a LaCassiere, I would be, too," Jane deducted. "Have I been followed my entire life?"

"You have, in one way or another, yes."

"But," Oliver interjected, "how do you communicate with these other immortals? These watchers? Surely you don't rely on written or verbal messages."

"Absolutely not." With that, the knight stood and approached Oliver. "One of the benefits of creating an immortal is the bond that forms between the immortal and his creator." DeSain stood behind Oliver's chair, his hands rested on Oliver's shoulders. "Your mind becomes forever linked to mine. Your thoughts," DeSain slipped his fingers into Oliver's hair, "your words, your actions are all mine, no matter where you are."

Jane leaned back in her chair. "You know every move made by every immortal?" She found that hard to believe. "Oliver said there could be hundreds."

"There are." DeSain ran his fingers through Oliver's hair a final time. "But soon, only one will matter."

"Which one is that?" Oliver asked, his hair askew.

"You know which one, my boy." DeSain looked down at him, as a father would a child.

From Oliver's mind came the words *Jane Marie.*

That's it! Jane thought. *Mother knew he'd use the name. That's how I know...* But, again, she didn't dare think too much for fear DeSain would notice the change in her mind.

"You see," DeSain patted Oliver's hair down, "your friend knows more than he lets on."

"Did you know we were coming?" she asked.

"You know the answer to that."

"Did you summon us here?"

"No." He was adamant. "You arrived at my doorstep of your own accord."

He interfered. Jane heard another strange, ghost voice again. Was it male? Female? She couldn't tell.

"You said I would be rewarded." Oliver sat with folded arms.

"What are you talking about, Oliver?" Jane asked, but Oliver's eyes were glazed. "Oliver?"

He didn't respond.

"What is he talking about, DeSain?" Jane sat forward. "What reward is he asking for?"

DeSain tapped Oliver's shoulders, then turned to face away from the table. "Five-hundred years ago, the bloodline of LaCassiere was in jeopardy of extinction. There were only two." He paused.

Jane sensed he'd been one, but the other... She couldn't quite see.

"My oath was to protect the bloodline until the threat of annihilation was overcome." He walked to the glass-walled ledge.

Jane knew there was more. "And were you promised something in return?" she called from her seat at the table.

Yes. He thought it clearly and didn't scold her for hearing it.

"What were you promised?" She rose from her seat. "And what does Oliver have to do with it?"

DeSain's back was to her, but she sensed his expression was riddled with torment. "There was a seer here that night. The night I took on the life of an immortal."

Whatever happened five centuries ago, she thought, happened here in this room. She looked quickly at Oliver. He had found his hat and was anxiously twisting its brim again. What had the knight done to him? She didn't like leaving his side, but she wouldn't go far.

"The seer took my hand and squeezed it," DeSain was making a fist in the air, "and she said someone would come for me."

From the line of LaCassiere, the unknown voice droned in Jane's head as she approached the knight on the ledge.

"She said it would be a woman like no other."

Jane was close to him now, as close as he'd been to her earlier. Her hands reached up to caress his shoulders. She pressed against his back.

"A woman like me?" she whispered.

"Yes."

Jane pressed her face against his back, hoping her thoughts were hidden. "You must have been lonely, waiting."

"I've had servants to pacify my needs, and I have found ways to fill the time."

Yes. He'd watched generations of immortals—his children—play through their lives like pieces on a giant chessboard. "Were you always certain I'd come?"

He turned slowly to face her. She crossed her wrists behind his neck. "The first time I saw you, I knew." His hands fell to her hips. "Time would reveal more in you than simply beauty."

She held her thoughts tight as she rested her cheek against his chest. "So you waited for me to grow up."

The knight sighed, remembering. "You were stubborn. That was the first sign. Strong-willed and opinionated, combined with a complete lack of fear. Centuries of politically-driven breeding had long ago robbed the LaCassiere line of its cunning, but with you all the old characteristics returned. You were as unique in body and spirit as the seer had foretold."

He shouldn't have interfered, the mysterious voice whispered in Jane's mind. She could hear DeSain's heart beating.

"Is that why you made me immortal?" she asked.

His hands slid up her sides. He took her hands and held them tightly to his chest. "With your father and brother no longer a hindrance, I could not see the sense in waiting, knowing you would one day be mine." DeSain leaned down to kiss her.

It's your destiny, the voice declared. Jane lifted her face to meet his. She accepted his lips and let fate enshroud them.

•

"I must have my reward," Oliver blurted out. He was dazed and groggy, as if he'd been unconscious, but he hadn't forgotten the real reason he'd brought Jane to Casa Vienna. "Your promise, if I'm not mistaken, Sir DeSain," he said as he stood up from his chair, rubbing his eyes, "was to grant me knighthood and the one thing I desire most." He pivoted to face them. "I fulfilled my end of the bargain. Now I'd like to collect."

"Oliver?" Jane looked confused, but Oliver knew she was bright enough to catch up once her lust cooled. Not that he was upset with her. It was obvious DeSain had her under some kind of spell.

The knight stepped away from Jane and strolled toward the table and Oliver. "You're absolutely right, my boy. We should have settled up the moment you arrived." He placed an arm around Oliver's shoulder.

Oliver could have done without the physical contact. "So if I understand you correctly, Sir," he said as the knight led him across the stone floor, "you said I could choose anything as my one request."

"Anything. No price is too high for what you've done for me." The knight had stopped before a wall display where two swords marked an X against the dark gray wall. Oliver hadn't noticed them before, perhaps because the monstrous centerpiece had blocked his view. "The sword of LaCassiere is what we'll use. The same blade that bestowed my own knighthood." DeSain reached forward and tore the sword from its mount.

"What is the significance of the other sword, Moncado?" Jane asked from behind.

So she was calling him *Moncado*, now. Wasn't that special. *How long have I been out?* Oliver wondered, knowing Jane and the knight would hear him. But he didn't care anymore. He asked, "Shouldn't there be witnesses?"

The knight shook his head. "We have the word of DeSain and the lovely Jane Marie. No one will dispute that."

How was Jane handling all this? Oliver wondered. But what did it matter? "Where, then, shall I stand?" Oliver just wanted it over, so he didn't have to pretend anymore.

"I would say there," DeSain pointed with the sword, "near the intersecting glass." Grasping the hilt with one hand and the sheath with the other, the knight freed the sword from its brilliant cover. The blade reflected a thousand rays from the afternoon sun.

Oliver took a step toward the ledge.

The knight grabbed his shoulder. "You should know you surpassed all my expectations."

It was nice of you to notice, he thought.

"I sincerely mean it." He draped an arm over Oliver's shoulder again, like a father, and started walking. "My immortals don't often know their objectives. They follow instructions subconsciously. It's a perfect system. But I could not have chosen a better watchman, a better guide, for this woman than you. Your subconscious as well as your conscious mind worked in tandem. You never wavered. It was brilliant."

Why would DeSain think Oliver's conflicting objectives worked in tandem? All this time he thought he'd been deceiving the knight. Had he actually been doing his will? But, Oliver remembered, he shouldn't think so much.

The knight stopped ten feet or so from the cliff's edge. Oliver imagined what the spot must have been like when DeSain was knighted. The glass walls surely hadn't been there.

"In my time," DeSain read Oliver's mind, "there were marble pillars supporting the rooftop. As you suspected, there was no glass."

"What was the significance of this place?" Jane asked. She was standing to Oliver's right, looking as beautiful as the day he'd met her. Afternoon sunlight glowed on her skin.

"In ancient times, it was suspected to have been a lookout as well as a ritual site. The LaCassiere legacy began on this spot when the seer received her first vision. The Knights of St. John were defeated here. All my ancestors were knighted on the sacred ground beneath our feet."

"Then I am in good company," Oliver said, "as I receive the honor." With Jane beside him, he knew he could see this through.

"You are indeed," the knight said. "Now, down on one knee, dear Oliver."

Oliver bent his right knee to the floor and, keeping his back straight, placed his palms on his left leg.

DeSain took a solid stance before him. "I ask you now for your wish, so as your title is bestowed, so will be your greatest desire."

Oliver took a deep breath and exhaled. *Now or never*, he remembered. He didn't look DeSain in the eye, instead he kept his head forward, his eyes focused on the gleaming sword the knight held pointed to the floor. "I ask for Jane Marie."

"Oliver, no!" Jane erupted beside him.

DeSain's silence caused Oliver's breath to hitch. But he had promised anything. *Anything*. Oliver was relieved when DeSain spoke again.

"Although your question does not surprise me, your bravery does."

Oliver felt a sudden chill. Beads of perspiration formed on his upper lip and forehead.

"But," the knight continued, "I gave my word." He raised the sword and pointed it upward. The blade shimmered, inches from DeSain's face.

Relieved, but still cautious, Oliver bowed his head.

"By the power granted me by my ancestors and those who fought bravely in the defense of Malta and her freedom," he touched the sword to Oliver's shoulder, "I give you the title..."

A loud knock on the door stopped him.

Oliver lifted his head. The short Italian man who had met them when he and Jane arrived was standing in the doorway. "My lord, your other guests have arrived."

"Ah," the knight said, "exquisite timing." Oliver couldn't tell if DeSain was speaking sarcastically or not. The knight looked down at Oliver and gestured toward the door. "Your witnesses have arrived after, all." DeSain addressed the servant again. "Show them in."

The servant seemed hesitant. "They've brought another, sir."

"Another what?" the knight asked. "Another imbecile? Show them in, Dominic. It will be good for them to see this. Gives them something to aspire to."

Although kneeling, Oliver could see the doorway above the banquet table, thanks to an incline in the stone floor. Dominic motioned to someone in the hallway. Three figures responded to his call and entered the room. Oliver shifted his weight to his front leg and rocked forward to stand, but the knight was one step ahead of him and shoved him down.

"Stay, my boy."

"Rand!" Jane's scream exploded in Oliver's eardrum, almost knocking him over as it did earlier. "What's happened to you?"

Oliver rubbed his head and wondered what bizarre chain of events had brought Jane's husband, along with Coop and Ozzy, to the castle.

DeSain rushed to Jane's side. "You stay calm, too. This is a surprise, but there will be time for greetings and explanations when we finish here." He called to the new arrivals. "Come, join us. Our friend Mr. Chatham is about to be knighted, and he has waited long enough. Leave us, Dominic."

"Your lordship." Dominic bowed and disappeared down the hall.

"Come closer." DeSain waved the three guests in. No one argued. The trio entered quietly, somberly, as if in a trance. Surely the knight was controlling them or they would have stumbled in running their mouths like mother hens.

Coop and Ozzy each held an arm of the man in the middle. He was taller than either of them. There was fear behind his blank stare, but from what he could tell of his countenance, Rand was a decent man. Jane had chosen well.

Too bad.

"Shall we resume?" The knight took his place before Oliver. He pointed the sword again to the ceiling. "Your desire remains?"

"Yes." Oliver bowed his head. With all the power of his mind, Oliver strained to see the act as if he were a spectator, to watch the transference of his reward as the others around him could.

"By the power granted me by my ancestors," the knight again touched the sword to Oliver's shoulder, "I hereby give you the title of Sir Oliver Chatham of Louisiana, and with it, all the privileges that this revered title holds."

Oliver's consciousness swam from his body in time to watch DeSain lift the sword high above his head. *She is finally mine*, Oliver thought. Now she would know all he ever wanted was a forever with her.

You can't have her, the knight's mind whispered. The blade, no longer suspended in the air, sliced quickly down like a pendulum.

Oliver saw no more.

•

Jane screamed and brought her hands up to shield her face. "What have you done?" she cried. The smell of blood filtered into her nose. She pulled her hands back. They were splattered with red.

"Mr. Chatham thought he was being sly. Instead I have made a lesson of him."

Jane watched in horror as the knight stepped up to the vampires and Rand—*Oh my god how did Rand get here?*—and wiped the blood from the sword across their shirts.

"We will find out exactly what these Spaniards were doing here in good time, but first," he whipped the sword in the air and pointed it at her, "I need you to know something."

"What?" She was afraid to ask.

He moved forward, brandishing the sword as he crept closer. "You were created for me. You can belong to no other."

He took you, Jane was starting to understand the voice. *Not voice*, she corrected, *voices*.

Rand needs help, she thought, but the knight was coming toward her, pointing the sword. His eyes reflected the fiery red of the setting sun behind her.

"I will have you," he said.

Jane took a step back.

"Or no one will have you." He jabbed the tip of the sword at her. She inched backward, to the glass. "I never forgot what it was like to touch you." He smiled. "To pierce you." The tip of the sword pressed against her chest. She slid against the wall to the corner.

"What did you do to me?" she asked, but long-repressed memories were surging back. Reminding her.

DeSain braced himself against the wall, holding the sword steady over her heart. "I am the only one who can create an immortal, and do you know how I do it?"

"How?" She couldn't breathe.

"By simply placing my hand on a mortal's head and allowing the energy to pass through my fingertips. I will it to happen and it does. No blood, no damage. Do you find that amazing?"

"Yes."

"You should. It is an extraordinary gift." He leaned in close. The tip of the sword broke through her shirt and cut into her skin. "I would give it to you if you asked." His breath was cold against her face.

"I don't want it." *Not without Rand*, she thought, hoping DeSain couldn't hear. She'd been backed into the corner again, as far as she could lodge herself. Far below, she imagined water lapping at the cliffs.

"What do you want?" he asked. "There is nothing I wouldn't give my queen."

She immediately thought of Rand and the reason she had come here. Afraid to taunt the knight further, but wanting to know once and for all if the reversal were possible, she uttered her request. "Return my mortality."

"Why would you want that?" He twisted the tip of the sword. "Don't you know what would happen if someone did this?" He plunged the blade into her chest. She heard the tip strike glass as the pain shot through her torso and limbs. "If you were mortal, you would be dead. I cannot allow that." His face was expressionless. "Choose something else."

But she couldn't choose. She couldn't think. Her vision was blurred.

You are an immortal, she heard his mind say.

Then the mystery voices. *Don't fall asleep.*

And you are mine, the knight's voice trailed off.

Stay awake, the spirit voices were faint, *you're more vulnerable...* But Jane's consciousness couldn't hold on anymore.

The knight and his sword disappeared.

CHAPTER 31

SACRAMENTO, CALIFORNIA – NOVEMBER, 1870

From a corner of the darkened bedroom—her bedroom—DeSain stood watching his chosen one sleep. He would take her tonight, but not yet. And not quickly. For now, he'd savor the sweet taste of her mind as it slept. Naïve and vulnerable. He grinned. Two of his favorite flavors.

She was alone now, and that was good. Her mother gone. Father and brother dead. Her one love vanquished. He liked her best this way. Isolated. Separated from the herd, so to speak. It would make her stronger. More determined. More of a challenge. But that would come later. Tonight she would give in to him without struggle, because he'd found a door to her soul by invading her dreams. Finally, their long dance would begin.

Winter had fallen on Sacramento, and the night was crisp and clear. The air was cold in the valley. But not deadly so. Not like in the high Sierras where so many westward travelers paid the ultimate price…and then some.

But so went the hardships of mortals.

Three large windows illuminated this corner room: two flanking the head of her bed, facing the river to the west, and one on the north wall overlooking the town. But he wouldn't be discovered. His stealth was unrivaled. His senses unmatched. He approached now without a sound and leaned against the tall, rich-colored post at the foot of her bed. He could smell her, like a predator smells its prey. It was sweet and feminine, but not like the scent of a woman. No. She was pure still. A virgin. All the more reason to savor the moment.

His eyes, accustomed to the din, traced her body's silhouette under the pale, quilted bedcovers. She lay motionless on her side facing him, eyes closed. He followed the curves made by her feet and her legs, her hips and her waist, her shoulder and her arm. Moonlight trickled through sheer lace curtains, revealing the smooth, clear skin of her face and her neck. One delicate hand, visible through the sleeve of her modest, ruffled nightdress, lay palm up near her lips on the pillow. The other rested gracefully on the quilt beside her. Her fingers twitched. Her eyes raced beneath closed lids. She was dreaming, of course, or he wouldn't be here. But he would waste no time guessing at the imagery of her subconscious. It was inconsequential. Whatever her dream, it would pale in comparison to the visions she would conjure hereafter. His desire swelled at the thought.

Show yourself, sweet maiden.

His mind reached out to hers without effort. She moaned and stirred, her body shifting under the blankets as she rolled onto her back. He glided along her bedside and grasped the bedcovers with a firm hand. He tossed them backwards, through the footposts, and they cascaded silently to the floor. Her hands moved slowly to the topmost button of her nightdress. He watched her pry it loose and move down to the next.

Standing close now, close enough to hear her breathing, he bent down and kissed her forehead. Her hair, loosely bound in a single braid, smelled of lilac. Ah, but the braid wouldn't do. While her hands continued their task, he removed the strip of fabric holding the braid, and carefully released the dark, waved tendrils. His fingers combed through her long hair, now flowing freely on the pillow. That was better.

She released the last button her arms could reach while lying down.

You're doing well, my queen, but keep going.

DeSain removed his black, floor-length overcoat and draped it over the bedpost at the foot of the bed. Never taking his eyes from her, he removed the links from his cuffs and pocketed them. He circled the bed, pacing slowly, unbuttoning his own shirt and rolling up his sleeves as he watched her. His footfalls audible, but only barely. She sat upright now, unfastening the last buttons below her knees. He kicked the blankets out of his way as he paused in front of her, chin raised, feet planted firmly. Her eyes remained hidden behind closed lids. Her head slightly tilted. The expression on her small, oval face was calm. Her hands, their chore now completed, fell limply in her lap.

He felt the chill in the room, but didn't shiver. He had a learned impartiality to temperature. But his prey, being mortal still, did not have that luxury. Beneath the now unbuttoned garment, her full breasts reacted instinctively to the cold. As if begging him to touch them. To suckle them. To bite them.

In good time, he assured.

He moved his hand between his legs, gripping his erection beneath his trousers. He'd always been proud of his size. He could take her now and it would fill her. Expand her. But not enough. Instead, he would wait for desire to engorge him. Her innocence not simply be taken, but ravaged. He opened his arms wide, and his fingers slipped around the posts at the foot of the bed.

Reveal yourself.

In her trance, she obeyed, releasing the nightdress at her shoulders. DeSain's grip on the bedposts tightened. Her light skin and firm, unspoiled breasts were hidden no more. She gently freed her arms from the sleeves, allowing the garment to fall around her. Her hands rested again, this time at her sides.

She was a masterpiece. Full lips, elegant neck, ample bosom, slender waist, firm thighs. DeSain had always possessed fine taste, but truly exquisite creatures were not plentiful. He'd been brilliant to follow her. To stay close and protect her. To claim her while she was young. This way, she would be forever youthful. Forever a masterpiece. And he could have her at his whim.

Lie back. Allow me to explore you.

The mortal—Jane Marie, she was called—eased herself onto her back. Her hands moved up her sides, slipped over her shoulders, and rested, wrists crossed, on the pillow above her head. Her legs inched apart, not too far, but far enough. He looked there, between her thighs, admiring the shape of her. Such innocence. Such perfection. How he reveled in his triumph.

He looked at her as she lay on the pillow. "I want you to see me," he spoke aloud, his voice as commanding as those of the gods of Malta.

Her eyes sprang open, traveling slowly from his hips to his face.

"You have been chosen." He held her stare, still gripping the posts of the bed. "Tonight I will give you the gift of eternity. Have you any objection?"

She wouldn't, of course. No one did.

He imagined himself as she would see him. With his high, furrowed brow. Muscular forearms. And the broad, strong chest exposed beneath his open shirt. He was powerful. Her conqueror. Her knight. Releasing his grip from the bedposts, he bent forward and grasped her ankles, one in each hand. With practiced ease, he brought her legs together. Allowing the heat between them to smolder.

Her eyes, wide but vacant, were still upon him as he crawled onto the bed. He moved catlike above her, brushing his cheeks along the skin of her legs, her belly, her chest, her neck. He came to rest at her side, propping up his head with his hand. His boots rubbed against her feet.

"Look at me, my beloved," he told her, gently turning her head with his hand. "You desire me." It wasn't a question.

The fingers of his right hand touched her wrist, and he delicately traced the skin down her arm, past her elbow, beside her breast, and along her side. Her skin erupted in gooseflesh. Her erect nipples hardened all the more.

"See?" He gently pinched them. "Your body prepares for me."

His open hand glided about her torso. He caressed her. Petted her. Enjoyed her. He moved about, cradling and suckling her. Kissing her lips, her neck, her navel. Her scent was intoxicating. He would need to take her soon.

Her gaze never left him, and he was pleased he'd allowed her to watch. This ritual wasn't necessary. He could bestow immortality without it. But why deny the satisfaction? Her loss of innocence was a small price for eternity. And wasn't she nearly his already?

He placed his palm atop her dark pubic hair and burrowed his fingers between her legs. Heat and moisture surrounded his fingertips. She was ready to receive him.

"It's time, my chosen one." Straddling her below the hips, he worked one knee between her legs and then the other. "I am going to take you," he said confidently, moving his knees apart to shoulder width, "and you will remember when the time comes." He unbuttoned his trousers and released his manhood, now fully erect and throbbing. "Look how it aches for you. Beckons to you."

Her eyes lowered obediently from his face to his groin. He reached down and spread her legs wide.

The scent of her was strong now, and he breathed it in hungrily. With his fingertip, he touched her, carefully outlining his virginal prize. He was tempted to penetrate her this way. To deflower her savagely with his hands. But her wetness seemed to plead for him. How could he refuse?

"Watch closely, my pet," he commanded, and, pulling her up by her buttocks, he plunged inside her. Her muscles constricted around him, spurring him on to move faster. Deeper.

"Does your knight satisfy you? Look into my eyes and speak."

"Yes."

"Louder."

"Yes."

"Are you ready for your gift?"

"Yes."

"Say please."

"Please."

DeSain loved to hear them beg. "Then breathe, my child, breathe deep." She did, and he erupted inside her, watching her face in delight as she opened her mouth to scream, her eyes no longer vacant but alive.

But she didn't scream. Not out loud.

His thrusts continued until the last drop was spilled. But before his erection subsided, he pulled her body to his chest, and keeping her tight with one hand, he brought his other hand to her head.

"From this day you will be immortal," he said, and touched his fingertips to her temple.

Her muscles tensed.

He kissed her forehead, then lowered her onto the bed, slowly pulling his spent member out. "You see what you've done?"

Her trance-like expression had returned, her eyes obediently stared into his.

"What a good little girl."

He buttoned his trousers and crouched between her still spread legs. There was a small amount of blood and she was torn, but it would heal. And, though she wouldn't feel it until later, hadn't her pain been part of the pleasure? He climbed down at the foot of the bed and stood, admiring her as he straightened his clothes. He brought her legs together again and pulled her bedcovers up to her neck. Then he brought her arms to her sides and kissed her gently on the mouth.

"Sleep now, my dear, and rest."

Her eyes closed. Her breathing calmed.

"Until next time."

Removing his coat from the bedpost, he allowed himself one last lingering look at her. Then he silently left the bedroom, descended the stairs, and exited the house.

The last of the night stars were fading as he made his way along the river to the docks. His interest in her wouldn't end here. No. But she needed time to blossom. Time to grow. He would have her again, and for much longer. DeSain was patient. He would watch her from a distance and wait.

And eventually, as he knew, she would find him.

It was worth waiting for.

And he had all the time in the world.

CHAPTER 32

"Get away from her!" Rand yelled, coming to his senses. He sprung forward, breaking free from the strange men who'd snatched him at the airport in New Orleans. He'd faded in and out of consciousness, and had no idea where he was—*could this be a dream?*—but he wasn't about to stand back and see his wife murdered by a lunatic with a sword.

"Stay back," the lunatic snapped, pulling the sword from Jane's chest and swinging it around to point at Rand. There was blood on the tip. Janie's blood. And hadn't there been another?

"This doesn't concern you," the man hissed.

"That's my wife!" Rand stood firm. His eyes darted from the man with the weapon to Janie and back again. "What the fuck's going on?"

Be careful, he thought he heard Janie say, but he'd been staring right at her and her lips hadn't moved.

"Your bravery will only hasten your death, mortal," the psycho growled.

Rand wondered if he'd heard correctly. *Mortal?* Who does this guy think he is? This had to be a dream. Rand's limbs were sore, and his breathing was heavy, but he knew adrenaline was kicking in. Dream or not, he'd experienced enough of life without her. "I'm leaving and she's coming with me." What did he have to lose?

The lunatic brought the sword up over his shoulder. Sunset glowed behind him. "You've wasted enough of my time," he said and lunged at Rand.

As if pushed in the chest, Rand fell to the floor. He rolled to the banquet table and pulled himself up on a chair.

"*No!*" Janie's voice rang out from behind the advancing man.

"It has to be done."

Rand shot around the table.

"No! He must be spared." Jane was rising to her feet. The front of her white shirt was stained red. "You say you'll give me everything, but yet you deny my every request."

"This mortal is nothing to us."

"Then let him go."

The man leapt onto the tabletop. Rand shuffled backward, wondering how far the guy could jump. He didn't wonder long.

"You had your time with her, but your time is over." The sword's tip was inches from Rand's face.

Back up, Jane's voice whispered in his ear. But how could that be? He slid his foot behind him, and retreated.

"Are you hearing voices?" the lunatic asked, keeping the sword pointed at the center of Rand's head.

Rand continued to move backward.

"What are they telling you? That even if I allow you to live, you have nothing to return to?" He jabbed the sword at Rand's stomach.

Rand jumped backward, arching his body away from the blade, but not quickly enough. He didn't dare look down to see how bad the cut was, as the tip of the sword came back on point between his eyes.

"If you go home," the crazy man continued, "you will be executed for murder." He looked elated. "Having a body conveniently wash up on the beach was a nice touch, don't you agree? It was only a matter of time before the detective made a connection. It was, after all, his duty to restrain you."

How did this strange man know about Rand's plight in Palm Beach? "I didn't murder my wife. She's right there," Rand pointed, but, when he looked, Janie wasn't at the window. A second later, he saw she had instead snuck up behind the man with the sword.

"Put the blade down, Moncado," she commanded. Her hand brushed the arm that held the weapon. Was she caressing him? Why? Could all this really be happening?

"Janie, how do you know this man?" Rand asked.

SSsssshhhhh, a choir of voices sang in his head.

Stay here, Janie was telling him—but how?—*don't think, just listen and do what I say.*

"If you must kill him," she continued in a hypnotic tone, "at least allow him the honor of knowing the reason for his death."

There was something different about his wife, but Rand couldn't place it. The man lowered his sword. Jane stood close to him, her hand resting on his palm as his fingers gripped the hilt. There was blood on her hands. And didn't she appear a little too healthy for a person who'd taken a sword in the chest just moments before?

"The fools who brought him should be attended to," the man said. "He'll know the reason he dies before I'm finished with them." In two short strides the man stood nose to nose with Rand. "You will die tonight, mortal. Make no mistake." And then he was gone, led away by Rand's angel of mercy.

•

In hibernation, as DeSain referred to it, the Spaniards stood fast at the scene of Oliver's knighthood ceremony. The only remnants of the event were Oliver's shoes, rumpled suit, and hat, which came as no surprise to the knight. Nothing ever remained of the fallen.

Jane Marie settled in at his side as he took a solid stance before the short, round immortal who had defied him. "What justification came to mind, Antony, when you decided to bring this secret gift to me?"

"He wasn't where you thought he was, sir. Coop and I…er Miguel and I, we thought you'd like to punish him for running away."

"And how would you know any of that? Do you presume to know what I think?" Leaving Jane's side, DeSain began to circle the frightened Spaniards.

"No, sir."

"Because, if you do, that would make you as smart as I am. And you know what that is?"

"What?"

DeSain crept behind the imbecile and screamed in his ear, "*IMPOSSIBLE*!" His voice thundered against the glass walls.

The Spaniard shivered.

Good, DeSain thought, *I'm getting through*. He shot a quick glance at the mortal he'd left huddling along the dark wall near the door. How *had* the husband managed to escape DeSain's sentinel? Why hadn't the detective sounded an alert when he'd been unable to contain the man? The knight had been led to believe every precaution was taken. *But I digress.*

"And then there is you." DeSain turned to the taller of the two idiots. "Do you agree with your friend? Did you work together in this?"

He stuttered. "I d-didn't think it was a g-good idea, sir, but he s-said you told him on the phone we—"

The knight grabbed the immortal by the throat. "You're saying Antony lied? If that's so, then it seems he's betrayed both of us, wouldn't you say?"

The lanky Spaniard made a gurgling noise as he tried to speak.

"You trusted him and he led you here under false pretenses to become the object of my wrath." He squeezed harder. "And now you dangle within inches of death, knowing it was he who put you in this position, and so I ask you," the knight released his grip, yet remained intimately close, "doesn't that make you angry?"

Miguel rubbed his neck. "Yes, sir," he mumbled.

"Doesn't it?" He took a step back. "If I were you, I would want revenge for what Antony has done. I'd want him to know beyond a shadow of doubt that he is in the wrong." The knight swung his blade to the lying Spaniard's neck. "Have you anything to say in your defense?"

"All we wanted was a little more rank on the chain, m' lord. You know? We been loyal a long time. I thought—"

"Now, you see," the knight sliced through the skin of the immortal's neck, "there you are thinking again." Blood dripped down his chest, soaking his shirt and denim jacket. "Haven't you learned by now, dear Antony, that thinking is your greatest weakness?" He dropped the blade from the Spaniard's neck. "But, fear not. I have a cure."

Tossing the sword to the ground behind him, the knight grabbed the Spaniard by the collar with both hands. He dragged him to the window and slammed his body against the glass. "Maybe," he pulled him back and slammed him again, "with a few knocks," he did it again, "you'll learn not," and again, "to think so much."

Spidery cracks fanned out in the glass as the knight battered the Spaniard's head against the wall.

"Doesn't this feel good, Miguel?" he hollered back at the sniveling imbecile behind him. "Is it not satisfying to see someone get the beating he deserves?" The final crash sent ice-like splinters fluttering to the sea below. DeSain pulled the breathless Spaniard from the window. "Can you hear me, Antony?" He shook him. "Last chance to redeem yourself. Oh," he looked back at Miguel, "but I should give you a turn. Would you like to toss him a bit as well?"

Miguel shook his head.

"No? I think he's had enough, anyway." The Spaniard's head was crushed. His features and blond hair were barely discernible beneath the blood. His body was limp in DeSain's arms. "You'll not betray me again, my friend." DeSain mustered the strength of five-hundred years of anticipation and threw the lifeless immortal against the glass wall. It shattered. Antony's body broke through and dropped below the recessed ledge.

"It wasn't my idea," DeSain heard the other Spaniard whine.

The knight turned from the window, brushing his hands together. "Oh, but Miguel, you seem frightened." He approached the whimpering fool. Wind howled through the broken glass behind him. "Surely you don't think your penalty will be as high as your friend's? He betrayed us. Both of us. You understand that." DeSain wrapped an arm around the Spaniard's shoulder. "Don't you?"

"Yes," Miguel snorted, "but I shudda known better."

DeSain smiled. "I'm delighted you recognize that, my friend, because that means you have potential. Are you familiar with potential, Miguel?"

"I think so."

"Potential is what a man can do after he realizes his capabilities. But maybe Jane Marie can explain it better." He looked around for her. She'd been close by when he'd first addressed the Spaniards. Ah, and there she was. She'd only moved away from the damaged wall. How beautiful she looked, silhouetted against the glass. "Would you say that's an accurate explanation of potential?" He hugged the Spaniard tight.

"Yes, I thought it adequate," she responded. He was glad she hadn't fled while the delinquent fools had distracted him. Apparently, she was coming to terms with her destiny. With that thought, DeSain was reminded of his five-centuries-long wait for her. His patient vigil, overseeing the LaCassiere line until it produced a woman whose powers matched his own. He grew suddenly anxious to finish his business with the Spaniard.

"So there you are, my dear Miguel. No matter what happens from this day forward, just remind yourself you have potential. Can you say it with me?"

"Potential," he complied.

"Very good." DeSain patted him on the back, then grabbed him by the collar and belt and hoisted him above his head. "Now, go demonstrate your potential with your friend." He ran to the broken window and flung the screaming Spaniard into the sea.

•

"Was all that necessary?" Jane's voice was cool, but she meant for it to be. "Is this how you rule, my Knight? By throwing your subjects through windows and lopping off their heads?"

"Why do I feel your tone mocks me?" DeSain wiped his hands on his shirt and pants and straightened his collar. "And what makes you speak so assertively? We are not equals, you and I. You will be wise to remember that."

As she stood near the intersecting glass walls, Jane felt his mind reaching out to hers. No more, she thought. Her wounds had healed. This needed to end. "And if I forget, what then? Will you fling me into the surf? What brand of destiny is this that you offer me?"

He walked toward her, his arms outstretched. "My dear, I desire only happiness for you."

"I don't want you near me."

He didn't stop. "You know how long I've waited for you. Nurtured you."

Nurtured? Her hands balled into fists as she thought of her mother. "You tortured me."

"Think of how much stronger you became after losing the ones you loved."

Was he admitting it? "You orchestrated everything, didn't you?" Her mother. Her father. Eddie. Oliver. He was reaching out to touch her, but the thought of his skin against hers made her nauseous. Still, she held her rage and allowed him to caress her face.

Soon, but not now, she thought. She would have answers first. "My entire life was played like a game."

He didn't respond. He stood in front of her, holding her face in his hands and prying hard with his mind.

But Jane wouldn't let him in. She sidestepped out of his reach and felt the cold blade on the back of her thigh.

"What's this?" the knight blinked. "Are you hiding something, my dear? I think we've had enough betrayal for one day, don't you?" He was trying to be demure.

Jane wasn't buying it. In an instant he'd learned about the sword and what she planned to do with it, but she wasn't about to let him learn anything more.

She swung her arm over her shoulder and grasped the hilt of the sword firmly and yanked it straight up and over her head. Had she worn anything but a long skirt, she couldn't have pulled it off. Before the knight had a chance to defend himself, Jane skewered him through the heart and rammed him into the corner of the glass walls. She felt the adhesive between the two panes give as the tip sank in and held fast.

"I must confess," DeSain said, showing no anger, "I didn't see this coming. You are clever." He shoved her backward, knocking her off her feet, and brought his hands to the hilt of the sword. He tugged, but the blade held firm.

"It was my mother who was clever. She taught me how to defeat you. And she used your own words to do it." *Jane Marie.*

The knight tugged again. "This makes us even now, doesn't it? Pull this off me." And tugged again.

Jane scrambled to her feet and watched the knight's desperate attempts to free himself.

It won't budge, she told him, standing five or six feet away. Images of her mother and father and Eddie and Oliver swam through her mind, all of them singing a chorus of revenge.

"Free me," he demanded. His cheeks were flushed. His eyes burned in fury.

No, she thought.

Don't feed my anger, he warned.

"When I was a little girl," Jane said, stepping past Oliver's remains to the table and grasping a chair, "my mother used to tell me the story of an evil sorcerer who was destroyed by a beautiful princess. Would you like to hear it?" She placed the chair in front of him, sat down, and crossed her legs.

"I don't know what you think you're doing," the knight's efforts to pull out the sword doubled, "but you can rest assured what happened to the three immortals before you will be nothing in comparison to the fate that awaits you if this continues. Loose me and I'll show mercy."

Jane feigned irritation. "Do you want to hear the tale or don't you?"

You'll pay for this. The knight's eyes were filled with anger.

"Then I'll give you the *Reader's Digest* version." Jane ignored his menacing gaze and wiggled in her chair pretending to get comfortable. "So, there's this crotchety old witch who gives a warning to the evil sorcerer, and wouldn't you know," she slapped herself playfully on the forehead, "his name just happened to be DeSain. To be honest, I thought you'd be taller."

The knight carried on struggling with the sword, but it continued to hold him captive.

"Anyway, the warning went something like this," she inhaled theatrically before reciting,

Your chosen will find you
If to the line you are true
And born will be an heir
From the blood of LaCassiere.

The knight no longer tended to his trap. "Where could you have heard this?" He was sweating and out of breath.

Jane cloaked her amusement with pretended disappointment. "So you know the story already? Why didn't you tell me?"

Enough with your games.

"All right, I'll stop." She stood and walked toward him, dusting off the memories and gathering the courage her mother had said she would have when the time came. "But do you know the rest of the witch's warning? I always thought it was the most exciting part."

"The prophecy was meant for my hearing only. It's not possible to have learned this."

"Oh, but it is. My mother told me, and she'd heard it from her mother, who'd heard it from..."

Stop!

No. She stepped close to the hilt of the protruding sword. "'But interfere with the natural trail,' the witch said, 'And an alternate fate will prevail.'" Jane held DeSain's gaze with her own. "You interfered." She backhanded the hilt of the sword.

"Aaaahhh." The knight struggled to stop the wobbling.

You interfered, the voices of a choir filled the room. The shock on DeSain's face told Jane he'd heard them, too.

"You're a witch like your mother!" He tried pulling at the sword again. Blood saturated the front of his shirt.

"Yes, and more powerful than you want to admit."

"You lie."

"Do I? My mother knew I wouldn't have her long, so she trained me very young. She taught me to read minds and hide thoughts and see the truth in people just as she did. She told me about you and about Oliver, and she taught me how to keep my thoughts hidden, as though they were completely forgotten—until the moment they were needed. Always. Even when I slept. Even as I dreamt. But now the moment has arrived."

"I don't believe you."

"Don't or won't? She told you I would defeat you."

"She was a liar."

"So you killed her."

You interfered with the line, the choir resounded.

"Why are the spirits helping you?" he asked.

Jane reached out, grabbed the hilt of the sword, and pulled. The tip broke loose of the glass and the blade slid free of DeSain's chest. "The voices of your ancestors say you interfered. They want revenge."

DeSain held his chest and dropped to his knees. "I did not interfere, you came of your own will."

"Not my will, Oliver's. An immortal created by you." The sword was heavy in her hand, but for a second, she considered ending it now. *No*, she told herself. *Not this way*.

"Oliver was your protection," the knight explained.

"He was my courier," she argued.

"I will hear no more of this."

As if realizing for the first time that he was free of the sword, Jane watched the knight try to rise, but he lost his balance and fell back into the corner. Broken glass rained to the floor as he struck the wall.

"What is this power you wield?" A sudden look of surprise flashed across his eyes. "And where is the mortal?"

Jane guarded her thoughts. "Gone. Stashed away from your prying mind and deadly temper. But he's the least of your worries."

She boldly stepped close to him. The wind blowing in from the damaged window swept across her face. The burnt orange and violet sunset painted the sky around them.

"Your fate was decided the moment you chose power over blood," she said, her face close to his. "You chose unwisely." Confident the spirits held him tightly in the corner, she touched her lips to his. "Your alternate fate has prevailed." She dropped the sword.

An evil sneer crept onto DeSain's face as he felt the spirits set him free. "I'm going to enjoy watching you die."

"Fuck you," she said. Jane turned and ran, knowing the knight would follow.

•

Breathless, Rand hid behind the suit of armor in the hall as he'd been instructed. He couldn't begin to understand anything that was happening in this strange world. Any minute he expected to wake up and discover it had all been a dream. Or a nightmare. Or whatever else existed outside the scope of his reality.

And what should he make of Janie? The pain of her loss had been debilitating, something he'd never expected to get over, but the past few days had been enormously more bizarre and frightening. Not only had his wife escaped death somehow, she'd traveled here to... To what? To fight some quasi-Count Dracula character? It was like some kind of crazy *Superman Meets Lex Luthor* only terrifyingly real.

But he had to stop thinking. Jane's instructions had been clear, and the other voices, the ones that appeared in his head from nowhere, were telling him it was time.

Be ready.

"I am," he answered, and immediately realized he hadn't needed to say it aloud.

Jane's footsteps pounded toward the door. In his mind, an image flashed, showing him that the man the voices called the knight was close behind her, brandishing a sword. Rand's heart quickened. He would have only one chance.

He backed up against the wall, clutching the hilt of the sword to his chest and holding the blade close to his forehead, just as the voices told him to do. "I hope you're with me," he whispered. None of this made sense to him, but he wanted reassurance that he wasn't alone.

We are with you.

As the voices echoed within his mind, Jane bolted past him at a dead run to the stairs.

Close your eyes, she told him.

He did and jumped into the path of the angry knight.

•

Jane didn't dare look back until she reached the stairs. But when she did, she turned so quickly she nearly lost her footing and tumbled to the landing beneath the crest tapestry. DeSain was unnervingly fast as he bounded through the doorway, waving the sword, and screaming in his mind, *I will chop you into a thousand pieces.*

Summoning all the energy within her, Jane joined the spirit choir in guiding her husband's hand. The man who had once said he would love her forever. For an instant, Jane saw the knight's eyes flicker in recognition as he noticed Rand, but by then it was too late.

•

Something he could only describe as instinct swung his arms back and Rand let go with a swing he never thought he had in him, not even in college. He spun so hard, he was sure he'd turned around twice before he came to a stop and fell to the ground. He opened his eyes. The sword had landed on his shoe. He kicked it off when he saw streaks of blood on the blade.

•

For a second, Jane thought Rand's swing hadn't connected. DeSain's speed even appeared to increase as he approached the end of the hall. But then the sword fell from his hand. His eyes wandered. His stride faltered, and he stumbled. When he fell to his knees, his head wobbled, then toppled to the floor.

Jane screamed.

•

Rand jumped to his feet to run to Jane. *"SHIT!"* he screamed as a stabbing pain in his groin knocked him back to the floor. He tucked into a ball and rolled, suffocating, sure he was going to die.

Please, God, he thought, *not now*. Not after things had come this far. *This has to be a dream. This has to be a dream.*

•

"Oh my God, Rand." Jane skirted the knight's disintegrating remains and ran to her husband. There were so many things she had to tell him. So many things she should explain. But first, she reminded herself, he had to make it through the change.

She ran to his side and fell upon him. He was writhing in pain.

"Say something, Rand, say anything." She stroked his hair, hoping he was strong enough physically to endure the rigors of becoming an immortal, especially one destined to assume the role of a protector. Moncado had been in his early twenties when the power was transferred. Rand was almost fifty. Keeping the secret had been easy, but carrying it out had been the hardest thing Jane hoped she'd ever have to do. She touched his forehead and prayed he'd be all right.

"Don't count me out yet," he whispered through chattering teeth.

He'll make us proud, the spirits sang.

The heaviness in Jane's heart lifted, and she bent down to hold him in her arms. She couldn't wait to tell him how long she'd waited. And how vampires brought him here, believing it was their idea. And how funny Rand's face had looked the first time he heard her voice in his head.

And she would definitely tell him about Oliver, and how it was he who reminded her she was strong enough to defend herself and ultimately win her battle with the knight. The one her mother had always called the evil sorcerer. When Oliver fell back in his chair, after feeling the mental sparks fly from Jane and Moncado in rebuke of his interruption, he'd sent a flash of a message to her. Jane immediately stuffed it away in the safest corner of her mind, but she would never forget his words: *Itwasloudreallyloudanditknockedmebut...you were louder.*

You were louder.

Dominic startled her. "Will the master recover, m'lady?"

"Oh, Dominic," she sat up, but kept a hand on Rand's shoulder. "I'm afraid your master is," she nodded her head, "gone."

"I see that," he smiled. She thought he looked a little embarrassed to do so. "But my inquiry is for the new lord of Casa Vienna, Master Rand."

Master Rand? "How did you know?"

"The spirits from the ledge told me." He pointed down the hall to the Terrace Room.

Rand's body slumped beneath her hand. She rolled him onto his back and pressed her ear to his chest. His heart wasn't beating. She hoped it was normal. But what was normal, really?

Then thankfully, blessedly, Rand stiffened, took in a massive breath, and opened his eyes. As he exhaled, his muscles relaxed. He took another breath, this one smaller. "That's a helluva ride, but I wouldn't recommend eating beforehand. What the fuck just happened to me?"

Jane couldn't believe it was over. She didn't even try to hold back the tears. "You're okay?"

"I'm okay." He pulled her down on top of him and held her closer, Jane thought, than he'd ever held her before.

EPILOGUE

SUNDAY, MARCH 25, 2006

Palm Beach Post, front page

ACKERTON WOMAN FOUND, PHOTOGRAPHER CLEARED

Palm Beach, Fla. (AP) — The murder and fraud charges against famed photographer Randolph Ackerton were dropped yesterday after police received a surprising phone call from the alleged victim, Ackerton's wife, Jane. Mrs. Ackerton contacted Palm Beach police just after 6:00 PM EST Saturday to say she was safe and with her husband in New Orleans. N.O.P.D. officials met with the couple and confirmed the woman's identity and general state of health.

"Mrs. Ackerton has no memory of last Monday's boating accident, nor does she remember her train ride to New Orleans," said Sergeant Terrance Benson, head of the Palm Beach Detective Bureau, "but her spirits are good and she's anxious to go home."

What started as a missing person's case for Detective Patrick Janson turned into a possible homicide when Ackerton suspiciously left the state on Thursday.

"At the time, we believed we had a body and a motive," Janson said. "We weren't taking any chances."

Ackerton told N.O.P.D. he "wasn't thinking clearly" when he left Florida after learning his wife had turned up at a friend's house Wednesday. His only explanation for the delay in notifying authorities was "time got away" from them.

Mr. and Mrs. Ackerton are scheduled to return to Palm Beach this afternoon. (*Continued on Page 8A*)

•

OCTOBER 8, 2006

Palm Beach Post, page 6D

MUSIC SCHOLARSHIP ANNOUNCED

Washington, D.C. — In a ceremony held last night at George Washington University's Cafritz Conference Center, Jane Ackerton, wife of photographer Rand Ackerton, presented the National Association of the Arts with a check for $700 million in order to establish a nationwide scholarship fund for music students in public schools. Among those in attendance were representatives from more than three hundred middle and high schools across the nation, whose travel and hotel expenses were generously provided by the Ackertons. No cameras were allowed at the event.

The money was discovered earlier this year during a homicide investigation involving the Ackertons, but Mrs. Ackerton maintains it doesn't belong to her.

"The courts say it's mine, but I really don't need it," Ackerton said to the crowd of educators, whose collective sentiment was that The Oliver Chatham Scholarship Fund could not have come at a better time.

Printed in the United States
76041LV00002B/175-222

9 781595 07161